COMPRADOR
DAVID R. CUDLIP

"AN EXTREMELY WELL-WRITTEN STORY OF DECEIT, TREACHERY, CHICANERY, AND WORLD POWER."

ALA Booklist

"CLEVER, STYLISH, DEMANDING...DISCOMFORTING! THE U.S. PREDICAMENT SEEMS ALL TOO PLAUSIBLE."

The Washington Post

COMPRADOR

DAVID R. CUDLIP

AVON
PUBLISHERS OF BARD, CAMELOT, DISCUS AND FLARE BOOKS

Grateful acknowledgment is made to the Paramount
Music Corporation for permission to reprint excerpts from
the song "I Remember You" by Johnny Mercer and Victor
Schertzinger, copyright © 1942 by Paramount Music Cor-
poration. Copyright © renewed 1969 by Paramount Music
Corporation.

AVON BOOKS
A division of
The Hearst Corporation
1790 Broadway
New York, New York 10019

The E. P. Dutton edition contains the following Library of
Congress Cataloging in Publication Data:

Cudlip, David R.
Comprador.

I. Title.
PS3553.U275C6   1983   813′.54   83-20772

First Avon Printing, April 1985

Who travels best travels with those who are no strangers to the road. Nice luck sent me deft companions: Bernard Wolfe, my fine friend and a fine writer, who watered me with good advice along the way; Marilyn Sorel, for doing away with excess luggage; and Joe Kanon, my editor and publisher, who patiently dragged me into town.

Owed and deep thanks.

For Carolina and Bobby

com·pra·dor \ˌkäm-prəˈdo(ə) r\ *or* **com·pra·dore,** *n*
[Pg *comprador,* lit., buyer]: a Chinese agent engaged
by a foreign establishment as an intermediary in business
affairs.

—WEBSTER'S NEW COLLEGIATE DICTIONARY

When goods don't cross borders, armies will.
—FREDERIC BASTIAT 1801–50

COMPRADOR

PART I

1

South China Sea
Beverly Hills

A groan turned into a shriek, and it could have come from anywhere: from the violent wind lashing the huge spread of canvas above, or even from one of the women below in the staterooms. You couldn't tell, not in that nervous sea.

And now sharper gusts beat against the black junk. Fifty meters long, three-masted, the big Hong Konger heeled hard over and plowed stubbornly against the water. Jolted suddenly, Piet Van Slyke, a heaver of a man, almost lost his footing on the fantail. He grabbed quickly for a slippery railing, nearly missing it.

"Bowels of Christ!" he swore.

"And in God's name, what are we doing outside?" chided Liu Wai.

"A little fresh air. Good to think in."

"Good to get sick in, you mean. There are a dozen cabins below."

"Hollanders don't chase women from their comforts."

"Rot in hell then. I'm Chinese."

"Who are well known for their abuses of women." Van Slyke boomed a laugh, enjoying the Singaporean's discomfort.

3

Sitting in a chair anchored to the deck by a chrome shaft, Liu Wai fussed like an old crone, trying to ward off the spray. He was finagling a trade with the Dutchman.

"Must we stay out here like beggars?"

Van Slyke ignored him. Looking up the creaking masts, he saw how they warped under the heavy pull of wind. "Too much sail for this weather. We ought to reef."

"You were the one demanding a fast return to Aberdeen harbor."

"Ya! Three days in this weather is too long for these meetings."

Liu Wai sighed. His massive belly rose and the thick eyelids closed as he said, "Well, do you want the Malaysian tin or not? It's the best quality. I can sell it anywhere. The Russians. Even China."

"At your idiotic prices they can have it, though I might give you dollars for it."

"I use dollars for wallpaper in the toilets of my staff . . . Look at you. A disgrace!"

Van Slyke took the mild insult good-naturedly, as he did whenever the others scorned the red woolen caftan he wore at sea. Or joked about his thigh-high boots, calling him the Dutch Devil-Kisser, sometimes Exalted Jade-Gater—this last because he often slept with two women at the same time, with enough stamina, apparently, to exhaust both. Standing almost seven feet tall, he towered over the others, his size enlarged by the pioneer-style cut of his flaming hair and the rusty spade of beard hanging off his huge jaw. But why should he mind jests? He was Shan Chu—Chief of Hill—of Shang-Magan's Council of Six this year. He could do as he damn well pleased. Almost.

"It is not the same without him, is it?"

"Cul-sjane?" answered Liu Wai.

"Ya. Clever, and pretty tough, too. He might know what to do with these dampt Russians."

"Shang-Magan survived for three centuries with and without the Russians. They'll come knocking on the door . . . Quit worrying."

"I worry plenty, Liu Wai. Their dampt armies have marched on you in the Middle East. Their claw is on Muldaur's Africa. They threaten me in Europe . . . That's three trading zones under their whip."

4

The obese Singaporean waved Van Slyke off. "We still control the important trade. Cul-sjane's House is the only true failure."

"Dampt lucky for you you no longer trade in oil."

"I diversify. I never trusted those sheiks anyway . . . Any more than I thought Cul-sjane was ready to run the American zone." Liu Wai shifted his gorilla belly as it growled. "Too young, still a pup."

"He came closer than any of us to unscrewing the OPEC cartel."

"And failed there too."

"Be reasonable, man!" Van Slyke glared.

"Reasonable? Many of us lost heavily in the U.S. And what hope of recovery? The whole zone commits suicide on the installment plan."

"Exactly my point. Who better than Culhane to see it through? Look what he did to break up that silver jiggering of the Texans and Arabs . . . And he held the North American markets until the very end. Who could ask for more?"

After a pause, Liu Wai said, "Joe Rearden is our man. We should have brought him in years ago instead of the pup."

Van Slyke shouted back scornfully, "Rearden. Bah! He is a known flusher on his trades."

"Misunderstood, perhaps. Besides, Cul-sjane is against me."

"He's against any Shang-Magan trading in opium and the White Dragon Pearl heroin. You've heard his argument—trouble with the governments someday."

With a loose grin, eyes slitting, Liu Wai said, "I deal with government officials in ways they find pleasing, even the American agents . . . I need no advice from infants."

Wind whacked hard against the stays. The Magan flag—six dragons in six brilliant colors against a field of white—cracked loudly, snapping loose from its mast. Off it fluttered like a bill-gull before disappearing into the roiling sea.

"You will vote to suspend then. Is that it?" asked Van Slyke.

"I'd rather vote to expel him and clear the way for Joe Rearden. He's our best bet."

Van Slyke thought of Culhane's humiliation and fierce

difficulties, wondered whether the American would ever be seen again in the Shang-Magan.

As if reading Van Slyke's mind, Liu Wai cut in. "How much do you think Cul-sjane lost, Puy-et?"

"Another man's losses or gains are his own business."

"In dollars, what would you estimate?"

"As you said, you cannot measure anymore in dollars."

"In Dutch guilders then?"

Van Slyke thought hard, working his beard. "One billion perhaps. Hard to figure."

Liu Wai knew it to be a larger amount. Rather than be toyed with by the big Dutchman, he pushed himself up with enormous effort. Narrowing his already small eyes, he said, "Rearden has invited me to Cap Ferrat for a fortnight. He's bringing actresses. Like to join us?"

"No."

"Might take your mind off the Russians."

"No."

"As you wish. If you've no objection, I'll join the others."

Watching the Singaporean waddle across the fantail, Van Slyke smothered a laugh. Gotten up in black satin pajama pants, scarlet jacket, and mauve slippers, Liu Wai looked like a circus hippo. No matter, Van Slyke thought; the man was a classic trader and did fine work running the Shang-Magan's Asia zone. Until a few years ago, Liu Wai could and did exact a six percent commission on every barrel of crude oil shipped from the Middle East to Japan. In return, the way was cleared for Japanese manufacturers to sell their cars and electronics to the West. A Shang-Magan interzone agreement, brilliantly successful, it had produced astonishing profits for several years. But it ended in a trade war, with Japan and Europe pitted against the U.S. A mistake no one had figured on.

Trade worked in a circle, like the earth itself. Van Slyke considered it the first duty of the Council of Six to ensure that it stayed that way. He sighed inwardly, thinking of the hundreds of millions in lost commissions. Tokyo now did its dealing for oil directly with Moscow, a dangerous and worsening situation.

Van Slyke hunched over the taffrail. He looked out at the sea swelling up against the horizon. Warwater, he thought, as Culhane came to mind again. The most ingenious speculator he'd ever met—iron-nerved, daring, a

6

loner and a natural. In thick trouble now, beaten clean down to the bone. And Van Slyke knew that just a few yards away four men waited for him, and wanted a vote taken so they could go home. Hard-bitten traders, the best in the world; with a pad, a few pencils, and some telephones they could liquidate half the countries in existence.

Van Slyke hated this day. Cursing into the wind's teeth, lurching across the deck, he forced open the door and stepped into the ebony-paneled saloon. Hurricane lamps swinging on gimbals flickered light against the faces of the others. A woman coughed, another tittered, and the air tasted sweetly of opium vapor.

He told the women, the Senegalese boy-whore of Liu Wai's, and the galley steward to leave. Feet spread, boots dripping onto a priceless Afghan rug, Van Slyke looked around in the barely relieved murk. He glanced quickly at the Gauguin painting given by Culhane to enliven the black walls. He ignored the art, but not these Shang-Magan traders.

There, by the mah-jongg table, sat Baster Muldaur idly fingering a playing title. As tough as he looked, the Afrikaner was built like one of his prize bulls, low to the ground, barrel-chested, thick-necked. Sire of five daughters, some of them raving beauties, but no sons. Muldaur was easily the richest man in all of Africa, which made some wonder why he served so devotedly as a deacon of the Dutch Reform Church. Yet a man's religion, if he could afford that sort of mistress, was his own conscience.

Across from Muldaur was Muir Tomlinson, whose trading zone began in Australia, stretched across to New Zealand, and covered all other Pacific islands. The oldest Shang-Magan alive, at seventy-two he still harpooned sharks off the Great Barrier Reef. Beautifully mannered, shy, and handsome, Tomlinson had made his first fortune by salvaging tons of abandoned materials left by the Americans after their winless 1945 victory in the Pacific.

Augustino von Grolin Camero, who chaperoned trade throughout South and Central America, leaned unsteadily against a wall. Tall for an Argentine, thin-featured, cool-eyed. With Culhane sidelined, Camero could lay claim to being the world's most potent grain trader. Some envied this aristocratic caballero his women and his immense pampas fincas. Van Slyke infrequently wondered if the same people would show jealousy over Augustino Camero's sexual affair with his first cousin, better known as His Eminence Tomas Cardinal Camero of Buenos Aires. A trivial matter, though.

As his sight adjusted to the darkness, Van Slyke accounted for Liu Wai. The Singaporean slouched on a divan in the far corner. Smoke drooled from his mouth as he exhaled the delights of his opium-filled water pipe.

As he had with Liu Wai earlier, Van Slyke spoke to them in Cantonese:

"Now you've had your say. Separately, in private, as it should be in a matter so delicate. We are a curious group. Elitists, I suppose, but elitists with great responsibilities. You have all sworn deep oaths to Shang-Magan—its code, its traditions. As your elected Shan Chu, I've sworn other oaths to you. To protect your interests, the settlement of territorial disputes, our very future . . ."

Van Slyke paused, wiping his mouth. Moving into the middle of the saloon, he continued:

". . . Our whole future depends on bringing along newer blood. No one can deny that Culhane succeeded brilliantly in developing the North American zone. But is he to blame for the trouble? We all suffer for it. Culhane fought bravely to hold his markets open. He is of wide sight, as some of us have remarked in the past. Also, he is our only American Council of Six member . . ."

The rocking motion stopped. The junk was luffing up into the wind, coming over on a new tack. The traders sat stone still, listening raptly to the only authority they ever truly recognized.

"It is time now," Van Slyke said. "Two of you wish to expel Culhane. Two others call for a year's suspension. Afterward, he can regain his Council of Six seat by again posting one ton of gold or an acceptable equivalent to his reserve account—our Rule Three provision."

Silence. All crossed glances with one another. Tomlinson sneezed politely into his handkerchief.

Van Slyke fished in his caftan and retrieved five joss sticks: eight inches long, of brightest red lacquer, tipped at each end with platinum leaf.

"If we're here to vote, Piet, which is the issue? To expel or suspend?" asked Muir Tomlinson.

"Only to suspend, I've decided."

Liu Wai snorted loudly into his opium pipe, but was powerless to overrule the Shan Chu.

"Vote now, at once!" instructed Van Slyke.

The sticks snapped, two of them, in the hands of Camero and Liu Wai. Baster Muldaur tapped his gently on the mahjongg table, then rolled it across the playing tiles. Tomlinson put his stick into an inside coat pocket. They all looked at one another again, deep and searching, before their faces met Van Slyke's. He still held on to his joss stick, unbroken.

"It is up to you, Piet," urged Augustino Camero.

"Obviously."

"Does anyone wish to change his vote? Or say anything else?" asked Muldaur. His voice was calm enough, but his chest moved out and in. No one answered him, but Van Slyke wondered if the Afrikaner suspected anything.

"How vote you, Piet?" asked Liu Wai.

"Soon enough, you will know."

Van Slyke waited, counting more silence. Abruptly he turned, went through the door, slammed it, and bucked his way down a long passageway. Two doors later, he reached the communications room and gave an order to the signaler.

"There's transmission problems today. Everything garbles." The signaler adjusted a knob until an orange dot was centered inside a green triangle. "Might do it," he said, as he leaned over to depress three red buttons on the radio console. The marine operator spoke just as Van Slyke motioned the signaler to leave.

He growled another command, fumed, and waited. A roar of sea slugged against the hull, pitching Van Slyke against the console. Shaking a painful elbow, mouthing other oaths, he suddenly remembered the voting stick in his hand. He hadn't really voted, had he? The others wouldn't know, only assume, wouldn't they? Yes, he was Shan Chu, and time no longer allowed for the luxury of candor. Better this way, he thought, than to get trapped in a double lie later on.

"Culhane here."

"A close vote, Rushton. I'm sorry to be the one—"

A blast of static, like an angry hornet, intruded; then nothing at all except for a pinging echo until the marine operator queried:

"Are you through?"

* * *

"The dice already passed," replied Rushton Culhane, fighting to control himself. Carefully, he anchored the telephone to its cradle; not so carefully, his hand trembled.

Culhane's nerves seemed to lift out of his body, as he felt the light-headedness that comes with shock. *Completely through, thanks to men I've worked with most of my life. I need air . . .*

Slowly, he walked to one side of his office. Parting the embossed green drapery, he opened French doors and stepped out to the terrace. Wilshire Boulevard was almost empty. A patrol car, red light flashing and siren shrilling, racing off to somewhere. Farther on, two delivery trucks chugging along on battery-powered engines. Only a few passenger cars.

He stood there for a time, letting the cool morning air wipe his moist face, before returning to his office. Walking through his small museum of paintings, he went over to the deep couch of Brazilian leather, loosening his pale Charvet tie on the way. He opened the lid of an onyx humidor and withdrew a Honduran #7 panatella, lighted it, then sat down. Mulling, he recast the golden rule: *Those who have the gold do the ruling.* He'd been done out of three tons of it.

From the outer hallway came the sound of padding steps on thick carpet. Then the little man with the island music deep in his voice appeared in the doorway.

For every one of the 7,326 days they'd been together, Rushton Culhane had never seen Herbsant Saxa dress differently for business. Always a three-piece suit, a snowflake-white vestette under the vest, blue shirt, white tie, a red carnation, and patent-leather shoes you could use for a shaving mirror.

And gold. Saxa wore gold as Nefertiti had, down to the tiny globe of the metal piercing his left earlobe. Part Haitian, some French, the rest of him Spanish Jew, with his woolly white hair and short stature he looked like a character actor. And in some ways he was.

Chanting, he entered the room: "One dollar bid, now two, now two, oh! Now I got three, hear four, now four . . ."

"So early?" said Culhane, forcing his smile.

"I sleep at Beverly Wilshire. Otherwise I must change bus three time today. Too old for nonsense."

"Expensive, isn't it?" asked Culhane, a question that wouldn't have occurred to him a year ago.

"Hotel? Eighty Swiss francs, one hundred German marks, or eight hundred American dollars. Take choice. And you look shit."

"Van Slyke called. I gather they went through it. I'm suspended or worse."

Saxa's face shook. Loose skin tinted the color of Drambuie wobbled, then tightened, and the cushions under his eyes almost vanished.

"Virgin Jesus, they know Washington don't pay us."

"That's my problem, not theirs. What's left of my Shang-Magan bond is in dollars, as you know so well."

Saxa rolled his eyes until only the whites showed in the dark mask of his face. It was one of his Haitian voodoo tricks, often done in fun, but not this time.

"Can't make us a temporary loan of gold?"

"They don't operate that way. You have to pay your own dues."

"What is you told me before? A year? Something?"

"I guess. Anyway, they'll write it up in Chinese, tinsel it, and probably send it by carrier pigeon." Culhane leaned over and stubbed out his cigar in a Baccarat crystal bowl. He needed movement then, any movement at all to ease the pressure in his lungs.

"Ain't possible for recover in year. They must know that."

"Maybe we can find a banana republic that'll freight us. Or a church. Know any good churches, Sant?"

"Be serious, Jesus sake!" Saxa squirmed into the chair facing Culhane, his feet barely scraping the carpet.

"Things were serious when others couldn't pay what they owed us. I'm stripped now, so it's no longer serious. It's done, fucking absolutely done." Culhane flushed deeply.

The phone rang. Two more times, yet neither man bothered answering it.

"Ah." Saxa brightened. "But they come to senses soon. Who else they got?"

"The New York Corporation."

11

"Everybody take your word on face . . . Rearden, he be birdshit in basket to them Magans."

"He's survived and I haven't. That's all the birdshit that seems to count right now."

"Creeping of Mother, the bastard a thug! Never hold to trades if market go against him."

Culhane shrugged wearily. "I'm going home. Send closing notices to the office here and in Chicago and Winnipeg."

"That easy done. Not so many people left," said Saxa, though shaking his head in unconscious protest.

"I'll send personal letters later."

Saxa gestured toward the walls of the large room and said, "You sell out paintings and them others at house. Easy. I promise good price in Europe. Safe money, too."

"No, Sant."

"Why not? Is a fortune here!"

"Because they're history, and that history *ain't* for sale."

Culhane got up from the deep couch, went to Sant Saxa, and gripped the little man's shoulder, before passing through a door to his private dressing room.

Saxa wanted to go with him, but that wouldn't do. He wanted to cry, but that wouldn't do either. Like watching your only son go through an amputation; and the son's future nothing more now than a floating toss-up. Saxa choked back a sob.

2

Washington

"Go over that once more," said Halburton, swinging around to face Joshua Squires, the Secretary of Treasury he'd inherited and was stuck with.

"Piegar of the Bank for International Settlements made the call himself."

"No, no! I mean the rest of it, the critical part."

"Well, effective ninety days from now, neither dollars nor U.S. Treasury obligations will be honored any longer as reserves for the other central banks. That includes our own Federal Reserve Bank . . . They promised not to announce it publicly until we're ready."

"We expected this possibility. We did, didn't we?"

"Not this fast, Mr. President."

"Where does this impact us most, the quickest?"

"We can't use dollars to settle our foreign accounts. Nobody else can, either. The dollar is . . . Well, it's like the zloty or the rupee. A *nothing.*"

"How much trouble? Can we pay our bills?"

"Not for anything we have to import."

"What do you recommend?"

"No good answer for it. The country hasn't faced this sort of catastrophe before."

Not exactly true, thought Halburton. During the American Revolution and the Civil War it was barely possible to pay the army, let alone foreign debts. Not important, though, and he asked:

"Why don't we just bypass this Bank for International Settlements?"

"We can't," replied Squires, shaking his talcumed head. "That's the only method existing to settle accounts among all the government central banks. You'd have to rearrange the whole international payments system. Just isn't possible."

"No clout, you mean. We're second-benchers, is that it?"

Squires made no comment, while remaining inordinately calm—and concluding again that this President wouldn't get by the first turn against turtles. Outclassed, a duffer.

Halburton paced twice around the Oval Office. Passing a couch, he felt an overpowering urge to lie on it and sleep away this newest crisis. Or to swear down on his God, or on someone. But his sense of order, taken from the law, and his Methodist upbringing, taken from his mother, lured him back to reality.

"The credit of this country was unsullied for a hundred years or more. They can't do . . ." Halburton's voice trailed off as he ran a shaky hand through his hair. His tired face thinned into a slack chin under a nose taking air at twice its usual rate.

Squires watched as the President shuffled over to the windows overlooking the Rose Garden. Halburton stared off through the glass panes, uninspired, angry, trying to fathom his position.

"I'll want a daily update. Hourly, if necessary."

"Naturally."

Halburton continued on with his morning séance. His gaunt frame slumped, coming apart at the seams on him now. And he found it very curious that the call to California was so blithely ignored.

That very afternoon in every financial market still operating, mostly foreign, the rumor was waterfalling: the U.S. had hit the wall running.

The dollar had become a leper, untouchable.

3

Bel Air

Culhane loped along, going easily, as he rounded the corner of Rodeo Drive. He barely noticed Giorgio's shredded yellow awning, the smashed front window of Gucci's, or the boarded-up doors of Hermes. He dodged litter everywhere. Spilled trash receptacles, soiled rags, a torn work boot, bent beer cans—every day it seemed dirtier.

Later, sweat darkening his jersey, he dashed down Sunset Boulevard, pushing himself, blood thrumming in his ears. Hearing them, he slowed down.

The mob, rabbling and cursing, seemed larger today. It spilled across the boulevard from Bel Air's east gate to the fire station on the other side. Shouting, their arms hoisted, some were throwing stones at the helmeted guards dressed in combat uniforms.

Others slowly chanted, "Bread . . . bread . . . bread, you bastards!"

A young black woman, her hair dyed ocher, shirtless, with her tattooed breasts brazenly exposed, spat at one of the guards. A bearded older white man threw a brick at another guard, hitting his knee. The guard cut loose with an aimless burst into the air from his Uzi machine gun, which did nothing to quiet the crowd.

Recognizing Culhane, the guards separated and made a

15

quick and narrow opening. He sprinted through, ducking as a rock glanced off his shoulder. Screams followed as he pounded up the winding road.

He ran very hard, with anger and fear crowding him all the way. The hungry mob wanted his life—he was Bel Air rich—and the sane thing to do was get out of their way. Culhane knew about hunger. He'd seen it many times and in too many places. Hungry people he understood, but not their politicians. Those he despised. The mob was stoning the wrong targets.

His children. Culhane eagerly wanted the feel of them right then. Those faces, innocent and fresh for a kiss, were the only solid hope now. Sara, eleven now, slim and golden-haired, and showing signs of her mother's beauty. The boy, Rush junior, just turned eight, the little heller for whom Culhane planned endless adventure and a strict bringing-up. He loved them both with a depth that sometimes actually frightened him. To fear anything, he knew, was to lose it. Or to lose to it.

White-bricked and appearing low-slung under its tiled roof, the huge residence rambled across the highest ledge of a glade sloping easily toward the Pacific blue. Stone walls edged the vast lawns. Oak and jack pine stood against the land, and there were towering firs with fanned boughs reaching skyward. In these tallest trees the birds nested, and on this morning they sang their piccolo sounds to the breezes.

By the eastern stone wall was an immaculately kept cutting garden. Squatting barefoot on his haunches, a Taiwanese tended a row of vegetables. Later in the day, in another part of the garden, he would snip fresh roses or fresias or perhaps chrysanthemums for the many rooms of the house.

The garden was the Taiwanese's life. He knew every living thing in it and exactly how it survived. It was as close to the Kingdom as ever he would experience on this earth. The old man stood now, rubbing his gnarled hand on a dirt-streaked apron. He waved as Culhane trotted up the pea-graveled driveway, making a sound like teeth crunching on celery.

Culhane stopped, his chest heaving and sweat pouring off him. He came toward the Taiwanese, saying in the man's dialect, "Your earth blooms are sunrise itself."

16

Bowing, the Taiwanese replied, "You honor a humble servant." Pointing to the early sun, he added, "In one hour the blooms will be locked in the cage of gold."

"And I can hear you bring the happy song to your birds."

"And they to me. The mouse and the frog by dark. The birds by light. Ai-ee, it removes the burdens of a thousand years."

Yours maybe but not mine, thought Culhane. He said, "Listen for the wisest frog. Watch what he eats and tell me. I must go now."

"And with you take the blessing of the blue cat who sleeps by the lotus."

"It is my gift to you, old father."

Culhane returned the Taiwanese's friendly smile as he headed down the driveway toward the paired oaken doors of his home.

The old Taiwanese watched carefully, thinking of the clouded look he'd observed in his master's sapphire eyes. Cul-sjane was Tai-pan and understood how to dignify even a poor man's work. Generous, too, at the time of both New Years; only now there would be no help from that source either.

Much lately had sorrowed the old man. From kitchen gossip he knew these were lusterless times for his master, that trouble loomed everywhere. Even trouble with that goddess to whom Cul-sjane was married. Was it not only three nights earlier that she could be seen running naked in the moonlight? Uttering strange, perhaps dangerous sayings while the master slept? Ai-ee!

Seeing Culhane disappear through the high-arched doors, the old man slowly inserted his warped fingers into his baggy, mended shirt. Searching there, he extracted a gummy brown pellet of opium. Lodging it next to his tooth-less gum, moistening it, he began slowly to suck its dream juices.

Another troubling thought entered his head as he put to trowel the radishes. His days of steady rest, for which he'd worked these many years, were moving beyond reach. In cold fury he remembered how the American bank had swindled him of his life's savings. One day the little book had said thirty-six thousand dollars, and then, without warning, he was told by letter that while his money was insured he must still wait for it.

17

He'd waited, and while he waited the value of his life's work had turned to the droppings of an earthworm. Soon it would be time to return across the ocean to his place of ancestry and prepare himself for death. Now it was only a receding hope. Highest insult, threatening to break a centuries-long chain of family tradition, and face would be lost.

His wages were now paid in food, shelter, and some silver coins. The joy weed and snow powder he'd secretively sold in this wealthiest of neighborhoods were now things past. No money. At least not enough gold money to satisfy the man who had brought the precious cargo, when delivering milk for the children of this big house.

The old man counted on one thing: Saturday would come soon. He'd take the necessary three buses to downtown and walk the remaining distance to Chinatown. He would visit his social club, his tong, and there, among old friends, he would implore favor by cagily insisting upon his rightful claim to respect. The respect due an elder, a person of age.

Then he would ask his tong brothers for errand work, anything that would help recover his losses at the cheating bank. Surely they would understand. His fidelity was unblemished and his dues, until lately, were always promptly paid. One very long turn of loyalty deserved at least a short one.

Annoyed, the old man slashed out with his Wyoming skinning knife, neatly severing a beetle nursing on a radish's leaf milk, the clean cut bringing instant death. He took pride in the simple task; no bank could steal his eyes, or his hands.

Culhane stepped through the foyer into the spacious front hall. A massive crystal chandelier hung from the ceiling two floors above, throwing its dancing rays across the black and white diamond shapes of the marble floor.

Difficult now to see the color nuances of the Dufy, the Renoir, the other Pissarro, and the three works by Monet. But even in the dark he knew them down to their smallest brushstrokes. Lasting friends, each representing one of his great market coups of the past; vanities that he loved.

Karin Culhane's silk pants made a swishing noise as she came down the spiral staircase, all in white except for the green bandanna that bound her auburn hair. A finely sculpted face, gently Nordic except for the mouth, which was almost Arabic with its chiseled lips.

Quite stunning, though with dark circles under her eyes, she was tall, willowy as a palm under breeze. Once her looks had been described as truly extraordinary, but now they were considered only beautiful—a haunted beauty, the beauty of shallow moonlight on the terrace of a decaying Mediterranean villa.

Culhane looked up. "You're up early. Where are the children?"

"To school at the hotel. Tuesday is the early session."

Now he remembered. Tuesdays and Thursdays they went very early for classes at the once fashionable and now converted Bel Air Hotel. Most things he could remember easily, in clean detail, yet somehow the trivial matters were irritatingly blurred these days.

"Long night. I lost track."

"A new morning. Where's my kiss?"

He held her for a long moment, saying, "I'm perspiring. Didn't want to muss you."

"What difference does it make?"

"It does to me, Karin," he said, trying to keep the smile on her face.

"What would I do without you?" asked Karin, looking into Culhane's blue eyes, feeling the raw strength of his arms pulling her closer.

"Continue as Norway's greatest princess."

"Not a real one."

"For me you are. Any food around?"

"Some tea and fruit . . ." Then, in one of her odd deflections, Karin added, "There's a new baby next door. Maybe we could buy it." Her eyes glazed.

"Sounds fine but I'm starved." He took her hand, walking her down the long hall toward the kitchen.

"Another one of those awful doctor's bills came yesterday. I'm sorry." A little quake in her voice.

"Worry about nothing, and forget the rest."

"Remember when you had your *Eastern Light* and we could sail all night? And we had stables. Wasn't it fun? Can you tell the bank to get my jewelry out?" Karin tugged at his hand. "Can we go to Santa Anita this afternoon and watch them run?" She was pitched up, almost breathless with excitement, and her eyes glittered.

He swept an arm over Karin's shoulders, drawing her near. "The track is closed, darling." For two seasons now, he thought, and your jewelry is probably around the neck of a solvent duchess.

"I'm going to vomit."

She pretended to gag, and Culhane wanted to thrash her, walk out, hold her—a dozen reactions at once. Chill tested his spine for the third time that morning.

"Let's have the tea."

Karin turned, throwing a brilliant smile at him. "I did Perdita from the *Winter's Tale* last night. Want to hear?" And before he could answer, Karin began:

"That wear upon your virgin branches yet / Your maiden-heads growing, Prosperina."

He felt a thunk in his belly, as if an anvil had dropped on it. "Karin . . . Karin!" He gripped her arms, shaking her very lightly, then whispered, "Do Perdita later. Tea, let's have the tea now, and maybe take a swim." Anything to humor her.

"There's no tea, there's no anything!" she screamed, a hand pulling loose and flying to her mouth at some imagined horror.

"Okay, let's just go easy."

Now the same hand fell to the top of her blouse. A quick yank, a sound of fabric ripping, and she stood there as naked as the young black girl Culhane had seen at the gate. A low keening moan came from her mouth, no longer beautiful, but harsh like the frozen look on her face. A long minute later her face regained its composure, her eyes emptied.

"I did it again, didn't I? Oh, Rushton!" Whimpering, collapsing into his arms. "I'm so frightened."

"It's all right, s'all right."

"I'll go ba-back to the clinic."

"Not ever again."

"I'm no use to you," sobbed Karin, her head shaking. "My God, we can't even sleep together!"

"It'll come right, Karin. It needs time."

They had spent twelve years together. He wanted to tell her of Van Slyke's call: what it really meant and that Culhane & Company would be forced finally to shut its doors.

But that can of herring couldn't be opened now. Not in her state, and not on top of the other shocks she'd endured. Worse, Karin adored the flamboyant Dutchman. She would never understand.

"That call last night?"

"What call was that?" he asked, gently yet surprised.

"From the White House, trying to reach you . . . I called you about it?"

"Oh, that one. I'm a little beat and just forgot," said Culhane. What the hell was this? He'd been there all night, awaiting the message from Van Slyke. No sleep, not even a doze, his nerves jumping around like loose power lines. There had been no call from Karin. Of that he was absolutely certain.

The White House? From whom? He knew no one personally on the new President's staff. Even the man himself was an enigma. In office for only three months or so, chased into the chair after the other one died from a coronary or too much thievery. Arkansas. Wasn't this Halburton from there? Maybe his staff came from the Ozarks and knew a little more about honesty.

Culhane felt Karin turn in his arms. A composed smile marked her mouth as she modestly began to cover those breasts he once knew so well. But her silk shirt wouldn't fasten. Giving it up as a poor try, she moved to the counter where the tea canister was kept.

He doubted that any call from Washington was to inform him that the government had relented, that they would now pay over the gold for the cobalt he'd secured from Zaire. Washington's refusal to pay had only brought him to financial ruin. That was all. The bastards. He tried to wipe it from his mind for a while so he could concentrate on Karin. But it was like wiping away a birthmark with your finger.

4

Zurich
Moscow

Nothing to celebrate about, but not bad either. The numbers tied out correctly, too,

Satisfied, Ambros Piegar initialed the ledger and tossed it into the auditor's tray. He was chief foreign-exchange trader for Braunsweig und Sohn, a private bank catering discreetly to a very rich clientele. Another erratic day in the markets. Yet, with the help of his four assistants, he'd still swung a profit of two million Swiss francs for the bank. A few more months like the last and he'd earn enough bonus to buy his own bank—a very small one.

Yawning, rubbing his stiff neck, he stood and walked to the window. Rain had washed it a dozen times that afternoon, and threatened to do it again.

Eleven stories up, on most days he could easily see over the old part of Zurich, across the grayish steeples and gabled roofs, all the way to the Zurichsee. Today, it looked to Ambros as if he were floating in a fogbank. Just like the money markets, he thought.

He turned for another look at the black electronic trading board: to the line with the day's last quote for the South African rand. Something happening there. The rate had been skittering around for days. Maybe, thought Ambros Piegar, I'm going to the right place to find out why.

Touching a yellow button on his intercom, he asked his secretary to call the garage and have his Porsche delivered to the Limmatquai entrance.

In the elevator he wondered again why his father was here in Zurich unannounced. Life must be getting soft at the BIS, or maybe he was homesick, thought Ambros, though God himself knew that Zurich offered few, if any, diversions over Basel, not even a flashy mistress. Ambros was sure his father believed that secret was safer than the number of a Swiss bank account.

Traffic crawled through the jammed streets, and Ambros slugged his way along until he reached the outskirts of the city. A blast of thundering sound rocketed through the bowl of mountains, shaking the Porsche's windshield. Ambros responded with smooth double-clutching; he flew now, snaking through the lighter traffic the way he sometimes skied the slalom course at Davos.

As the Porsche streaked through the arched entrance of the driveway up to his family home, Ambros speculated wryly about this hurriedly called meeting. A good word? Doubtful. A complicated errand? Probably. With Panzi off in summer training, whatever the reason for the summons, it might even relieve another dull evening. No, probably not, thought Ambros; it would be more like a very long hour with a tedious preacher. Grueling, nerve-racking, full of brimstone. And no laughs at the end of it, either, since he knew that his mother—one of the liveliest women in Zurich—was inventing every excuse imaginable to prolong her holiday in Burgenstock. He envied her.

Leaving the car, he sprinted up the front steps and walked through the vestibule, brushing rain off his suit. The door opened and an old Alpenseiler, bent now, his green loden-cloth jacket hanging loosely, greeted Ambros warmly.

A hallway like very few in all of Switzerland. The floor was of gray limestone, with a thick runner of Oriental design covering its length. Outsized yellow candles fixed in wall sconces bounced their light off iron maces, truncheons, and fighting lances hung against the walls. Overhead were flags of all the cantons in a glory of pompous color. Reaching the hall's end, Ambros braced his shoulders, was about to knock on the oak door, decided the hell with it, and entered.

Hans-Otto Piegar stood with his back to a fire flaming high inside a small cave. Perched above on the long deep mantel were mounted hunting falcons, beaks opened, wings flared, talons curled for the kill.

Erect, even-featured, though with a florid face, the elder Piegar's thinning yellow hair was streaked fast to his broad head. A skilled tailor had stitched up prize-winning work in camouflaging his girth. Hans-Otto Piegar waited: it was his son's duty to pay out the first greeting.

"You look well, Father," said Ambros amiably. "I was surprised to hear you were in Zurich."

"So," said Hans-Otto Piegar, "you're punctual for a change . . . Care for a drink?" Piegar lifted his glass in invitation.

"Thanks, no."

"Still seeing that barmaid or whatever?"

Ambros puffed his boyish cheeks slightly, answering, "Panzi is the best woman skier in Switzerland. She'll get a silver for sure in the next Olympics, possibly a gold." He wished he hadn't come.

"You'll never run Braunsweig und Sohn unless you get your duty and your standing straight. Sit down. We've business to discuss, and I've a plane waiting at Kloten."

"Going to Basel?" asked Ambros as he sat down on a wing chair across the room. Jesus! What a grand welcome, he thought.

"To Warsaw, then Moscow."

"More Russian roulette?"

Hans-Otto Piegar's fingers tightened around his glass. "You'd do well to listen!"

"I've tried ever since before puberty."

"Ambros . . ."

"Go ahead. Sorry, really."

"You're not to repeat a word," warned Hans-Otto Piegar. He waited until Ambros nodded. "There's every chance the Russian ruble will be banded together with the other European currencies soon. All except for the British pound . . ."

". . . And Switzerland? Surely not us." Ambros's face drained to a lighter shade.

25

"I speak as president of the BIS, not as a Swiss. But this country's neutralism may have to change."

"Never. And you'll never get the Americans to agree on a currency like the one you're talking about."

"America's finished. Kaput. It's vital that we find a stable international unit to replace the dollar," said Hans-Otto Piegar.

Tongue-tied, Ambros barely heard his father. The dollar might be finished, yet it was staggering to think of some new currency slicked up with Russian promises behind it. Comic opera, I'm hearing.

"Are you listening?" demanded Hans-Otto Piegar.

"It's a lot to accept in one pass."

Piegar came away from the fireplace. "Well, be damn certain you absorb this—tomorrow, and every day thereafter, until told differently, you're to begin short-trading the dollar again. You're to take short positions for all the Rearden accounts and all of ours. Got that straight, Ambros?"

My own father, thought Ambros. The entrusted guardian for international credit and currency. He's supposed to keep a long distance from personal dealings in any currency. He could be disgraced, jailed even, and he wants me to front for him. Chrissakes, he's even talking of scuttling our Swiss franc.

"Would this include the St. Gallen Trust as well?"

"Of course it does."

"Just wanted to be sure. How about the other American accounts?"

"Not advisable. We don't want to attract attention, do we?"

"Possibly I'll switch them into South African rand," said Ambros, hoping to draw his father out without betraying any unusual interest.

"That would be asking for it. Just leave them be."

"Any particular reason?"

"None I care to discuss."

Ambros was sick, impressed but sick, as he said, "Russia doesn't have the reserves to back her share of a new currency. Europe would end up carrying all the luggage for Moscow."

"Russia produces more gold and platinum than anyone else in the world. Those are prima facie reserves."

26

"If they would pledge them, you mean."

Hans-Otto Piegar sighed. "Leave those questions to us at BIS. Have you got my instructions clear, Ambros?"

Ambros nodded, then asked, "Do you suppose the Reardens would sell their interest in Braunsweig und Sohn to us, or to a Swiss syndicate?"

"It's the key to their empire. Why in hell should they?"

"You know, the bank is handling some very strange money . . . We ought to change that, clean it up."

"A good Swiss banker has blind eyes to the origin of money. Any money." Hans-Otto Piegar stepped over to a trolley-bar and refilled his glass.

Ambros pressed again: "One further point, Father . . . Those other American accounts? If the dollar falls, really goes, they'll be wiped out. And Braunsweig will gain at their expense. Something like what happened to the Jews years ago."

"A dead man can hardly reveal his account number, can he?"

"Except these clients won't be dead." Ambros looked at him, thinking, He's a for-hire money-gun who's power-crazy.

"They may as well be. Most Americans deposited money with us to avoid taxes. If they protest, they'll reveal their tax dodges."

"And what of the Mafia's deposits and the Unione Corse's. You think they'll play dead?"

Hans-Otto Piegar flushed. His fists smashed against the table. A lamp teetered, then fell.

"Never use those names. Have you learned nothing, damn you!"

"I like to know what side of my back to watch. You're at the BIS, safe as the sun. I'm here."

"And well paid for it, I might add."

Just like that it ended, with nothing more to say to each other. A set of instructions, illegal or at least highly questionable. Ambros felt like a thief and debated whether to throw in his resignation. Throw it in right now, right into the drink going down his father's gullet.

Hans-Otto Piegar strode toward the door, stopped briefly to bone-crunch Ambros's hand, and warned once more, "Not one damn whisper of it."

For the first time in over a year, Ambros yielded to the

desire for whiskey. The hell with the ulcer, he decided—
I've just heard something only a handful of people in the
world could possibly know about. I could ruin Braunsweig.
Or my own father. I could also make enough money to hide
in the African veldt with Panzi forever. The old son of a
bitch is going for me again. For what!

Zurich still gulped rain the next morning. The digital
clock on the wall facing Ambros displayed the numbers
0748. He fingered a switch; the video screen flickered to
life and the latest rates for the world's prime currencies
were quoted off the Hong Kong market. Another switch
and he saw that the early rates of the Moscow Nvrodny
Bank were somewhat higher. He might try a little arbitra-
ging. He placed a call to Munich, another to Brussels, finally one to Amsterdam. Too early. No action yet. He
picked up the morning sports page to search for news of the
Swiss skiing team, training in New Zealand.

Panzi. She's safe, thought Ambros, and well away from
this family buggery. It was a new day but it was an old device. Ambros didn't like getting used, family or not, and
his back rode up as he thought again about resigning.
Panzi would resonate with bubbly pleasure if he quit the
bank. She would rag him without remorse to come live in
Davos. And besides, he thought, there were still a few
things worth watching from a ringside seat, so why not
watch them?

Twenty minutes later, a green light on his board beck-
oned to him. A direct-wire call from Julius Baer & Company, an active though small bank with a reputation for
shrewd dealing. Pleasantries, a raw joke, then the trader
asked Ambros to quote him a D-mark rate for French
francs. Ambros quoted 3.42 francs to the mark, slightly below the Hong Kong market.

"How many will you take?" the trader wanted to know.

"All you've got," answered Ambros. Julius Baer & Company rarely dealt in sums over two million in any currency.

"Thirty million?"

"Sorry, I can't go that high without an okay from the
top."

"What can you handle, Ambros?"

"Five is the tops."

"Done. At three point four two francs to the mark."

Ambros scribbled the trade on a ticket and handed it to a young clerk across the table for entry in the money-position ledger. In quick succession, he laid the francs off in Paris and Rotterdam. Lights were flashing rapidly now and he was immersed in another day with the Philistines.

What the hell would Julius Baer & Company be doing with a mittful of Frenchies like that, he wondered. Acting like big players, enthusing over the thirty-million figure. A fool thing to do. You never even hint that you're carrying a big position. Ambros felt a little nerve twitch in his neck, as if a needle had entered it.

"Schroder Bank calling."

"Morning," replied Ambros.

"Quoting dollars for sale?" A worn joke by now.

Ambros hesitated, then quickly said, "I'll buy dollars against rand," disregarding his father's warning.

"Rand!"

"Yes, rand, R-A-N-D," spelled out Ambros.

"I'll get back. Five minutes, okay?"

"Sing or sink," said Ambros, trying to gauge the Schroder trader's appetite.

"Your quote?"

"Five hundred to the rand."

The Shroder trader whistled. "Size?"

"Four hundred million."

"You think I'm the Prime Minister of South Africa, you fucking comedian. You're balmy. I'll do a third of it . . . maybe."

"All or none," said Ambros, feeling it coming on.

"You're done for. You're nuts!"

The light disappeared.

He couldn't help himself. Ambros doubled over with laughter. The rest of the traders paused, startled, trying to figure out what had come over him. He didn't care. The world was going mad. A lot mad. So why shouldn't he?

An amateurish try, perhaps. But Ambros knew that the word would fan throughout the continental money markets—Braunsweig is buying dollars! And the market for dollars would inch up. A feint and he'd sell the dollars Braunsweig und Sohn didn't have. Classic and dangerous risk-taking, as were all short-trading operations. Up to a

29

point he'd carry out his father's black plans. He had other thoughts about his own.

He didn't know all the shades of legal larceny that central bankers were capable of, but Ambros thought he knew something about America, where he'd spent six years off and on. Instinctively, he was certain that someone was making another historical error, and he had no intention of getting burned by it.

Hitler had tried it. Now it was Moscow's turn. Control, iron-fisted control, Genghis Khan style. The four winds were blowing, none of them warm, and his father was sailing his kite on the one from the east.

Another light flickered on the board. Ambros wondered: What's to become of my American friends?

Moscow. Within the city a bell pealed the hour at nine into the dark night. A night no darker than the talk going on in the Kremlin's largest office, where Gregor Metzilov was coating up his latest scheme. Unwise, he decided, to push any harder, risk a rebuke or even a flat turndown. Not with Piegar as good as netted, a big fish too, the biggest.

Across the green baize table sat Kyril Nyurischev, immobile, pensive, all the clues of his face masked. Heavy eyebrows crawled like caterpillars over the frost of slate-gray eyes that sometimes put the taste of pennies in Metzilov's mouth. A face etched with grainy ravines, old yet still hard. Hard enough to have sent thousands of Russian dissidents to an arctic gulag or, if they were lucky, into the stillness of deep earth.

Metzilov shifted in his chair. He had posed several questions, and Nyurischev was taking his time answering. He rubbed his thin nose as Nyurischev finally decided to speak.

"I would not underestimate the American response."

"Their banks are closed. Their financial markets, too. What can they do?"

"Open them."

"Please, Comrade President, let me repeat. These Eurodollars were part of Europe's credit structure. All we have to do is sell dollars short. We're bound to make a huge win."

30

"This *shorting,* go over that for me again. Sounds foolish to me."

Once again Metzilov explained the trading device, long accepted in Western markets, for selling what you never owned in the first place. Those who judged any currency, commodity, or security as overpriced would sell to investors who thought differently. If the seller was right, and prices eventually dropped, he stepped in and bought at the lower price, thereby covering on his earlier sale. Profits were often enormous, and the beauty was that you could arrange the whole business with very little money up front, though you did make a full gift of your nerve.

"Our nerve," said Metzilov, his manner silky with persuasion, "is stronger by far than the U.S. dollar."

"You are talking of gambling hundreds of millions in Russian rubles!"

"Except," argued Metzilov, "it is not a gamble. We will sell the dollars to European banks, forcing them to sell back to us later if necessary at some fraction of our cost. The difference we pocket. And the difference is what we'll contribute to the Bank for International Settlements as our reserve pledge behind the new currency . . . We go in for free."

Nyurischev chilled a smile, answering, "Nothing is for free, Metzilov."

"We can put the blade to the Americans again. Unbearable pressure. I'm sure of it."

"They could always abandon the Eurodollar."

"And what little credit they have left would be forever ruined. Besides, their pride wouldn't allow it."

"I don't see why European banks will cooperate in a venture like this."

Metzilov made a small twisting motion with one hand. "They either go along or we shut off their oil. It's quite simple, really."

"And the British?"

"In time, Comrade President, we'll deal with them," said Metzilov, triumph evident in his face.

"And the details of this plan. Have they been thoroughly reviewed with the Finance Ministry?"

"I've personally gone over every point with them."

Nyurischev slid a small rectangular silver case from his coat pocket, opened it, and took out a brown Turkish ciga-

31

rette. Tapping its end against the case, he waited for Metzilov to light it.

Then he asked, "What of their bullion?"

"Europe's banking gold is still held in New York at the U.S.'s Federal Reserve Bank. Some of it is in Switzerland. The rest is kept in the custody of the various central banks in various capitals."

"How will it be moved to Russia, then?"

"That's stage two. Once the dollar is flushed out of Europe's system, the *last* link with America will be broken. Then we squeeze Europe for its bullion."

"There must be some risk to it," said Nyurischev, breathing smoke across the table.

"No one says where it is. We've gone over it and over it. Though I understand your concern . . ."

Metzilov left his reply unfinished. A subtle dig was enough. Nyurischev was a practiced survivor. He wouldn't care to be on the wrong side of a good thing.

"Tell this man Piegar we insist on one-third representation at BIS. For the time being, the European bullion can remain where it is. But we reserve the right to open that question in the future."

"And the operations against the dollar?"

"Yes."

A loop formed in the corner of Metzilov's mouth. He smiled as he gratefully replied, "It will be a grand triumph, Comrade President. Another shining hour."

Nyurischev only nodded. Still uncertain about the mechanical details of the plan, even the need for it, he decided to approve it anyway. Anything that spelled more trouble for the Americans was bound to be greeted eagerly by the Politburo.

Metzilov shuffled some papers together, and was about to arise from his chair when Nyurischev stilled him. "I'm not through yet." The caterpillars over his eyes jumped down. "These grain-production reports. The shortages are unacceptable."

"It's the weather, Comrade President. Not enough rainfall. We're unable to divert sufficient irrigation water from the Volga and Dnepr—"

"What are you doing about it? Who are you coordinating the problem with? And when do I see options and solutions?"

32

"The army has first priority on the necessary mat—"

"Get more materials."

"We'd have to purchase them abroad."

"Do it."

"We don't have the ready credit. Perhaps after we complete the dollar operation—."

"You are head of State Central Planning, Metzilov. Get moving. Our citizens aren't bargaining for hungry winters every year."

Meekly now, his wind slipping, Metzilov answered, "We can buy grain from Australia or Canada, perhaps the Argentine. It all depends on the dollar oper—"

"You will drop everything until the problem is settled," warned Nyurischev.

"I will assess it again immediately."

"Good," said Nyurischev, rising. "Your future depends on it." Then he turned and limped toward the door that led to his private office.

Gregor Metzilov sank back into his chair. Wiping corn-colored hair off his troubled brow, he reconsidered his position. Hard to gauge Nyurischev's true support for gutting the dollar, cutting away the last of that cancer from Europe. This grain business was a problem that might require hellish amounts of credit. Or rain. Everything else is going so smoothly, why in hell won't it rain on time?

He had planned everything else so well. His arguments were the telling ones that had counted before: step by step, grab the vital unprotected resources to the south. America? No, she would never fight thousands of miles from her shores again. Not until the spiritual wounds of Vietnam were healed, and that would take years. Nor could her Indian Ocean navy pose any honest threat. How, comrades, how . . .

He'd been heard, then heard again when laying out his plan for disabling the American banking system. Making utter fools of the Wall Streeters had taken nothing more than sowing discord among the OPEC cartel members, pitting them against one another, causing a modest price war. When oil prices fell there was less money earned to pay off the billions loaned by the American banks to the OPEC countries and to other nearly destitute third world nations. And when forty crack Russian divisions rolled into Iran, then Saudi afterward, oil shipments declined by

33

half. The money flow almost stopped, and the banks were forced to call in their shaky loans. But no one could pay them. Not Mexico, Brazil, Nigeria, Israel, Korea—none of the big borrowers had the money to make good. A liquidity problem became a solvency crisis, ending up in the Panic when Moscow forced the OPEC countries to withdraw their remaining funds from Wall Street. The banks, demolished, shut their doors with a clang heard round the world.

Metzilov sighed. His finest moment, most brilliant coup, winning loudest praise from the Politburo and promises of high promotion when the time was right.

At a distance, when possible, he studied the crafty methods of the Shang-Magan. Of how the weight of this world was swung by those controlling its real wealth. Yes, Russia had armies to secure her needs. The Magans had no armies, only their cunning tricks. Soon, Metzilov reminded himself, he'd have to supply Monte Carlo with another report of some sort, a carefully phrased one.

Rain, you whore, he thought. Nyurischev wants grain, does he? What better way to finance it than with the money in Europe's bank vaults? But it was time now to do some raining on Hans-Otto Piegar, waiting at the Metropole across Red Square, for the past twelve hours.

5

Washington

Groggy after all the hopscotch flying, needing a shave,
Culhane's attitude toward niceties was subzero and dropping. Tired, too, of the months of stonewalling. This
government owed him three tons of gold—the entire capital
of Culhane & Company while it still drew breath. He
wouldn't beg, though. Burn maybe, like now, but he was
damned if he'd beg from this crowd.

Nearly missing a step, he followed the blue-uniformed
guard up the bluer-carpeted stairs into the West Wing.
Then the guard pointed and stepped away as Culhane entered the Oval Office. Going directly over to Halburton, he
shook his hand. Then he was introduced to Joshua Squires.

One glance at the complacently superior look on
Squires's face, the Racquet Club tie and Sulka shirt, the
dyed hair and unsteady eyes, and Culhane's earlier doubts
about the man were confirmed. A Rearden man, the New
Yorker's masquerading doll, who had been artfully manipulated into Washington through the play of sheer political
weight.

"You're very good to come all this distance," said the
President quietly.

"No more direct flights, so you can see a lot of country."

"Very inconvenient, I hear."

"Tiresome, anyway," said Culhane, who continued to study Squires. A Back Bay fop, he decided, and probably with watermelon juice for blood. Squires looked away.

Halburton moved closer, seating himself in a wing chair facing the other two men as they sat down. "I was discussing a problem with Secretary Squires when you arrived. I asked him to stay on for a minute."

"I'd prefer discussing my business in private," said Culhane, observing Squires clench at the very direct reply.

"Yes, but first let's clear up this misunderstanding over the gold you claim is owed."

"Misunderstanding? Zaire shipped cobalt for this government's account and the terms were for gold. I paid them when you wouldn't."

"Yes, I know, and perhaps Secretary Squires can explain our situation."

Both men looked at Squires, who fidgeted, then began, "Under the Emergency Powers Act, the President is lawfully empowered to suspend any contract that runs counter to the national interest . . . It was that same act that enabled us to reestablish the Gold Commission to determine whether our currency should once again be backed with gold specie. Congress agreed to go along only if all further transactions in gold were stopped pending the findings of the commission."

Culhane swiveled his eyes from Squires to Halburton, knowing that at least one of them was a fraud. He thought: You sons of bitches ought to hang for a while, then be shot at first light.

But instead he insisted, "This government has a gold obligation to me. Period."

"The Treasury's lawyers don't consider it binding," said Squires, offended by the Californian, trying to guess exactly why he was here anyway.

"Without first advising me or the government of Zaire?" asked Culhane of Halburton.

"An oversight. You'll remember that the White House was in transition then."

"The government broke its word. That's hardly an oversight."

"There was no choice in the matter, I assure you," said Halburton, testing, still wary.

"Welshing is always a choice."

36

Halburton's back arched. He was saved from a reply as Squires said: "You can always file an action in the Court of Claims."

"I haven't got five years to dawdle away."

"Well now, that's your problem, isn't it?" asked Squires sullenly.

Culhane covered Squires with a grapeshot look. *"You* may become my problem."

"What's that supposed to mean?" asked Squires, riveted by Culhane's stare.

"Just that I've every intention of collecting what I'm owed. Treasury lawyers or not."

"Not very quickly you won't, but then, you could always accept cash and be done with it."

"After you and your crowd destroyed it. Not likely, Squires . . ."

"All right . . . all right," said Halburton nervously, standing up, trying to dampen the tension. "Perhaps, Mr. Secretary, you should leave us now."

With Squires gone, Culhane asked, "Am I supposed to accept that drivel? Is that why I'm here?"

"You've no written contract. As a lawyer, I'd say you have a case, since the Pentagon has the cobalt . . . I agree, though, it would take years—"

"Sorry, Halburton. That whole trading arrangement was done through the back door so the Russians wouldn't get wind of it. I don't need written contracts, and I had the word and handshake of the man you replaced."

"Quite possibly you did. But this is now, isn't it?"

"You're reneging again, is that it?"

"In a moment I'd like to explore a possible solution." Halburton rubbed his palms together, searching for a place to begin. Then he told Culhane of Squires's report of a week earlier about the Bank for International Settlements' drastic ruling on the dollar, finishing with "What's your opinion?"

"I don't have one."

"Try a guess, then."

"Someone's pulling the chain tighter, forcing this country into isolation."

"Who besides Russia? You must have access to—"

"I'd guess the European banks are involved somehow," said Culhane idly, unwilling to say more.

37

"You think they can make it stick?"

"Ask Squires and his banking geniuses. They pumped a trillion dollars into Europe's money pool. Europe's just now returning the favor."

"How we got into such a mess, I don't know."

"The government was warned of a trade war. You served on the U.S. Trade Commission, so you must have seen it coming."

"Did you, Culhane?"

"Put it this way—I *thought* I went into gold."

"I'm told you know a great deal about commodities. Grain, particularly."

"I'm a trader. Or *was*."

"Maybe we can arrange a bargain, then," said Halburton, very cautiously, before adding, "I realize I wasn't expected to have this job, but I've got it, and I admit to needing help."

Culhane's attention sharpened to a pinpoint. "Is that why you've got a lightweight like Squires around?"

"He was already here. And I can't get rid of him without offending the Reardens."

"Why are you telling me this?"

"So you'll believe me when I say no gold can be released until the question of a new currency is decided. I've been trying to get the Currency Reform Act out of Rearden's Senate committee for weeks now. Throwing Squires out won't help anything."

"That's your fight, not mine."

"Oh, I think it's yours too. Your interests and mine are quite the same."

"You mentioned a solution of some sort." Culhane got up to stretch. His muscles were tired after the trip from Los Angeles. He wanted a shower, a shave, and some sleep. Mostly, though, he wanted to hear more about Halburton's bargain.

Halburton pointed over to two thick volumes lying on his desk. "I read those reports you prepared for the government three years ago. Also, the speech you gave before the Club of Rome . . . You predicted it all, mostly."

"And it made its biggest noise when it hit the ash can."

"Just so," said Halburton softly. "In your report you stated that eighty percent of our minerals must be imported."

38

"Less now. You have twenty million people unemployed, and half the usual rate of industrial activity."

Halburton tapped his reading glasses on the desk in a series of impatient clicks. Coming out of his chair again, he said, "How long would it take to remedy the stockpile program?"

"You're short platinum, manganese, chrome, antimony, vanadium. Short across the board. You'd have to barter for everything unless you use gold. Hard to bring off . . . Damn near impossible."

Pacing, Halburton turned around, stopping suddenly. His face was taut, white lines showing around his mouth. "Some of our military are threatening war without the approval of Congress or myself. They're afraid we're getting cut off."

"You'll lose it, too, the shape we're in."

"I'm determined to avoid war," said Halburton. "All war—including the civil war this country is headed for if we can't find a solution soon. That would spell the end, the end of it for us, the end of democracy, our liberties, everything we've stood for. Brother killing brother again to eat, survive."

Abruptly, Halburton stopped in the middle of the room, looked up somewhere on the ceiling, and said, "I'll be back . . . And remember, this is *your* country too!"

Culhane surveyed the empty room. It seemed like some worn-out mausoleum. A man could bury himself in here, he thought, and under problems he couldn't really see or touch or even smell. How had any of them ever operated a nation while locked inside this place? A place where you could play with yourself, or where Kennedy supposedly played with his girls, but you were always fenced out.

Halburton is wrong about this being my country. One's country, any country, is an accident of birth. Someplace that stamps you with its citizenship, gives you a number, regales you with its myths. Taxes you to the grave and beyond, and steals what it can't tax.

Six times now he'd been in this room, never once really understanding any of its occupants. The place needed sprucing up, too; the blue-and-gold carpet was coming apart around the edges; a brown stain shaped like Florida marred one wall; the curtains were faded and the windows smudged.

Still, the remains of his fortune were in the clutches of

39

this very House. And, beyond a doubt, he knew his trading leverage was nil. So if Halburton's got a deal to offer, why is he walking around on cat's feet? thought Culhane.

Coming back through the door, Halburton went to the windows overlooking the Rose Garden. Near the windows a door was ajar, admitting air thick with humidity.

"Would you clarify something for me?"

"Possibly. I don't know," Culhane said.

"I've been told you helped engineer the OPEC oil embargo against us back in 1973 or so."

Culhane let the statement hang as he studied Halburton with care. "It's the Russians who call those shots now."

"You did it, though."

"I've no comment on it, Halburton."

"Well, it is right to say you had a hand in private talks with the Middle East countries about forming their own trading bloc? Joining the Arabs and Israel into one sphere?"

"Something like it," Culhane said. "It went off the tracks when this government, along with Europe and Japan, got scared and poked their long noses where they didn't belong." He remembered it all quite clearly. Bitterly, too.

"A matter of opinion, I'd say."

"You think so? Here's a matter of fact, then—we almost had a first-rate deal glued together. One that would have settled old scores and made for a sparkling future. Instead, you got a Sinai war and no oil for a while."

"You really think governments, this one anyway, sidetracked you?"

"They were afraid . . . Dumb, but there it is."

"Afraid of what?"

"None of you wanted a couple of hundred million people forged into a new world power . . . Not one with all that oil, with lands that could be made arable, with the real possibility of becoming industrialized, like Japan."

"So we were warned with the embargo?"

"You were warned, all right."

"I see."

"I doubt if you do. But your problem isn't what I think or don't think, is it?"

"In a way it is."

"Why?"

"Culhane, I need you here in Washington to restore the strategic stockpile reserves. Help me get the materials

40

this country needs to survive and I'll sign an Administrative Order authorizing your gold payment when the time is right."

"You really expect me to get waltzed twice?"

"Perhaps you don't have the stomach for the fight . . . the only fight making any sense at all."

"I fight alongside people I trust. Unfortunately, that doesn't include most governments."

"Why not try me?"

What's he really asking me for? To bail him out, and with what? Violin music. I'd need the whole Magan system, the Monte Carlo Inspectorate, all of it, to even have a chance. Culhane lit a Honduran #7 panatella, thinking more, trying to figure out the other side of Halburton's offer.

"I might try you if you try me with the three tons," he told Halburton through a bent ring of smoke.

"I can't go against Congress. When the climate changes, I will sign a release. You've my word on it."

"I'm afraid you're whistling. It would take a miracle to bring it—"

"Those books you wrote"—Halburton pointed over at his desk again—"you said it could be done. I read them."

"That was *then.*"

"Three tons of gold, Culhane. Anyone understands those numbers. Just help me and I'll do the same for you . . . Tell me, what would someone need to even attempt it?"

Culhane decided to risk some truth on him: "A map of the unknown. A blue-ribbon method of putting information together. A crack staff. Credit or a freeing up of the U.S. gold to trade with." Culhane aimed another stream of smoke toward the fireplace. "And you'd need very, very good dice."

"And if there is no U.S. gold to trade with?"

"Probably impossible without it. I don't know."

"Care to find out for your three tons of gold? I'll keep my promise," repeated Halburton, "if you'll get behind me on this."

Halburton went to his desk and wrote a note. Afterward, he walked over to Culhane, offering his hand and saying, "Think it over."

Standing, Culhane examined the lined, soft face. Halburton's mouth twitched nervously at the corner. His eyes and the flesh around them were hounded, and his hand-

41

shake was given with spare strength. He looked frail, as timid as a defrocked bishop.

"Now, let me ask you one," said Culhane. "Is it true the Russians have offered to let up if you'll agree to dismantle the entire U.S. missile capability?"

Halburton tensed again, seemed almost ready to shudder, saying, "That's a corner we can't get backed into, what has our military so frightened . . . Pure blackmail!"

"Blackmail? I'd say they passed that point some time ago."

"Will I hear from you soon as to whether you'll come?" said Halburton.

"You'll hear." Culhane moved toward the door. "Maybe you should try the New York Corporation."

"No. That wouldn't do at all."

"Who knows? I hear they at least have options on certain—"

"No. I've enough Rearden problems right now."

Closing the door, Halburton leaned against it, his head lowered. He felt cheapened somehow. Culhane is entitled to his fair due, and we're doing him out of it. A false bargain I've offered, and therefore one with no standing whatsoever. Yet I need to noose him. To regain three tons of gold most men would cannibalize their own mothers, commit treason, sell out their most sacred beliefs.

First, trust him. Tell him everything important. Drive him, push him as if you were all the elephants in Africa. You will see . . .

Halburton remembered Van Slyke's words exactly. Asking questions, then for other references, he had been cautioned to stay calm, stay silent: Culhane was nobody to trifle with. And of the laws against extortion and conspiracy to defraud, the Dutchman had only told him, rightly, "A President must turn that coin over for himself."

Coin. The very word hoisted Halburton's worries a notch higher. Quite aware, he was, that the U.S. Government had no accurate count of how much gold it really owned, free and clear.

6

Chicago

Fourteen hours and two flight delays later, Culhane arrived at O'Hare in Chicago. His suit hung on him like a mussed blanket. He'd slept on a bench at LaGuardia, then on the tight-seated American Airlines 727 operated, as were all commercial flights, by the Air Force. All he'd had to eat was a bowl of greasy chicken soup, some tea, and a hardtack biscuit.

The terminal tunnels were empty, their lights bony. Billboards on the walls were stained with graffiti. One bit of scrawl, *Jesus Saves,* had been amended to *Jesus Sucks.*

Going through two security checks, Culhane found no coffee shop open, no newsstand, not even a bar. At the counter for check-in to Los Angeles, a listless agent told him to count on a four-hour delay. And, yes, all airport hotels were shut, had been for months now. That was it. You flew the Air Force version of commercial aviation or you didn't fly. He found a bank of seats and flopped out on three of them.

Culhane groaned inwardly at the folly of it all. Only a few years ago, when the country was bailing itself out of the worst trouble since the Thirties, he had pleaded with Washington to stop it. Stop the drunken spending, quit

43

squandering the assets, and please Christ put the precious stockpiles right for a change.

Polite smiles; distant ones, too.

And begged every top industrialist he knew to look down the line, over the horizon, fix the future sensibly.

More smiles, backslapping, offers of drinks and more business. You're sleepwalking, he had told them, and the window you're headed for is twenty stories up and wide open. He could have forced some to listen closely, but inevitably and ironically they would have cried foul to Washington. And once Washington went into heat, with bureaucrats sniffing about, he would have needed to pray up a long litany with the Council of Six as to why Washington was falling out of its tree again. So he hadn't pushed it, and should have, when the chance was dancing right there in his hands. How you learn, always the hard way, Culhane thought, as the past sin of omission scolded deep inside his ear.

He missed the Gulfstream II that used to run him anywhere in the world on a moment's notice. To Chicago even, once a month, to talk with his grain traders and to attend the Board of Trade meetings as a governor. Closed. Hard to believe the greatest trading market in the world was boarded up now. He missed the boisterous hollering of the trading floor, all the friendly cursing, elbowing, even mild hysteria as the brokers traded billions of dollars in futures contracts each day. Nothing had ever excited him more; neither winning ocean races with *Eastern Star,* nor his horses capturing the big purses in California, New York, or France. But now the horses and the yacht were gone, he reminded himself, just like the Board of Trade.

Halburton had asked for a *guess* as to who, besides the Russians, was behind the operation to finish the dollar off. Seven, no, eight months earlier, Culhane had seen a report done up by the Monte Carlo Inspectorate. Very revealing, too, as it detailed how Moscow, using third-party agents in higher circles of American banks, had favorably influenced massive loans to Romania, Poland, Nigeria, Argentina, Mexico, and other wanting countries. And how the Russians were busy plotting stronger strangleholds on those same countries, in turn forcing loan defaults and leaving the banks with huge losses. Clever maneuvering

44

from the Moscow sidelines—not a shot fired, none necessary—with the snare working perfectly.

Is Halburton really naïve enough to think he can recover this country by playing with the strategic stockpiling program? That's like catching Niagara Falls in a paper cup. Yet Halburton must act. With a lady's maid like Squires at his side? No help, no gold is what he implied, the pretty bastard.

The obscure chalklines of an idea worked their way into the corners of his mind. There is always a way. Always. He began to think about the Straits of Hormuz, that passageway of water formed like a liquid question mark, through which half the world's oil moved. Somewhere inside the pulses ticked away. He knew the signals by now; later, they might even tick louder in a coherent pattern.

He rolled over, trying to find a comfortable position. Hungry, God, he was hungry all right. But he had been hungry before, and so he tried to stop thinking about it.

An image of Hormuz returned. Oil was the lever, wasn't it? Oil and grain. "Always trade for the main lever" was what Ken-chou Ming had taught him in Hong Kong those many years ago. And beautiful honey-skinned Jia and her brother, Richard, who were in Shanghai now and probably knew the gospel of survival by heart. A haze closed over Culhane, and he slept.

7

New York

Ah, there she was! Clay Flickinger saw Andrea Warren crossing Fifty-eighth Street, looking like a sexual hurricane ready to mow down everyone in sight. Something, no matter how small, would always move in him whenever he observed her. She'd be just right: classic breeding, nicely educated, a clever way of winning over confidence.

He had heard once of a comment made by the Duke of Abruzzi at a pigeon shoot years before in Deauville: "She's the finest woman wingshot in America and has the best balls I've seen—thank God they're on her chest!" A chorus of laughter from the other hunters, men, soon disappeared as Andrea Warren wiped-the-eye of every one of them; she shot seventy birds inside the ring without a miss.

No denying she was frivolous, even wayward at times, and maybe it was the residue of her bluish blood. Her mother could be like that, yet Flickinger didn't care just then to think about Andrea's mother, or her father either.

Andrea wore sky-blue silks under a wide-brimmed straw hat with a flowery scarf tied around it. A breeze molded the dress against her breasts and swirled the filmy material around her long-striding legs. He watched her sure glide, how she walked in a straight line, head high, moving lithely.

Full of verve, her face excited, Andrea Warren came closer. Flickinger stood up, answering her with his own smile, which needed more mouth and less chin.

"Clay, oh, you!" Flying the last few steps, she took both his arms in her hands, pressed, then raised and hooked her arms around Flickinger's rigid neck. The straw hat tilted up, and he could see the canary hair feathering across her brow and, underneath, the almost unlined green eyes.

"You look like an ad for danger."

"I'll do the flirting here, thank you," Andrea said, cutting a wide smile. Releasing him, she went on, "What brings you to Gomorrah? Awful, isn't it?" Her voice was honeysuckled, though deep for a woman.

"Been over a year now. How's your mother?"

"She's in Florence mooching off the Count Valfiore. She just couldn't take it here anymore." Andrea's smile vanished. She found it slightly embarrassing to discuss her mother, especially with Clay Flickinger.

"So," Flickinger said, "tell me what goes on with you. Sit, shall we?"

"Living my life in the closet, like everyone else. One of the nouveau poor. There's scuttlebutt the *Times-Herald* is thinking of closing down the New York bureau. Food lines, the UN gone, crime waves—all that stuff isn't fresh enough to print anymore. That's what goes on with me. And you?"

"I'll come to that presently." He might as well tell her now. "The *Times-Herald is* going to close its bureau here."

"God! If that doesn't ring the last bell. I don't want to seem rude, but is this going to take long?"

"I doubt it. Why?"

"Someone in the office lifted my food coupons. Right from my purse! I have to sign a thing at the Control Board."

No trivial matter, but she wasn't whining about it, and Flickinger liked that side of her. "A situation's breaking in Washington that's tailor-made for you."

"Move there again? Uh-uh."

"Why not? You think you could land a slot with another newspaper?"

"You couldn't buy one if you were Walter Cronkite incarnate," Andrea said, a little uneasily.

"What's to hold you here?"

48

"A nice sportswriter I know who just lost his job. That's all . . . It's all so damn depressing. You'd think the government could do something." Andrea put a thumbnail against the edge of her teeth, looking past Flickinger to a strolling policeman, and stayed silent.

"That Tim Rearden business still got you corkscrewed? Is that it?"

"Done and gone years ago."

"Still got your father's . . . I mean your apartment in Georgetown?"

"The last tenants beat me out of three months' rent. State Department people! Can you believe it?"

Flickinger smiled sparingly. "Teach you not to consort with the enemy."

"Yeah. Tell it to the mayor, if you can find her. And why me in Washington?"

"Does the name Rushton Culhane mean anything to you?" The supple animal presence of her aroused him, and Flickinger shifted sideways on the bench; he couldn't help it.

"From California? We did a piece on him, I think, when he bellied up . . . Married an actress or someone."

"The same. Halburton signed him on as an adviser to run the strategic stockpile program."

"What is it? Materials and stuff?" She frowned, with a thin furrow showing over her nose.

"Yes, exactly. The country requires thirty-six types for industry to even yawn. We produce eight."

"And how do you get involved?" Andrea asked directly. An ingrained habit by now, but still a nervy question.

"I'm to be Culhane's batman," Flickinger replied dourly, "run errands and lay on logistics."

"How do I fit in?" asked Andrea, hoping she didn't.

"Same sort of thing. Just like drawing up those profiles on the UN-ers. Start interviewing Culhane, develop him as a news source, get as close as you can."

"Clay, I don't think this is my gig. Not at all. Really I don't." The large straw hat partly hid the perplexed look on Andrea's face, but Flickinger caught it anyway.

Flickinger's thin, arrogant face hardened. "Your New York bureau closes, then where'll you be?"

"Up shitto creek," answered Andrea stiffly, "and of course you know it."

"So let's get down to it. Here's some background material on Culhane," said Flickinger, pointing to a blue vinyl folio on the bench. "Some of it's public, some not."

"Well, *there,*" said Andrea, "looks like quite a lot. Is he one-legged? Anything juicy?"

Christ, how fast they change. Threaten their security and it's all milk to the puppy. With no real need to cull his memory, he answered her with:

"Born illegitimately in Honolulu in 1937. His mother came from Boston and she taught mathematics at the University of Hawaii. Seems she was also the top call girl in the islands in those days. The father of record was some Australian Royal Naval captain . . . Culhane's mother died in the Pearl Harbor bombing. He was raised for a time in an orphanage, later on ran off to sea. Around 1957 he shows up in Hong Kong, where a Chinese family, name of Ming, taught him a thing or two about trading in world markets . . . He came back here and eventually marries a middling-to-good Norwegian actress. Three children, I think, but one died somehow . . . He's a real gee-whizzer, speaks five languages, and reputedly is a member of the Shang-Magan. They say that's the largest trading club in the world . . . Made and lost the kind of money I never heard of before. Racing stables, jets, even with his own schooner. Somehow he stayed clear of the bored-and-beautiful set. Matter of fact, he's anonymously financed twenty Hawaiian orphans through college every year and supported a starving tribe in the Sudan . . . Those are the short and cracked ribs of Culhane's life. There's more in the file there."

"Yachts and racehorses, is it? Interesting," said Andrea, thinking that she'd have to reread the *Times-Herald* article. "What's his . . . his personal signature like?"

"Very unpredictable, they say. We don't know much."

"You're the one who's going to be working with him. Why do you need me?"

"Better that way, that's all. And that's also enough."

With one large, capable hand Andrea picked up the blue folio, putting it on her lap. She felt like a trapped nun desperately wanting to pitch out the vows. And the oath she wanted to utter stayed put behind her generous mouth.

She had to get to the Control Board soon. Clothes, her

sportswriter, closing and opening apartments, all the other . . .

"When am I supposed to be in Washington?"

"Next week is sufficient."

"Christ! What about my clothes and all the other—"

"Besides, it might be healthy to get out of here."

Flickinger pointed up to a large belch of smoke staining the sky. They were burning refuse over on Park Avenue, and the drifting odor smelled faintly of fish oil. Andrea's nose wrinkled as she stood up, taking another look at Flickinger's wiry narrow body, short gray hair, gray suit, almost gray eyes. Neutral gray, she thought, the perfect human advertisement if you were selling very old chrome. She said nothing more, just regarded him coolly, then got up and walked away with that walk better poetry sings about.

He sat there quietly for several minutes, estimating how to find his way back to LaGuardia. Taxis were as scarce as loose airline seats, and buses never went out there anymore. A caravan of Salvation Army trucks circled through Sherman Square, coming to a stop near the Plaza Hotel. Soon, the noon-hour feeding of the worn and weary would begin—hot soup for a cold coupon. Five policemen formed up in a rank on the corner; they wore white helmets, and batons dangled from their wrists for controlling the often unruly crowds.

Flickinger wondered. Was she pretending she didn't know, just taking the payments and shutting up, letting the past keep its thin layer of dust? Was that a legible bet or not? The one killing had barely escaped the lens as it was. Two would be unthinkable.

Culhane. A continent's distance away and the son of a bitch was already a nuisance, reflected Flickinger, who looked around two times, saw nothing unusual, then coughed roughly from the Park Avenue smoke.

People were appearing now.

Time to get out.

8

Bel Air

A magical charm had prevailed there once. Anyone ever invited to the Firehouse Club didn't forget it quickly; some had called it the closest thing to a salon existing in Southern California. Reckless and sometimes inspired talk was encouraged. Notions of the bizarre were explored, and it was fun, exhilarating fun at times, and somehow the Culhane pool house seemed the perfect place for it all.

Only two rules were ever enforced: no talk of politics or religion; insulting behavior meant permanent exile. That was all. You could drink as much as you could hold, lie as much as you were believed, eat until your liver rebelled, play cards for money until you fainted. You could dance, lecture to yourself, even slip upstairs if you were very sly.

The regular members, who had met on the third Thursday of each month, were a hazardous bunch: four of the more sane members of the Hollywood mob, three good painters, the maestro of the Los Angeles Symphony, the chiefs of the police and fire departments, some industrialists, a blind poet, a top novelist, a professional stuntman, a retired astronaut, Willy Shoemaker, two professors from Cal Tech with Nobel prizes to their credit, Sant Saxa, Pepe Ruiz, who ran the bar at Chasen's . . . the list lengthened. No politicians were allowed in, and few lawyers, since their well-known habit of arguing when drinking ruined the fun.

Even when Culhane was traveling, couldn't be there, the festivities, and the laugh talk and the serious sort, flowed till the early hours, always. On those occasions Karin and Sant Saxa had directed the traffic. Quite skillfully, too, and they kept a sharp eye out for anything that would make for any newspaper talk.

The pool house stood on a flat of ground just below the rumpy ridge occupied by the main residence. An old firehouse, once, with a mansard roof, and brick walls now painted white. Culhane had bought it years earlier at public auction, restored it, then altered the interior to its present style.

Sliding glass replaced the old wooden doors. Inside, where flashy red engines once rested between fire alarms, the refurbishing included a marble-topped soda fountain, a wet bar, a small kitchen, several groups of bleached-leather lounging furniture, and a piano. He had kept the brass sliding pole that ran straight up through an opening into the second floor, which was divided into two large bedrooms, a huge bathroom with sauna, and another bar. Culhane's children had insisted upon the pole, and he agreed with them whenever he could.

Early evenings, like this one, and fresh breezes usually skipped through the live oaks and the taller firs; boughs and leaves rustled, quiet came. You were reminded of faraway countryside up there in the Bel Air hills and canyons.

Below, in the scooped basin of Los Angeles, you were reminded of a battleground. Vicious gangs roamed. Hospitals were in trouble, schools vandalized; watchdogs were fed better than many people. On the floury rim of the city no morning passed when bodies, snarled in sea kelp, failed to wash ashore. Suicides. Murders, too, even of infants. The law hid, when it could no longer cope. City dwellers went out into the night and stole crops from enraged farmers in the surrounding counties. You survived by agility, or by training and instinct, the way a jungle fighter or a smart wharf rat did.

Karin Culhane knew about the trouble down there, though she hadn't been off the property in months. She'd been in the hands of so many clinics, doctors, and healers that when the day arrived to come back here, she'd sworn

54

never to leave again. This was refuge. Culhane was her rock. Her children were all the other melody she needed.

She loved this room. It held a thousand memories, the ones of intimacy, laughing nights, the cliques of amusing people who had trooped through it. For now, it was a comfortable patch where she could go back, back more, and relive the magic times.

Across the room against one wall hung a rare collection of Comanche wood carvings under a row of feathered war bonnets. By her side was a chrome-bordered glass table mounted on elephant tusks: a gift from an Ivory Coast chieftain, a houseguest, who had made a serious offer to buy her. Checkering another wall were eleven framed studio photos commemorating feature films in which she had appeared in the lead role. Among those glossies were others of directors, some producers, and a few big-time male box-office draws, each picture inscribed with a flamboyant signature.

She had become quite good at blotting out the unpleasant, cruel images. It was so easy to invent one-act plays in her head. She could act out anything up there. Alone, no critics, not even a script to learn; it was much better than playing out scenes with some psychiatrist. Or she could remember the lavish parties that had once dizzied the main residence; nights a sultan would envy. And of how some of the younger actresses would sneak down to this pool house, go to one of the upstairs bedrooms with some producer, there to hear lies that no scriptwriter in the world could dream up.

With no more cocaine for fluffy dreams, the memories and invented plays in her head were the best party in town. Karin heard his sounds then. Her smile widened as she thought of another scene, far away in Paris, a long time ago. She would ask him.

Stepping out of a dressing room, toweling his thick dark hair, Culhane spoke to Karin. "Where'd our party go?"

"Sant and the children took the dishes up."

He walked over to the bar and poured the white of Mendocino Zinfandel into a balloon glass. He heard Karin ask, "Play it for me, Rushton . . ."

"Like some?" He raised the glass. "It's good."

"Just the song."

"On my way."

And he crossed the room, stopped, kissed her, then went to the piano bench. Leaning over, he turned a switch, then a dial on an instrument that could duplicate drums in six different sound combinations.

No glaze tonight in those haunted eyes that peered out from the haunting face. Classic beauty, badly bruised mind. He looked up at her and thought, It would take a very good painter to capture those delicate hollows in her cheeks and that smile with the chandelier in it.

Clinging oyster-white satin traced Karin's slender body. Thin puffs of white fur bordered the collar and the bottom of three-quarter-length sleeves. And from the light glowing behind her, Culhane could tell she wore nothing underneath the gossamer frock. With her coppery Norse hair, it all seemed so perfect, so right. But it was a dream smashed, and they both knew it.

Fingers strolling across the keyboard, he waited for a moment to mesh with the drumbeat. Then he nodded to Karin, who leaned against the piano.

"I remember you . . . You're the one who made my dreams come true . . . A few kisses ago. I remember you . . ."

As she sang, his memory swept back to that night at Maxim's when he first saw her. Two tables away, she had been surrounded by some hotshot Hollywood types and two well-known European directors. Loud talk of another film together (laughter); other talk of how the one they'd just wrapped up was bound for rave notices (nervous laughter); waiters gadding about, corks popping, two table captains preparing flambés. Among them only Karin had seemed bored, her wonderful mouth looking like a stepped-on worm.

He'd been alone, passing through Paris from Beirut on the way back to Los Angeles. Seeing her that way, lovely and so sad, he called a table captain over and sent her the oldest bottle of Champagne in Maxim's cellar. With it went one dahlia from his table vase, and his card, on which he'd written: "Nobody Ever Died of Laughter—Beerbohm (Max)."

A smile, like a diamond spray, lit up her face when she read it. Two or three shy looks later, seeing that he was alone, Karin had excused herself and come over. They talked. They talked and made a circus of other talk for

56

days straight. Cutting rolls of red tape, bribing a magistrate heavily, they had married in Venice ten nights later.

Twelve years ago, almost to the night, a slick Algerian pianist had played this song, and Karin had claimed the lyric as if it had been written only for her. Maybe it had, thought Culhane, as he worked across the treble keys.

". . . And, baby, when those angels asked me to recall . . . The thrill of it all . . . Then I will tell them I re-memmm-ber you."

Clapping his hands, Herbsant Saza came through the glass doors like a blue ghost. With his cinnamon skin, a frilled blue shirt, a dark velvet bow tie, and a midnight-blue smoking jacket, he looked like an operator of one of the old Havana nightclubs. But he gave it away with his gold ear bead and the rest of his glittering trinkets.

Culhane stopped playing. She would sing only for him. No one else, ever.

"I'll go up now," said Karin.

"Oh, but no, my lady," said Sant, moving into the room. "More song. God ask for more, and so does Saxa."

Karin smiled, slipping out of the brighter light, replying, "The power goes off in an hour. I have things to do for the children."

"I'll walk you up," Culhane said.

"You don't have to."

"I want to, babe." He said to Sant, "I'll be back in a minute."

They went out by the pool, climbed up several flagstone steps, up the brow of the ridge toward a path leading to the big house. Early stars showered the blue Pacific night, the last orange rays of sun having slipped well to the west now.

Reaching the path, she turned, saying, "A wonderful afternoon. Sorry about the food."

"I don't really miss those big dinners anymore. Do you?"

"Sometimes. I get damn tired of vegetables."

"Sant's got a line on some beef and—"

"Kiss me."

She took his lean face in her cool hands, brought it to hers, then ran her fingers through his coal-black hair, smoothing it, soothing him. Her hands built a cup under his square chin. And afterward, when they broke, she told

57

him, "I'm sorry that we couldn't be in bed tonight. I've been a terrible woman to you."

"Nobody can help it, Karin. It'll all come right, you'll see." But he knew it never would or could. Only a half lie, Culhane hadn't minded saying it.

"Just hold me for a minute. I can't bear to see you go, Rushton . . ."

He whispered to her, "Just a month or so. And Sant will be here."

"Maybe we can try. I don't mind if you—"

"I'll come up later."

"If we're just careful or you lock the door."

A hundred doors, he thought, and Culhane met her mouth again.

Down in the pool house, Sant Saxa had tipped the last of the Zinfandel into a glass. He sat on one of the lounge chairs, thinking, recalling, and staring absently at the pictures of Karin and the others.

Seventy-three years of life gone by, he thought, and the haywire of it all. And now the dogs of night are howling louder.

He could feel it in his marrow, and the doctors kept telling him about a tendency for fluid to build in his lungs. Some second sight of his Haitian blood told him it wouldn't be long now. A small thing to do for Rushton Culhane, thought Sant, and it might be the last one.

Rolling the wine in his mouth, Sant Saxa remembered glimpses of the Hong Kong days. Almost twenty-two years ago. Jesu Christo, flown where?

. . . Damn lucky to make it . . . Luckier Hong Kong take me after gunrunning in Venezuela and real estate in Mexico, would have worked too if bitch of governor's wife not so goddamned greedy . . . On the run I went . . . Had to . . . And if not for Ken-chou Ming giving me job there in his trading house, I still be pushing second-rate textiles . . . Then the kid come . . . A star-walker and we run it good until come this fuck of crash . . . Remember when Ken-chou tell me go to California with the bright one . . . Help him, restrain him, old Ming say to me . . . What a thing we put together . . . Too big, maybe . . . Hong Kong . . . Women . . . Be forty or thirty year old again for month, and be with those women . . . Young women and old whiskey . . . Their mother teach them those things . . . Grand-mothers too . . .

Saxa heard the panther-soft sound of Culhane's bare feet coming through the glass doors. He turned, saying, "Jesus, I have old dream of Hong Kong come back. Right in my head like one of those." Sant pointed toward one of the photographs of Karin.

"Peel me a copy. I'll bet it was of girls."

Saxa's grizzled head nodded vigorously. "Maybe you peel old man a hard drink?"

"Some Izarra?" A liqueur that Culhane favored, it was nail-hard and made by the Basques for igniting holidays and stopping tanks.

"That horse piss. Make me want to eat hay. Let me have please."

Culhane went to the bar and made drinks. He was running low on the Izarra, a case or so left, and couldn't get it anymore. He said, "Santo, we've got business to discuss. You ready?"

"Twenty-two year I be ready for you."

"That you have." Culhane brought the drinks and the bottle over across the thick green carpet. Sitting down, he looked steadily at this man, who was a hundred hands, and a head to go with them.

"Pray up me, all mothers," said Sant, who went into conference with his drink, sliding the Izarra into his impatient mouth.

Going more easily on his, Culhane said, "Tomorrow or the next day I'm off. So we better square away now."

"How you get there?"

"Air Force courier plane. They shuttle them back and forth with stuff that's not for the mails."

"Ain't be the same," said Sant.

"Just for a couple of months maybe. A damn nuisance, but Halburton has played it fair so far."

"We done okay so far. Thank to Jesus the red phone they put in."

Culhane nodded. "The big thing, Sant, is that I'll be able to get my hands on the government grain reserves. That may help a lot, you know."

"I don't like," said Saxa, finishing another tilt with his glass. "They bastards, you know."

"It's the best way to get our gold payment. Halburton is the only keyhole we have."

"Ain't you the one though? I think Shang people can't mess with government positions. Shit in horn, man, they got you—"

"I'm not taking any pay for it. Just a place to live while I'm there."

Saxa slumped forward a little toward the table. He poured more Izarra, the strength of it catching him. The idea of government, any government, bothered him. He'd run from at least three of them, and still had four passports, two of them bogus, in case he had to run again.

"You already know what's up with Tomlinson in Australia," continued Culhane, "and Baster Muldaur in Johannesburg. You'll have to keep all the dummy companies straight. I'll have some more for us to use when I get to Washington."

"Whose?"

"CIA has a bookful of them, I'm told. We'll get ten or twenty and use them just once, and only for the three-corner trades."

"Them bastards get too close."

"It's just an option, Sant. And they have information sources we might need and no longer have."

"Why not Shang-Magan help? Christ, you do plenty set up Monte Carlo."

"No." Culhane shook his head wearily. "You've got to get it straight, we're out of it for now. We're like any other outsiders." Culhane still found it hard to accept.

"Shang-Magan have Russian agent?" asked Sant Saxa. He'd never before explored these matters with Culhane, knowing how sensitive they were.

"Piped right in to Nyurischev, as a matter of fact."

"Make any sense me to see him?" asked Sant, quite seriously, and quite serious in the amount of Izarra he knocked back into his throat just then.

"We might never see you again . . . The key, Sant, the best play, is to keep working through Richard Ming in Shanghai as much as we can. Then Muldaur and Tomlinson."

"I guess CIA fronts work," observed Saxa, frightened a bit. "We mark up trades some and catch a profit."

Culhane shook his head again.

"Don't be damn fool," argued Sant. "Why not? We doing the work."

"It's a government game. It's their stockpile, their assets. It's not the same, and you know it."

"They owe us, and they never know if we mark up."

"But you and I would. Besides, I don't want the slightest chance of any trouble, Sant. I want the gold they owe us, and that's all."

Saxa went for the Izarra again, splashing some into Culhane's glass this time. Some of the clear fluid dripped onto a magazine cover before he uprighted the bottle.

"I appreciate, beyond words, that you'll stay here with Karin and the children until this thing is over."

"Tomorrow I go for beefs and milk," Sant said.

"I'm leaving two rolls of Krugers for you. I'm taking one, and that's the last we've got."

"I got some gold."

"You'll use mine, Sant, or what I've got."

"Only I take charity from who I hate."

"It's not charity, dammit."

"We all in a hurt, Rushton. Why you not let me sell paintings . . . Christ, I get a bank of gold in Europe."

Sant Saxa's olive-dark eyes moistened, their lids drooping slightly, and he rolled his eyes until only misted ivory showed; he was thinking again.

"We've been over that, so do me a favor and let it go."

"Don't be pig in the head."

The art was a deep-down part of Culhane, for keeps, a very high article of faith. He said, "They're our poetry, Sant. How can you sell the house poet? I wouldn't sell you for anything."

Saxa's eyes went white again, like miniature Ping-Pong balls, and Culhane couldn't tell whether he'd really been heard or not. It didn't matter. The art was a sort of legacy and would stay put, except for those paintings from the office that were crated to go with him.

Again, the dark hand around the neck of the squat bottle. Culhane hadn't seen the aging wire-puller take it in like this in years. The little man toyed very briefly with his drink before throwing most of it down the hatch.

"Save some for tomorrow," Culhane said.

"I fine . . . fine."

"The stuff explodes at that rate."

"Don't show it . . . Karin, she look fine tonight." Saxa threw open an empty palm, sat up, tugged at the Izarra with his other hand. "What do if she strip, run bare-ass again?"

"Get her inside and call Frank Henry on that list of phone numbers in the library," answered Culhane.

"Some sight, a woman that beautiful."

"That's not too funny, Sant."

"Sorry . . . she jus' so damn boot-i-fool. Ah'll be awful good those kids."

"Thanks."

Culhane wondered how much of tonight he'd have to repeat in the morning. Sant's head was weaving now, the eyes hooding heavily. He had intended asking the little man to keep an eye on the Taiwanese groundsman, who ran off frequently and was showing signs of returning to his old habits with opium. He had warned the Taiwanese once that his neck would get shortened if he pushed the narcotic toward Karin again. He'd go over it with Sant tomorrow.

"Y'ever think of Hong Kong?" asked Sant.

"Lots of times I do."

"Best time, eh? Think of Jia?"

God, how I remember her, thought Culhane, who tried to imagine what that narcotic of womanhood looked like now, what she was doing, how she lived in China. Married? Children? What?

"Ri-chad say you talk."

"It's just twice now we've talked. Just business."

"Jes-ush, you had good women."

"A taste learned at your knobby knee."

"Stay indoor, fuck for your country so you don't have to go fight for it!"

To Culhane's utter astonishment, the words had floated out without a missed beat and hardly a slur. But Sant Saxa toppled to one side, his glass of Izarra falling to the floor, his head angling awkwardly on the armrest. Out. He was out like a swirl of dust in front of a broom.

"Good night, you little genius," said Culhane to the elfin's deafened ears.

He went over and began to tidy Saxa up. Soft snores oozed through raspy breathing. Culhane stripped off

Sant's velvet bow tie, opened his shirt, and struggled the dinner coat off the slumbering, lifeless form.

Going to a closet, he took two beach blankets from one of the shelves. After two vigorous minutes, he had Saxa swaddled in wool, safely under for the night, and maybe for the whole of the next morning, too. Culhane knelt beside the couch and looked down into the tired, sad, wise face of this man he loved. Lowering his mouth, he kissed Sant's forehead.

He stepped outside under the blue canopy of night. Stars shone radiantly, dense paths of them chasing high over a quarter moon. He walked to one edge of the patio, turned, and craned his neck slightly so that he could see over the lip of ridge to the rambling house above. No lights were on in Karin's rooms. He ached, ached for her.

He remembered, then, the last time. Nearly a year ago, on Karin's first return from the clinic in Santa Barbara, and they'd made love one night. And, as they found each other, she had rolled abruptly from beneath him and cried out like some scolding child.

Racing for the door before Culhane could recover his senses, Karin had vanished somewhere in the vast house. Later, after a search, he'd found her downstairs in the library, huddled naked in a desk chair, telephone in hand, bawling, telling the West Los Angeles Police she'd been raped.

Culhane returned to the pool house, listened for Sant, found the other blanket and the other couch. He wouldn't think about the rape ever again, a promise he'd made before and knew was useless. He tried not to think of anything just then.

An hour later he was still trying. The thought of leaving was grinding stones in his heart. He gripped the blanket, then a seat cushion, knowing how bad it would get, being alone again. He'd have to watch it or it would seize him the way it had in the past. If he couldn't stay close to his blood, what the hell was the reason for anything . . .

And fudging it with Karin, telling her he'd only be gone for a month. Three or four of them was more like it. A sorry bitch of a job back there. How lovely. Much easier if he had the old commercial-intelligence team at Culhane & Company; easier yet if he could access the Shang-Magan Inspectorate in Monte Carlo, the best system ever built, like a hundred Rolls-Royce brains pulling for you every minute.

Still, with Sant here handling the ropes, it might work for a time. They had swung a four-sider last week: U.S. metallurgical coal against forty-seven million board feet of British Columbia plywood, the plywood crossed against Malaysian tin, the tin traded to Mexico for silver, the silver bartered back to China for titanium. It took a whole week, though, for a deal that could be transacted in a few hours in other days.

None of it possible, either, without Richard Ming in Shanghai agreeing to stick his neck out. A stroke of luck there. China would help, the way he'd tried to help them in the past when few others would.

Mings. No holding them down, no matter what the odds. They bounced back like rubber boomerangs. Wonderful people, some special strain in the blood, an immunity against defeat.

Culhane thought of Ken-chou Ming and the Hong Kong of the fifties, the city wide open and awash in deals. You could bargain anything except your name. Lose that and you were through. Sant was right. What days those were, a fairyland of excitement. Learn, learn, work, work, getting richer by the month and never having time to care or count it . . . Jia swimming him through the nights in her arms and thighs of purest bliss.

Fabulous, and I'm fabulous out on my ass, Culhane thought, rolling over and pulling up the blanket again. He was afraid, hollow and cold, and thinking helped it go away. Alone, back there, it would be like swallowing iodine. Every damn day of it.

Wind shivered the trees outside, tempting him to go up and sleep with the children. His last thought before sleep beat him down was to chuck it—tell Halburton to fly it by himself, because the Culhanes were headed out for Macao to start over.

Which was what would have happened had he known that tomorrow would be the last he'd ever see any of them alive. The last except for Sant Saxa, who snored away in peace a few yards away.

PART II

9

Washington

"Some nice pictures here, mister. Better'n those old lithos we took down," said a maintenance man, standing back to admire the Pissarro. "That sumbitch could handle a brush all right."

"Move to the right and the light will show his blues and oranges better."

The buzzer droned again.

"That be all?"

"You've been a real help," said Culhane, offering his hand.

"Anytime. And thanks for this," said the man, thumping his pocket with a stained hand, then stooping to pack his tools in a canvas case.

"I've got to get the door," said Culhane, and he moved off as the maintenance man looked around at the rest of the pictures he'd been hanging. He thought they were copies, and didn't really know the names of the painters anyway.

Opening the door, Culhane looked at the burr-headed man standing there, carrying a woven straw hat and a briefcase, and wearing a blank look.

"You must be Clay Flickinger," said Culhane, whose attention was diverted as the maintenance man came into the hall from the suite's other door.

"I am."

"Come on in. I've been rearranging the furniture in your place. At least I was told it's yours."

"It's leased by us," returned Flickinger, stepping past Culhane.

From habit born of long training, Clay Flickinger observed Culhane with a scientist's passion for detail. Mildly surprised that Culhane looked younger than his reported age, he was struck by the raw presence of the man. He looks like he could train heavyweights without using a mouthpiece, thought Flickinger.

"Those must be yours," said Flickinger, pointing at one of the paintings, glancing at the others.

"You like art or music?" asked Culhane.

"Never had much time for either one. It must be nice," said Flickinger with a slight edge in his words. "You've managed to get settled fast enough."

"They said you'd be out of town for a couple of days, so I thought I might as well put the laundry away."

"Loose ends in Florida," said Flickinger.

"How are you called? Clay . . . Flick . . . something else?"

" 'Mr. Flickinger' will do."

So it's going to be like that, thought Culhane. Well, fine, you can have it any way you like it.

"Your trip here go all right?" asked Flickinger in his curious monotone.

"My seatmate was a mailbag, though I appreciate your getting my gear here."

"You were Class A priority, Mr. Culhane. You have to know four bureaucrats with the right stamps to get that tag," said Flickinger, who looked with barely concealed envy at Culhane's bench-made shoes and the immaculately cut line of his suit.

Taking a chair, Flickinger leaned over and unsnapped his briefcase. Fumbling for a moment, he withdrew a slim envelope and laid it on a table.

"That's a White House pass, four books of food coupons, and some gas stamps. You've already seen your office, I hear."

"Yes," said Culhane, "though I don't know how much

I'll use it . . . And I've got a shopping list for you, and first on it is a secured phone line between this room and the White House signal board."

"You'd need an okay on that from the Man himself or his staff chief."

"It's in the works, and I'd appreciate it if you'd sort out the details. Also, I want it checked every day for security."

"Anything else?"

"Quite a number of things. You'd better get pencil and paper."

Flickinger fished in his briefcase for paper, then pulled a pen from the inside of his suit coat. He made the movements leadenly, chafing now, feeling strangely cowed.

"We'll want systematic watches on all primary and secondary ports and airfields in Africa. If you can get them, copies of the bills of lading for everything that's shipped out of that continent to anywhere in the world. I'll give you a list tomorrow of European trading companies to study up on."

Flickinger looked up and asked, "Where would they be located?"

"Luxembourg, Switzerland, Lichtenstein, and London. I'll take care of Singapore and Hong Kong in another way."

"We may already know about some or all of them."

"Maybe. But I want to compare what you have with what I already know. For example, one I left out is Rearden's New York Corporation. I want everything you've got on that operation."

Flickinger shook his head, pursing a smile. "That's domestic. Under law, we're not permitted to gather domestic intelligence without specific permission. Or didn't you know?"

"I used to brief some of your analysts. They certainly knew about my company's operation."

"Universal data collection. Background stuff," lied Flickinger.

"Please see what you can scratch up anyway."

"I'll try. Anything else?"

"Do you like cigars? Hondurans?"

"I chew on a pipe sometimes. I'm trying to stop. Go ahead, though."

Culhane went to another room. Flickinger gazed around

at the paintings, the two long davenports against the walls, and the deep-sided chairs flanking the small fireplace. He'd never been in this one before—plenty of others, but not this one. He didn't like this discussion, the way orders were getting rapped out, and he wondered if the paintings were hoax art. Probably. They said this bastard went broke, so they couldn't be the good ones.

Wisps of smoke from the panatella and the sounds of a recording of Hoagy Carmichael's "Stardust" trailed behind Culhane as he returned. He crossed the room to a window, opened it, and looked briefly across Lafayette Square to the White House.

Measuring Flickinger again, deciding the man ought to be retailing funeral services, he told him:

"I'll need a terminal strung to the computers of the National Security Agency. And I'll want to interview at least three of their systems and programming people."

"No. You'll be better off using us."

"I'm told their equipment is more advanced."

"Why the computer access? What's that supposed to do?"

"Probability games, regression analysis if there's enough data to base them on. Things like that."

"We can do that sort of work quite easily. We've got the people," claimed Flickinger.

"Much of the time I don't know what I'm looking for," evaded Culhane. "So please set it up the way I've asked."

Miffed, Flickinger recoiled inwardly at the scorching he'd be getting from the Director. Culhane was trying to cut them out of the information circuit already.

"I want a linkup," Culhane was saying, "to the best and the friendliest of foreign intelligence services represented in Washington."

"I'd advise using only one. The British," said Flickinger, thinking it might even work to his advantage.

"Fine. We can start there."

"I'll need to know your purpose."

"When I know you'll know. Meanwhile, just get it going, if you don't mind."

"That's hardly an explanation."

"Have to do for the time being."

"You might be overstepping your charter, you know?"

A circle of silence as Clay Flickinger realized he didn't

know very much about Culhane's authority or of what limits, if any, Halburton had put on the man.

"I was told you want the use of our corporations of convenience."

"About twenty of them," Culhane said.

"Outside the United States?"

"Yes, and with no possibility of an ownership trace."

"I'll need more details."

And so began Clay Flickinger's limited education on how multisided bartering trades worked. Culhane took him through several examples, though he made no mention of what he was doing with Richard Ming in Shanghai. He explained how very large commodity trades were often broken up into smaller ones, and the why and wherefore of dummy companies. That tax dodges had nothing to do with it. But keeping, say, the London market guessing about the availability and price of Chilean copper did. You camouflaged your moves. People contacts were critical, as was the role of Sant Saxa, who would orchestrate the details. "You work in the dark," Culhane told him, "or run the risk of getting skinned at the stake. It's tricky sometimes."

Intent now, Flickinger's mind was absorbing it all like a sponge. It all bore a striking resemblance to the craft of intelligence work—the manipulation of knowns against unknowns.

"This man Saxa. We'll have to get a security clearance on him."

"He's my responsibility. Forget about him."

"Sorry, that just won't fly."

"It'll have to," said Culhane, giving Flickinger a look that would bruise stone. "There's no chance, none, of handling this problem without him. Wouldn't think of it."

"That's your business, but we'll have to check him just the same."

"Check all you want, if you can, but he's in to stay."

Flickinger didn't comment. His pained expression telegraphed all the message necessary. Control, he was thinking of control, and not liking it when recalling how Culhane had been described as a *wayward*.

"Now here's the easy part," said Culhane, running a thick smoke ring into the air. "Do you know the Metropolitan Chief of Police?"

71

"No, I don't. How in hell does he fit in?"

"Meet him. Find out who's the best black-marketeer in the District. The one under police protection."

"You're missing me there."

"This hotel is short on food, and this hotel is where I currently live. They need some help."

Flickinger's mouth opened; an astonished look made its slow journey across his narrow face. "It's a very poor way for a government employee to do things."

"Correction, I'm not an employee . . . But the question is, can you do it?"

"Why can't you?"

"I suppose I could, but I thought you were here to help me."

"Not that way I'm not. And it could get embarrassing if the word got around I was."

"Look into it, please. Just get the name and whereabouts of the right person," said Culhane. "I'll do the rest."

Culhane eyed Flickinger evenly. He didn't want to alienate the man, or falsely nourish his hypocrisy, either. The sigh he made was hidden by another pillow of smoke.

"When the CIA buys information, turns a foreign agent, or plants one of its own agents abroad, you call all of that Sunday-schooling."

Flickinger shifted uneasily in his chair. Feeling put upon, his imagined grip on the situation fading, he said, "It's different. You know it is."

Culhane sat there as quietly as a sphinx. A locking of wills, with the turf and rules different for each of them. One man a spy, the other a speculator, who cared not a whit about espionage shenanigans. Child's play-stuff was how Culhane regarded it mostly.

"Is that all?" Flickinger asked.

"Just one more thing," said Culhane, getting up. He waited for Flickinger to come out of his chair. "I'd like a full dossier on you. You're going to be working in close with me. So I'm going to need to know how you think, what you won at and didn't . . . You can have the same on me, if you don't already."

"It's simply not possible."

"Make your choice, Flickinger. Either help make this thing work or please go away."

Flickinger reached for his hat, crushed it onto his head, and bulled his way to the door. As it slammed, Culhane was thinking about his family. How was Karin bearing up? The children? He went over to the telephone. For a personal long-distance telephone call he'd have to get the operator to reserve a time.

In the corridor, Flickinger leaned an insistent finger into the elevator button. No response after two minutes. He was tense, angered; his scalp crawled. Like some schoolboy, he'd been consigned to the corner, a pants wetter, and then shown the door. He pressed the button again. A moment later, stiff-legged, he went down the hallway until he found the exit door to the staircase.

Comes this assenheimer, this whore's son, thought Flickinger, and I'm getting poured onto the scrap heap, laid aside, because some poseur gone broke is in town. He'll make a balls of it. Going outside normal channels, telling me what to do, making the whole sideshow twice as hard to follow.

As he reached the lobby of the Hay-Adams, still moving at pace, his blare of thought turned to Andrea Warren. She'd better come across this time; nothing halfway now. Flickinger would think about it more. He glanced at his watch. There might still be time to stop by the bookbinder's.

10

Washington

Andrea Warren finished jotting a note to Italy, telling her mother of the reassignment to Washington. Everything was fine, distorted Andrea, except that the autumn heat was a killer without air conditioning and the light and power were shut off promptly at ten every night except in a few government buildings. Naturally, the fertility rate was reaching unrivaled heights; she drew a comical face at the end of the sentence.

A soft peal from the telephone stalled her closing lines. Unconsciously, she buttoned the top of the frilly wrapper she wore, concealing her perspiring breasts in a chaste feminine act.

"Hello."

"You've been out."

"Shopping. Four places to find decent soap."

"You settled in?"

"So-so. Have you met him? What's he like?"

"I think the bastard is nothing more than a well-connected gangster."

"Really. How divine," said Andrea.

"You remember the little bookbindery on Eye Street, close to your office?"

"The funny little Bulgarian man. He still there?"

"He'll have a diary for you. Put your observations in it. Drop it back there whenever you have something for me."

"That's all?"

"I'll call when there's anything new."

Back at her desk, Andrea unlocked a lower drawer and drew out the file Flickinger had given her in New York. She read part of it again, wondering to herself what it might be like to have a mother who sold her allurements. So had half the countesses she knew in Europe, and not a few American women she could think of. So has my own mother, she suddenly realized again—and I'm gaining on all of them.

Thumbing to the back of the file, she scanned the photographs of Rushton Culhane. Taken at a distance, they showed little detail, though she could pick him out in a crowd without difficulty. Well, he's tall and dark, thought Andrea, and probably a pain in the ass. And I'm tall and blond, and I've knocked down bigger men than you, Culhane.

She snapped the file closed, plotting avidly how to get next to the Californian. Why not the direct, no-holds-barred approach, she asked herself. Yet not too fast or pushy! An inside curve, sort of.

Tired. Plagued by a sharp headache, too. Culhane three-gunned it, going hard, doing mental wind sprints.

Early on, he found the core truth of what he'd suspected from the beginning: a mud slide with no defined borders to it.

From dawn's light until after midnight, he worked in the cubby-office in the White House basement or in his suite at the Hay-Adams. Endless streams of visitors, everyone pleading for materials—always the ones in short-est supply—and they embroidered the most patriotic arguments heard since Patrick Henry's time. They needed everything.

One man from General Electric arrived with elaborate charts and argued that if he couldn't get tungsten for Carboly-tools then half the nation's remaining heavy-machinery industry would shut down. Culhane gave him part of what he needed.

Others, like the trained pros of the Pentagon, hollered for the whole basket. An entire, faltering military machine and its supporting armaments industries would crash unless action was taken. Not tomorrow, now!

All argued, wheedled. On occasion, they threatened him, because they felt threatened by events they couldn't quite grasp. Culhane listened patiently, made notes, sometimes but not often signed an authorization to release materials from one of the stockpiling warehouses. Shipping problems were serious; terms of payment added more hours of haggling.

Halburton wanted reports. Culhane wanted different reports. He'd been getting the first computer hard copy from the National Security Agency. The trouble lay in deriving timely input data from the CIA to feed into the computers. Flickinger advised that the Agency was moving the moon to get reliable information on port movements in Africa. No quarrel with Flickinger on that one; a tall order, and Culhane knew it.

But he wondered why there'd been nothing about Joe Rearden's New York Corporation. Three requests had ended in three runarounds.

Sant Saxa was getting limited cooperation from Baster Muldaur in Johannesburg. And Tomlinson Ltd. of Melbourne was helping. Both would act only as agents for certain of the dummy companies Culhane operated, trying to disguise that the U.S. Government was behind these vital trades.

Culhane was now talking to a client, as he eyed a two-inch stack of urgent messages piled up next to the telephone.

A beefy Air Force colonel from the Air Material Command, his chest splashed with battle ribbons, sat on the other side of the desk. His wide buttocks were pinched into a narrow chair, small enough to fit into the crowded office.

"We need vanadium, and we can't have you tying strings to it," complained the colonel.

"We're down to a hundred thousand pounds," replied Culhane, "and the Navy is in line for one fourth of it. Go get the priorities changed."

"Yeah," growled the colonel. "Unsnagging kites at night from tall trees is easier."

"Give me your surplus aluminum at Wright-Pat and I'll try, *try*, to get the vanadium for you."

77

"You got any idea the amount of paperwork that takes? I'd have to clear it with three layers of the Air Staff."

A valid complaint, yet Culhane stood firm. If the departments and agencies wanted access to the stockpile, they'd have to agree to return any surplus materials they weren't using. A constant skirmish.

He met the colonel's eyes levelly and said, "My offer stands. You agree to swap and I'll get your vanadium, if I can."

The colonel stood, absently kicking a battered brown briefcase. "We might have to zing this one over your head."

"Go to it, Colonel. I intend to go over you and get the aluminum back. I was just trying to make it easy."

"How do you know we have it?"

"I call God every day. The connection gets bad, but the story is usually straight."

The colonel strained his shoulders until the ribbons moved a good inch. "You're shaking your cold stones if you think we're giving up anything we've already got."

"Scarce stones," said Culhane, "and I've got 'em, so get used to it."

"No way. We wouldn't do it."

"Betcha . . . Use some ingenuity now and we'll put you in for another ribbon. The better-judgment ribbon, maybe."

"You're a real laugh, Mr. Culhane. You oughta do jokes for the USO, like Bob Hope used to."

"It's an idea all right," replied Culhane, standing, ready to show his visitor out of the barren office. "I wouldn't need his writers, not with all the laugh tracks walking around this town."

"If we can work out something on the aluminum, how soon could we expect the vanadium?" A change of tactics now.

"With luck, in two weeks. Not including shipping time. You might hurry it up if you can get the Canadian Air Force to do an end run and help out."

The colonel pulled a long face. "I'll get back to you."

On the desk, on the floor, and on one small table were reams of paper. Requisitions, delivery schedules, orders for release of warehouse materials needing his signature. Halburton had insisted he use a White House office, to be

78

close by. But it wasn't big enough, and he felt like a cave rat on some days. Before the Air Force officer had arrived, he'd been leafing through a report of the National Security Council dealing with estimates of the Warsaw Pact nations' grain production and livestock ratios, and the outlook for both.

Culhane returned to his desk to read more of it. After an hour or so, he switched on the video-display terminal at one side of the desk, wired through a modem-system to the National Security Agency's computers at Fort Meade. He could call up certain data with surprising speed. Circling around Flickinger's protests, he had met with the NSA people several times, showing them what he wanted in the way of an information book; what the computer programs should do; and what else would be nice although not essential.

Tapping at the keyboard, making three entry errors, he finally called up the program he wanted. Punching away, referring to the report, Culhane eventually got what he was looking for. The powerful computers at Fort Meade made their microsecond computations, whirling precise rows of green numbers back onto the video screen. He kept going at it, comparing what he knew with what he guessed at, and then both against several assumptions.

Next he called up agricultural statistics for Canada, Australia, and the Argentine. Pushing other keys, he grouped and compared, looking for patterns.

He locked the information in, called up yet another analytical factoring program that would cluster, then separate random data, like cream from milk. He worked away in silence, concentrating fully at his favorite pastime—trying to manipulate U.S. economic and production indicators into a credible yet false format.

The red phone purred twice before he picked it up.

"That you, Sant?"

"Think maybe Ghost of Christmas come back?"

"Karin and the kids around?"

"They come in minute. Good news for you. That tantalum. Tomlinson in Australia get it and dummy it through Djakarta . . . A big hitch. We got to take back seventeen troy ton silver, too."

Culhane thought for a brief moment.

"You there?" asked Saxa.

"Partly. Tell him we'll need thirty days on the silver, and tell him thanks."

"Dunno, Rush. He tell me he rifle bank to get tantalum for us. Ain't too easy over there, he say."

"Remind him of Libya three years ago, when we got his buttons back for him on those oil trades."

"I try."

"Sant, see if you can get hold of Richard Ming in Shanghai tonight. Ask if they'll front another trade for us in vanadium. If they'll do it, then put the trade through Baster Muldaur, in Johannesburg with shipping instructions to follow."

"What for pay?"

"Four million pounds of Argentine beef."

"Jesus! Send here. I buy California with it."

Culhane laughed, then asked, "You all right?" Saxa didn't sound right. There was a deep hacking sound in the middle of his voice.

"Fit as whorehouse cat. This place too goddamn big. I feel like I running in old Santa Anita Handicap to make one trip down hall . . . Here they come. I talk you later."

Breathlessly and vaguely, Karin came on, and after her the children. One by one they clamored out what news they had for him, asking for his, and he almost had to make it up. When the call was over, sadness worked unsparingly, though the pleasure of their voices still sang beautifully in his ear.

Karin had told him the old Taiwanese had wandered off for a few days. Probably on a drunk in Chinatown, thought Culhane, giving it no more attention. And she had said there was some woman reporter who'd been calling the house. He let both thoughts pass.

He was lonely, too lonely. It was getting to him in the night, and he was sweating again.

Gathering up stacks of paper, he fitted them into two black dispatch cases, each the size of a small overnight bag. He left the office, wound his way through the twisting basement hallways, up three steps, past the guard seated behind a desk.

"G'night, Shorty," he said.

"And to you, Mr. Culhane. You want me to call for some help with those bags?"

"I've got them, thanks."

80

The guard opened the door, and Culhane welcomed the moist cooling air that caressed his face. He stood for a moment, drinking it in, then walked past the east gatehouse, nodding once to another blue-shirted guard.

Moonlight, cold and distant, reached its pale fingers down through the starless night, the light working a trick. He could see how it made the treetops of Lafayette Park shimmer strangely, almost growing taller and widening somehow. The buildings were blackened, and only every fourth streetlight glowed weakly. Sparse traffic and few pedestrians made the city seem anemic. Rain would come tonight; he could feel it, as he had once learned how to sense it at sea long ago.

He reached Lafayette Square. Across it he could see the Hay-Adams. She loomed up like an old dowager dressed in faded grays, chin up, durable, waiting for better days. Her entry lights threw a dim beam back into the murk.

Passing the Jackson Monument in the center of the square, Culhane quickened his step. La Danielle, the hotel's restaurant, would be open tonight. There'd be nothing interesting to eat, he knew, but at least the food might be warm. He'd find out and have Frédy send something up, while he trudged through the paperwork he deplored, had to force himself into every day.

Entering the lobby, he checked for mail, then made for the elevator. Even the light inside was toned in faint russet, and though the lobby was almost empty, he barely noticed her until she suddenly blocked his path.

"Mr. Culhane," she said.

Stopping, his eyes went right to the tall woman with a good voice.

"I'm Andrea Warren of the Los Angeles *Times-Herald*'s Washington bureau."

He tried to close on her with his eyes, but she hung back in a thin dagger of shadow. "How are you . . . Miss or is it Mrs. Warren?" Blond, well upholstered, dressed in denims with a lime-green sweater under the jacket. He could see those things but no real details of her.

"Miss. Andrea, actually, and I'm fine. I'm almost fine, that is. I've been waiting here for two hours."

"For me?"

"Yes. I've been trying endlessly to get an appointment

81

to see you. No one in government seems to know where your office is. So I couldn't call you there."

"What can I do for you?" He moved closer.

"I'd like to interview you for the paper."

"How did you find me here?"

"I bird-dogged. No luck. Then I called your home in Bel Air. And here I am." A tentative grin played across her glossed mouth.

Culhane nodded. She must be the reporter Karin had mentioned earlier. "It's pretty late for an interview, and I've got night work to do." He shrugged his shoulders, and the heavy dispatch cases began to sway.

"Tomorrow. *Please.*"

"Sorry, but I've nothing to discuss with the press. No offense."

"Mr. Culhane, my bureau chief is on my neck to get a story, or at least a statement, from you."

"There's no story to get," said Culhane, with half a smile, a very quick one. "Give him that for a statement."

This woman, whoever she was, had voltage in her. A sugary, low-floating voice and an unwavering look from the eyes, whose color he still couldn't tell.

"I need a break. They're talking about a staff layoff. I'm short on seniority. *Please.*"

"I'm sorry. Maybe in a few months I'll have something for you. At least a mildly good joke." By that time, he hoped, his days in Washington would be distant history.

"A man like you, with your background, doesn't come to Washington just for the hell of it, does he? I mean, we know that and—"

"Excuse me now," said Culhane politely. "Got homework to do."

He looked again at the woman. Interesting, not a classic Scandinavian beauty like Karin, but tall and with an aristocratic face of clean line under the fleecy hair. Yet she looked like a rich hippie in those tailored denims. Probably one of those limousine liberals, he thought, and big-bosomed, too. Press people! He abhorred them and their inability to measure fact, and he turned away.

Andrea watched him go, the drill of anger biting into her. She recognized it for the frustration it was and, underneath it, a feeling of rejection that she rarely knew from men.

I'm going to get to you, damn you, Culhane. She walked brusquely to the lobby's front door, went outside, and felt the dribble of raindrops against her flushed cheeks. I'll get your laundry number even if I have to cruise through those lavender eyes. What in hell kind of man has eyes that color anyway? Like African violets. A faggot's eyes, eyes that belonged on a necklace, not in a man's face.

No taxis were about, and she had no raincoat with her. Nor, Andrea remembered, feeling idiotic, did she have enough cash to pay the thirty-dollar fare to Georgetown.

11

Washington

A small celebration was gathering in honor of the Queen's birthday. Flickinger passed around the cars dropping off members of the diplomatic corps, gadflies, and senior bureaucrats, then eased up the wrong-way lane of the driveway, turning in to a parking space behind the British Embassy.

Cutting the engine, he said, "We'll go in the back way. Save time."

"Would you prefer to handle this thing?" asked Culhane.

"I'm not even sure what it is you want."

"It's only the digging out that's hard. But not that hard, if they'll try."

"Yeah, well, that's your ball game. I'll just sit and play with my pockets."

"Let's go then."

Cowperthwaite's office was at the end of the third floor in a separate building from where the party saluting Her Majesty was going on. Paneled in oiled oak, with a high ceiling and wide windows, it looked like a room where any prominent London merchant might spend his day plodding away for profit. Or how to beat a few pounds out of the Inland Revenuers this year.

Fiftyish, portly but not short, a lock of his sandy-gray hair slanting over one eyebrow. Cowperthwaite wore a fine-check houndstooth suit and ankle-high jodhpur boots that shined almost as brightly as Sant Saxa's shoes.

"Tea?" asked Cowperthwaite as they took their seats. Both men declined.

"Ah, well, to the Queen anyway," said Cowperthwaite. He began to core at the bowl of his pipe with a penknife.

"As I said earlier, Crispen, this is an unofficial visit," began Flickinger. "Mr. Culhane here is acting as an adviser to the President. He'd like some help on a matter."

In concise terms Culhane told the second-Secretary what was needed. It took less than two minutes to get through all four points. Even Flickinger, alert to every word, seemed impressed by the model briefing.

Cowperthwaite, setting his pipe down, penciled notes on a pad. He paused, looked up, covered both men with a quick glance. "You want a listing, you say, of the dollar position of Europe's banks. That the size of it?"

"Yes," said Culhane. "Who's long and who's short and by how much."

"*All* the banks?"

"Just the major ones."

"A Treasury matter, isn't it?" he asked.

"We'd like to verify through a third party," said Culhane.

"Bit irregular, isn't it, not to have the request come through your Treasury channels."

"The times are irregular, Mr. Secretary," returned Culhane.

"This isn't quite in my line, you understand, Mr. Culhane. I'll have to run it by the appropriate ministry."

Culhane understood both the slight rebuke and the artifice Cowperthwaite was playing at. He said simply, "We'd appreciate whatever assistance you can give."

Never one to pass up an opportunity, Cowperthwaite asked, "You know the Moncotta brothers of London, Mr. Culhane? I had occasion to talk to one of them today. Told him I expected to see you, and they asked that I convey their respects."

Culhane relaxed into a smile. "I know them well. The best gold traders in the world. How are they?"

"Fine, I should hope. Slow these days, things are . . . Still and all, they seem to be holding up."

"We did some interesting things together once."

"I gather . . . And, oh, by the way, I'm curious about something—are you somewhat familiar with this organization calling itself the Shang-Magan?"

The question caught Culhane totally by surprise. Hesitating, he skimped it with "Very familiar. An informal group of traders founded about three hundred years ago by the Chinese compradors, who served the British, among others."

"Quite so. I gather it's not all that informal," probed Cowperthwaite.

Culhane swept a frozen glare across to where Flickinger sat, thinking, If you've set me up, you bastard, I'll swing you, then answered, "Depends upon your point of view, I guess."

A high chuckle, like a woman's, before Cowperthwaite said, "Yes, yes, as in so many things. You must know Piet Van Slyke?"

"Well and favorably."

"You wouldn't think of him as a contrabander, or would you? A drug dealer?"

"Not the slimmest chance of it."

"How can you be so sure?"

"Know the man, then you know what he will or won't do. Van Slyke wouldn't."

"And Liu Wai of Singapore. Do you know him?"

"Quite well. A very important trader. Also Shang-Magan, there's no secret to it."

"You mean," asked Cowperthwaite, "his penchant for drug dealing?"

"You'd better ask him," evaded Culhane, who knew a fair amount about Wai's drug operations in the Burmese corner of the Golden Triangle. A very sore point between the two of them for a long time now.

"And, of course, you wouldn't say if you did."

"Not about something like that and where I'm short on facts."

"A pity." Cowperthwaite cored his pipe again.

That seemed to end it. Culhane experienced a clawing feeling that his reluctance to talk might well throw things off the track with this Britisher. If so, he'd find another way. He wouldn't break Shang-Magan rules of confidence, for the British Crown or anyone else. He had seen documents in possession of the Shang-Magan that implicated the CIA, half a dozen other security services, the Vatican, and plenty of foreign governments in various drug operations. About as legal as incest.

Flickinger spoke up. "I've one or two things to discuss, Crispen, if you've time."

"By all means."

Getting up, Culhane said, "I'll go toast the Queen. See you downstairs." He turned to Cowperthwaite, already rising from his chair, and thanked him.

He left as he'd come, feeling uneasy about the whole situation. It was a risk. He didn't like bringing government into his plans, or anywhere near them. Too much loose plumbing. Better trying it this way, though, than involving Squires and his bunch over at Treasury.

Leaving the elevator, listening, he went down the hallway toward a reception room. Frills and trills as people milled about, chattering emptily. Culhane edged his way toward a long buffet table at the far end of the room, and found it not worth the effort. The canapé trays were barren. A long finger-sandwich, as if in hiding, lay tilted against a silver-bellied tea service. A huge tureen offered some sort of fruit punch with rinds of oranges and limes floating on the surface.

He wanted a drink, but there was no whiskey in sight. The British were too practiced at the diplomatic arts to lay it on in the usual way. Not with the American press fussing about, ever ready to report high doings when others were dodging the rent collector.

A small man with a razored military haircut, wearing a white butler's coat, served him a glass of punch. One thirsty sip and Culhane could tell that the juice was spiked with rum. He toasted the Queen, whose portrait hung high on a bright wall at the window side of the room.

He saw her then, standing in a knot of people not very far away. She was dressed in a pink suit, the pink of a child's Easter egg. That was where the child thing ended, though. Her hair was the color of day-old champagne, feathered across her forehead, the rest of it falling almost to her shoulders. She was taller than some of the men gathered around her. An upturned nose, retroussé, and in her cheeks the rose of snow crab that you often see in Celtic or Chinese countrywomen.

Full of vitality and flow. And something else, too: that "I dare you" look of mischief in the green eyes. Cheetah there, in this woman, or the sleek and bunched strength of a puma. He heard the roll of her deep laugh autographing the air through those glossed lips.

Excitement crackled through him as if a dangerous rumor had just circulated. He turned back toward the table, replacing the punch glass on it, his thoughts running loosely.

Culhane wasn't sure if he sensed her breathing first or just the words. "How do you say hello in Cantonese?" she asked.

"Chao hu," he answered without thinking, smiling, then turning toward her. Culhane saw there was a tiny chip missing from one front tooth in her slightly parted mouth. He liked it, and her for not overdoing her vanity.

"It's unfair."

"What is?"

"Your eyes. Men aren't supposed to have eyes like yours."

"I know a man who can actually turn his white."

"You're a speculator, aren't you?"

"Sort of."

"Then I'll bid for them," bantered Andrea. "How much?"

On the off chance, Culhane replied, "A hot kiss carefully applied."

And he was wonderfully surprised, when she leaned into him and brushed her moist warm mouth near his; all of it done in one eccentric instant. "I'll settle for an interview. I've been studying up on you," Andrea said pulling back, her face eager and very alive.

"Know anything that I don't but should?"

"Just what's in the files. Not enough scandal to be fun, but lots of mystery and things like that."

"Bored you backwards, I'll bet."

"El-wrongo," said Andrea. "May I call you Rushton?"

"Or anything you like." Now he could see the delicate downy fluff on her smooth cheeks.

"And then I'll *call* you for an interview and you won't refuse me, because this is 'Be Kind to Working-Girls' week."

"It always is, they say."

"And you'll tell me how you became a big trader."

"Past tense. They say that, too."

"Won't you . . . puh-lease . . . I'm accurate, I'm fair, and every punch is thrown in plain sight, above the belt."

"But why? What's the interest?"

"You're from Los Angeles. That's where my paper is published. Hometown interest and that sort of thing . . . You're the only Californian in the White House."

No mystery to where he hung his hat, but Culhane wondered how she'd become aware of it. He wasn't listed in any government directory. He saw Flickinger then, sliding through the crowd. And how in hell does she know I speak Chinese?

"Talk to me," insisted Andrea.

Why not? Better than another night alone. "Like to come for dinner tonight?" he asked. "Leave now or pretty soon. I've got a Smithfield ham."

"You're serious? A ham? Where'd you get it . . . I mean yes . . . Yes, I'd love to." Her rise of excitement put a bolt down his spine.

Culhane thought he detected a flicker of recognition in her eyes as Flickinger came up to where they stood. But it wasn't so much that reaction as it was her way of greeting Flickinger when he introduced them. She hadn't said "How do you do" or "I'm delighted" or "It's a pleasure" or any of the usual exchanges when strangers meet. Andrea simply greeted Flickinger with "Nice to see you," as if they had known each other before. Only a vague impression. He let it go.

"The lady and I are going to the hotel for dinner. We need a lift. You ready?"

Flickinger arranged a satisfied, even cheerful look on his face. "Never more so. I hate these damn things. A royal pain in the ass," he said, in a weak attempt at comedy.

They bumped their way out through the crowd. Halfway to the door, Andrea circled away briefly to tell someone that she'd be catching another ride home.

In the White House a harassed Halburton was finishing an unpleasant session with a high-ranking Air Force general.

"We're getting our throats cut inch by inch. Half our

90

squadrons are grounded. No parts, no spare engines, and fuel supplies are abysmal."

"I've got a new man here helping on that problem," countered Halburton.

"A hundred magicians couldn't solve our problems."

"Give it a chance."

"We're out of time, Mr. President. You've got to decide on the Hormuz question, and soon."

"Hormuz is hardly a cure-all."

"It's part of it. This is a battle for resources, and you take what—"

"You take it a step at a time is what you do. And I won't have the military pressuring me prematurely."

The general made a small ceremony of examining his manicured nails, then looked into Halburton's seamed face before saying, "Sir, that choice may be taken from you."

"And you'll be sacked and worse," said Halburton.

"You can't fire the whole of the armed forces, can you, Mr. President?"

Halburton stood, indicating that the meeting was over, that he'd had enough, but knowing he had no ready answer to the Air Forcer's last question. He felt as if he were swimming among knives half the time, losing his weight and invested power; rankled too by the general's implied and not so subtle defiance.

The dinner was over. Talk had traveled in unshaped orbits, mostly of art and music, places they'd both visited, a few people they knew. Andrea slipped her questions in like a well-trained welterweight. Flick, move, dodge, punch. Nothing had really hit home yet. Still, she peppered away at any part of him that seemed vulnerable.

Pretty silky, decided Culhane, finding it enjoyable listening to her work out. And those legs. Sitting directly across from her, he was bewitched by their graceful length and nicely toned shape. She would be stronger than she looked; he tried to guess by how much, and the guess fell flat, but the rest of her came on like censorable poetry.

"Whatever has quieted you?" he asked, amused, ready for more.

"I was wondering what it's like speculating for a living. Like gambling, I suppose."

Culhane laughed.

"Tell me. I'd really like to know," said Andrea.

"Roulette with your nerves. Most of the time you're buying things you never see from someone who doesn't even own what they're selling you."

"Sounds underhanded."

"It's every human wish in its first phase . . . And the hell with this sort of talk anyway."

"How about college, where did you go for that?" She couldn't remember if Flickinger had mentioned anything about it; there had been nothing in the file, either.

A blank look from Culhane, who answered, "I didn't. I was trying to learn a trade, or how to."

"You get harder to believe by the minute."

"I could've been a good reporter maybe."

"Bait me another day . . . How did you educate yourself?"

"In alleys that have no names and in places where you keep your name to yourself."

"True? Is that it, really?"

"Partly, though I sent away to Stanford and Dartmouth and to Cambridge in England. I asked for their curriculums. Then I wrote the professors who taught the interesting stuff and asked for the names of the textbooks they used . . . And when it was lonely and cold at sea, and there were no dames within a thousand miles, and none at all with legs like yours, I made love to the textbooks."

A blush rising on her throat, Andrea said, "That is remarkable."

Arising from the nubbed white davenport, Andrea went over to inspect the small Cézanne again. Impasto, thickened with oil from the artist's hand: it captivated her. She wanted to reach out and touch it gently, but resisted the impulse.

"All these and a dinner of Smithfield ham . . . I would've come just for the etchings," said Andrea, around a soft smile.

"I didn't know, or I could've saved on the ham."

"Pooh!" She made a clown's face, then asked, "You still haven't told me what you really do here for Halburton."

"I run his warehouses. All the stuff you can't get with food coupons."

"That's hard to accept."

"It's your job to get the truth, isn't it? Isn't that what a journalist does?"

"And that man who drove us here from the Embassy. Who is he?" said Andrea, without skipping a beat.

"Flickinger? He's a grumbler from the intelligence community."

"He must be some grumbler, if he's entitled to a car." Ah-ah! thought Andrea, this is going to be some doozy of a report for Clay Flickinger. Culhane doesn't fib even when I open the door for him with white gloves on.

"The grumblers always get them. Way of the world." He stood up. "I need more music, and maybe a drink. How about you?"

"Is it strong? The drink?"

"Izarra. It's Basque and they use it to fuel their boats."

"And some more of that Tommy Dorsey music, too."

"You got it." Culhane departed for the small pantry, where he kept the Izarra and the few Honduran cigars he had left.

Strange, she thought, those damn eyes of his never leave you. An invasion of privacy somehow. Art, he knows a lot about art. That Cézanne is genuine, I bet. I'd like to know for sure. And music, too. Eddie Sauter and Fletcher Henderson and Joe King Oliver—God, who even remembers them anymore. And under all those California or Hawaiian easy airs is an unmothered soul on steel wheels. He pumped me dry all the way through dinner and I hardly realized it. A charm-boy, and he is too, dammit! I wonder what a man like him dreams about when awake. Or who he dreams about when asleep. Probably naked grain barges.

Andrea heard the mellow strains of Tommy Dorsey's "I'll Never Smile Again" before noticing his footfall. He handed her a globe of the Izarra, keeping the other in the hand that held the slender Honduran #7.

Lifting the clear liqueur to her mouth, Andrea hesitated, a brief sniff, then took a wallop of it. Her eyes closed into two tight creases. Shoulders wiggling, she choked out, "Ggrraad," then gasped. "Jhoosus! It's Draino!"

"It's like Italian grappa. You don't gargle with it," said Culhane, laughing. "There's some wine in there, I think, if you'd rather have—"

"No, no! Never let it be said that Andrea Warren failed in her duty to the Basques."

The lights went out. None of the usual flashing on and off to warn everyone that the power was going off until morning. Sudden blackness, just as if a fuse had blown.

"My God," said Andrea, "what . . . oh, God, what time is it? Don't they let you know?"

"I don't know what happened. Feel around until you find the drawer in that table next to you. Candles are in it."

"Oh! Bloody hell, there won't even be taxis now."

"Relax and find the candles."

Culhane heard her rummaging in the drawer. His eyes were not yet accustomed to the darkness, and he closed them, while thinking.

"I've got them. They're sort of small, aren't they?"

"Just hold on. I'm waiting for my eyes to adjust."

"You think I'm taking off for Paris or somewhere? Damn, how am I going to get home?"

"Someone waiting up for you?"

"It's very awkward, you know, in the dark and everything."

"Easy. The bats don't fly for an hour or so."

"I am easy, dammit."

Crossing the room, banging his shin into a coffee table, a soft curse. He could tell he was close to her breathing. So close now he could fix the outlines of her dark shape.

"Hold out one candle and I'll try it with my Honduran."

"I assume that means your cigar."

He felt the touch of her wrist, then moved his fingers over hers until he got a hold on the candle. Building the cigar up to a redder ash, he met it with the candle's wick.

"There," he said, "that's one. Let me have the other." And then he did it again.

Reaching into another drawer, he found two glass holders at the back of it, and planted the candles in them. He smelled her fragrance again.

"Jasmine. From Floris."

In the bare light, Andrea swiveled her head back and forth. In disbelief she said, "Not one man in a thousand would know that. How would you? Does your wife wear it?"

94

"No." But he'd known a Chinese woman once in Hong Kong who had.

"You really clam up when it comes to your wife, don't you?"

"Yes."

"Yes, no, this and that. Rushton, I've got to find a bed tonight, and that's not a proposition."

Her thoughts just then were much less convincing than she hoped the words sounded; a thrumming feeling inside, and moisture, too. Imagining that a flush was creeping over her skin, she was glad for the darkness.

"I can ring the desk," said Culhane. "They probably have an extra room. At about five hundred bucks."

"That's out of the question. Criminy!"

"Or you can use the spare bedroom here. I'll lend you a robe, and I know I've got a fresh toothbrush."

"Would you?"

"Sure. Besides, this place needs a little scandal."

"It's no time to be funny."

Taking one of the candles, going to his bedroom, he found a yellow silk robe that he'd worn possibly twice, never remembered even packing when leaving Bel Air. In the bathroom closet, almost scorching the papered shelves with the stubby candle, he located the toothbrush, still in its cellophane wrapper.

He saw her in the vague light when he returned. "I've got the duds," said Culhane, holding out one arm with the yellow robe draped over it.

"My color even."

"Some redhead made off with the blue one." He had meant it as a joke, but could tell she didn't take it that way. No velvet laugh issued.

"Better take the other candle." Culhane led her across the room and through a short hallway that ended with a door to the bedroom.

"Thank you," said Andrea. "I mean it."

"Extra towels are in the closet, and the warm water comes on at seven. It's never hot."

Later, Culhane lay in bed, his head creasing the pillow, a candle flickering on the nightstand and the last dram of Izarra in his hand. He thought about Crispen Cowperthwaite, then found his mind drifting toward Andrea Warren.

Amusing, rather innocent, more handsome than beautiful, and pretty bright. Candid. Christ, was she candid. And with it all, flighty, a sort of advanced sophomore with high heels on. Schooled in Europe and America, familiar with Cap Ferrat and Deauville and Capri and elsewhere. A Fifth Avenue filly, the daughter, as she put it, of some deceased diplomat. Seems to know a hell of a lot of people, but not too much about herself. Thirty-five or six, he guessed. One of those coy delighters who would say, "A woman who tells her age will tell anything." Didn't matter anyway. A jasmine-and-julep kid, really, despite the latent animal lurking in those wildly promising loins.

He blew out the flame, but not the images of her; those continued to flirt, making sleep a stranger.

12

Washington

Flickinger angled his way along Eye Street, rounding the block on the opposite side to the bookbinder's. He stood there for a long moment by an abandoned flower stall. All he could see was a man peering through the iron mesh of a haberdasher's window, then a clutch of small children escorted by three women.

Moving slowly down the street, an olive-drab Army truck coughed oily exhaust into the clear morning air. A mean-looking Negro soldier, his helmet as shiny as a billiard ball, with a carbine slung on his shoulder, rode on the truck's running board. On his field jacket he wore the joyless yellow stripes of a sergeant.

Otherwise, the quiet of Saturday morning in heavily patrolled Washington.

Observing the bookbinder's store before crossing the street was an unnecessary act. But then, Flickinger's wariness was founded on experience; the experience bought and bought again in the swamp of human perfidy.

Who knew about the Bulgar? In the end, thought Flickinger, who really knows about anybody? Caution was Flickinger's obstinate vanity. Crossing the street, jaywalking against a red light, he moved like the squirrel that never lets anything come between it and the nearest tree.

He knocked at the Bulgar's quaint little factory, and heard the heavy steps shuffling up to the door. A green shade was pulled aside, and Flickinger saw the genial face staring back at him through the glass. A bolt slicked back almost soundlessly, and he entered through the opening door.

The Bulgar stepped back. With the dark brown walrus mustache, the twinkling eyes, and the heavy features, he looked like the gravure on a tin of straight-cut Balkan tobacco. A grappler for a hand at the end of a heavily muscled arm came toward Flickinger. Two fingers were missing up to the second joint.

Almost snorting, the Bulgar said, "Vilkom. Good to see." Behind the strong accent was the stronger breath of garlic.

Flickinger shook the outstretched hand, afterward wiping his own absently on the side of his trousers. The Bulgar made no pretense about wiping his lamed hand twice on the ink-stained apron he wore over black, chalk-streaked trousers.

"Having a problem with the paper, I hear."

The Bulgar's face darkened. Stepping around Flickinger to lock the door again, he said, "'S' not good. I make a compare. Not good."

"Exactly what is wrong with it?"

"Cuba goven-a-men paper hasa more rag in it. Leetle more silk also."

"Where did your present paper stock come from?" asked Flickinger.

"E-spana."

"I'll look into it. I'd like to read the book now."

"Kom," suggested the Bulgar, who ran his gimp hand through oiled hair of shiny ridged waves.

They moved across a clean-swept hardwood floor, going by an old-fashioned counter of beveled green glass, through a brown pleated curtain, to the working area behind the shop's customer area.

Two long benches were surrounded by several stools. A large skylight poured morning light into a room that smelled of fixing glue, compound oil, beeswax, and cured leather. Flickinger was led over to a stock shelf. The Bulgar reached up and pulled down the diary, which was bound in apricot-dyed leather and bordered with scrolled lines of deep orange.

"Always here, the one mosa to the left," said the Bulgar, pointing. The shelf held another dozen or so diaries of the same design, their color so bilious that no one had ever bought one.

"Fine. I'll just ask for some privacy and read it here on one of the stools." A puzzled frown swept the Bulgar's gargoyle face until Flickinger added, "I wish to be left alone."

"Yah," and the bookbinder lumbered off through the curtain, his broad back and loose shuffle reminiscent of a trained bear.

Flickinger pulled a key case from his pocket, opened it, then inserted a duplicate key in the diary's brass lock. Going to the nearest stool, he sat and read Andrea's neat handwriting:

I've seen him twice now.

No real facts and, if there were, no way to verify them.

You listen long enough to the man (and I could do it for hours) and the feeling prints that he is indeed different. Is he the ultimate risk-machine? I don't know. What I do know is that he is no one-trick pony. Yes, he dares, probably thrives on it, searching perhaps for the limit which he can withstand.

Human? Compassionate? I think so. He is caught up by art and music. People with souls of granite don't camp out in museums, and he does or did. I studied both in Europe for years (as you well know) and I feel like a lighted match next to his floodlight.

Throw the glass on him and you see shades inside other shades. You've seen, I'm sure, that easy and smooth charm of his. I think it's genuine. I think it would work fine on the King or the King's bootmaker. He learned about people somewhere . . . in the orphanage or as a runaway to sea . . . though somehow I doubt it was either of those places.

99

Yet he's coiled, cruising around like a shark in shallow water. In that breast beats the heart of a born revolutionary. Even money or better, I would bet you he is capable of manipulating events as well as anyone in Washington. Sleight-of-hand! And those damned eyes of melting sapphire.

Women would find him attractive. Hellishly so. He gives off that delirious feeling that makes the little hairs of your neck stand up. Why? Adventure, I guess. And an honest-to-God man for certain. Any real woman would like a crack at taming it all to size.

I cajoled him like the very devil to discuss some of those historical speculations of his. Fascinating! I never realized he was the one who broke up the infamous silver cartel attempted by the Texans and their Arab friends.

Make no mistake about one thing. You are dealing there with a first-rate brain. Very different radio waves work up there.

More later . . .

A popping sound as Flickinger snapped the diary shut. He shifted his weight on the hard stool, momentarily thinking that whoever worked in this room would need inch-thick calluses on their ass.

Womb talk! Not a good fact in the lot. Still, it was early. She'd need time to penetrate, anybody would. She'd done the right and professional thing not to refer to Culhane by name. She'd done the wrong one in mentioning the silver business. The smallest slip could lead to the most serious, even fatal outcome. And he recalled again Andrea's father, who had sniffed at the wrong pot once too often. Too bad.

Arguing with caution, he gave way to it and opened the diary again. Carefully, Flickinger ripped out the pages Andrea had penned so precisely. From his coat pocket he removed a small blue card with three questions typewritten on it. *More later,* he thought, relocking the diary and replacing it at the very left of the others on the shelf.

He went through the curtain and reentered the shop's

100

small reception area. Hunched over the counter, the Bulgar was looking through a magnifier into the face of a complicated rubber stamp used for Polish entry visas.

He put it down, shifted a foggy gaze in Flickinger's direction, and reminded, "Vill see about paper?"

"Vill see," Flickinger parroted in a hard voice, then asked, "Was the book brought here by a woman?" Glad now that he was far enough away not to be smoked again by the garlic.

"Messa-ger. Wrapped in box. You want box?"

"No, I want a surgeon's mask."

A cold one, rarely smiling, this Flissa-jer, thought the Bulgar. And too thin in the belly, which would make him even thinner in the heart.

Flickinger went to the door, threw the bolt, and faded away into the rest of Saturday morning. Two steps away, he heard the bolt slide into place behind him. It reminded him of a rifle being chambered with a round of ammunition.

13

New York

Joe Rearden's nerves are shot, decided Guido Grasselli, who leaned back into his chair. Bored, he dialed out the swarms of words buzzing around. Someday he would run the New York Corporation, and there wouldn't be any of this quibbling, either. A few well-chosen words, a gesture, the right sort of look would suffice.

It wasn't enough, he thought, to have power: you had to use it, plant and grow fear, reap it. Why make it so complicated? Culhane wasn't a threat. Look at the Chief skittering around like some hen in heat . . . And Squires, who considered himself so goddamned smooth and necessary . . . Even the kid over there, who retained his Senate seat with a smile and money and more money, and had kitty litter for brains.

Caught up in Joe Rearden's heated glare, Squires was searching around for an answer. Grasselli tuned back in.

"Joe, none of us can tell Halburton who he can talk with."

"From Arkansas," answered Joe Rearden drily, "we get a hick who should never have gotten on the party ticket. And he pulls in Culhane, for chrissakes!"

"Mr. Rearden." Guido Grasselli came alive now. "What can Culhane really do? He's broke. He even owes us. There gotta be ways to enlighten him." Grasselli moved to ease the weight of the .38 Colt Special in his shoulder holster.

"Do! Culhane can block us from selling our inventories into the stockpile . . ."

A wild card of thought, and Joe Rearden leveled his attention on his son. "Tim, can't the Senate investigate? Can't you figure out a way to bring pressure, embarrass Halburton, force him to get rid of Culhane?"

A dreamy, almost empty look on Tim Rearden's face. "Culhane doesn't even appear on a government payroll. More to the point, the White House hasn't even asked us to authorize gold to pay for the stockpile program. So there's nothing to investigate."

"When was the last time the Treasury audited the gold stocks?" asked Joe Rearden of Squires.

"Years ago. I'd have to check the date. The books don't balance, though."

"Be a hell of a row in the papers, I suppose," observed Joe Rearden, standing up.

He walked to a window overlooking Park Avenue, idly rapped his knuckles against one pane of glass. A truck, no cars, and scattered pods of people. Trash in black refuse bags was piled up in front of the buildings across the avenue. Some of the mounds reached as high as the first story, and would stay there until the fire department burned them on the islands separating the wide avenue.

Joe Rearden spoke at the window, though loudly enough for the others to hear. "I want Culhane out of there. Now what are your thoughts, if any?" he demanded, swinging around to face Grasselli.

"As I say, the guy is broke. He closed down, didn't he? Plenty of ways to tie rocks to him."

Squires arched his neck backward. His mouth tightened so that it became the color of his pallid face. Tim Rearden diverted his eyes to a far corner of the room.

Realizing that he'd been misunderstood, Guido Grasselli attempted to smooth it all over, "What I mean is, we make him a deal. A skiff, a sort of silent partnership."

"Cut him in?" asked Joe Rearden in disbelief.

"Sure," said Grasselli, "we splice him in for maybe six or eight percent. We can also cancel out his liability on what he owes us on the grain paper, which we may never

104

collect on anyway. And, if we have to, we fix him up . . .
No, that won't work at all. Just the first two."

Christ, thought Grasselli, I almost recommended we tie
Culhane into Braunsweig und Sohn. I damn near said it in
front of flint-nose Squires.

"He might buy it," Joe Rearden said. "Then again, he
might not. What then?"

"Let's see what he says. There's always other ideas we
can think of," Grasselli said.

"Such as what?" asked Joe Rearden of the lawyer.

"We get him to do a few big buys from us. Without him
knowing about it, we credit him with some big commissions. He's made to look like he's on the take. We leak the
word, we compromise him, and whoosh—he's gone. He's
finished."

"We thought he was finished months ago."

"It's just a nuisance thing. We can fix it," assured Grasselli, adding, "Mr. Rearden, I got a meeting across the
river tonight. Got to start out soon."

"On your way then. And check with me tomorrow."

Casting nothing more than a sidelong glance at Joshua
Squires, he passed by Tim Rearden and said in a lowered
voice, "See you soon, Senator. Keep it all the way up."

Through the door, and Guido's thoughts leaped to the
meeting that evening over in Jersey City. The food, the
booze, and the broads would be good. The jokes a scream,
but loud arguing about the cut. Two *capos* would be there.

No matter how detailed the accounting records sent in
each month, they always had questions. Always the fucking questions, like they'd forgotten how to count. "Why
can't we reconcile the Montreal account?" "There's no entry for the transfer from Curaçao to Switzerland." "The
exchange rate at Braunschweiger"—they never said
Braunsweig—"looks like someone cooked it in shit." In the
end, the genuflections done with, the ledgers would
square. Maybe a small adjustment here and there, but
with the huge sluice of money funneled offshore over the
years, what the hell could they expect?

As the door closed behind Grasselli, the agenda took a
new direction. Joe Rearden stood by the large mahogany
partner's desk, streaked by a shaft of late-afternoon light.
"In a month, perhaps two, we should have enough stock

105

accumulated to control Citicorp. How does the bank-refinancing legislation stand?" he asked Squires.

"The Treasury is ready whenever the Senate is. The working drafts of the bill are done."

"Tim?" asked his father.

"All hung up on the question of reforming the currency with gold backing," said Tim. "Halburton wants it one way, the rest of us another." He spoke listlessly, another void look decorating his face.

"What are the chances of getting Congress to reopen the banks by issuing gold guarantees?" Joe Rearden asked.

"Fifty-fifty. All depends on how the U.S. gold reserves are ultimately allocated. You can't consider one bill without the other."

"And what about this *external* dollar you mentioned the other day?" Joe Rearden asked Squires.

"It won't go far. It's an old plan that Halburton wants dusted off again."

"Sorry. What's that again?" asked Tim.

"A two-currency system," Squires told him. "One for domestic use, the other for foreign transactions."

"I haven't been briefed on that one," Tim said.

"It's an old study, Tim," said Squires. "Nothing to concern yourself with . . . Yet the biggest problem is still the enormous pool of dollars in Europe. Unless we get those back, you can't back a new dollar with gold. Europe would have Fort Knox in its pocket in one day . . . But I wouldn't worry about it."

"You think Culhane's meddling in it?"

"I don't see why. He can't do anything."

"Check into it. You'll be wanting to get back to Washington," Joe Rearden said to Squires. "Talk to Halburton again. Maybe, he'll change his mind about Tim here."

"I can try," said Squires haplessly.

"Do better than *try*, Joshua. Now if you'll excuse me, I have family business with my son."

And, like Grasselli before him, the Secretary of the Treasury was dismissed. But then, Joe Rearden had rescued Squires when the New York banks closed. He'd loaned him gold, saved his mansion in Glen Cove, even salvaged the man's faltering reputation. In exchange, he only asked for Squires's soul, and found that it could be bought pretty cheaply.

106

Still sitting quietly in the wing chair, Tim Rearden had hardly opened his mouth. Like a fly on the wall, he saw, he heard, but he didn't really grasp the talk. With none of his father's cunning, for most of his adult life he'd been a wheel spinning around inside the larger machinery operated by Joe Rearden. The best staff, a remarkable public relations team, wealth, a real power in the Senate—he had it all, provided by the iron-minded man in front of him now.

All this mummery for the White House. Tim Rearden wasn't at all sure he could stand up to its rigors or the scrutiny that came with it. His closet sexual life, the foreign-aid kickback schemes, Mafia affiliations—what if any of it were to come under a hard probe by the media? They always fingered somebody who would talk.

Tim's thoughts were rudely invaded when his father mentioned, "Squires thinks he's a lead-pipe cinch to come back to Citicorp when we reopen it, eh?"

"Isn't he?"

"The carpentry for his cross is almost finished."

"Then why," asked Tim, "do you want him pushing this Bank Refinancing Act?"

"A cheap way to get capital. Let him run with it and see where it goes."

"A compromise, you mean."

Up and down, slowly, went Joe Rearden's head. "Right. Just like all the other crap that gets passed down there. All we want is our share of the gold guarantees, if they're legislated."

"So how do you expect this gold business to work out?"

"Ten percent to get the banks on their feet again, the rest to back a new currency."

"Then why not signal it to Halburton?"

"Because unless we hold out, there's no leverage on him to take you on as Vice-President." Joe Rearden looked very squarely at his son.

"I can look after our affairs better in the Senate."

Chin hardening, Joe Rearden said, "I'll judge that one, Tim. You might never make it to the Presidency. But in the next election whoever does will have to come right through us."

"I get a little tired of being the—"

107

"Oh, you do, do you? I put you in the Senate. I made you rich. And you're getting tired, you say?"

"Yes, all right, I've heard it," Tim said impatiently.

"Just remember it. We're in a time of crisis. And out of its ashes will come the greatest empire this nation has ever seen. Better than Morgan's or Rockefeller's or any of them. That's what the New York Corporation will be. And if I need you in the White House to assure it, that's where you'll damn well be."

"Are you planning lunch here?"

"Your mother would be pleased to eat with you, I'm sure. I'm to attend a meeting of the Archdiocese's Finance Committee with the Cardinal."

"Don't tell me they're in trouble."

"Nothing that can't be handled," Joe Rearden said, dismissing the question.

Tim Rearden unwound from the wing chair, centered his tie, and calculated how he might dodge a long, boring luncheon with his mother. Endless questions, new charitable crusades to hear of. He would plead some excuse or other, he was adept at that. And Grasselli, where the hell did he get off—"Keep it all the way up." Horrible, swaggering prick.

14

The Ukraine
Washington

An old man, so old and bent that now he must firm his short steps with a wooden staff, gazed sadly across the fallow plains that lay flat beside a village north of Stanislav. His long face, as ridged and dark as a walnut, saw death. The death of his land. Where once there had been an endless golden carpet of wheat, now it looked like an infected carcass. Even the wolves passed it by; and, greatest insult, so did the birds.

And he knew in the way peasants always do that down the length of the Ukraine it was the same everywhere. Murmurings from the other villages—cousin to cousin and landsman to landsman—were always the same. Another year of scorching, with the sun pounding down like a blacksmith's hammer.

A scourge. It was the scourge visited upon a country that closed its churches and denied its rightful God, thought the old man. A saying from his tattered Old Testament, hidden under the steps of his daughter's log cottage, came to him:

"Has the rain a father? Who sired the drops of dew?"
He knew.

Three seasons now. Wagons empty. Tractors stilled. Women sulking, men as hot-tempered as the sun above, and their children bewildered. An old story written many times over the centuries. As far back as man's beginning.

He spat. Nothing but juiceless air came from his cottony mouth. The old man knew he would die soon; it gnawed that he wouldn't see this land in flower again. He was ready to die, and even to see how death would catch him. But the land wasn't supposed to die.

Turning around on the humped knoll, the old man dug his staff into the parched ground, catching it in a small hole. He looked down into a nest of starved field mice. He knelt, the effort hurting. With gnarled hands, he scraped baked dust over them.

The sound drove deep into Culhane's stupor before he heard it. He groped into the blackness until finding the culprit.

"Mr. Culhane?" came an unfamiliar voice over the telephone.

"Um-hmm."

"I'm Guido Grasselli. I'm in-house legal counsel for the New York Corporation."

Strange sensations ran along Culhane's ribs. He'd heard Sant Saxa refer on past occasions to Grasselli, but had never met the man. Rearden either, for that matter.

"What is it?"

"Apologize for calling so early. We've an important matter to propose. Can I see you?"

"Time is it?"

"Ah . . . five twelve."

"What matter is that, Mr. Grasselli?" Culhane sat up slowly.

"Private. We'd need some privacy," said the voice, lowering.

Culhane paused, trying to recall his schedule. Intrigued, too. "Is it about those open grain contracts you hold of mine? Until the markets open again—"

"No, no. Maybe those, but something more important."

"Five this afternoon might work out."

"No good, Mr. Culhane. I've got an afternoon reservation for New York. Impossible to change," said Grasselli, coming across smoothly.

110

"I'm leaving to go across the park in twenty minutes or so. You can walk along if you like."

"Jesus, I ain't even dressed yet!" The voice not so smooth now.

"Make it twenty-five minutes. I'll look for you downstairs at the reception desk."

"Yeah, sure," came Grasselli's glum answer.

Culhane replaced the phone. Curiosity fanned his interest. Joe Rearden obviously wanted something. Untangling himself from the bedsheets, he went to the window, pushed aside the curtains, and looked out across the low skyline. A burst of eastern light, like an immense lemon rind, peeled away at the gray dawn.

Culhane's eyes traveled down to the statue of Andrew Jackson in the center of Lafayette Square Park. A smile crept over his mouth as he recalled a crack made by Andrea Warren two days earlier. They'd sat in the park sharing a puny lunch of apples and imitation Grana Padano cheese.

Dangling a bright ripe apple by the stem, Andrea had looked up at Jackson's face and said:

"You suppose Eve could have tempted that tough old bastard with one of these the way she did Adam?"

"She'd have to go carefully. Somewhere I once read that Jackson's two deepest regrets in life were that he hadn't been able to shoot Henry Clay or hang John Calhoun."

They'd laughed. Laughs were scarce. On that day they'd been scarcest: Boston was engulfed in another citywide food riot, which even the National Guard couldn't control, and prairie fires were reported in the Dakota grainlands.

A thought blacker than India ink, there was actual talk of censoring the news. Halburton possessed the authority under the Emergency Powers Act. Nobody really knew whether he'd invoke it to calm the country. Andrea worried about it.

"Don't fret," he remembered telling her.

"You scare the water out of me sometimes," she'd said. "Why?"

"Because you're too . . . I don't know, cool, I guess."

"You're looking at the most frightened person I know."

"Rarely, I bet."

"Always, you'd be safer betting."

And that was the way he felt, turning now, away from

111

the freshening sky. Alone. He drifted into a loneliness that squeezed his insides.

Fairly tall, in good physical trim, and dressed in a dark worsted suit, Grasselli's cold eyes contrasted with the fluffy hair ringing his smooth-featured face. A lean face except for the mouth, which was wide and puffy. Culhane felt the eyes cover him like a search warrant, and noticed, too, that Grasselli hadn't found time to shave.

"I'm Culhane."

"Grasselli. Guido Grasselli." Taking Culhane's hand, he felt the force of its grip right up to his elbow.

"Shall we go," Culhane said.

They left the hotel, crossed Sixteenth Street, and made their way along one of the crosswalks in the park.

"Mr. Rearden sends his respects," said Grasselli, trying to break the ice. He skipped a step, to keep pace.

Culhane looked into the distance, listening to Grasselli's voice. Mostly it came smoothly, persuasively. But every so often it would jerk.

"What is it Joe Rearden wants?"

"Some accommodation of interests, a little business. Can't you slow down?"

Culhane braked his step, pointing to a bench by the Jackson monument, thinking again of Andrea. "We can rest it right here for a couple of minutes. Then I'm off to a meeting."

Grasselli narrowed it down: "Mr. Rearden thinks the New York Corporation can provide real assistance to the stockpiling effort. We've still got our foreign offices, and we've got access to materials that are tough to find these days."

Culhane dearly wanted to know how, but couldn't bring himself to ask. Pride got to him. He answered, "Submit a list of what you have, the quantities and price quotations. If we need it, we'll trade for it."

"We'd rather have you submit the government's requirements, then we'll answer to—"

"We do it the other way around now."

Grasselli smiled, almost boyishly. "We're not going to let you shop us. We're not amateurs, you know, Mr. Culhane."

"I never thought you were."

Grasselli moved slightly on the bench, catching Culhane full in the eye now. "We can offer credit terms."

Culhane's interest rose. Credit!

"What sort of terms?"

"Depends on how much of the business we can have."

And when you get enough of it, thought Culhane, and I'm beholden to you, and other sources dry up on me, then there goes the credit and there goes me right up the Swanee River in a one-way canoe.

"I repeat, Mr. Grasselli, put your proposal in writing and I'll gladly discuss it."

Grasselli shook his head. "No, you don't understand. We're offering real help here. I mean, even Congress might get interested in our idea."

Culhane could fell the pressure stroking now, the hint of an investigation, prompted, no doubt, by Tim Rearden or one of his cronies.

"A hell of an idea you have there," he said. "Maybe Senator Rearden can explain why his appropriations committee wouldn't fund the purchase of critical materials for the past three years . . . Of course, in those days the government could pay in dollars, and maybe he'd like to explain why that doesn't work anymore either."

Grasselli reddened, and nervously scraped one heel against the pavement. He pitched his last point, saying, "Mr. Culhane, consider this from another side. We could forget those Culhane & Company open contracts we hold. More, we could even help you personally with some well-earned finder's commissions. Something like that. Nobody has to be the wiser, you know."

Humiliation scalded Culhane. His eyes turned their telltale methyl blue, uncontrollably, as anger rose. A damn jackal like Rearden, a man who never understood the rules, has sent this bush leaguer to remind me I'm a church mouse now.

"I suppose, Mr. Ass-elli"—he couldn't resist it—"that I can be bought. But tell Rearden if he's got other errands with me to come himself."

"You're making a mistake," warned Grasselli.

"This meeting is one of them, too." Culhane arose from the bench. "Send me your list and we'll see."

Grasselli watched him walk away. Fuming, the lawyer decided a little checking around out on the Coast couldn't hurt. Who was Culhane but a has-been? Arrogant son of a bitch, too.

Culhane left the elevator and walked down the second-floor hallway to the Treaty Room. He saw the secret service agent who had the duty that night: a hulker, with a thick neck and enormous sloping shoulders, a former footballer from Alabama.

"Morning, Billy Joe. The Man up yet?"

"You bet," Billy Joe Rowels said. "He did his walk already round the grounds . . . Say, the boss got sent some Panamas the other day. You want a few? He don't smoke 'em."

"Whatever you can spare I'd love to have."

"He'll be right along, if you want to go in. I'll have the 'gars ready when you leave."

"I owe you one."

Of all the rooms in the mansion, Halburton seemed to prefer the Treaty Room. Except for their meetings in the Oval Office, this was where they always talked, and where Culhane sometimes briefed him. He supposed it was because of its staid decor or maybe its history, or that it reminded the President of his former judge's chambers.

Victorian furniture, two tremendous candelabra that reached from the floor to the mantel on either side of the marble fireplace, and a gilded mirror large enough to catch the whole room in its reflection. Green-flocked wallpaper and burgundy drapes against the high windows. Paintings on the wall of Lincoln and Grant in conference, another of Zachary Taylor, and a third of Andrew Jackson. Men who'd done the business of state in here once.

Treaties, several important ones, had been signed in this room. And ripped up when another generation found that it didn't like its inheritance so much after all.

A soft double knock. A serving cart put its linen-draped prow through the door, followed by a tan-coated black man. Greeting Culhane quietly, the steward set two places at one end of the massive table in the center of the room. As quietly, he left.

From another era this room, so traditional yet tired—the way Efram Halburton looked as he came through the door now.

"Good morning."

114

"And to you . . . and to you," repeated Halburton, courtly of manner. "Eggs, I see, and prunes. How you know you're getting old is when they give you prunes every day. Hear from your family? They all right?"

"Fine, thanks." He wondered if Halburton knew anything at all about Karin. Probably not.

"Good. Let's fork these yolks, then, and talk. I'll start. You eat. I've been hearing good things from those Pentagon people about what you're doing for them. They aren't crying every split second. I appreciate it."

"We're on a bear hunt with a slingshot. The stockpile quantities are insufficient to keep this game up." Culhane started on the eggs, the first he'd eaten in two weeks.

"Trade the wheat."

"We haven't got the shipping capacity. Besides, the wheat is too important to trade."

"You're not going to get gold, if that's your idea."

"You're not going to get out of the hole, either. Not this way."

"I know it," said Halburton, mopping up some egg with a bread sliver. "What're your ideas about this Hormuz"—he faltered—"incident?"

"Interesting."

"That's all? Interesting? That's all you can say? Why—"

"It's military high jinks. It won't stop Russia. It cuts Europe's throat is all it does."

"Some are in favor of just that. Europe's been no friend to us."

"Europe can be dealt with later," said Culhane. "Hormuz is a flat gamble . . . Gamble you can't, and spilling blood is senseless."

"The military don't think it'll cost one life. Very few, anyway."

"It might be the right place. But it sure as hell is the wrong time."

"They make a convincing case."

"So did Hannibal." Culhane put his hands at his sides. "And a hundred others you could name." His hands closed into fists.

"Even the Russians wouldn't be mad enough to go nuclear over Hormuz. It wouldn't be worth—"

"They're getting everything they want without it. And

115

they must know you can't touch them . . . No, Halburton, they've pushed us to the edge of the paper."

"Whose side are you on!" Halburton's hand shook the cup against its saucer.

Culhane had struck the nerve he wanted to avoid. How could he tell Halburton that he was on no one's side? His own side certainly, but no one else's. So he tried mollifying the President with:

"The Straits of Hormuz idea only goes partway. It has to fit into a much larger scheme to do any lasting good."

"That may be so. Or it may not," Halburton observed, going crusty. "I'll have to be the judge of it."

"You'll have lost the prime advantage of maneuver and surprise if you move too soon," argued Culhane.

"You're against it then!"

"For now. Later on, it could have real possibilities. As could the Treasury study on *external* currency . . . It's all got to be put together somehow."

"Well, how?"

"I don't know yet. Some sort of a giant leapfrogging operation, but what kind I'm not sure."

"The two-currency system is a godsend. We can put the domestic dollar on a sound footing—"

"You mean," interrupted Culhane, "you can cheat every other holder of dollars in the world. You cheated me. Go ahead and cheat them."

"I resent that. This country is entitled to put its house in ord—"

"Order?" Culhane nearly shouted. "Leave everyone around the world holding the bag because the politicos spent us bankrupt! Your house in order? Is that what you said? Tell me, what exactly does the house stand for? Has it got balls? Does it pay off its debts? Or do you run out, the way the government did on Social Security . . . You people in Washington and the banks allowed the world to become flooded with dollars, and *you* have to pay them off . . . Or you can run. But how far?"

Halburton threw his napkin in the middle of the table. Culhane stopped talking. For a moment, they stared, frozen, the silence almost ringing. Culhane wanted to discuss his plan for a Blue Dollar—a piracy really of the Treasury's idea for an external currency. He had read up on the plan, which was unfinished yet intriguing, in some government interagency memos that Halburton had sent his way. This was the wrong time to bring it up, and Culhane decided to let it pass.

"I thought you could help. I thought I could trust you to give me an objective view." Halburton spoke forlornly. "And I was willing to get your gold back and—"

"I can try helping you. There may be a way to give Russia something to think about . . . 'Hi-yo, Silver' by the Pentagon, done now, won't help."

"I don't know how long I can hold the military. They're threatening to go ahead, and I think they could do it."

"Timing is all you've got. Your only crowbar. Don't throw it away."

"You always say that, and I'm damned if I understand," said Halburton, pushing, digging, never convinced.

Culhane shrugged, thought, and said, "If I'm the alligator and you're the bear, then I win in the water but you do on land. It's all timing and it's all terrain. That makes it nearly identical to a carefully worked out trading operation."

"Or a military operation. Correct?"

"I suppose," said Culhane, swallowing some egg. "You can't win that one, though."

"And which will we be? The gator or the bear?"

"Neither."

"I'm sorry, Culhane. It's still early in the morning for me. I don't get it."

Culhane met Halburton's eyes earnestly. "And let's hope neither will anyone else. Let the Russians oil their guns and the Pentagon sharpen its steel. Our job is to work out the ambush. Confuse, disorient, and surprise them. It's the best way to go—there's no way we can beat the Russians on land, not eight thousand miles away, anyway."

"You sound like an army general."

Culhane smiled. "Well, Moscow's been outmaneuvered before. But you'd have to be willing to play on the finest of fine edges. Have to think about a few other things, too."

"Such as."

"Put Senator Rearden in as your Vice-President so that

we can settle this currency thing," Culhane said flatly, not batting an eye.

For a long minute, Halburton gave Culhane a searching, skeptical look. "You can't be serious. I wouldn't have that Rearden crowd in to mow the back lawn."

"I don't go for them either," said Culhane, thinking of his meeting with Grasselli. "But it might solve the problem, one problem anyway."

"You don't understand the politics of the matter. You couldn't, after saying that."

"Your politics. It's a game of charades, of posturing . . . And it's not the issue here. A new currency is. Worry about Rearden later."

"Even if I did forget about him, what about those Eurodollars? How do you propose dealing with that damnable problem?"

"Give me a few weeks. Let me have some time," said Culhane, "and I'll give you an approach."

"An approach!"

"That's all. Look, we're advised by the British that the European banks are shorting the dollar hard again. I'm a trader, and they're begging for trouble over there if we help them along . . . I want your help to feed falsified data to the newspapers that we're in worse shape than we really are."

Puzzled, Halburton asked, "Whatever for? It's bad enough as it is."

"Because it'll be picked up by the Russians, and Europe, too. No big waves, just a few bubbles."

"You want to influence opinion?"

"Something like that. Reinforce it, really."

Halburton made a steeple with his hands and looked off, frowning. His head waved slightly, like a slowing pendulum. He hadn't said no. Was he sending a signal through his sleeve?

Half a minute passed before Culhane said:

"A very good man once told me the idea that works best is the one that people *think* is the truest one. It won't necessarily be true, because nobody knows exactly what that is. So it's the *perception* of what is true that counts. I found out he was right."

Culhane reached for the silver coffeepot, seeing his fuzzed reflection in its bright belly as he poured. As in other times of stress, his thoughts went back to Ken-chou Ming:

"You talk trade and you talk peace. You talk war and you bargain bones."

15

Washington
Amsterdam

The flasher blinked. Culhane picked up the red phone, motioning Flickinger to keep his chair.

"Good, and you?. . . Cuban sugar . . . That much? . . . No, ask Richard Ming first, and do the back end of it with Muldaur. Work the balance against Japan for the tantulum carbide powder . . . No, through Hong Kong covered by Lichtenstein-Sirius and then shut it down for good . . . Say it's for London or Prague, nobody will know . . . Mine too, and I'll call them tonight."

He hung up and stared into space, then at Flickinger, who with his gray looks and grayer ways reminded Culhane of an embalmer.

"Okay. Tell Cowperthwaite we appreciate what he's done for us."

"What are you going to do with that information?"

"I haven't decided. Maybe nothing." And maybe everything, thought Culhane. "Do you care?"

Flickinger shrugged his narrow shoulders nonchalantly. "I suppose not . . . I couldn't help overhear your conversation. Something about Cuba, I believe."

"Yes. Sugar. They're unloading a surplus. Imagine having a surplus."

"Would you have any way to obtain a special grade of paper used by the Cuban government for official travel documents, visas and so forth?"

Culhane paused, then answered, "My interest might rise when I see what you've got on the New York Corporation."

"Oh, yes," replied Flickinger mildly, then lied, "We're still looking through the files. If we had anything at all, it might have been purged by now."

No sale, thought Culhane. He couldn't figure a way to get at it. Elusive, like the dossier the CIA had sent over on Flickinger's service record. Thick as boiler steam and about as informative.

"Incidentally, tomorrow they'll have your other office ready," Flickinger said.

"I got a notice already. Takes a while, doesn't it."

Flickinger gestured toward the red phone next to Culhane's desk. "Wiring those things is quite a job, you know. The Army accounts for every one of them, and they're all linked through someplace in Missouri."

"Really? Well, I'm through if you are," Culhane said, indifferently.

Flickinger got up. "I'll be going across the river for the day, in case you need me."

"Pick up the Rearden stuff while you're there."

But Flickinger was almost through the door. If he heard Culhane, he gave no sign of it. Hurrying, he had things to do before catching the shuttle wagon, which went four times daily across the Potomac carrying the White House staffers and Pentagon and CIA personnel. Awkward, but it saved precious fuel.

On the desk were four sheets of stapled paper showing what Cowperthwaite at the British Embassy had come up with. Across the board the story was pretty much the same. All the great banks of Europe—German, French, Italian, Swiss, Dutch, a few British—were shorting the dollar to absurd lengths. By the scores of billions of dollars. It would take a man spending a thousand dollars a day over two thousand years to run through just one billion alone. Ludicrous. Culhane shook his head as he surveyed the list.

He plowed into more paperwork, like a bank teller

counting notes. Sometimes he would relieve the boredom by taking a stab at where some of these sacred materials were found.

Here was one. Chrysotile asbestos. From Rhodesia now called Zimbabwe. A rare material with amazing electrical and thermal conductivity qualities, it was used in missile and submarine construction.

Rhodesia. He remembered going there on a buying mission for Ken-chou Ming many years before. Twenty-two years old then, and his first real test by that brilliant, generous comprador.

He began to think about Hong Kong, trying to recall his small apartment up by Magazine Gap. The furtive hours spent there with the heavenly Jia Ming, essence of all Chinese feminine fragrance; hour by the patient hour, she would teach her way of lovemaking. Incredible.

In China now someplace. Doing what? Living how? A husband? Surely there must be.

I wish golden joss, thought Culhane, for you, Jia, and for Richard, your brother, who is saving my ass at some risk to his own.

An hour later he left the White House for the eight-block walk to the National Archives. Culhane knew he could have requested the information he was after from the Treasury Department. Yet it might have raised eyebrows, and it was a matter, anyway, on which he wanted to do his own homework.

He was becoming fond of the place. Museums were a drug with him, and the Archives were special. The biggest pair of bronze doors in the world; prime documents on display that showed how a nation was founded. Other things, too, like films concerning everything from toothbrushing to childbearing. The magnificent and the absurd, all under one roof.

A pant of warm breeze filled the late afternoon as he made his way along Constitution Avenue, heading for the hotel. His third visit to the Archives, and Culhane had most of what he needed. It was all there: the payments made by various European countries on their official debts to the U.S.; their unpaid loans from the war. Only Finland had settled up in full. Interesting.

Attractive women were on the stroll, some of them

housewives, he imagined, bargaining their favors for rationing coupons. True trade, illicit perhaps, but very real. Some young boys and girls sold flowers and, astonishingly, in Washington, avocados. Transported how? he wondered.

He counted seven bars that were boarded up. Early lines of people formed at the locked entrances to a few bakery shops and grocery stores. Sullen looks. A few line jumpers muscled in toward the front of one line. An argument ensued, then a scuffle.

Going into the Hay-Adams lobby, he called for his mail at the reception desk. A cheerful-looking girl dressed in a green jacket and dark skirt handed him two postcards and a letter.

"Excuse me," she said, "Mr. Frédy left a message asking you to please come see him when you came in." A very nice smile, teeth like luminous chalk.

"Did he say what he wanted?"

"Not exactly." She hesitated. "I heard the hotel is running short on food again."

"I've got a long-distance call reserved. Tell him I'll check with him later."

She nodded understandingly.

"Are you new here?"

"My name is Jenny Carruthers, Mr. Culhane."

"Hello, Jenny. This desk never looked better or brighter."

Now a leaping smile from her that disobeyed all laws of optics.

Up in his suite, he checked on the call to California. Twenty minutes or so, he was told. He loosened his tie, threw off his coat, and sat, thinking up a new litany.

He drew imaginary boxes in his mind, putting problems in various compartments: one for Karin; another for Halburton; a third for Russia and Europe; the Reardens, of course; China. Mexico he didn't think would present a real problem, so it didn't get a box. The grain reserves might become politically difficult to use in the way he thought best. The Blue Dollar would be a test of luck more than skill, a bluff that could fall flat. Or one that would bring on a banshee wail. Possibly Halburton's wail. He felt like having a drink.

The phone rang, startling him. Culhane reached over, wondering if there were problems now with the black-market deals he'd made for food deliveries to the hotel. Was Frédy in a corner again?

The hotel operator said: "Mr. Culhane, an overseas call for you."

"Thanks." Who was this?

The overseas operator came on: "For Mr. Culhane. A call from Amsterdam."

A roll of deep laugh like bass drums before the curtain lifts for the dancing girls. Van Slyke! No other laugh quite like that in the world, or at least none that Culhane knew of.

"There you are, my friend. In that city of shame and fools. Tell me of yourself."

"Hello, Piet. My God, it's good to hear your voice. How'd you find me?"

"Your man, Saxa, that brown bastard who trades like a Canal Street whore. And our ambassador in your god-struck city confirmed it. Why are you there?"

"A long story. Just be for a short while."

Van Slyke's English sounds better on the phone, Culhane thought, less thickened and guttural—though it has never been that bad. Better than my Dutch.

"Are you employed now by government?"

"No, Piet. No violation. But I am advising them . . . Without pay," he added.

"Goot!" Now the accent. "I hear from Muldaur, then Tomlinson, that you trade together. And with some profit. Is so?"

"No profit for me. But yes, we're doing some things together." Damn, thought Culhane, feeling uncomfortable having this conversation over an open line.

"I can hope you would come to me when there is business to be done . . . Nothing personal, you understand the Council's decision."

"I know that, Piet. And don't worry, I'll come to you first when there's something very important to be done." And there will be, hoped Culhane, who was unsure but forced any trace of it from his voice.

Another bellow of laughter, a roar. "Goot! Now tell me, Rusht, tell me what you think the chances of you coming back to us are?"

"Fifty-fifty."

"No better?"

125

"No better, Piet, but I wouldn't say that to anyone else."

"I also call to tell you I have confidence no matter your trouble. And I call to find out what you want done with your reserve account. Is netted at eighteen million U.S. Not much, I'm afraid, but even so, it's yours. I can arrange for a draft on one of the good banks to be sent."

One hundred million down to eighteen. His whole Shang-Magan reserve account riddled into worthless pieces.

"Just hold on to it, Piet."

"No interest paid. You know that."

"I remember."

"Goot, for that business then. Now, please don't accept personal-service money from your government. Come see me if you get to Europe. Things are getting bad here. Rooskies want it all . . . I'm your friend, please know that. I will help as long as the Rules aren't broken."

"You bet, Piet."

"Come back." And the lines carried no further sounds, only emptiness, and he was cut off again from his people. Those he had known, striven to be part of, the best traders on earth.

A picture of Van Slyke grew in Culhane's mind. The huge, red-haired human beast, almost a man from another age, color enough there for a dozen marching bands. He knew very little of the Dutchman's ancestry. Probably conceived by two earthquakes, and God help the woman who'd had to labor him into this world.

Culhane remembered back to when he was first tapped for the Shang-Magan, its very first U.S. member. Then his first cruise on the big sailing junk from Mombasa in Kenya, and his surprise at the presence of women and young boys on the boat. An old custom, Van Slyke had advised him, and one that began with the Shang-Magans at least two centuries earlier. The whores and the boys were there to keep things relaxed, loose, the mind and body free of other needs whenever business was discussed. A safe drug, Van Slyke had told him.

Dismissing this reverie, Culhane went into the other room to turn on some music. Selecting a tape he'd brought from California, he threaded it through the head of a Sony tape deck. Soon he heard the soothing vibes of Lionel Hampton.

He'd been tempted sorely to ask if the Shang-Magan's

Russian agent was still in place. Still Metzilov, was it? Placed where now in Moscow's castles? Bad form even to ask such a question. Van Slyke wouldn't have answered it anyway. If it was still Metzilov—and it might not be—it raised possibilities. Culhane had helped recruit the man, knew how and what he was paid by the Magan to furnish inside advice about Russian trade policy.

Culhane was unaware of the identity of the Shang-Magan's North American agent. Who might that be? None of the Council members knew the government agents placed within their own trading zones. The rule, a good one, lessened suspicions about unfair advantage, or unseemly complaints over conflicts of interest. It was a first-class system for obtaining trading intelligence for use by all Shang-Magans. All benefited equally.

And all knew only so much about these worldwide agents. Culhane had recruited agent candidates for Europe and Russia; Muldaur for the Far East; Van Slyke for North America; Liu Wai for Africa, and so forth. Carefully laid down, intricately woven, the system of information—for it was a system—worked. All of it was tied together in Monte Carlo, under the tight control of an Albanian who ran a pool of talented researchers.

Metzilov! Culhane remembered the Russian vividly now. A cold cobra, but clever and ambitious, on the rise evidently. Metzilov had fit the silhouette the Council of Six used to select and recruit its advisory agents—reasonably honest, buyable, never notable themselves but always linked closely with others who formed real government policy.

What is Russia's choke-price? Moscow would have one, like anyone else. Russia might be capable of quick military responses. But he doubted if she would act fast in a trading crunch, at the crucial moment, when the art of timing counted so dearly. They were too paranoid, stodgy, inelastic, didn't grasp open-ended speculation, with its advantages and traps.

The odds were staggering, but the fascination of his craft rarely failed to bring up his blood when a big play loomed. Any huge trade like those he'd engineered once in the world grain markets, with billions at stake, would run his blood up to the boiling point. To try the greatest trade ever, or the illusion of it, stretched his curiosity no end.

Culhane snapped out of it. Where was the call to California? He lifted the phone, asking for the long-distance operator. A wait. He looked at his watch. She came on.

"I had a call reserved to California."

"The lines aren't cleared yet."

"When do you think?"

"Can't say. We're backlogged two or three hours as it is."

"Goddammit anyway!" he cursed softly.

"I beg your pardon!"

The hell with it. He'd use the red phone. Culhane went over to pick it up. An Army Signal Corps communicator intervened.

"I've got to get through," Culhane said.

"The lines are preempted for military traffic, sir."

"How long?"

"Several hours at least."

"Beautiful."

He replaced that receiver too, went back to the hotel phone, got through to the White House operator. No luck there either.

It slugged him then. Unexpectedly, the way it always did, and his back shook as the feeling down in his feet went away. Culhane couldn't tell whether the moisture on his face was cold or hot. Marble, it felt like stone up there. He tried to steel himself. More trembles came. It was happening again, and he couldn't force it down. Two deep gasps.

Alone too long, and now it got him again. Ever since his mother died as fast and as big as you can ever die, in front of his very eyes, these fears had hounded him. He took a step, then two, froze. A scream in the center of his soul. Crush it, dammit, he told himself.

But one of the terrorizing images appeared anyway.

He was back in deepest Africa this time. The time he'd gone there exploring for Ken-chou Ming. Up there in the Congo, where the Luba trackers, leading him, had suddenly gone to ground, vanishing utterly. He'd wandered, lost, thrashing around in the jungle for days. He ate grubs, roots and berries that made him physically sick. The jungle so dense he couldn't find his shadow; so strange with noises he couldn't listen for water; so thick and heavy he couldn't take star bearings or even see the sun sometimes;

128

so eerily quiet he swore he could hear the heartbeats of insects. Ostracized, until the Pygmies had found him . . .

The trembling stopped, the fear passing now as it always did, just after leaving another invisible gash. Culhane shook himself, tasting drops of salt on his lips. He moved and it felt all right. Africa! Christ almighty, he thought.

Pain, like the pain of Karin's sexual frostbite, he could get around. Not this, though. It clamped on like a lifetime barnacle, the way it did for others who feared heights, the dark, or confining spaces.

Piet Van Slyke sank his lantern jaw into the palm of one meaty hand.

Ach! A trench of trouble out there. He slammed the flat of his other hand down on an oak table, a huge table, a huge hand, and both jumped from the impact. With four long strides—seven for a normal man—he crossed the floor until he reached the bowed window overlooking Leidsestraat.

The expensive shops bordering the street were closed now, had been for hours. A pale light from the streetlamps was barely able to cut through the fog slithering off the nearby canals. Through the haze below the giant Dutchman could see the large Golden Cricket circled in wrought iron swinging eerily over the front doors to his house. The Cricket, his chop: the most famous in Europe, more respected now than Rothschild's, but not as old.

Standing there, brooding, his wedge of red nose almost even with the top of the window, he barely heard her words.

"Will there by anything else, Myjn heer?"

A west Hollander accent. The woman was very tall, almost level with Van Slyke's shoulder. A heavy flow of dark hair was caught behind her head in a big cushion of bun. A wide face, gentle, watched his through cautious eyes. She'd been with Van Slyke for almost ten years. Highly trusted, his *little-mistress,* and like Sant Saxa a sort of good luck charm, only more so.

Van Slyke sat down on the wooden heating register under the window. It groaned under his nearly three hundred pounds. He crossed one booted foot over his other knee.

"See to raising Muldaur in South Africa. Wherever he is, I want him tonight."

She nodded, hardly able to contain the affection she felt for this gianter. Not the Golden Cricket at all, she thought, but rather a magnetic lion. A magnetic king, and so blind at times.

"And after, do you wish the other call to Washington?" asked Marit Toorenaar.

"Tomorrow is soon enough. Though I wish you to call my house and advise the Countess that I'm detained. Give my apologies, tell her to proceed with dinner . . . I'll be two hours, perhaps more."

Again the woman nodded, then ventured with, "A word, Myjn heer?"

Van Slyke smiled, although it was impossible to see it through the heavy beard.

"This Countess woman," she began, irritated, "will only bring us trouble."

"All women do except you, Marit," replied Van Slyke, studying her face for the jealousy he knew was in her heart.

"It is madness to invest in those boutiques in times like this. We are not retailers. Besides, I've been over her accounting reports a dozen times. They are a farce," said Marit, in the fearless voice of a woman speaking her mind.

"I know."

"Then why?"

"Because her father was intelligent enough to restrict her income from the trust he left for her. Because she cannot come up with the capital required for this frivolity. But we can . . . And because, Marit, her trustees control the directorship of Stahlwerken Bruges and I want their steel, all of it I can get."

"Do not cheapen yourself, Myjn heer."

"These are cheap times. Need I remind you of what is happening here in Europe? We are menaced from the East, which will shit on us when it suits them. Look here, right now, in Europe—your Europe and mine—talking détente! That is a whore's word, meaning, I take you and keep me . . . My work as Shan Chu is sleepless. And when it is never done, never, I must look to our own affairs in this House! Now I need steel, not words, but steel, not prayers, but steel, not simpering politicians, but hard steel!" Van Slyke thundered the words until Marit Toorenaar was certain the leaded window behind him would crack.

With a firm grace, she said, "I have said my words. I'll call Muldaur now and tomorrow Washington again."

Van Slyke stood now and fitfully tapped the chandelier made of a hundred chamois horns. Swaying on its heavy chain, its lights threw a shower of polka dots against the high bookcases, the massive floor globe, the biggest Eames furniture ever made, and ten Van Slyke merchant ships in model under glass.

Culhane, I wonder if you can do all this, thought Piet Van Slyke. I could not. I do not have your instinct for the big play. I am only blessed to know men and their weaknesses. Now is your test, the biggest. How will you face it? Moscow, the thieves, what of them?

Van Slyke thought back to his ruse of conversation with Liu Wai, the Singaporean, on that stormy afternoon on the South China Sea. How, as Shan Chu, he'd craftily gotten the Council of Six to suspend Culhane. Could the American mend the trouble over there?

And where do I find time to meet with the Black Pope, waiting now at the Europa Hotel? The Superior of the Vatican's marines, the Jesuits, had come for a private loan, on the quiet, of two hundred million guilders. The American plate collections were a thing of the past: that rich source of revenue as dry now as a dehydrated apricot. They'd get their loan all right, thought Van Slyke, but not until he could figure out what he wanted in return. And it wouldn't be a papal blessing, either.

Yes, my friend Culhane, we will soon learn if you are a Shan Chu. Then your worries really begin. Holland is small, yet once it ruled a third of this planet. Founded even your New York. Through trade alone and smart alliances we achieved, fought the world for the right to trade wherever we wanted to. Now you fight it. You in America were a thousand Hollands. Now let us see if you can survive as well and for as long.

"Are you that shrewd? God help you if you are," spoke Piet Van Slyke aloud, as the call to South Africa was announced.

Piet thought of the Belgian countess staying at his home. She would, he was sure, want one of her tiresome games with the pony whip tonight.

131

16

Washington

Andrea ended a brief note to her mother, who had moved from Florence to the Capri residence of Count Alberto Valfiore. How very damn jolly for them, she thought, looking over at a travel clock, checking the time.

It was 7:28, and he was late.

Andrea walked back to her bedroom. For the second time now, she shucked off the low-cut peasant blouse, unhooking her bra. She hated the damn things, and this one didn't look right under the filmy white material. Too dark, and besides . . .

Feeling better, she tucked the blouse back into the waist of the full-length sand-colored suede skirt. Pirouetting once before the closet mirror, she thought, Well, if he doesn't like, he doesn't.

But Andrea knew she looked enticing, abundantly so. Her blush of natural skin tone, her feathery hair alive and shining, her wide mouth only slightly rouged, the eyelashes barely shadowed. A quick riff of hand fluffing her hair, another glance in the mirror, and her spirits lifted.

Usually so punctual, where was he? Always there right on the minute for their campy lunches in Lafayette Square. And the other time, too, she thought, when he took me to La Danielle at the Hay-Adams for a private lunch. Only ten people, Frédy's patrons, in that whole gorgeous room, and soft-shell crabs from the Maryland shore. Ecstasy, and illegal, too, which made the dinner tastier somehow. Forbidden fruit.

She strode from the bedroom through the living room, and beyond, into the kitchen. The smell of chicken baking in herbs, sherry, and real butter—for which she'd bartered an old litho—wafted into the air. Andrea grabbed a potholder, stooped, reached into the oven to check on her creation, and found it plopping and smelling divine.

"Ouch, shitto!" she yelped as the edge of her hand grazed the hot grill. Closing the oven door, she kicked at it with one golden slipper.

Cooking eluded her. So many nights in restaurants, palaces, villas, and dining salons; she had learned how not to cook, never once considering it as any sort of deficiency.

Candles? Were there enough of those, in case the power was tripped off early tonight? She went into the next room to check. Sitting down on a pale yellow couch, Andrea wished there were flowers. Again, him, more thoughts of Culhane. Married to a Hollywood princess-bitch. Watch it! she told herself, and in the next instant, Forget it! Thoughts were sniffling warily at one another like strange dogs who'd just met—I mean, my God, look at him, and the really good mind, so tough and yet gentle, and what he's been through. But so damned independent, like a biological cell that splits and reproduces itself, again and again.

And me doing notes about him for Clay Flickinger. What if I don't? Here's what, you ninny. You lose your job at the paper, that's likely, and you lose the tab-off from CIA. You lose the moon you are now sitting on that ought to be decently covered with panties.

That cold-blooded humper. A disagreeable memory surfaced then. Andrea was aware that Flickinger had flirted his way into a shabby affair once with her mother. In Berlin, where her father was posted there as the CIA station chief, where he'd met with mysterious death.

Oh well, she thought, a long time ago and Clay has tried to help, *has* helped, generously. Still . . .

The door chime rang. Yes! Excitement rippled along her vertebrae, then other places. Nimbly, she fled across the room.

"Sorry," said Culhane, smiling, as she opened the door.

"I had to come the roundabout way and couldn't stop to phone."

Wilting, she asked. "What happened, Rushton?"

"I was in Maryland at Fort Meade, and the shuttle was late . . . Dropped off a few people before my turn came."

"Over there with all those crypto types?" asked Andrea, impressed. It was, she knew, the headquarters of the National Security Agency, the holy of holies, so sensitive it was rarely mentioned outside the intelligence community.

"Compliments of Frédy." He handed her a small sack, brown and wrinkled.

She looked at the brown package and asked, "Don't open till Christmas or now?"

"Something for dinner, unless you've something else."

He stood with her in the foyer of the apartment. A parquet floor, white walls with smoked mirrors on them in whitish gilded frames. A small, sparkling light overhead throwing narrow rays of prismed light, softly holding a moment neither of them could see.

"Oh, you treasure," said Andrea, almost breathlessly. She had opened the bag and pulled out a bottle of Perrier-Jouet, 1955. "Wherever . . . I mean the year and all . . . How did you?. . .

"Trade secret," said Culhane, "and a wonderful year. The year the angels waltzed on the grapes." He was charmed by her obvious delight.

"Be perfect with the chicken. How neat!"

She hugged him, clinging, igniting, until they broke apart. She became wet, hoping, though knowing, it wouldn't show like the erect nipples studding her low-swept peasant blouse.

"Touch my tongue again, quick," said Andrea, who stepped away before Culhane could. "God, I'm—"

"A sugar tease." Culhane smiled, reaching for her. But she was leaning back, on a dreamy cloud, contagiously flustered.

"I'd better ice this wonder," she said, looking at the Champagne bottle. "If they shut the power down early, I'll scream." She thought of darkness, and that maybe she wouldn't scream after all. "C'mon." Andrea tugged his hand. "A drink. I heisted some Scotch from a friend at the Peruvian embassy . . . Over there," pointing to an antique

135

armoire, wormholed and waxed up to a high sheen. "Be with you in a jiff," and she glided away.

Culhane walked into the room, seeing the smooth lines of chintz curtains, valanced, over a wide window. Branches from the maple tree, he'd seen when arriving, bounced their shadows against windowpanes lighted up by a Stiffel table lamp. A white shag rug, more white walls, some white furniture, and English period pieces. Good satinwood. On the walls were silk fabrics framed in chrome, also a grouping of Greek icons.

A cared-for room, thought Culhane, as he went to the armoire. He spotted the bottle immediately. Highland malt whisky, worth crown jewels on the black market. A careful pour into both glasses, ice in hers but not his, than a taste. Stirring the ice in Andrea's glass, he thought of how stirred he was by her embrace. Almost woozy, his blood heating, doing its work, reminding him of the flesh's truest message.

"I like your room," said Culhane, as he saw Andrea return.

"Some me, some my mother."

"Nice."

"Come sit." She could feel it coming on, only a little stronger, or worse, now. "Tell me about your day," as they walked toward the long green couch.

"Nothing big," he said. "Just fussing with computers and game theory."

"A who?"

"A way of trying to predict likely outcomes against known or unknown odds. You build a series model, then jam it with hundreds of possible cases and see what happens," Culhane tried to explain.

"Try it in French. If it's math, then to me it's mud."

He laughed. "As I said, it was a sort of nothing." Another taste. It was so godawful good.

"And how is our President Halburton today? Tell him we can use some advertising revenues." A bite there in her words.

"Didn't see him."

"You see him a lot, though, don't you?"

"More than he'd like, I'm sure. And more than I want to, I know."

"You don't like him either?"

136

"He sings from a different songsheet than I do and he likes to lawyer you until you're crazy. But he's okay. A rough job."

"And a wrong man for it," replied Andrea.

"Give him a chance. You press people blame things on him that began ten or twenty years ago."

Andrea returned almost toughly with "Did you see the article today in the paper about this Bank for International Settlements business? I mean, dammit, not even a croak out of the White House. That's our leader?"

He couldn't tell her what a huge break it might possibly be. Maybe, just maybe.

"He never got to the honeymoon. Only been in the chair for seven months, so give him a break."

"He's a disaster chasing a catastrophe."

"We've survived those before."

"This is the worst, though, isn't it? He's going to ruin us. Just like this BIS thing, where nobody will take our money anymore."

"The way you press people write him up, I'm surprised he doesn't go after you for libel."

Andrea heaved the deep breath of the annoyed, as her spectacular breasts threatened the stitching of her blouse. The nipples, he saw, had gone to sleep.

"Be a darling and get us another drink. I'm thinking of becoming a strict alcoholic. With a sign on my back and a rosary in my teeth," Andrea said.

Her voice became lighter, the mouth making a smile again. He got up and walked over to the armoire, as she lofted a thought that had badgered her all day.

"Do you know Hans Piegar? Excuse me, Hans-Otto Piegar—he always insists on that—at the BIS?"

"Of him," said Culhane over his shoulder. "I don't personally know him."

"I lived with his family for eight months in Zurich once. He's not worth knowing, even if he is Jesus Christ these days. His wife is a saint and his son, Ambros, a loverly killer of a boy. A peach."

Surprise, a tug in Culhane's belly.

He dropped the ice into her glass. It sounded like a car wreck. Lived with him? All day he'd been working on money on the National Security Agency's computers, trying to test the BIS's ultimate capacity to be drowned, backed against the ropes, and take Europe's banks with it.

"How'd you get to know the Piegars? Newspapering?"

"Oh, way before," said Andrea, "way before. My father was stationed in Bern. I was about sixteen and had mild dyslexia and read everything backwards. The best doctor was in Zurich then, so I went there for most of a year and lived as a sort of au pair girl with the Piegars, and studied there, too. My father knew him from the forties, in the war, when he was in Switzerland with Allen Dulles."

"OSS?" Culhane had somehow thought that Andrea's father was in the State Department.

"Yes. He was . . . My father was a lawyer, but he just kept going to war. A really wonderful man . . . He died in Berlin, and I was numb for a year at least."

Culhane watched as Andrea drank nervously, wishing he hadn't asked the question, but still glad for the answer.

"You must miss your family," said Andrea. "I remember seeing your wife in the movies. Very beautiful."

"Sure I miss them. Before long I expect to be back with them."

Andrea's heart thumped. "What'll you do then?"

"Damned if I know. Close my eyes and ride the skies," replied Culhane airily.

"Mind if I ask something?"

"You will anyway, so go ahead."

"What would be a big trading day, when you were really rolling?"

"Two or three billion. About as big as I ever got, anyway."

"Is that right? Really?" Andrea asked, disbelief etched on her face.

"Sometimes."

"Does it hurt not to be rich anymore? My family used to be, and my mother never got over it. She lives now with an Italian count."

Culhane looked off.

"As long as I had my own work to do, I was rich enough. I never went in it for money."

"I don't get you."

"In my game you can't play it just for money. You'd go sour. The money end was just so many decimals, because it

138

came fast and went fast. One year I had a negative net worth of seventy million. Now I'm all the way up to zero."

"You're not busted, though. Look at that art you have. Don't you worry about keeping it there at the hotel?"

"No, I don't worry about it. Anyone trying to steal it would have a hell of a time selling it in this country."

"I'd worry. Your Cézanne is to die for."

"Awful good," agreed Culhane over his drink.

Andrea leaned back. Her eyes traversed the room, then fell on him again. "My father moved around so much. We lived on Long Island on my grandmother's estate. Horses, duck shoots, pinafores and patent leather shoes, dances, a nanny even. Pretty poshy until the money went . . . I suppose it was dreamy growing up in Hawaii . . ."

Miserable, remembered Culhane, though he replied, "Pineapples, palm trees, and big blue water," and did not let on how terrifying it was to be alone there during his childhood. How he'd hated the orphanage.

"Beautiful, I suppose. I've never been."

"I lied my way onto a tramper when I was sixteen, sailed away, and never saw Hawaii again," answered Culhane tonelessly.

More to it, certainly, thought Andrea, catching the undercurrent instantly. But she was too practiced a journalist to chafe away at a raw wound, knowing it would only fester if she did.

"Must have been some lie."

"A beaut. My best ever."

"You're not a liar. Are you? Say no."

"I'm a fair bluffer. That's almost the same. Not quite, but almost."

"Probably learned that trick in Hong Kong."

"The Chinese are good teachers, and I got some memorable pointers from others later on." He could remember a few of those lessons, especially the expensive ones.

"I'd like to know about those Shang-whatever sometime," Andrea said.

Culhane gazed steadily at her. Andrea conveyed something like electrical flame that lured, then burned up the summer moths. Who was she really, and made of what? He couldn't decide yet. "Ever faced a really make-or-break problem in your life?" he asked.

"Well, there was school and deciding to take a crack at

journalism . . . Then deciding *not* to get married twice . . .
And handling my mother . . . Things like that. What's so
damn funny?"

"I was talking more of a walk-or-die kind of problem."

"Well, I don't hang around with the French Foreign
Legion anymore," said Andrea, giving off one of her beguiling laughs.

Almost an hour had run by as they traveled along in conversation, enjoying the whisky, feeling for the deeper flow
of each other.

"Jumping Phoebe!" exclaimed Andrea, leaping up, dart-
ing across the room. "The chicken! I'll be right back."

Am I a what? wondered Culhane. A case study? I'm forever on the grill with this woman. Just her way, perhaps,
and she is trained to ask, ask. Odd, and so are a few other
items.

Andrea returned, a mopey, irritated look straining her
face. "Rushton, it's cinders. There's just some rice." On the
verge of tears.

"Not to worry. Okay?"

"It's just so stupid of me . . . All those damn coupons
wasted."

Culhane got up and went to her. "Hey," and he smiled,
"let's shake hands with Perrier-Jouet and wish on the
stars for a while."

He followed her to the kitchen. On the counter lay the
earthenware casserole dish, its insides a black crust of
hardened soup. Inedible. He opened the Champagne and
returned to the other room, where he poured the wine into
other glasses at the armoire.

"For tomorrow and the next one," he said, touching his
glass to hers. Culhane bent toward her and kissed her
lightly across the eyes, then hard around the mouth.

"I want you," said Andrea, very openly. "Brazen of me,
isn't it?" He still had one arm around her, his hand touching the warm softness just below the back of her neck.
"You've the right to remain silent, because anything you
say now can and *will* be used against you."

"I'm not free to love you," said Culhane.

"I don't care. Later I will, but now I don't."

He felt Karin, he felt awful, and he felt thrilled, with his
temples pounding furiously. Their mouths mingled again.
Later, they couldn't remember who began undressing the

140

other first; clothing puddled about their feet, they just moved together, as insistently as early wind. Eagerly, they burrowed into their own mist of urgent murmurings. The outside world vanished for Culhane, especially the part of it asking whether he was engaging in pardonable infidelity.

And later, Culhane whispered, "You've really got me going."

"There?" Delicate, intimate strokes.

"Yes . . ."

"More there?"

"Can't s-stop."

"Hurry, darling, deep, go deep."

"Ai ching mei jan." The words sang out from him in the Chiu Chao dialect, as his conscious feelings completely whited out.

Night brought them no betrayals. Cool Champagne on the lips that later turned hot inside them. Hunger, much hunger, though none of it caused by the spoiled dinner, and Culhane knew that only time would reveal the best and many different ways to celebrate Andrea sexually.

Everything about her intrigued him. Her unabashed lust, the raw strength, her sensitivity everywhere to the tiniest touch of his tongue. She was female, and very magnificent to him.

Much later dawn came. Culhane slid quietly from the warm and tossed bed. Trying not to disturb her, he moved soundlessly to the window and observed the rose-gray light pushing against the tail of night. Naked, immobile, he stood there and thought for a long time. He was deep into it and didn't hear Andrea stir in the bed, reaching over for where he should be.

"Rushton," she murmured, her low voice made deeper by drowsiness.

"Yes, love." He turned toward her.

"S'wonderful night."

"The very best. Thank you for it."

"Me too."

Even in that dim light, her eyes caught a sparkle. Christ, God! thought Culhane, mesmerized and naked and a little loony at the dairy-fresh sight of her just then.

"I don't wan' . . . get up," she mumbled into the pillow. "Don't."

141

"Go . . . t' work."

"The hell with the work. That's all we seem to do . . . In the day," he said, grinning.

"I'm behind on—"

"You've a gorgeous behind. Very athletic." She heard him chuckle.

"Stop! No, don't stop."

He moved toward her then, saying, "What do you say to staying home today?"

"M'velous. I need to figure . . . excuse."

"That's where I come **in.**"

Andrea came alive now. The *Times-Herald* could hang its Washington copy without her, as they had before and would after. She turned, feeling him, pressing.

Belly to belly, they surfed again with enough exquisite heat to make the cool of morning fly away.

17

Washington

Couldn't get enough of each other on a day that seemed to soar off into space somewhere. Andrea no longer denied that she was falling for him. She knew it would be fatal to finagle anything like the same admission from him. Sometime, naturally, but not now.

Still, making love that morning, and in the earlier night, opened the gate for other intimacy. For days now, Andrea had mildly niggled at him to tell her about the Shang-Magan, a topic he had touched on only sparingly in the past. Just enough, though, so that curiosity ran away, demanding that she follow. Now that she had him in bed, under the eternal handicap, she pressed her advantage as she pressed her body to his, nudging and asking, going straight for his bones.

And Culhane wanted to show her what he hoped would keep them both satisfied: Andrea because she might feel she was really getting something; himself to pretend that he was still one of the chosen apostles. Yet some of the story he would never tell, wouldn't dream of imparting to anyone, not even to Karin, whose faraway voice flayed at him now.

"I can give you some background, if that's all you want," Culhane was saying to Andrea.

"Could I dig up any of it by myself?"

"Some of it, maybe, but you'd have to know exactly where to look."

"Where, for instance?"

"That I wouldn't tell you."

"How much of this stays off the record?"

"All of it, far as I'm concerned."

"Then don't tell me."

"Okay. I'd rather hear more about you anyway."

"I'm just kidding. I'm dying to hear about it, Rushton."

"Not an iota for print though. You promise?"

"Not ever?"

"Not ever. I mean it."

"Why would you tell me anything, if it's all out of some hidden drawer?"

"It's nothing secret, Andrea. Just that the Shang-Magan deplores publicity, always has."

"So tell me, I'll be Betty Button Mouth . . ."

In a spurious way, thinking about it helped. Talking about it might even remind him of where he really belonged, which was not here in Washington astride this halo of a woman.

"Shang-Magan goes back to the sixteen hundreds," he began, "when the Dutch and English wanted to run the Asiatic trade. Colonizing everything in sight, too. Indonesia, Malaysia, South Africa."

But it was the Portuguese who first put a heavy footprint on China, he said, staring straight up at the ceiling, focusing old memory cells. They sailed up the Pearl River to Canton, anchored, and sent emissaries ashore to sue for trading privileges with the Middle Kingdom. They came at the right time: the beginning of the Manchu dynasty, when the emperor Ch'ung Ch'en had knocked the Ming dynasty off the throne.

Andrea snuggled closer, listening for the nuggets that might interest Flickinger. She hoped it wasn't all going to be some obscure history lesson.

"China was ready to deal. The Manchus thought the time was ripe for China to lower her barricades and do a little rain dance with the West—you know, see how it would all work out."

"Just like that?" asked Andrea. "No little deals on the side with the court princes, like the Saudis do it?"

"Sure, sometimes. But to make damn certain the Portuguese or anyone else didn't infect China, the emperor laid
down an edict: the Western barbarians were to be confined
to a walled patch of ground on the quayside of Canton. Go
outside the walls, and the penalty was death. Any dealings
inside China had to be handled by persons of Chinese
blood, no one else.

"The Portuguese raised hell, swore in purple, but com-
plied. So they looked around for Chinese middlemen to get
the trade going, start the action. The Portuguese called
them *compradors,* which means buyers or negotiators . . .
fixer-uppers, you could say. The word stayed because the
idea of using middlemen worked. It was all new, a different system."

Culhane paused, lacing his hands behind his pillowed
head, locking one leg with hers. Fun to remember it again.
It took place such a long time ago, yet it seemed so real and
vivid to him. As if he had actually been there, seeing it all
unfold.

Compradors were carefully screened, he went on, and
were men of high standing in their community—bankers,
businessmen, a few professional gamblers. Men who knew
where and how to bend the rules, what was possible, what
wasn't. Both buyers and sellers, it was up to them to see
the teas, silks, camphorwood, porcelain, and everything
else got delivered on time to the Canton wharf. There, the
clipper ships waited for the wind-tides to sail those cargos
to London or Boston or wherever.

"Were they all Sunday's children, so handy and all?"
Andrea asked.

"Very sharp, and sometimes had even sharper women
doing their thinking for them. Sort of people who had
fighter-pilot mentalities, attacking every opportunity in
sight."

Andrea heard excitement rising in his voice.

Soon there were dozens of these compradors and they
formed a guild, a typical Chinese tradition, and soon the
whole game began to change. While the foreign owners of
the trading hongs squabbled and fought among themselves for markets, the smart little Chinese compradors
were up to a different trapeze act altogether.

"What do you mean, doing what?"

"Learning what was really going on and what the for-

145

eigners wouldn't dream of sharing among themselves—
information, the key! The compradors knew who needed
what, sent where, when . . . And the Shang-Magan still
does."

On their journeys from Canton into deepest China, the
compradors met secretly in Nanking or Foochow, anyplace
they could. The information they exchanged gave them
power. Greater power at times than their foreign employ-
ers down in Canton, and later in Hong Kong and Shanghai. Big things began to happen, and as the China trade
expanded, everyone wanted a slice. The trading hongs
wanted the goods, the Chinese provincial warlords wanted
duties on every load of merchandise crossing their fief-
doms, the Manchus up in Peking demanded other tribute.

"I knew the old green grease was in there somewhere,"
chided Andrea.

"Impossible, though, to pay off everyone and make a
profit."

So the guild elected a council to deal with the situation—
the graft, corruption, heavy taxes, the foreign trading
hongs who were cutting each other up to survive. The
council modeled itself after the one ruling Venice in the
1300s, when Venice virtually controlled all the Mediterranean trade. It was made up of six men, very senior, the best
of the bunch. The other compradors swore oaths of fealty to
the council, promising to abide by the rules and promising
to shut up about council business.

"Tough gents, too, because if you broke your word, once
given, they had you garroted or worse. I've heard, but
don't know if I believe it, that when the Mafia was estab-
lished in Sicily in the late seventeen hundreds they modeled it after the compradors' guild. Death penalties for
finking, and so on."

Is he part of a criminal syndicate, thought Andrea, the
way Flickinger once suggested? God! "What does the
name mean? Shang-Magan?" she asked.

"Sort of pidgin Chinese. *Shang* is shorthand for Shanghai, which means 'above the sea,' and *Magan*, loosely,
means 'merchants' association.' Anyway, now the Shang-
Magan had a real say in the China trade. They kept all the
wheels oiled, and no one can do it better, with greater fi-
nesse, than the Chinese."

"How do you fit in? You're not Chinese."

"Well, it didn't stay Chinese. They elected an amazing Shan Chu in the early nineteen hundreds—"

"A what?"

"Shan Chu," repeated Culhane, and spelled it for her. "Means Chief of Hill, and he keeps the books and is top fox on the council. The one I'm talking about was called T.V. Soong."

"You're serious, are you?"

"Yes, and his father called himself Charles Jones Soong, and for a brief time he lived here. A rug peddler down in Alabama and Mississippi, where I guess he picked up the first two parts of his name. Later, he came back to China and fathered not only T.V. but three daughters too.

"One girl, Ching-ling, married Sun Yat-sen, who tried and damn near succeeded in making a republic out of China. Another daughter, May-ling, married Chiang Kai-shek and you know about him. What a trio! But it was T.V. Soong who owned the steady brain. I think he was the best finance minister any government ever had, a boy with a real stroke.

"His brothers-in-law, whose greed was surpassed only by their blindness, fiddled him out of the government. Not smart, but a big break for the Shang-Magan. He was the one who branched the Magans out, insisted on admitting non-Chinese to the organization. A hell of a row took place, I read, but T.V. survived it somehow. This was just before the outbreak of the First World War. T.V. warned the Chinese compradors that trouble was coming, to diversify, get rid of their European holdings. They didn't listen, and only grudgingly let a few new boys in. Round-eyes. Sassoon and Fessenden and Patino of Bolivia, who looked after the South American zone.

"But the war hit and hit hard. Those Chinese who had invested in Europe were drained empty. Afterwards, it was the foreigners of the Shang-Magan who kept it together. They had credit, lots of it, and they put the guild back on its pins . . . For a price, of course: election to the Council of Six. That almost started another war among the guild members. But it happened . . . Their election, that is.

"And it went on that way for another decade or so, until the late thirties, and then the Japanese invaded China. All the trade with China died overnight. Goddamn shame, that was, and the end of the real China trade. Shanghai was shut down, Nanking, Foochow, then Hong Kong. The Council of Six removed all the books—the archives—and sailed off to Lisbon. They operated out of Portugal, which was neutral, during the war.

"Only Hong Kong was to come alive again. A friend of mine, who taught me, he's gone now, blew air back into Hong Kong's lungs after the Japanese were whipped. He was a Council of Six member, a wonderful and great man. His name was Ming, and I loved him hard."

"Loved him? I'd like to hear about that one," Andrea said.

"The finest, a real vicar."

"And, let me guess, he endorsed you into the club?"

"I was the first member ever elected from North America," he told her. "Quite a thrill, an honor really. Ken-chou Ming pushed for me before he died. A legacy, perhaps."

"But how does it all really work?"

"Managing the largest trades, Andrea. The ones where the zeros really count, and others can't swing them."

"Why? Why can't others do it?"

"They don't know how to bring the immense capital needed up against the smallest window of time. Nor are they skilled at creating the right mirage."

"Mirage?"

"The illusion that once the Magan is in there is never any limit on money. That frightens most people, you see. Me too, sometimes."

For a moment, it was as quiet as the Sabbath, until Andrea asked him for a specific example. Culhane hesitated long enough for his memory to travel over past horizons.

"Well, I'll tell you one that's over and done with now," he said. "Still, keep it to yourself . . .

"It was in London, some years ago. A meeting was called to settle a threat to the world diamond market. De Beers, who monopolized the trade for decades, had called on the Shang-Magan for help. The cartel was mortally afraid the Russians were going to flood the market with high-quality yet low-priced stones. Russia wanted in. Needed the money to pay for imports.

"Wanting privacy, the Shang-Magan took an entire floor at the Connaught. A tricky act in itself to manage in that place. Muldaur came for the great diamond-mining combines of Africa. Van Slyke was there to uphold Europe's interest, De Beers being in London and so part of his trading zone. I attended for North America, because this country consumed the largest amount of diamonds annually. At that time, anyway.

"And from Russia came a man called Metzilov. An ornery bastard, but a shrewd one.

"It was a dogfight, nothing less, and it went on four days running. Somehow the British government got wind of it all and requested consultations. Van Slyke refused Her Majesty's government, telling them it was a private matter. Even the State Department here in Washington wanted to know what was going on. And we had to tell them to butt out and stay out. All to be played, you see, on a very short hand. And with no outsiders to muddle it.

"Came the fourth day, very early in the morning, and we were about ready to throw in the towel when Muldaur suddenly worked out a deal: De Beers' Central Selling Organization would agree to sell Russia's diamond output; North America would buy any diamond surplus for two years so as to stabilize prices; De Beers, in return for getting its monopoly again, would pursuade the British Government to allow U.S. oil companies into the North Sea oil play; the African diamond-mining combines—Muldaur's turf—would share in U.S. oil production from the North Sea for five years, to make up for any losses South Africa suffered by allowing Moscow into the trade circle. Everybody won. And we shoehorned the American oil companies, who would pay us dearly, into one of the richest prizes of Europe.

"Before the crows stirred in London that morning, Van Slyke rousted the chairman of De Beers out of bed. Swallowing slowly—as Van Slyke later retold it—the world's king diamond merchants bought the idea. With one proviso: I had to promise to enforce it on the North American end, where the real selling action was, to stop any possibility of Russian undercutting games. So I agreed, of course. Had to. For a while there I had enough diamonds to pave a small town."

"How very dreamy," said Andrea. "I could've spent them for you, if you'd only called me . . . Then what? Did the Crown knight you or something?"

"Afterward, I told Metzilov that Russia was in. And told him that Moscow must abide by De Beers' rules, so we could keep everyone's diamond mines running. Metzilov wanted to know why the hundred-eighty-degree turnabout by De Beers.

"But there he was on his own tiller. So you probably know more about it now than he does. All he had to do was meet with the Central Selling Organization to iron the rest of the linen. And he did, and it worked until this country fell down the stairs.

"Jesus, that Metzilov," said Culhane. "Coldest face I ever saw. Paralyzed his mother's heart, I'd bet.

"That's how the Shang-Magan works sometimes," he went on. "It's the know-how. Always staying in the background, and nearly always with a full grip on the big ones. De Beers didn't exactly bounce for joy. But it was fair. And, of course, if they refused to go along, they knew we could set up another cartel, which would finish them.

". . . What's that again?" he answered to her muffled question.

"Cartels? You can't mean you're in favor of them. God, they'd own us all if—"

"Cartels are all right for some things," he stopped her. "You can't get greedy, like OPEC did. And you can't open and shut diamond mines depending on the marriage rate, either. Too expensive. So you balance the flow by market control. Governments, after all, monopolize currencies. Just don't know what they're doing most of the time, as we're finding out the hard way."

"Go over that again, would you? It can't be what you really believe." Saying it, Andrea tilted away, a foot or more, so that she could see him fully. See whether he was joshing with her now.

Culhane repeated his point, wondering, all the while, what it was that seemed to upset her. Was she the nun of naïveté? A schoolgirl still gowned in pink innocence? Couldn't she understand that your beliefs had to spread a dozen ways or you would never achieve even the small miracles?

In other times he had formed temporary cartels to support shaky grain markets. His paper losses sometimes running into heavy millions, but he knew those would eventually be recovered. You did it when you had to, or the farmers of the world would be selling their tractors at the next sheriff's auction. You kept it going with whatever help you could beg.

But then, how could she know of those struggles?

Yet he hadn't been trying to educate her. He strived only to capture again for himself what it really meant to be of Magan weight: his communion with the real thing. Not the Knights of Malta or belonging to the Paris Jockey Club, or that sort of social fakery, but much more—the highest curia of the daily religion that outlasted all the others. Trade, the milk breast that fed everyone by the hour.

And his hours, he sensed, were melting away, and his plans were still without a spine to hold them up.

18

New York
Washington

Pole-thin, standing very straight, aging muscles sagging in his face, Joe Rearden looked down the length of Park Avenue. They were at it again down there, he saw, and it did nothing to lighten his humor.

"Why are you forcing this thing?"

"It's the best way to do it," answered Guido Grasselli.

"I don't like partners. You know that."

"This thing won't stand up by itself, Chief. It needs help. The Doney brothers can set it up."

Grasselli had learned that a little buttering with the word *Chief* here and there would usually pay handsomely. So easy to say, and easier yet not to mean.

"I don't like it. My arrangements with those *people* are for Swiss banking only. And not for joint ownership of anything."

"To swing this thing correctly, we'll need help. West Coast help. That's top of the line, a given."

"They were already paid plenty," said Joe Rearden, irritated, though not enough to completely dismiss Guido Grasselli's view.

"The California Coastal Commission and three city gov-

153

ernments need looking after. We can't do that, Chief, without the Doney brothers. They can tap in where we can't, so they think they're entitled to a larger share . . . And they managed all the spadework on Culhane."

"How's that again?"

Just manipulate the sequence a little, thought Guido, he'll never check it out.

"Sure, the Doneys have friends up in Bel Air, where Culhane lives. A hell of a big place. The wife, a couple of kids, Saxa—that's Culhane's man—are there. And some old Chinese guy for the garden. The Doneys had the Chinaman followed a few times. He goes into Chinatown to the Kung Liet . . ."

"What's that?"

"A sort of Chinese social organization. They're in all the Chinese-American communities. There's one here in New York. They speak the old tongue, gamble, find jobs . . . A club," said Grasselli, opening his hands as if to say, That's all.

"Go ahead."

"Well, the Doneys do a little business here and there with the Kung Liet."

"And?" Joe Rearden leaned forward, intent.

"They found out that the Chinaman—actually, he's Taiwanese—is one very pissed-off chink. Apparently, the guy wanted to retire back to Taiwan but couldn't when the banks closed, so he's mad. They open him up a little and find out Culhane's got a very pricey art collection in the house . . . The Taiwanese comes smarter after a few talks. For three kilos of gold, and one more paid to the Kung Liet, he agrees to a little job for us."

"I've heard about that art collection. You can't steal it. Everybody in the art world knows who the owner is."

"I know, Chief," said Grasselli, alert now, ready with the clincher, "but how about this—we get the chink to destroy a painting or two."

A moment passed. "Interesting . . . Very interesting, Guido."

"Make Culhane sweat over what happens next. Maybe he'll learn to listen for a change."

"Are we completely out of it? No chance of tracing anything?"

"As I said, Chief, it would be the Doneys' pleasure. We

got to put up half the gold and pay the chink's way out of the country. They do the rest."

"But we can't be involved, not the slightest thread of any connection," insisted Joe Rearden.

"It's a one-shot. The chink will be long gone. We're thousands of miles away. The Doneys aren't gonna talk, and sure as hell the Kung Liet won't. They get part of the gold as it is. It couldn't be cleaner."

"Except," replied Joe Rearden, "the Doney brothers want half ownership in Sparkle-Clear."

"Fair is fair, Chief. They've got a lot of city officials to grease, and they're assuming all the risks if there's trouble."

"It's got more holes in it than a sink strainer," complained Joe Rearden, wheeling his chair around so that his back was to Grasselli.

"Think it over a few days? After all, the water company isn't earning anything for us. And then there's Culhane thrown into the sandwich almost for free."

Another screw in Culhane's coffin, a kick right to the balls, thought Rearden. Grasselli's getting to know too much, thinks he's one of us. Yet his connections are unbeatable.

"We'll discuss it again tomorrow."

"Whatever you think is best," replied Grasselli somberly, restraining a smile. He took one last glance at the bald monk's circle on the back of the Chief's head. Bull's-eye.

After Grasselli left, Joe Rearden pulled his spindle-thin body up from the chair. Business was terrible. The inventory positions alone were bad enough, but the carrying costs were pure banditry. He needed a way to sell off to the strategic stockpile, and soon.

Under the shallow light of a floor lamp, Flickinger sat in his small den. One hand was wrapped around a mug of acorn tea; in the other he held the few pages of Andrea's second diary entry. Earlier he'd gone by the Bulgar's, torn out the recently inked pages, and been savaged by another attack of garlic breath.

Sipping the acrid tea, he read:

Why do you rip out the pages? Never mind, I've torn up

your blue cards with the vague questions on them. As to those: First, yes, you must already know he meets with Halburton more than is necessary to give advice on rare earths, etc. He gives no hints, no details, and never will, I suspect.

Second, he despairs of State authority and can run you through brick-tight arguments of how it has failed. He says, "When the elephant runs, always the ant gets stepped on." He points to the food riots in this country, the ones in Africa, Poland, and elsewhere. What can authority do when this earth has six to eight billion people to feed by the end of this century?

Control the food and you control the game is the point he makes. And he doesn't think war is inevitable. He does admit, though, that like England at the start of World War II, we are alone. Yet he somehow reasons that Russia has reached its high-water mark. The way you tackle Russia, he thinks, is the same way they whipped Napoleon and Hitler. You retreat, and keep it up, until the opposition is stretched thinner than an eggshell, and then it cracks easily enough. The trouble is, he says, that American "authority" cannot square up to the idea of retreating as a tactical gain.

Thirdly, there seems to be no really deep secret about this Shang-Magan organization. Well financed, apparently with massive influence, it has certain rigidly enforced rules binding its members. Publicity is avoided at all costs. Their one aim is to advance world trade by any peaceful means necessary. To hear him say it, you'd think it was a sort of a nuclear-powered chamber of commerce. But, of course, there is more to it. He mentioned that he rceived a call recently from a Van Slyke, who is, I gather, the highest priest. He was pleased. Very.

I don't know exactly what that means. Not yet. Could use extra food coupons, if you're not feeling stingy. He's tough-fun, if you know what I mean.

Absently, crumpling the pages, Clay Flickinger gazed into his sparsely furnished room. He recalled Clarissa

Warren, the woman from whom Andrea had drawn her looks, and quite possibly her irreverent nature, too. Blissful days there were, eventually heaved up into a treacherous kiss-off after Frederic Warren was ground into dust. Superbly executed, no trace left, after he had picked too close to the bone. And now that double-dealing bitch, Clarissa, was sunning herself on the hills of Italy.

What of Andrea? Plainly, she was seeing Culhane on some regular basis. An affair in the making? Already made? Quite likely, he thought; he wouldn't mind her layer of cake for himself.

His mind rolled over what he just finished reading, snubbing up at one sentence: *Yet he somehow reasons that Russia has reached its high-water mark.* What was the meaning of that statement? Did Culhane know something? Very doubtful, decided Flickinger, whose cautious nature dug a foot deeper. What would it take to put Culhane under harness? Moscow might up the ante for that brilliant ten-strike.

The file concerning the New York Corporation was an unstable bomb, floating around in nitroglycerin jelly. Made all the worse, knew Flickinger, because in times past the New York Corporation had given friendly assistance when asked. Releasing the file's contents would mean Rearden trouble, and other kinds as well. He rocked his head back against the chair, closing his eyes, spinning more webs.

19

Moscow
Zurich
Washington

Nyurischev's ankle bothered him today, the left one, where he'd caught the shrapnel in the bloody siege of Stalingrad, more than forty years earlier. Harsh stabbing pains shot up to his knee whenever he moved too quickly. Doctors at the Moskova Medical Institute had offered to operate again but, of course, couldn't assure the outcome. Any more, thought Kyril Nyurischev, than could his top aides assure him of anything less than another cloudy horizon of problems.

Nyurischev's instincts told him that things were moving too fast, much too fast for the economy to contend with. The immensity of Russia's war machine had been achieved at huge cost, taxing the planners, causing a mass of other projects to be delayed. New unrest was surfacing among the people, too, and the poets were whispering their taunting verses in the streets again.

More of the same now as Nyurischev looked across the table at Gregor Metzilov's sinister face. You have to be more nimble than a ballerina, he thought, with these younger men. He listened to Metzilov reeling off figures, analyses, promises. Nyurischev knew a great deal about promises.

The reports out of the Ukraine and other regions bothered him deeply. One district after another complained about meeting harvesting goals, or coming anywhere close to them.

Over his wattled neck, Nyurischev's mouth moved, the voice strong. "This one, Metzilov, right there!" One stubby forefinger pointed at a book of charts lying open on the green baize table.

"Comrade President, you cannot shift that volume of water from the Volga. The Ukrainian Civil Works Department calls it a two-year project. By that time normal weather cycles could solve the problems."

Metzilov repeated his answer by rote, sick of the question, tired of Nyurischev's constant prodding. Miracles were expected each month, and endless explanations if they weren't delivered with ribbons tied around them.

"And if not? What if we're in long-term drought? What then?"

Metzilov shrugged. "Then it's a wise investment. Otherwise it's a risk."

"A risk! What of this European money scheme and this"—Nyurischev threw up his hands in an impatient gesture—"this American dollar business?"

"All goes well," answered Metzilov, satin threading his every syllable. "Very nicely. In perhaps three months, four at the outside, we shall have profited hugely."

"And tell me how many of the American dollars have you . . . What is it, shortaged?"

"Sold short," corrected Metzilov. "A little over a hundred billion. We will ruin them."

"Selling what you don't own is a risk we can afford *not* to take."

"Well, you needn't worry. All goes exactly as planned and I—"

Nyurischev reached across the table, putting a surprisingly strong grip on Metzilov's wrist. A bottle of mineral water was upended, and Metzilov could feel the liquid soaking into his sleeve.

"You will suspend the project immediately."

Metzilov slowly turned the color of milk. "It cannot be

stopped before the sum of one hundred twenty billions. That was the agreement made with Bank of International Settlements. Comrade President, it forms part of the arrangements for our own currency linkage with Western Europe's."

"You will undo them, get rid of the problem," said Nyurischev forcefully. He released Metzilov's wrist.

"I'd need three months."

"Two, no more. Meanwhile, you will coordinate with the Ministry of Agriculture for the importing of grain . . . Look at me, damn you, Metzilov!"

Inwardly gagging, Metzilov thought, Two months! He apologized, "Sorry, I was calculating something."

"You would do better to calculate with the ministry what it will cost to pay for the grain. And let no Russian go hungry this winter because you fail in that task."

"Of course not," replied Metzilov, worried. "Yet the U.S. may be in worse trouble than we thought. Now is the time to send them down for good."

"I've already seen those estimates."

"And so?"

"And so, Metzilov, I'm interested in grain, bread, and not money."

"Let me spring the last trap. I beg you to reconsi—"

"You will see to your orders. You will see to the grain problem." Nyurischev's face deepened, the heavy eyebrows knitting together.

"We'd be doing it wrong. Russia marches untouched. Certainly, you see how—"

"Stop sniveling, Metzilov."

As if peppered with birdshot, Metzilov sagged. "Will that be all?" he asked.

"Not quite. What is the progress of our personal ventures? What of those?"

A quick reverse as Metzilov's chiseled face brightened. "Excellent," he said. "We have the largest part of the shoe market. Cosmetics and women's clothing are doing much better too. Our best year."

"And the rubles?"

"In the same place. Millions of them waiting to be converted. You understand, of course, that we must first link the ruble with Europe's currencies. That is why we must continue the dollar selling."

161

"For now all that matters is food."

"It isn't all that matters," protested Metzilov, barely under control. "Don't you see that—"

"You may go now." Nyurischev waved him away. He was tired. His ankle pained him. The dollar business could wait, and it would wait until he understood it better. A fool thing to allow it in the first place.

Metzilov moved for the door as quickly as good taste would allow, and hurried to his office. He urgently needed time to reshape his plans. Several crucial calls to Europe must be made. Two of them today. Piegar could wait for a while, but not the others.

Metzilov knew he'd have to pay closer attention now to the "personal ventures" that Nyurischev had just inquired about. The factories in Minsk, Leningrad, and Kiev were absolutely illegal under Soviet law. But it was accepted practice for the *vlasti*, the higher-ups, to produce articles for the Russian black market. Bribery, the diverting of materials, fiddling production schedules brought it off very nicely, and it was so profitable.

A private cache of two hundred million Russian rubles had been amassed under Metzilov's wizardry, was safely stored now in gray ammunition boxes at his dacha on the outskirts of Moscow. Ten percent his, the rest held for Nyurischev and three other senior Politburo members. As the junior member of the syndicate, Metzilov held the money, ensuring, of course, that if trouble arose he would bear the brunt of it.

But how to convert the rubles to a usable currency that Western banks would freely accept? He counted on the day when Russia's and Europe's money systems would finally join together. Then he could convert, be rich. Other schemes lingered in his facile brain. When the time came, he would make investments, own hotels, restaurants, perhaps a small bank or two in Lichtenstein. Why not?

Piling up the rubles was easier than anything he'd ever devised before. The Russian people begged for anything made of some quality, goods not otherwise obtainable in their war-based economy. Black market or Red market, it made no difference to Gregor Metzilov; take care of the right people, a kiss here or a threat there. And he worked with cool diligence to carve out his share of the juicy trade. Just as he dutifully passed along certain information to the Shang-Magan's Monte Carlo group, in return for platinum payments made to his vault account at Moncotta's in London. An impressive nest egg, four thousand ounces safely in place there. Four years of hidden earnings, and all begun only two years after first meeting those strange Magan men who whittled out the diamond negotiations with De Beers. Metzilov recalled another time, when he'd outsmarted Culhane, who had attended the same United Nations Trade Conference in Rome for no apparent reason other than to discuss the proposition. Culhane hadn't lingered more than a day in Italy after the details were settled.

"Attractive money for easy work" was how the American had put it. "All it takes is an updated view of the finer points of Russian trade policy. And we'll help you get what you want and sell your exports at the same time . . . No, we are not talking about commercial espionage. We are talking about good, straight advice."

He had checked to find out all he could about the Shang-Magan, even requesting a report from the KGB. Because of his position at the State Planning Committee, no questions were asked. Nothing much to be had, though: only three or four flimsy pages, of no interest, it seemed, to state security.

So Metzilov had plunged, and every month handed over a brief commentary to the British Airways manager in Moscow. Unsigned, simple, quick, and efficient, since there was so little to report. Russia, after all, had no lasting trade policy. Historically, the country exported hardly anything.

So why not throw the Shang-Magan a harmless bone or clipped feather occasionally? Good money there to be taken for the asking. The only loose end in the arrangement—the one causing Metzilov's stomach to cinch up sometimes—was the platinum he accepted for his advisory services. Naturally, he hadn't told anyone in Moscow about that; nor about how he used the platinum as collateral at Moncotta Brothers in London for a margin account to short the U.S. dollar.

Nobody ever accused him of idiocy, and Metzilov always reasoned to himself that as long as Nyurischev and other party chieftains were getting theirs, why shouldn't he enjoy something on the side? But if he were caught out excuses wouldn't stand any better chance than a wet match in a low wind.

Somehow he'd have to sidetrack Nyurischev's absurd orders. So close now, Metzilov was certain he could literally reach out and squeeze the last burp out of the dollar. Sheer madness to stop now. Another thought struck home: technically speaking, he should tell the Shang-Magan that Russia might soon become a big buyer in the world grain market.

Maybe, he thought, it would be wiser to inform Monte Carlo, keep his fences mended, and cover his ass with snow. Sooner or later they would learn of any large buy anyway. For now, he needed to figure some way to stall it; tie it up in the Kremlin bureaucracy, which could bury nearly anything except sunshine.

Gazing out his office window to Red Square, Metzilov scratched his neck, the one he meant to protect. Nyurischev's order to stop the dollar-shorting operation was a dangerous move in itself. Worse, reducing the pressure now on the dollar could wipe out his account with Moncotta.

His dilemma was real enough. It would require his best footwork and even better head work.

In Zurich, no flowery words passed between Hans-Otto Piegar and his son, Ambros, either. In the Piegars' fortresslike house they bruised each other at a late luncheon of oxtail soup, roast leg of veal, rostii potatoes, and salad. A half-full bottle of Mouton-Rothschild rested in a silver coaster near at hand.

Skipping the main course, Ambros fussed about with the salad. He sipped the wine, its ruby color reminding him of one of Panzi's ski jackets. He couldn't wait to see her that night in Davos. Ambros desired, right now, only her, only Panzi's powerful smooth thighs. Wonderment struck him again that he was to be a father. Would she be the only gold medalist in history to be pregnant? He hoped so. One day it would be a sort of headliner to discuss within *his* family.

"And so you defy better judgment and keep going in your own way?" Hans-Otto Piegar was asking, demanding, looking into his son's brown eyes. "You were instructed to make dollar short-sales on all the family accounts. I'm told you haven't."

"I did what you asked, for your account."

"But not for your mother's account or yours."

"You're not with Braunsweig any longer. Giving you that information would be against the law."

"Dammit, Ambros! I'm your father."

"But not my banker. Nor Mother's. She gave me her power of attorney two years ago, when you went to the BIS."

Hans-Otto Piegar reddened, then came harder at Ambros with "You're heading for trouble. I'll have you thrown out of Braunsweig."

Ambros smiled, the easy one that women liked. "Throw me a million miles, if you can. I think you're trying to plot the downfall of an already slaughtered U.S. currency, and you're supposed to be the protector of them all . . . I'm very proud to be your son, really brimming with pride."

Ambros readied himself for another blast. His father's penchant for tyranny had caused Ambros a severe stomach ulcer once. For almost a year he'd passed blood. The doctor advised him: If you have to take it you have to, but learn how to throw it off. Relax. Your father shits the same way we all do.

Ambros looked across at the portrait of his mother, that superbly fresh and composed face, and then at the three small Rodin bronzes set into white alcoves against the pale lemon walls.

"Your insolence will cost you, Ambros."

"Truth is usually pretty insolent, I find."

"Here's some truth for you, Ambros. Supposing I were to cut you out of my will?"

"I never expected to be in it."

A glare from the elder Piegar as he asked, "What is your net worth currently?"

"A very insolent question. And here's the same kind of answer—I'll show you mine if you'll show me yours."

"You ungrateful bastard."

"Don't say that in front of Mother. You've already won the trophy for insulting her enough as it is."

"You listen to me, Ambros. You're to take a short position in dollars for your mother's account by tomorrow at the latest. Is that clear?"

"It's up to her. Between Mutti and myself, we've got a long position in dollars of twenty million or more. And as much in South African rand. I think we're in great shape."

"I'm trying to keep you from making a damn fool of yourself and ruining your mother at the same time."

"I'm a hunch player, and quite well diversified at the moment."

"You're vacant is what you are," said Hans-Otto Piegar, exasperated and showing it.

"Maybe. Did I mention that I received a letter recently from Andrea Warren? She's in Washington now. Things are terrible, she said, but it's not lights out for good."

A faint but delicious memory of those wonderful, fumbling nights so long ago. His first time. So much like Panzi, thought Ambros, and wondered why he'd never thought of that similarity before.

"What in hell's name would she know?"

"Andrea's pretty smart. Anyway, I hope it gets better for her."

"It won't. Not there." Hans-Otto Piegar took a last swallow of wine. "Are you planning to be in Zurich this weekend?"

"Tonight I leave for Davos. I'll be staying there with Panzi and her family."

Piegar winced. "She's got you by the pants, has she?"

"And everything else."

Ambros kept his seat. He should get up, he knew, when his father did. That was custom. Courtesy. But he couldn't bring himself to perform the simple act.

"And I suppose you'll be marrying her one day."

"Right after the Winter Olympics. My regiment has drawn winter training this year. The maneuvers are near Chur, so at least some of my battalion can come to the wedding."

"Your battalion?"

"I'm a major now. I thought it was a gross error on the last promotion list. Apparently not, the damn idiots. I've got the Twenty-first Mountain Grenadiers. Mostly Appenzellers, and a very tough lot, too."

Not a little astonished, Hans-Otto Piegar said, "That's interesting." No more would he say or give to his only son, who was now the youngest major in the Swiss army.

166

"I'm off to Bern. You'll change your mother's account, as I've asked, won't you?"

"It's up to Mutti, and she leaves it all up to me," answered Ambros, resolutely, quietly.

Hans-Otto Piegar bit down on his lip, wheeled abruptly, and left the room. Ambros still sat. Taking another swallow of wine, he watched the red tears trickle slowly down the inside of the glass.

Culhane pored over the almost completed drafts of the proposed trade memoranda with China and Mexico. He would need two more visits to Fort Meade to crunch out more numbers in the computers there. Then the trickiest part of all, finding a word-processing operator who knew how to keep his mouth buttoned up. Two or three operators would be better, much safer.

Soon it would be up to Halburton and to fate. Would they be ready? He looked at a table of numbers, then over to some pages of a World Bank report on China. Excitement scratched at his imagination.

Russia must be shocked into a dead standstill, forced to face up to her own choke-price. Europe must be cut loose somehow from Moscow's stranglehold. Sealing up the Hormuz Straits could solve that problem. Yet Europe must pay its own levy, and how much was another question. What would Piet Van Slyke say about it all? Europe was his trading zone.

Culhane yawned, loosened his tie, and let these issues simmer as he studied his tactics. The light was better in these new quarters in the old Executive Office Building. Closer now to his small staff, the room more spacious, easier to work in, the office breathed new life somehow into his work. No more than a five-minute walk when Halburton wanted to talk.

A rap on the door. Culhane looked up.

Flickinger entered, a frugal smile twitching at the corners of his mouth. "Have you got a minute?" Though not asked, he sat down and continued, "I've been detailed to Florida for a few days to fix up some loose nuts and bolts. If you need me for anything, the duty officer can always reach me."

"Florida, eh? If you find any stray cigars, pick some up." Culhane shuffled some papers to cover a map of China.

167

"Have you, by chance, thought of any way to come up with that Cuban paper we discussed?"

"Have you a spare copy of the New York Corporation's file? The one that always seems misplaced?"

"No, I don't." The lie again. Flickinger got up and started for the door.

"Just a minute." Flickinger turned around. "Try Leopoldo Maxaculi in Caracas. His number is 44-81-16. Use my name. He might help you."

Instantly, Flickinger whisked out a pocket notebook and pencil, asking for a repeat of the number. Scribbling it down, he looked up and asked, "Can he be trusted?"

Wagging his head, dumbfounded, Culhane said, "Do it or don't do it. It's up to you."

"But if it doesn't work, would you try it with Van Slyke when you talk again? It's very—" Deep from within Flickinger's subconscious the words had simply slipped out.

Culhane went dead still, before asking, "You people fooling around with my telephone? If you are, by Christ—"

"Not at all. I swear." Flustered, forced to think fast, Flickinger knew he'd be hard pressed to explain.

"Stay in Florida as long as you can. Now scram."

"Look, I just assumed you'd be in touch—"

"Get going while you've still got two feet."

Hapless, feeling idiotic, Flickinger made a hasty exit.

Culhane regained his seat. His mind pumped at flash rate now as coils of suspicion formed. A dozen questions arose, all of them angling against the recent call from Piet Van Slyke. How would Flickinger have guessed at it?

". . . would you try it with Van Slyke when you talk again?" Those were Flickinger's words. Exactly.

He had told Andrea of Piet's call. No one else, not even Sant Saxa. So how did Flickinger get wind of it, if I'm not tapped, as he says I'm not. Someone at the hotel? Who? Andrea? Then his mind spun backward. Wait! And he recalled the night at the British Embassy on the Queen's birthday, and the meeting with the British closet spy, Cowperthwaite. Afterward, he'd met up with Andrea downstairs at the reception, later introducing her to Flickinger. The manner of their greeting was so casual, so odd, as if they'd *been related, known each other before.*

Her father was once an OSS officer. A connection there?

168

A better one than any hotel telephone operator, certainly. Has Andrea infiltrated my life for another purpose? Think. My God, I've been sleeping with her for days and days now.

20

Bel Air

The old Taiwanese sat on the edge of a bed, sucking for more courage on his third opium pellet.

The room where he slept was down a hall that ran straight off the kitchen. A very still night with a moon throwing its half-blush across Culhane's residence. Some of the light leaked through the window, painting a silvery blotch on the black cotton pants the old man wore. He was barefoot and would dress more suitably later.

His few possessions were already packed in a blue laundry bag. His shoes were out, and his windbreaker was strung over the back of a chair. He could leave very quickly now.

All the arrangements made so nicely, he thought. Three bar of gold, ticket from Vancouver to Tokyo to Hong Kong to Taipei. Honor. I die like man instead of dog.

Slipping one hand into his pocket, he pulled out a small penlight. A flick of its switch and the pale beam showed that his cheap wristwatch said 1:34.

Soon time to cut master's color picture. But he go away now. Picture no good anyway. Otherwise sell to eat. Not good picture like in Taiwan. Pay so much, these stupid ones, for me to cut away worthless picture.

He stood up and reached across the blanket until his

gnarled fingers gripped the familiar handle of the Wyoming hunting knife, made for gutting hunted game. He had found its hooked blade perfect for garden work. That afternoon he'd sharpened the surgical steel so that its edge could cut air in half. The old man padded on his bare feet out the bedroom door, then as silently through the kitchen.

Karin Culhane tossed fitfully in the wide bed up in the master bedroom. A thirst burned in her throat, deep and dry. Then it burned elsewhere and the ache came back, a deep throbbing inside her delicate walls. Lazily, almost unconsciously, she rolled onto her back, and with two fingers plucked lightly at an excited nipple. A soft moan, while her other hand sought the tiny organ hidden under the puff of reddish hair. Expertly, she loved herself.

There was nothing silly about it anymore. Just urges, pounding away, that needed quieting. She brought up an image of her husband doing these beautiful, playful things to her. But he was a million miles away. She did not touch him anymore, was not good for him, dreamed Karin, since the baby died. I killed her. It was me.

Both hands were there now, fingers and knuckles doing a frenzied samba, and soon the muscles along the whole length of her body squeezed, focused, arched before the gorgeous detonation slapped her flat against the sheet again.

Yet the other thirst, the one in her throat, kept biting away. Karin rolled off the bed, standing nude and lovely in a shaft of moonlight. A breathy sigh as she thought of going downstairs to the kitchen. She wanted milk, if there was any, or at least a squeeze of lemon in water. She could do it easily in the dark, as she had many times before. There would be no light at this hour.

The old man wouldn't have known one painting from another even with an art book. Already narrow strips of canvas drooled down like tangled confetti from the frames that held Pissarro, Monet, Seurat, Corot, and Cézanne. Just the Renoir to go and he'd be done. The knife worked efficiently, just as it did in the garden, hardly making a sound.

A night noise then. He stopped his surgery, though the small penlight still played its beam against one wall. Feet!

He heard quiet and rhythmic footfalls on the carpeted circular staircase.

A little one? The Missy?

"Who's there? Is that you, Rushie?" asked Karin into the black, thinking it might be her son.

Paralyzed, fear narrowing his already frail chest, the old man squirmed against the wall. He wanted to be the wall, disappear into it. May God's Thunder come now, he thought, as he pressed himself tighter against the plaster.

Naked, unafraid, her mind actually clear, Karin walked into the murk toward the origin of the light. "What's the matter? Why are you down here at this hour?"

The opium pellet was sucked away down the old man's throat; fright made his scrotum shrivel; a squirt of urine trickled down one leg. A nervous reaction and the light beam changed angles so that Karin saw, in one fast glimpse, three of the shredded paintings.

"Oh, dear God, what's happ—" she shrieked, then moaned, "You're crazy! What've you done?"

Karin lunged forward, in a trot, believing she was in another nightmare and knowing she was not. Her heart raced, and her graceful body reached nearly to the Taiwanese as he threw the light beam on her.

All goddesses, he thought, seeing Karin's raw womanhood in the rim of light that showed her up like a ghost against the pitch blackness.

She plunged up against him. "It's you . . . you!" screamed Karin. "You awful—"

Petrified, seeing her hands rising up in rage, the old man struck out with the Wyoming knife. A deep slash cut diagonally through one breast and the hook came out of her body near the hipbone on the other side. Karin didn't feel the pain. She shoved forward again, trying to dig her fingers into his eyes.

The old man dropped his frail shoulder and rammed it against her chest. Searing pain now, a terrible burning, as he drove her against a curio cabinet. Glass smashed. He bloodied his arm, as a collection of hand-painted Chinese paper fans tumbled to the floor. Again, a high screeching yell from Karin, before he dug the blade deep into her throat and ripped upward in one curving stroke.

One last rasp of breath as she fell to the floor, blood fill-

173

ing her lungs, then spilling over the tile floor. She died as nakedly as she was born.

He ripped at her twice more. Overcome with fear, his mind fogged by the opium, shaking now, the old man saw his dream fading into other red mirages. What to do? He thought wildly and tremulously as another burp of urine spurted down his leg.

He picked up the penlight dropped during the struggle. Turning it on the Missy, the old man could see that death had rid her of all her devils. The coppery hair flew out into a pool of scarlet blood running along the tiles, soaking into the edge of an area rug.

He padded away, cradling his blood-streaked arm.

Crawling, he took each stair cautiously: up, listening, up some more. At the top, he aimed the light down another long hallway. Somewhere in there, he told himself. His knees turned to jelly, and the rest of his senses became muddled again in opiated clouds.

Lost, old and tired and beaten, he would do the rest of it now, so glad the black man wasn't there. The Wyoming knife was held at the slashing angle as he crept down the hallway, listening for life sounds.

21

Washington
Bel Air

"Take it with you."

"Why not leave it here?" asked Culhane.

"You're the collector," said Andrea, "so keep it with your others."

"Where'd you say you got it?" Culhane leaned over and tied a shoelace.

"The office gofer. I gave him two meat coupons and he fainted with delirium . . . And don't look at me like I was a thief."

"It isn't that at all." He finished knotting his tie and slipped into his blue blazer.

"It's just an old record anyway." Andrea pushed herself up on her elbows against the pillow. Her long smooth back was uncovered, and he could see the enticing drape of one breast.

"I don't want you giving things away for me. Certainly not coupons."

Culhane glanced at her, as if to reaffirm his point. He went over and sat on the bed, thinking how in the spreading light of dawn Andrea looked fresher than rained-on mint.

"You don't like people doing things for you, do you," said Andrea in a low, thoughtful voice. "It gets you some-how."

"You do worlds for me as it is."

"I didn't mean *that* . . . You go skittish or something when somebody tries to do a little paying back."

Andrea stretched and turned over. Now the bedsheet made a slanting margin across her hips.

"I've got to get going," he said.

"Halburton again?" Culhane nodded as Andrea teased, "I think you've *got* it for him."

"I've got it for him all right."

"Come back to bed and we'll make two left turns. Head if you want it."

She laughed impishly, watching for his reaction. Culhane gave out with a steady look, his eyes teal blue. A look that never failed to excite her, making her feel special, beautiful, important. Andrea felt her nipples swell.

"Don't try me twice. I feel the southern rise coming on."

"That's my healthy feller talking."

"That's your feller who'd better get his kickers moving too."

"What do you do with him at this insane hour anyway?" The sheet slipped down, until her thighs and blond belly fur were exposed.

"We start out with novocaine cocktails, then roll verbal grenades around . . . Working with him is like sculpting fog, and he needs a week sometimes to decide when to pee."

"Well, I hope I'm more fun than that in the morning."

"Someday I'll skywrite it for you." Culhane grinned lecherously.

"Ah, right now I'd settle for a ceiling poem."

"Jesus, Andrea, don't horse me this way. I've got to va-moose . . . And you've got the best-looking ass on both sides of the Equator."

"Maybe the readiest, too." Andrea looked at Culhane openly, quite seriously too, and added, "It's never been like this for me before . . . And you?" She waited expec-tantly.

"Never."

Not a flat misstatement, since it was always different

176

with everyone. But that little truth could sleep undisturbed.

Getting up, he bent over, smelled the jasmine in Andrea's hair, then very fondly bit her mouth.

"Please take the record," she reminded him.

On the way out the door, he stopped by the coffee table and picked up the tattered record jacket of the Bix Beiderbecke recording. An oldie, good stuff, cut by RCA Victor decades ago.

Outside, the crisp morning sang its own praises. He remembered other October mornings in other places: Beirut, where the autumn air seemed to have passed through vintage wine before you breathed it; or in Rio, where it was springtime now, with the warm breezes blowing against the blue mouth of Copacabana beach.

By the Potomac nature would soon undress as the countryside changed from red to lifeless brown and finally to empty white. And very soon now the great wedges of geese and duck would move from Canada down the long flyway, hide out for a while on Chesapeake Bay, then go south for warmer waters.

Culhane thought about these things as he headed for the Hay-Adams, some three miles away. He thought about Andrea, too, and their lives binding up closer by the day. Soon he'd have to come to terms with himself. A full-fledged affair, and it was wrong, for there was still Karin; and it was right, since there was no real Karin except in body. More, she was incapable of defending herself, even if she cared to, and that part of it was net, net wrong.

That Andrea might be somehow tied into the CIA didn't really bother him. Nothing actually pointed to her as the source of Flickinger's knowledge of the recent telephone call from Van Slyke. Just a hunch. Yet he'd once made scores of millions on gut hunches, when timing itself outweighed the availability of facts. Better to bide my time, Culhane told himself, and wait for another signal. Why accuse her of anything, and in any event, why would she consort with a Flickinger?

Culhane quickened his step, invigorated by superb air as light as thistledown. It was still quiet on the streets as he passed by the deserted Electrical Workers and Machinists' building. Boarded up, the lower windows taped, the lawns and shrubbery overgrown.

177

In two hours he would meet with Halburton again. They would wrangle more. A few days earlier, it had become necessary to explain again how sophisticated trading practices worked—this to a President who had served once as a deputy in the U.S. Trade Representative's office.

They'd discussed the usual forms of noncash countertrade: barter—straight exchange of goods for other goods; compensation deals—where one party sells equipment to make more product and then takes amounts of that product as payment; swaps—in which similar commodities, such as oil, are exchanged in various locations to save on transportation costs; switches—more complex transactions, where two countries incur an imbalance in trade with each other, and a third party steps in and resolves the difference by selling the creditor country something it needs and accepting payment from the debtor country in some export that it has an abundance of. He hadn't even tried to take Halburton through the more intricate ballet of four-and five-corner trades: those where you had to link six or seven trades at once. Gonad growers!

In the hotel, Jenny Carruthers, the new hire at the reception desk, put down the phone and, hurrying toward him, her face mottled with anxiety, said, "Mr. Culhane, oh, my goodness—"

"Morning, Jenny."

"A Mr. Saxa has been trying to reach you half the night. And the White House operator, too."

Now what? "Thanks. I'll see to it right away."

A reassuring smile as Jenny said, "I hope everything is all right?"

"I'll get right on the calls upstairs."

Jenny stood there for a brief moment watching his retreating figure. She wasn't sure things were all right at all. Too many calls, and the callers' voices so urgent. She worried her lip with her lustrous teeth. Everybody on the staff liked Mr. Culhane, knew he was somehow important, even a bit mysterious. It was even rumored that he somehow arranged for the hotel's food.

Entering his suite, Culhane headed directly for the red phone.

Three rings later, Saxa's voice blurted, "Rush? That you?"

"Right here."

178

A labored pause. "Better take chair."

"C'mon, Sant, give." Culhane laughed into the phone.

A heavy intake of breath, followed by a deep cough, as Saxa said, "I die myself telling you . . . But Karin and children are, are dead. I bad sorry."

Something inside Culhane jarred loose; then a heavy thunk hit the pit of his stomach. "What?" he said, quite softly. "When, where?" A voice inside him said it was true.

"Night before last one, right here in house. Crawl with cops now. Jack McTigue here with other police . . . Your family—they be murdered, Rush."

"Shot?" asked Culhane, feeling the blood draw down from his own head. The phone seemed to freeze in his hand.

"No," came the answer. "By knife."

A silence as the reality of it struck him. Culhane could feel some other cold blade skewering his own insides. He dropped to his knees. Karin? The children? No! Every bone in his body seemed to bend.

"You there?" asked Sant

"No," groaned Culhane, sickened now.

"Christ, I sorry . . . Awful," and now Saxa's voice was almost inaudible, on the verge of breaking. Another pounding cough came. "Police think it happen Saturday night. I down in Gardena to see Gillis. She be sick, and I not get back until Monday afternoon. I found them, call police. Been trying call you."

Culhane nodded to no one, thinking: And the reason you couldn't get me is because I've been shacked up with this new friend of mine.

"Somehow I'll get out there today. Don't know how yet."

Dead? Why? Not possible.

And his heart, soul, and mind hung up abruptly. His chest heaving, he stifled a cry. Murdered! Why? As always, the anger, the frustration, put magenta into his eyes. Something feeling like a snake's belly shivered down his back. His insides seemed stripped out.

For several minutes he knelt there, staring at nothing, dazed, his shoulders lifting a ton of concrete. Culhane wept silently. When the rim of his mind cleared, later, he could think only of the feral thing that frightened him most. Alone! By himself again in this world, no blood connectives now to tie his life together. Not one suture.

He dialed the number Halburton had given him for emergencies. Almost instantly, a resonant Southern voice answered, "Agent Rowels."

"Morning, Billy Joe," Culhane almost gasped.

"Shit fire, Mr. Culhane, half the world's lookin' for you."

"I badly need to talk to the President. He around?"

"Just hold." The line emptied for a minute or so.

"That you, Culhane?" asked Halburton, the voice graveled with morning rust.

Culhane proceeded to quickly relate what skeletal details he knew. To two questions, he answered the President with "I don't know" and "Apparently hacked to death." Then he said, "I need help getting a Priority One air pass to Los Angeles. Will you?"

"You stay right there. A car'll be there in ten minutes to pick you up . . . Now keep a hold of yourself. I'm struck dumb. That's all I can say right now," ended Halburton, with vigor now in his tone.

"I appreciate it. I do," replied Culhane numbly.

Again the line went dead. Everything in his world seemed dead then. Culhane fell onto the wing chair near the phone, his whole being soaked with shock. Everything that had counted, gone, dust!

And later, he thought, Shall I pack? No, there's plenty of clothes out there . . . Christ! Change my shirt? Are you going to a dance, you dumb son of a bitch? You're going home, home to a hell as empty of life as leukemia cells.

He didn't know how long he sat there watching the wheel of his life roll away . . . farther, farther still, until it spun off into a chasm.

A flock of homicide investigators dusted for fingerprints, examined the bedroom for traces of evidence, and took hundreds of pictures. One photographer, who had earlier taken photos of the bodies, now aimed his camera at the torn paintings. One by one he pointed his heartless lens against them.

Crude chalk lines were drawn on the tiled floor to show where Karin Culhane's body had fallen. Crusts of blood stained the corner of a carpet. And scattered about, still, were the priceless Chinese paper fans with their ebony and mother-of-pearl handles, some of them broken or crushed beyond repair.

Now the word was out. Only the red phone didn't ring insistently. A policeman walked to where police captain Jack McTigue and Herbsant Saxa stood talking, in the hall, near the door to the library.

The policeman spoke, "Cap'n, there's newshawkers down at the driveway gate. They're raising hell for a statement of some kind." His eyes lifted a little, awaiting a reply.

A bulky man, with graying reddish hair, known for his temper and his compassion, McTigue said to Saxa, "What do you think, Sant?" Their friendship dated back almost as long as the friendship of the police captain and Culhane.

"He not like it, Jack. You know that."

"They aren't going to vanish, you know. If we give them something maybe they'll take off before he arrives," said McTigue. He glanced at his watch. "Three hours or so and he ought to be here."

His face drooping, Sant said, "You do it, Jack. I not got the heart or balls."

"Okay," returned McTigue, who motioned the other policeman to follow along as he went down the hall toward the front door, then out to the long driveway.

Herbsant Saxa stepped down the hallway in the other direction. It was only late morning now in California, but he didn't care, he wanted a drink. Something to hold on to. He walked into the room that Culhane had renovated with a pub bar brought over from England years ago. A nice affair, though droll and barren on that morning. A hard cough bent him as he reached for the bottle he wanted. Just a little something to grip until his best friend, his *son*, arrived. It would be terrible to see him after all these months.

A whisper went to loud talk and then to a mild roar as the UPI wire service clacked away. Noise carried excitedly through the Washington Bureau of the Los Angeles *Times-Herald*:

. . . FAMILY OF WELL-KNOWN CALIFORNIA BUSINESSMAN FOUND MURDERED IN BEL-AIR MANSION . . .

Curious, her attention caught by the kindled voices close by, Andrea popped out of her small office. A young

181

lacquer-haired secretary—the subject of lurid bets around the newsroom—sashayed by.

"What's going on?" asked Andrea. "The Pope get raped or something?"

"Beats me. Some White House guy's family in California just bought the farm the hard way."

Andrea raced the few yards down the half-lit corridor into the small newsroom. Deftly, she pushed her way into the huddle of people crowding over the broad tape.

"Tell me," she implored, "who is it?" But she knew.

"The Culhane guy again," somebody shot back. "His wife and two kids found the wrong end of a blade. Gutted, it sounds like."

Andrea's knees jiggled. A fierce thump of her cranial nerves, and then the shattering grief that only a person in love can know for another.

"I'm coming in," she said. She elbowed her way to the ticker tape. Each printed blurb she read sank her lower.

Later, the gist of the story understood, she backed her way out. What seemed like a ten-mile walk back to her office made her legs feel as if they were chained in irons. Closing the door, she wept with a feverish passion so powerful it crushed.

That fabulous man, Andrea thought. Someone should torch the bitter balls of this country. Patch this horror. What more?

I love you so.

22

Bel Air

Culhane noted four squad cars and a van parked in front of his house. Death, his loves gone, and reality hitting at him again.

He had arrived an hour ago in California at Norton AFB. A blue car driven by a young airman brought him the rest of the way. Home now, he was in the worst hell he'd ever known; driving through the gates, he'd seen policemen shooing away strangers. His breathing had stopped. His chest tightened, then a feeling like his insides were coated with frost.

The airman said, "It ain't my place to say it, sir, but I know you been stoned good. I'm real sorry . . . Call the base, you need anything."

Culhane tried a smile. But it wouldn't come as he looked over at the airman, whose youth and innocence struggled there in the intent face. Then a brief handshake before Culhane left the car. Slowly, he walked to where Herbsant Saxa stood.

Watching through the car window, the airman saw Culhane and the dark little man throw their arms around each other. The smaller man hardly reached to Culhane's chest. But the airman saw that they stood there holding each other closely in front of the big house, bigger than the school he'd been to in western Tennessee. What was it like, he wondered, to be so rich? It couldn't be much different if you were a tall, hard-looking bastard like Culhane, who seemed okay and who ran his arms around another nigger like me. The airman threw the car in gear and headed down the driveway.

"Jack McTigue still here?"

"He here. Plenty others, too. You not going to like in there."

Culhane drew a deep breath. "Let's get it over with."

Through the door then, and Culhane jerked to a standstill as he saw the ripped canvases of those priceless joys. A furious rage flashed inside, yet he only shook his head silently.

Walking farther, he observed the chalk dust on the tile floor and didn't have to ask what it meant. He stepped carefully, with Sant right behind him, until reaching the library.

A guarded, appeasing look on McTigue's face as he greeted Culhane, who thought the police captain looked harassed. Tie undone, shirt collar winging out, a long ash ready to drop from the cigarette dangling from his mouth.

"Jack," said Culhane, reaching forward with his hand.

"Hello, Rush. You made a fast pedal here."

"I got helped. Where do you want to begin?" Then Culhane turned and said to Sant, who was about to leave, "No, Sant, stay here."

"Let's sit down," suggested McTigue. He pulled a small notebook out from his gray suitcoat.

And in about three minutes the captain recited the known and discovered facts: probable date and time of the crimes, the method of killing, where the bodies were found by Saxa, and so forth. McTigue sweated each word of it, skimming over the more gruesome details.

At the end, empty-eyed and perplexed, the captain asked, "It sounds absurd but I have to ask you—you got any idea who could have done this?"

"I've been thinking about it for seven hours, and I can't even guess," replied Culhane.

"Maybe street thugs go past gate guards," Saxa said.

"The homicide team think it was one person using the same weapon," explained McTigue. "We're trying to chase

184

down your Taiwanese handyman. No one seems to know if he stayed here that night."

"I don't either," said Culhane.

"We found a few bracelets and rings upstairs in the master bedroom. Was there any big jewelry? Important stones or anything?"

"Karin had to sell most of it a year ago."

There were several more questions. None of them poured even the slimmest light on the killings.

"Rush," said McTigue finally, "the remains of your family can be released anytime you're ready to make the arrangements."

"Don't I have to identify them?"

"Sant and I already have."

Culhane passed an appreciative look to Sant Saxa; no words, the look was enough.

"Is there anything I can do for you?" asked McTigue, wondering what had happened to Culhane's face.

"Hunt the bastard down."

"I mean anything personal."

"Can you keep a man by the gate for a few days?"

"That's easy enough."

"And maybe, Jack, you could loan me a police launch for a couple of hours."

"Bury them at sea? You want that?"

"Their ashes. I think Karin would want it that way."

"Just tell us when," said McTigue, who sprang from his chair, walked over, and rested one palm on Culhane's slumped shoulder. Culhane sat there with his head buried in both hands, his mind fogging up. McTigue turned and motioned Sant from the room so some details could be discussed out of Culhane's hearing.

Alone now, Culhane recalled oddments of their lives together. The nights when they would all picnic down on the cool beach, watching the waves charging in, playing a game of guessing which wave came from Tahiti, from Hawaii, from Guam or anywhere. Sometimes they would make up new names for the early stars. Borrowed names like Pinocchio, Minnie, or Popeye for the big one that was actually Sirius. Nutty, silly, wonderful games. Sand in the food and drinks, even in his cigar.

Or the time they'd sailed on his *Eastern Light* through the fjords or Norway, with Karin reciting the legends of her land. A grand month, ending in Finland, where he had the schooner taken down and shipped back to California.

Culhane held himself now, as strongly as he could, forcing control, feeling very old. Not this way, he thought, not with a scarlet gash across her graceful throat. He remembered her lightly accented voice and the way she could spin words, making you think you were the only person in the world who meant anything to her. A life that had gone rough, absorbing too many shocks. But a life that counted for much with him. Taken away, first by demons, now by murder.

Everything dropped violently inside him. He lurched up from the chair, almost stumbling toward the window. He looked down across the back lawn to a grove of pepper trees, just staring, not searching for anything at all, trying only to let the good memories flush away his agony.

Instead he felt his strength drain away; terror and despair in his heart, breaking it again, and him with it. He would fight anything and anyone for what belonged to him. Now, there was nothing left to fight for.

Alone, he stood there, bawling without tears, numbly wondering whether he could take one step, one more breath, and why do it anyway.

Sant Saxa, who had come back to the room, saw that Culhane had turned whiter than phosphorous. It badly frightened him; that, and the eyes that were of deepest violet now.

"Get me some drink, Sant, please."

For several hours Culhane stayed in the library, melting down the bottle of Izarra. Until, finally, the sun played its last light against the kingwood paneling of the room, raising it to a high sheen. Nightfall came and he slept for an hour before waking to hear Sant stirring around.

"I make barley soup for us. And vegetable from garden."

"Later maybe, Sant. You get everything straight with Muldaur on the—"

"All fixed. Don't worry about any that stuff."

"I've got some things to tell you. Then you'll have to forget them."

Culhane told Saxa of the plans in development, and of Halburton's way of dodging the hard choices. He went over it rapidly, including his ideas of cornering the world wheat market and how the Blue Dollar fit in. He had to talk, get his mind off death, and he couldn't think of anything else to say. So he kept talking to find out if he was still sane.

Awed, fascinated, trying to figure a place for himself in the scheme, Sant asked, "What is like there in Washington?"

"Like running with the whores. Except in Washington they sell their candy for votes."

"Halburton, he that way?"

"Better than most of them. But he'd be better off teaching priests somewhere."

"He got you to help him."

"I really don't know if anyone can."

"But you got this big plan."

"I can't break through to him half the time." And then Culhane's broad shoulders shook. His head lowered as he said: "Jesus, Sant, everyone's gone on us, aren't they?"

"I be here with you."

"But no family, Sant. Who's going to be around, carry on for us?"

"Start again. You still young."

"Yeah," said Culhane, his voice as muted as the faraway sounds of his children.

Sensing instantly the mood, the great torment gathering in Culhane, Sant switched channels deftly, asking, "Can bring this big idea off? Dangerous. Never hear of any like it."

"There's a chance."

"Shang-Magan?"

"If I can con them. But it's the timing that really matters, Sant. Just like the old big market plays."

"You be careful. You looking for big trouble," Sant offered.

"I know," said Culhane, taking another dram of the Izarra to anesthetize himself. "But I can't see any other way to do it."

"Go walking away."

"There goes our gold if I did. Or a long lawsuit, anyway, to recover it."

"You care?"

"Yes. It's a lot of gold. Besides," said Culahne, turning from the view of the back lawn, "I want to see if it can be done."

"You get kill maybe too," Sant said, blatantly.

"I want to see if something else can be pulled off. Something permanent."

"Is what? What you mean?"

"I'm not sure yet, Sant. It's just an idea I've been discussing with Halburton."

"Idea for death maybe."

Twice now Sant had mentioned killing and death. This time he saw Culhane nearly go rigid. But Saxa was a comprador, and would speak the best advice he could, no matter how brutal it sounded.

"How about soup?" Sant asked.

"Later maybe. I'm going to the pool house in a while. I'll sleep there."

Together for so long, they could read each other like a deck of marked cards. A whirlpool of questions and ideas swirled around in Sant Saxa's head. Somehow he had to get into this huge play Culhane was mapping out.

But how? And how to buy the time Culhane needed? Saxa promised himself that he would work on the problem.

23

New York
Washington
Bel Air

Joe Rearden burst out, "You good-for-goddamn-nothing fool!"

Wincing, Guido Grasselli stood there in Rearden's study taking it. He had to. The Culhane business had gone as sour as turpentine, and threatened now to ignite.

"Police. Federal investigations, you idiotic—"

"Murder is a state felony, the federals shouldn't get into it," interrupted Grasselli.

"They'll get into it if they're told to. What do you take me for, you stupid prick!"

"Mr. Rearden," pleaded Guido, "look, we're clear. There's no way to tie us into it."

"I want to know soon, very soon, where that chink is. You get me, Guido?"

"Please. Sure I get you." You old fart bag, thought Guido. "He's gone to ground somewhere. Air Canada has no record of him checking in through Vancouver. We've been looking all over for six, seven days now."

"And the police? Are they looking too?"

Timidly, Guido replied, "I'm told so."

"When they find him, that's link number one. But they're not going to find him, are they, Guido? And do you know why?"

Grasselli just shook his head, wondering what was coming now.

Rearden centered himself under an overhead light that cast its glare against his long face. His spittled mouth opened twice before he could say, "The why of it, Guido, you worthless bastard, is because you're going west. And you're going to find the Chinaman, and then you're going to shut him up!"

"You need me here."

"You go tonight!"

"I couldn't get seat space that fast. They'll run the asshole down. Give them some time."

But Joe Rearden would hear none of it. "Don't come back to New York until every trace is eliminated."

"Aw, for chrissakes, Chief, it's not as bad—"

"Half your rope is gone, Guido."

Grasselli just stared into Rearden's implacable gaze, knowing that he had no choice. He had no idea of how to find the runty old Taiwanese. The Doneys were taking care of it. But if the police got there first . . .

An airless, starless night in Washington as Andrea peeled down the bedcovers. Not a word yet from him! The *Times-Herald,* the wire services, television had all blasted the story for three days before running out of ammunition. Culahne wouldn't interview, and the police had released few details. The press had been closed out. No phones were answered at the residence; the gates were locked—she'd heard—and watched by the police.

A ring now! With an eager sweep of her arm, she reached for the phone on the bedside table. Him?

"A Miss Warren there?" asked an operator.

"Yes," breathlessly.

"Hold please." Then: "Here's your party, sir. You have three minutes."

"Andrea." It was Clay Flickinger. Her spirits sagged. "Yes."

"I'm calling from Florida. I've got a small job for you."

"When don't you?"

"We've less than three minutes. Now listen! The President hasn't heard from Culhane. The phones don't answer out there, and the police refuse to bother him."

"Good."

"Culhane can hermit out there for all I care. But Halburton is Halburton and he wants answers. It's on my lap. But I can't leave Florida now. I want you to get to Culhane and find out what's going on, when he's coming back, then let me know."

"This is a very shitto idea, Clay. You play it, and I'll just turn the pages."

"None of that, Andrea. Now listen. There's a letter from Halburton already delivered to my office. It'll be handed to you when you're picked up. That ought to get you through the gate guards at Bel Air, and we'll alert the police about your coming anyway. Clear?"

"No. Why doesn't the White House just keep trying the house number?"

"They do. Days of it. Even on that special phone that's patched through naval communications."

Andrea's forehead lifted. Why one of those phones out there when he's been here all the time? Puzzles, she thought, and asked, "And if I refuse to invade his privacy?"

Tonelessly, Flickinger answered, "Then say good-bye to those little gold wafers you've been getting, and those extra food coupons, and probably to your job at the *Times-Herald*."

Stung, Andrea replied hotly, "You wouldn't!"

"Try me and you'll see."

"I don't have any way to get to California."

"You'll be getting another call soon, so don't go anywhere."

"Clay, damn you, I can't just—"

"Good-bye. Be damn sure you fill me in."

She was dressed in pale yellow linen slacks, a white blouse, and a thin white sweater. A young officer gawked at her. An actress? A hell of a frail, anyway.

Reaching into the car, across the seat, she slipped an envelope from a side pocket of her purse. Showing it to the officer, Andrea said, "I'm supposed to deliver this. As you can see, it's not stamped."

191

The officer noted the addressee, and the typed legend in the lower corner, which read, "By Hand." Turning the envelope over, on its flap he saw "THE WHITE HOUSE" in royal-blue print.

Confusion scrambled the young man's face as he asked, "Miss Warner? That what you said?"

"Andrea War-ren."

"Sorry. I'll run this up to the house and see what they say."

"Who are *they?*"

"Mr. Culhane and Mr. Saxa."

"Oh. Well, why don't I run it up instead."

"Sorry, ma'am, I got orders, like I said."

"And I've got a few of my own . . . Can I talk to your superior? You were supposed to be told I was arriving."

"Sit tight, ma'am, I'll be right back. Just sit tight."

"I will, but please give the letter back first. Just explain where it's from."

The officer hitched up his gun belt and strode over to unlock and then carefully relock the gate.

A real rambler. Spanish, Monterey. What do they call this style? Big. I've seen bigger, but this is a lot of bricks. Near a wall, she saw the cutting gardens. Autumn flowers drooped on their wilted stems, and there were staked plants that might be vegetables, she guessed.

How is he? Mortally wounded? Toughing it out? Who is the other man? Sax—no, Saxa. Strange name. She stood there leaning against the hood of the sedan until she saw the police officer reach the front door. From the way his arms were moving, he was apparently talking to someone. She strolled over to the road, and began to survey the hillsides. Better than nice, she thought, and seeing other large homes down below, wondered if they were owned by movie people or dope kings. Nice places, but showy all the same. Out beyond, the turquoise of the Pacific looked back at her with its hypnotic wink. From somewhere ambrosia petted the air.

She took a brief walk, taking in everything. When she returned the officer was waiting. The gates were swung open.

Another hundred-pound smile from Andrea, and the officer gaped openly and said, "You're to go in."

The oak double doors were open. Andrea pulled the yellow sedan in close, got out, and walked right into the cathedral of the front hall.

Sant Saxa appeared, startling her, and said, "Miss Warren." It wasn't a question.

"Yes . . . Yes, I'm Andrea Warren. And you must be Mr. Saxa, is it?"

"S'right."

"Is Rushton anywhere near?"

"Pretty near. You have letter for him?"

"I do. I'd like to give it to him personally."

"He in no shape for company, lady."

"I'm sure he'll want to see me. Have you told him I'm here? . . . Look, I've come a long way. Okay?"

She looked, decided Sant, like one of those outdoorsy New Zealand girls with the magnificent breasts and pelvises that kept any sane man from chasing over the hill too often. A Culhane type for certain, right down to the few freckles on that coral skin.

"You come with me."

Sant led her through one of the rooms that opened onto the terrace, then down the flagstone steps to the pool house.

Who is this funny, frizzy-haired little man with the cedar skin and dressed up like a popinjay, she wondered. Talks funny, too, out of that crooked little face. And with a golden bead in his ear, no less. The butler? Rushton had never mentioned anything about him, not that he necessarily would have.

Andrea saw him lying there in a sweaty sleep, wearing a red turtleneck sweater and partly covered by a sheet. On the facing lounge-sofa some used Porthault bedsheets were bunched up in a pile. Three empty bottles poked their necks out from the tangle of cloth.

"My God!" said Andrea, "What's happened?"

"He's fighting the scorpion."

"Has a doctor seen him?"

"He don't ever go to them pill people."

A whip of rare anger at Andrea's mouth locked tight. Then, in a brittle voice, "You've got to get one. Look at him!"

"He okay, lady. Now you go away, eh?"

"Don't be a damn fool," Andrea scolded. "Who's the family doctor? I want the number. Right now, I want it."

193

Sant Saxa wasn't used to being ordered around by any-one, and never by a woman. Very calmly he answered, "Who appoint you anything? We plenty trouble here, lady, and we no need your kind."

Afraid their voices would awaken Culhane, Andrea stepped over to Sant, grabbed his hand, and marched him out to the patio. Unable to resist her superior strength, he scampered right along like an errant child.

"Has he been eating?"

"Soup and good whiskey."

"Brilliant."

"All he wanted," protested Sant, almost ready to let fly at her.

"It's not all he needed! Now, I'm going back in there and try to make him comfortable. And you, please, please, are going to call the doctor." Andrea poured on the honey now, and she could do it. By the bucket.

The famous medical facility was caught in the same vise that plagued most hospitals. Power was a problem; people were a problem; pandemonium was a problem; paperwork was impossible. No paperwork, then no drugs or supplies. The outpatient clinic was deluged with people wanting bones set after daily epidemics of muggings, of thuggery. The maternity ward had been converted to take care of se-rious illness. Intensive-care treatment had ceased to func-tion when backup emergency power couldn't be had. The corridors were lined with cots to handle all the overflow. Few could pay their bills.

But, in days past, Rushton Culhane had helped raise or given millions to the UCLA Medical Center. Frank Henry was not a man to forget another's generosity. Nor did he forget that even with the help of some of the country's top specialists he'd been unable to find any lasting cure for Karin Culhane's bout with mental illness. A failure, but a diligent and hard try nonetheless.

No hesitation at the gate to Culhane's driveway this time. Already alerted by Saxa, a new officer waved Dr. Henry right through, after seeing the large orange decal in the car's upper right windshield.

Carrying his bag of wonders, Frank Henry was met at the door by Saxa, who escorted him down to the pool house. Surprised at seeing Andrea, yet disturbed at Culhane's condition, Frank Henry, though an amiable man, waved aside Sant's effort to introduce her. He went right to work.

"Rushton," said Frank Henry, "open your mouth." But Culhane was sunk under and barely twitched. "One of you come here and help open his mouth for me."

Andrea bolted to Henry's side. "Like this," he told her, "just easily, and keep two fingers lightly clamped over his nose . . . That's it. Not too hard now."

She stooped over very close to Frank Henry, trying to hold Culhane's damp head still. Her breast pushed against the back of the doctor's head as he moved his head between her outstretched arms, peering, with the light and a depressor, into Culhane's throat. Out came a stethoscope from the bag; afterward a portable blood pressure unit. The examination went on for several minutes.

Standing up, Frank Henry just looked off through the glass doors and across the pool. Then he said, "He ought to be in a hospital. But there isn't one in the city that I'd put him into."

"How bad is he, Doctor?" asked Andrea.

"Hard to know without complete tests. But he's hurting."

"What does that mean?"

"How well do you know him?" Frank Henry candidly asked her.

"Well enough."

Frank Henry looked at Sant. "His vital signs are weaker than they should be. Blood pressure is low. Pulse weak. He's not fighting."

"What that mean, he not fighting!" Sant said.

"I see it every day," said Fank Henry. "Too many right hooks, and God knows he's had plenty, and the mind shuts down. The will to struggle goes to sleep. It happens. We don't know why."

"What you suggest?" asked Sant, pushing himself forward, alarmed.

"Keep him dry. Walk him twice a day, or he'll likely come down with pneumonia. Feed him. He must eat. Put him in the sun. Above all, keep him clear and moving and warm."

"Is there a name for his condition?" asked Andrea.

"Your Latin any good?"

"No."

"Then it wouldn't make any difference. He's in heavy shock. Trauma. Like shell-shock. That, and perhaps a punctured soul."

"Is it very serious?" Andrea asked.

Frank Henry shrugged. "Possibly. He's in a state of severe depression, I'd say. So are a million or so other people in this city."

"Well, what if he doesn't respond to—"

"I can only tell you he needs rest. Rest and quiet. He'll heal up or he won't."

"You mean *that's* it? You're not going to give him anything? What the hell kind of a doctor are you any—"

"I'd give him my blood if I could," said Frank Henry gravely, and offended, too.

"The booze okay?" Sant asked.

"Some is all right—as good as anything else. If you've any to spare, I'd like to borrow a couple bottles."

"For God's sake!" huffed Andrea. Her green eyes almost disappeared behind slitted lids.

They looked at her, strangely, then not so strangely, realizing that she was scared. Yet Frank Henry had seen a thousand cases like Rushton Culhane. The man was simply beaten down. You could hope but you couldn't operate, not on a man's spirit.

"Do you know how to take a pulse rate?" Frank Henry asked Andrea.

"Yes, I do."

"Check his regularly. If it drops below sixty-five, call me immediately, whatever the time." Frank Henry closed up his bag, let out a slight grunt, and said, "Sant, walk me upstairs so we can talk a little."

Andrea hurried inside the pool house. Culhane was tossing around on the lounge-sofa, one arm stretched out lifelessly. She'd straighten out the deplorable bed, then find out what there was to eat in this enormous home.

At least, she thought, knowingly or unknowingly, Dr. Henry implied that I'd better hang around. Maybe Saxa will relent now, won't think I'm invading his sanctuary. Unpack now? No, the hell with it. And Clay Flickinger, what do I tell him?

She looked down at Culhane again. He uttered grunts,

and the brilliant eyes were now dimmer than used nickels.

Walk or die, she remembered him saying to her. Somehow I must make him want to live again. He is mine, always will be mine.

24

Moscow
Bel Air
Johannesburg
Washington

The light dust of an early snow flurried across Moscow. If the same weather worked its way into the Ukraine, any hopes for more harvesting of the meager grain crop would be out the back window.

That notion did nothing to revive Gregor Metzilov, now on his way to the Ministry of Agriculture in a chauffeur-driven Ziv from his dacha in the elite Zhukova district, twenty-five miles west of Moscow. Traffic chugged along. The driver swerved sharply to avoid skidding into a truck up ahead. Nothing chugged very slowly inside Metzilov's head. He concentrated on the massive dollar-shorting operation going on in the European financial markets.

The prize was too great. Knocking the Americans off for good, bleeding Europe, gaining control of the world's monetary system should be enough to punch the lights out of the old men controlling the Politburo too. Yet Metzilov understood the nuances and pressures of the Russian apparat, and he knew he'd have to toe the line or else. With some satisfaction then, he thought of how a few years earlier he'd engineered the widespread protests throughout Europe against the U.S. deployment of cruise missiles on the Continent.

Could he engineer another grand coup?

He was so close now. The action was running in his favor, and with a little luck he could easily outrun his rivals for a key ministry. After that, he was virtually certain he could bid, given a few years, for Nyurischev's throne. Who could stop him? All the old power brokers would be kissing their graves.

Yet this annoying grain problem could upset everything. Metzilov knew he couldn't buck Nyurischev on the basics. Daily reports compiled by the Secretariat told of trouble in Georgia, the Urals area, Tashkent, and what was once Armenia.

Nyurischev's repeated warning still rang in Metzilov's ears: *No Russians were to go hungry this year or in any other.*

Metzilov tried to figure out how to wangle a little more time. He badly needed some luck, and some method of persuading Piegar and the BIS to exert more influence over the big banks of Europe. Would they agree to unwind the huge tranche of dollar speculations that Russia had undertaken? To do so would free Russian credit for the grain purchases Nyurischev was demanding.

But what of his account at Moncotta in London? Trading as he was on the thinnest margins, even a slight upsurge in the dollar would wash out his platinum holdings.

Time. How to find that tricky bitch: she was relentless, with no voice, never there when you needed her

Over a chorus of surly protests, Metzilov had called for a meeting of senior officials from the Ministry of Agriculture on this Saturday morning. A tactical discussion, it would set the stage for sending Russian experts to Canada, Argentina, and Australia to begin talks for purchasing grains.

Soon the Americans would crack, had to, then crawl on their knees, begging forgiveness for flooding the Euromarkets with their dollars, finally be forced into a harsh settlement. He would, therefore, do the smart thing and slow down the Russian grain buyers. Just for a little while. A few weeks at most.

Sweat ran everywhere in the seams of Culhane's body. Sometimes he would wipe it away, weirdly believing it was blood. His mouth usually felt cotton-dry, except when he flooded it with whatever whiskey was at hand. The sheets he used turned hot then cold, just like his body. He went down deep, ocean-floor deep, often unsure of where he was.

One afternoon, demented, he threw himself naked into the pool, pretending he was back in the warm juices of his mother's womb. He ate little, nibbling at what Andrea or Sant brought him, pushing most of it away. He would hold his breath, stare emptily at anything except the photos of Karin on the wall. His beard grew, his lean face thinned, his hollow eyes burned red at the edges.

It was death he loved, wanting it to come for him right now, come for caresses and seduction, come for argument, but come and not be afraid to. But he knew instinctively that it wouldn't, and so he hated it.

In the night, he screamed out for his children. One time he got up a rage and smashed a few dozen glasses against the marble soda fountain in the pool house. A chair made of eland horns lay broken in half.

A damn good thing, Sant had thought, that the grounds were so big the neighbors couldn't hear the ruckus. In his youth, Saxa had seen Haitians succumb to trances, drink chicken blood, dance crazily for days during voodoo rites until they dropped from exhaustion.

Culhane was killing something, Sant knew, and he would do it alone. The scorpion was stinging his son. Andrea wept, when looking at the gaunt face that said nothing, though it begged for help. She shuddered when he hollered out quite madly in two, possibly three strange languages, words or phrases all garbled together, as if a lunar force were shaking him by the brain.

Baster Muldaur was a brawny, barrel-chested man with pink cheeks, usually a pink humor, and a face that only a mallet could make. The rugged shape and weathered skin told of the Afrikaner in him. He was its purest form. A past player for South Africa's championship Springbok rugby team, he bore that honor proudly. A Springboker in South

201

Africa, though an unpaid athlete, was the rough equivalent of a Heisman trophy winner in America, or one of Spain's more select matadors. He was the Council of Six's man for all of Africa, a responsibility the Shang-Magan had conferred upon him eighteen years earlier. There were no mining barons or diamond princes in that fabled continent who did not actively seek his counsel and good graces. A fair lot of them also vied for the breeding rights to his five daughters and his renowned herd of prize bulls.

He looked out through a wide glass window, out across the sloping veldt to the white-painted corrals, where some of the herd was feeding. Beyond was a small village of light blue barns with orange-tiled roofs. On these two thousand hectares of spectacular land Muldaur spent his weekends, seeing to his daughters, his bulls, and his private game reserve.

An hour from now he would be off for Argentina to bid on the most expensive bull ever auctioned anywhere. Not a shred of doubt as to the outcome. Whatever it took, he would pay; the Argentine bull would become a South African citizen at any cost. Easily the richest man in Africa, Muldaur had quit counting his wealth a long time ago.

Now, listening to Van Slyke, digging the phone deeper into his shoulder, freeing both hands, Muldaur lit a fat black cigar.

"I'm trying to get more information," Van Slyke was saying, "but there seems to be a lid on it."

"Shouldn't be that hard to find out, Piet."

"You know Culhane. Silent as a clam's fart when he wants to be."

Muldaur exhaled a stream of smoke, watching it bump up against the window. "Certainly, he'll accept our help to find these . . . these murderers."

"I can't even get through on the phone."

"He's still in California, is he?" asked Muldaur.

"So I understand. But I don't think it would do any good to send someone."

Muldaur thought for a moment, then suggested, "Let's post a two-million-Krugerrand reward for information. That ought to get a result. If not, we'll double it."

"You suppose Liu Wai will go along?"

"Leave him to me," answered Muldaur. "I'll get that fat Chinaman to come to the fiddle."

202

"Very good. Have a pleasant trip to Buenos Aires. If you see Camero, give my respects."

"I'll see him all right. He has a bull I want."

A thunderous laugh from Van Slyke. "You must be leery of women, the way you chase after bulls, Baster."

"I should be. I'm surrounded by skirts. I'll talk to you in a week . . . A rotten thing this is."

"You have no idea. Now good-bye, and my thanks."

In Amsterdam at his town house, Van Slyke went grave of face as he put down the phone. A bad mistake over Culhane, he thought, and irreparable, too. The Magan should have helped him when it had the chance, and maybe this horrifying tragedy wouldn't have occurred. His fault primarily, and he knew it.

Hours later a sun, as yellow and full as ripened grapefruit, glazed the brisk air in Washington. Its generous light poured into the Treaty Room, warming Halburton's bones. He sat at the long table studying the drafts of Culhane's proposed compacts with China and Mexico.

As a lawyer, his mind and way were dry-nursed to the weighing of words and their meanings. Mostly, though, to look at intent, reasoning, and risk. Then, of course, to ferret out the loopholes.

A spotted hand traveled up to his snowy hair, ruffling it as he thought for a while. He'd seen many masterfully joined documents in his day, some of real poetry. But Efram Halburton admitted that he had never seen any quite like these.

In one cohesive plan, the whole thing came clear. How the huge trading scheme worked, where the credits came from, the methods of financing, how industry would be furnished with materials, and in what sequence U.S. commerce could be fired alive again.

Then the smaller document—the most highly classified paper in government—that told of the implications for Europe and Japan, but mostly Russia.

But the really fascinating part was the carpet-tight reasoning as to why China and Mexico would sign up. Culhane had spelled out the chief advantages for all three countries, with America's role an equal one.

Superb work, thought Halburton, and a mighty gamble. He was intrigued as to how a brain like Culhane's was made. What bit of physics in nature did that for one man and not for others?

An unforgotten refrain came to him again:

First, trust him. Tell him everything important. Drive him, push him as if you were all the elephants in Africa. You will see . . .

Well, I have pushed him, sighed Halburton inwardly, and he sure as the devil has done the same to me. Now look at what's happened. The man was a true credit, had done all and more asked of him—soon I must decide, and soon, I hope, he returns.

He studied for another two hours, so intently that he barely heard agent Billy Joe Rowels knock before entering the room.

Halburton looked up to hear Billy Joe say, "Sunday noon, suh. Ah brought the whiskey. S'break time."

"You think so?"

"Yessuh," said the big footballer, "we goin' to salute the Lord with some of his best whiskey."

Billy Joe stepped forward, put a silver tray on the edge of the table, and handed over one glass. No ice in it, just the aromatic whiskey.

They talked about nothing special, sipping away, with Billy Joe here and there raising a hint about Anne Fairfax, the pretty widow of a very popular Secretary of State.

"Should we do some poker tonight, say around six?" asked Halburton, changing the subject.

"Ah'll round up the boys. They'll be real pleased."

"Good. Same stakes?"

"Your pleasure, suh."

"I'll see you at six then."

Billy Joe stood up, took the President's glass along with his own, and replaced them on the tray. The big tank of a man disappeared through the door, carrying the tray, which looked like an oversized silver dollar in his giant hand.

Halburton sat and thought more. He thought about how good the whiskey tasted, and he thought of Culhane and of how the Californian might be bearing up under his terrific sorrows.

I'm already playing highest possible stakes poker with him and he is calling all the bets. The important ones anyway. One day I'll have to make good and release his gold to him. But not quite yet. I need him. I don't know as I like him, but I do know he is a vital gear. Yet no amount of gold will hold a man like Culhane for long. Too damned independent to stick with anything that doesn't interest him.

A loose remembrance then of one morning when Culhane had advised, "Militarily, Russia can't be beaten now, and it's a hopeless solution even if they could. Whip her by denying her the resources necessary to sustain her war machine. Make the bastards extend themselves and then geld them."

Halburton thought back to the time when he'd raised the question of involving Joshua Squires in Culhane's plan to manipulate the European money markets. The trader had gone livid. But this Blue Dollar business is no trivial matter either. A staggering idea, though possibly a brilliant one, too.

25

Bel Air

Andrea was near collapse. Going all day and half the night, she fed him vegetable purees when he'd take them, cleaned and walked Culhane when he'd cooperate. She had moved down to the pool house, sleeping fitfully on the other couch, ready at all times when he surfaced from worlds unknown.

She had never lived through a week as tormented as this one. Missing her monthy period by a couple of weeks for the first time in years had overjoyed her, then frightened the very wits from her. Culhane was calming down, sleeping a lot, yet there were times when he was like a loose wrecking ball. And Andrea reeled when glancing at the photos of Karin Culhane hanging so decorously on the wall; it gave her tremors watching the beautiful glossy faces looking back at her. She wanted to leave.

She had to stay.

Deep into night, and Andrea heard him roll, then the whisking sound of sheets being stripped off. Feet thunked on the floor. She felt around for a flashlight, found it, pointed it downward, and pressed the switch.

"Rushton." The light beam caught his feet.

"I'm thirsty," he acknowledged hoarsely.

"Lie down, baby, and I'll do it."

"I need to do it myself."

"Take the light then."

He nodded, reached over, and took the light. He appeared, thought Andrea, like an Arabian pirate with the dark growth of beard rimming his face. She watched as the light beam zigzagged across the floor, stopping when it reached the soda fountain. Water splashed against the stainless-steel sink.

He came back, more steadily; there was less wobble to the path of light. Sitting down, Culhane said, "I'm a linear catastrophe."

Andrea sat beside him, putting a hand to his forehead. "You're not sweating."

He breathed deeply, then voraciously.

"How long have I been down?"

"Almost ten days."

"Christ."

"Lie down and I'll give you an alcohol rub."

"No. I've got enough of that in me already."

"You almost drowned on it a few times."

"I needed it—needed something, anyway."

"I was here," said Andrea.

"I guess I wasn't."

"Been a bad time, Rush."

She pushed him flat, without resistance, until he lay face up. Culhane still held the flashlight limply, the beam grazing the blackness, then revealing Andrea's supple, strong body. Taking the light from him, putting it on the floor, she reached across to a side table and retrieved the almost empty bottle of rubbing alcohol. Slowly she began to stroke him with the cooling fluid.

As she worked her strong fingers into his hard body, he breathed evenly, dozing but not out. Culhane knew because he could feel her sphere of breast against him, her arm under his neck, her care pouring into . . .

Ten days, was that what Andrea said? Couldn't be. All he could recall were formless images in endless array. Had he been back to the jungles, out by Jupiter for tea and cake maybe, soloing in a limitless cloud bank? He didn't know. He cared, but right then he didn't care quite enough to ask. She had kept vigil over him. Sant, too, probably. Where was Sant-o? Here Sant-o, here, lover, c'mere, I need to see you.

He could breathe fine, move his limbs, hear everything very acutely. He dimly remembered awakening once with a straining erection, so those parts were reporting in satisfactorily too.

No, he wasn't dead because he could feel Andrea, angel of highest mercy, rubbing him gently as one wet drop from her face plopped on his lip.

Another two days passed. At midmorning, the sky outside was as blue as a peacock's eye and Andrea was cutting up vegetables in the kitchen. Her back faced Sant as he entered the long kitchen. He stopped, stood there soundlessly watching as she worked. She wore rolled-up dungarees, a man's white shirt hanging outside, a striped apron around her waist.

She hadn't raised her voice once since their slight tiff on the morning of her arrival. Resilient, humorous too, and he liked that. No doubt of it, thought Sant, she's made all the difference.

"Morning, Miss Andrea."

She jumped. "Ah, Sant," she said, turning around, "I looked for you earlier."

"Took a walk." Sant crossed the kitchen. Nearing her, he held out a small package.

She opened it, finding to her surprise a *Times-Herald,* a tin of throat lozenges, and something wrapped in butcher's paper. "What's in there?"

"Chicken breast and little veal."

"How do you guys do it? Really. Rush does it in Washington, too."

A crooked smile from Sant's little mouth. "Old trick for new time . . . I see you put cover over torn paintings. Good idea, Andrea."

"I couldn't stand looking at them anymore. And in this house . . ."

"Big before but too big now."

"Everything is changed now, isn't it, Sant?"

"You see it change many time before you pull your curtain." He flicked a little dust from his blue suit, earned during the long walk up from the Bel Air gate. "Let me have throat drops back again. I go down and talk to him."

Andrea gave him the tin, as he bowed to her slightly, saying, "Sorry it not go well for us first time."

"Well, we got by it all right, didn't we? . . . You might

209

like to see this," said Andrea, pulling an envelope from her apron pocket. "He read it this morning, and was about to crumple it up when I rescued it."

Handing the letter over, Sant took it, opened it, and read through his gold spectacles:

THE WHITE HOUSE

Dear Rushton,

Ten calls and no answers. Abraham Lincoln had the same trouble reaching his generals during the Civil War.

You've come to hardest grief. When my Gayle died seven years ago, I thought the earth had gone off its axis. I believed that I knew something about this world and how to live in it. Not so, I found out, and rather abruptly too.

Real grief is unforgiving. You learn how to duel with it moment by moment. You win on the day when you've seen and learned all of its snares.

You will.

Kind regard,
E.H.

P.S. I have your "Blue Boy."

Sant refolded the letter, handing it back, saying, "Nice thing I guess."

"Where should I put it?"

"Maybe in middle drawer of desk in library."

She knew where that was all right. The red phone was there. She'd used it, furtively, three nights ago to reach Flickinger in Florida.

"There's a large wicker basket of other mail. Hundreds of letters. He won't read them. What should I do?"

Sant shrugged. "Nothing."

"What do you suppose the President's reference to 'Blue Boy' is all about?"

Sant's eyes lifted up to hers as he replied, "Must be private joke." But he knew what it meant: Culhane's go-for-broke subterfuge.

Now Sant did go, his pygmy legs moving slowly, as Andrea watched the grizzled gray head disappear. She opened the *Times-Herald* to the front page and read: HALBURTON BLASTED BY CONGRESS. She hadn't seen a paper in a week. Strangely, it didn't bother her at all. But very soon, Andrea knew, she'd have to get back to Washington somehow, and found the prospect oddly unappealing.

It was especially odd after the strange look Culhane had given her earlier, when she'd handed him Halburton's letter. She had been so anxious to see him again, frantic with concern, leaving Washington so hastily, that the exquisite dilemma of explaining her arrival in California hadn't really occurred to her until she was halfway across the country. By then, it was too late to do anything but keep going, see it through. Andrea sighed audibly in frustration.

Culhane wore sunglasses against the spill of morning November sun that would do its work fast and leave. Swaddled under a light cotton blanket, his newly grown beard cat-whiskering over the top of it, he lay on a deck hammock. He leaned over and switched off a tape recorder playing some of his favorite jazz.

"Those glycerin drops taste good, Sant, Have one."

"I sucked out after all the asses I kiss to get them. You keep."

They laughed.

"Baster's people say be back from South America tomorrow. You want I talk to him about chromates then?"

"I don't really care, Sant. Just do whatever sounds best, then let Washington know."

"Andrea show me letter from Halburton. She want save it for you . . . I a little hard on her when she first come here."

"She get pushy?"

"Big lady. Good for you, eh? You think she here for newspaper business the way she say?"

"I haven't the faintest idea."

"Here she come with soup."

Culhane turned his head, seeing Andrea balancing a tray, coming down the steps. She had lost weight, he noticed.

Andrea put the tray on a glass-topped table and said, "Sant got us a paper. I can read you the interesting stuff."

Sant gave a little wave and left for the house.

Unfolding the paper, she sat next to Culhane. Once a great metropolitan daily, seventy or more pages per edition, now it was cut down to twenty or so. No real-estate section, some sports, no financial, very little society coverage. The great paper had become a small-town weekly.

Thinking it might disturb him, she passed over a four-inch article head: GANGLAND KILLING. It told of two bodies, one Caucasian and the other believed to be of Oriental extraction, bound together, and washed ashore on Catalina Island. The heads and the hands had been severed from both bodies, making identification almost impossible. (And it never would have occurred to either of them that the mutilated bodies were Grasselli and the old Taiwanese—neither of whom was known to Andrea anyway.)

So Andrea read a column, datelined London, about a rumored meeting among the European finance ministers and those from Eastern Bloc countries to discuss plans for a single-unified currency.

Blue Dollar! thought Culhane instantly. Andrea saw a vague film cross his lavender eyes as he looked into the distance. It was a look she'd observed before, when his mind was hammerlocking on something. She folded the paper and put it away.

"You're getting your color back," she told him, reaching for the soup.

"Looking in the mirror this morning, I awarded myself first prize for the best Halloween mask."

"Not so. And don't shave that beard off. I love it."

"You might change your mind."

"Maybe," returned Andrea, "but you always told me one fact is worth a hundred guesses."

"Trouble with you is you have a woman's perfect memory at the wrong time."

"If it was like yours, I'd be onstage somewhere doing mnemonic tricks."

He shifted in the hammock, the change of weight causing it to swing. "You've done a hell of a trick on this stage right here. Is that that jasmine essence you're wearing?"

And you told me you knew another woman who wore it too, thought Andrea. "Your voice is getting stronger, Rush." And it did sound less like the gurgle of bubbling water.

"Sant brought me some throat candy. It's pretty good. Takes the rawness away. Got some drug or other in it."

"Mr. Herbsant Saxa is quite an interesting flycatcher."

"If you only knew."

"Tell me what you've been thinking about down here." But Andrea wondered if she shouldn't be doing the real talking now.

Culhane's mouth parted in the cat's fur of beard; a narrow smile made of a pink tongue and white teeth glistened against the black hairs. "I wouldn't abuse your time for anything," he said with a touch of sarcasm.

"Tell your favorite newswoman and lover." Andrea almost didn't get the last word out.

"Later maybe."

"It might help to let go a little, you know."

Silence, for a long moment, and Andrea guessed she might have leaned too hard. Maybe he didn't want to talk. Yet he'd smiled moments ago, a lively shine fleetingly there in his eyes again.

Culhane just drifted into it:

"I've been wondering how in one life I can lose so much family. I hardly knew my mother and never my father . . . Then the Mings of Hong Kong faded away . . . Now my wife and kids gone . . . That's a lot of people to lose. The other night I dreamed about my days at the orphanage. I was terrified of that place."

"That was a long time ago, darling." '

"I think I could even smell the latrines and the carbolic soap."

"But you got away from it."

"I needed the sea badly then."

"And look at everything else you've done in your life."

"What really? I've tried never to cheat, though I've been rough at times." Culhane looked sharply at Andrea. "And the Bible. I've read it three times. A wonderful story, except I can't believe it all. To have a true faith, well, that's like having a private blood bank, I suppose . . . I don't even know if I can claim a country as my own."

"That's ridiculous. I hate it when you say that."

"What the hell do I owe this country or it me?"

"You can't mean that, Rush. Don't say it."

"You'd rather I fibbed around it?" Culhane paused, grappling with another idea before adding, "Take loyalty.

213

That cute notion doesn't mean a hell of a lot to most people, does it? Ethics are an invitation to disaster. You're better off making your own rules, aren't you? At least you know what you've got."

"Crooks are known for it, aren't they?"

"I can think of some highly placed crooks who can probably show something to us."

"Don't talk that way."

"Mark it down as probable truth. Go down some morning, early, and talk to that mob of shouters at the Bel Air gate. Ask them if they'd like a bowl of ethics today."

"Well, how about your Shang-Magan friends? You always said they're—"

"Bingo. There's my whole case in capital letters. Christ, when I think of what I . . ." But he left the words dangling, feeling hot pressure rise under his ears.

"Sorry I brought it up."

"Are you? You always seem so interested in the Shang-Magan."

"You'll admit they're pretty fascinating."

"Not half as fascinating as how you got out here, Andrea. How did you get an air priority? Who are you *in* with, anyway?"

"What do you mean?" Anguish cloaked her, along with the smell of trouble. She grated her teeth.

"How do you come to be carrying a letter from Halburton? You their pet messenger now?"

Andrea fidgeted. Twice she cleared her throat, then moved her soup bowl, which suddenly became cold to her touch. She gazed over at Culhane imploringly.

"I can still add," he said. "And it all adds up very funny. So hang it together for me."

"Let's not get into this right now, all right?"

"Got all afternoon. Just so you tape it together in one piece."

"I'm here. Isn't that what counts?"

"Most of what counts, but not all of it by any stretch."

"I don't think you really want to know."

"You don't mind if I do my own thinking, do you?"

He knows. At least he suspects, thought Andrea, as nervous pinpricks raked her entire being. And I love him and I can't stand it anymore. She wanted to cry, really cry, and in the same terrible instant wished herself anyplace else

214

but here, facing him, forced either to reveal herself or to conceal a deception already half naked.

"Too long a story, no beginning, no end, is that it?" Culhane goaded impatiently.

"It wouldn't thrill you very much either."

"And quit hiding your face, I want to look at you."

"Can't we eat first?"

"So long as you're the dessert. We'll start with you and work backward."

"Later, I promise," said Andrea, her voice faltering.

"Don't duck me anymore, Andrea."

She didn't know how to begin. A wave of dizziness hit her, before she regained herself. "All right. I do some work for the Agency."

"That much I can guess."

A sunburn of blush, as she said: "How long have you known?"

"What does it matter?"

"It matters to me. All along you've—"

"Let's get to the why of why you do it. The money? Old Glory? What?"

"You want to hear this, Rushton, or don't you?"

"From ground zero."

And so Andrea told him more of her father, who had read law at Yale and afterward was inducted into the OSS during the war. All the heady adventure somehow seduced him, and he had stayed on when the CIA was formed. After Korea, he was posted to Berlin, where he died. Her family was long on Old Westbury and Palm Beach, but woefully short on the money needed to keep that life up. Out of its vestpocket funds, the CIA carried the cost of Andrea's education at Vassar, doing so again when she was admitted to the Columbia School of Journalism. They found a position for her with *Women's Wear Daily;* later, with the Los Angeles *Times-Herald.* Both the CIA and the newspaper had paid her, and until the world's moorings broke loose, she could live well.

All she really had done, explained Andrea, was to write profiles of foreign intelligence officers masquerading as UN diplomats. It was fairly routine work, since she was assigned by the *Times-Herald* to cover the UN beat anyway.

The rub was that CIA was forbidden by law, without specific permission, to conduct operations within the United

States. That was the exclusive turf of the FBI, with whom CIA had all sorts of domestic squabbles.

". . . So part of what I do, and have been doing, is technically illegal," finished Andrea. "But I was paying the family upkeep."

"Working for those meddlers?"

"In a vague way. Doing something for my country. Getting helped and paid for it too." She hesitated. "I wrote some things about you. Gave them to Clay Flickinger . . . I agreed to do it before I knew you . . . Didn't know that you and I would, well . . ." Her face became bunched, tight, then innocent in repose, the expressions changing fluently.

Culhane's shoulders stiffened, but he only said, "Had me under your looking glass all the time. Be funny if it weren't so disappointing."

"I'm . . . I'm only trying to explain—"

"And you did, thank you. You're a spy. Keep a gun, too?"

"Stop it, please! I told you, and I'm glad I did. Bothered hell out of me for weeks now."

"Oh, you'll hold up. With a technique like yours, you can't miss."

She wanted to slap him. Sting him with a swift one, and whip the airy talk right out of his mouth. Instead Andrea said quietly, "Look, I'm sorry. Trust me. It won't happen again. Somehow I'll get out of the whole thing."

"Maybe you'd better stay with them. They can't have many Jezebels like you."

"Rush, what I did was really a minor nothing."

"Tell me, Andrea, how many minor nothings do you think it takes to put a screw hole in someone's trust?"

"You're twisting my words. You know you are."

"You're the twist specialist. You're . . . Hell, I don't know what you are."

"Not what you think, anyway."

"Who is?"

"I told you the truth, at least. Doesn't it matter at all? Don't I?"

But he didn't reply. He screened her out, indifferently, through half-lidded eyes, as if she were some nuisance unexpectedly in the way of a larger vision. Andrea's legs trembled. The calves of her legs tightened until they

216

cramped, and her breasts heaved. Exasperated, she tried speaking again, but the words died in the strangle of her rising emotion.

She left him, strutting off, feeling little shame, but enough anger to pack and get out even if she had to walk back to Washington.

For a time, he sat there trying to sort it out. What had she really told the CIA? That ring of fools could ruin everything and not even know it.

Andrea, lover who betrayed him. Or had she? Maybe she didn't know any better, had been coerced somehow or manipulated into deceit. Deceit is survival in these times. And Culhane's thoughts wandered on to some of the stunts performed so recently by Saxa and himself.

Bogey trades, shadow trading companies, deals carrying someone else's name. Richard Ming's, for example, or Tomlinson's and Muldaur's. Slipping in a fifth ace wherever he could find a chance, an opening.

Take her. No, don't take her, to hell with her. But she'd tried to straighten it out, hadn't she? Come clean, told all—or had she? Were there more word curves lurking behind that resolute face?

Culhane tried to escape his soured feelings. He drowsed, but not enough to avoid the near truth: Andrea had come, come and stayed, and pulled some life back into him.

What did that count for?

No price, he decided reluctantly, for the kiss of life.

And yet he was afraid, afraid of himself, and afraid that he had allowed Andrea to come too close to his ways. But here, once more, was that instant when he knew there was no longer any time left to be afraid.

On the second floor of the house, Sant Saxa stood in the room he'd been using for the past months. Comfortable, almost elegant, it was filled with Provençal furniture, had high-timbered ceilings, a large needlepoint rug on the floor, and flowery Scalamandre drapes in convoy against four opened windows.

Soon it would be time to leave. Sant knew the last bells were tolling for him; it made no difference, and there was nothing to be done about it anyway. Two things were factored into his plans: he would not make Culhane witness to another death, if he could help it; and his only son

217

needed time to carry off this almost surrealistic plan he'd concocted.

And I buy time for him with Russians, he thought. It not that hard. What in hell they know about real game. I do that for him. I get Gillis Prato do goddamndest acting job of her life. Gillis better actress than McTigue is cop.

Sant paced, calculating, looking for defects. I nap on it, he decided, and went over to pull the shades on the windows, where the sun was now quartering its afternoon light.

A day passed, then another. Saxa had waited, puzzled by the strange behavior of Andrea and by Culhane's aloof silence and flatly stated wish to be left alone. At times, he would hear Culhane thumping on the piano down in the pool house. Andrea made the meals; Saxa carried Culhane's down to him, wanting to ask what was amiss with the woman, but he was always warned off by Culhane's black moods.

Night came, the second one, and Saxa found Andrea soaking laundry in one of the kitchen sinks. She looked different—wan, unsmiling, a frown pleating her face with worry lines.

"You talk with me, eh?"

"Sure. Someone around here needs to talk . . . How's his majesty?"

"We drink two good ones, so that keep him."

"You know what Frank Henry said about the booze. Not too much."

"Fuck Frank Henry. We need it. I tell you in library, eh?"

Andrea couldn't restrain a laugh now. This little man who talked like a waif: one minute so courtly, funny, and the next like a pistolero. Tidying up, she closed the kitchen doors and went down the long hall. In the library she found Sant hanging up the red phone and looking lost behind the big desk.

Andrea sat in a deep chair of cherry-red damask, curling her feet under her legs.

"I go tomorrow, Andrea. He not know it," said Saxa with a drawn face.

"Leaving! Why?"

"Something very, very important be done."

"But how can you just run out, Sant?" And why not me too, she thought.

"I not run out. Just go away and help him."

"Then why not tell him? You can't just skip out."

"He forbid me go. Talk me out of it. But you see I help him."

"Where will you go?" asked Andrea.

"Not sure yet, child, but long way."

Sant left his chair. Roaming around the room, his patent leather jodhpur boots gleaming like black Vaseline, he did his eye trick with only the whites showing, like dabs of vanilla ice cream. Andrea couldn't believe it. That's impossible, she thought—he's fainted and he's still on his feet.

"What are you doing?"

"A way be alone when you with someone else."

"I'll leave, if you prefer."

"No, no," protested Sant.

"You really adore him, don't you?"

"He the best kind," explained Sant. "He blessed like Haitian, and Haitians sometime see around corner. He like that too."

"You really think that?" asked Andrea.

"I be with him many years. So, no mistake."

"What was Karin like, Sant?" Andrea nibbled on a knuckle, disturbed at what might happen if Saxa left now, wanting time to think about herself and some time *not* to think about Culhane.

A pause that seemed endless, like a wait in the dentist's office, and then Sant answered:

"She one of few movie women I ever like. Not stuck over herself like some. But fast all go to hell. They have baby child who die from something bad in Karin's milk. She blame on herself. She beg for movie part, maybe to forget. But Rush, he against it. Some studio keep asking for her and he let her go finally. She go on drug, lemme see . . ." Sant snapped his fingers, trying to pronounce it correctly. "Elly-es-dee. She go crazy up in Canada. Somewhere there. Rush, he all over the world when Panic come by. He move like crazy too. And he try to hold big grain market in Chicago when other people shut down. Too hard, too big, you know. He spend all his money. Sell boat, horses, the plane, her jewels go . . . Karin, she break down. Many doc-

219

tor. Clinic, everything. Nothing work for long . . . Very
good lady, though. Very fine."

"Thanks," said Andrea, gratefully. "He never told me
any of it."

"That his world and for nobody else."

"And if you go, Sant, what of him?"

"If I not go he might go Macao. He told me he might.
Packers come soon to crate this place up."

"Macao?"

"He got small apartment there. For long time now. He
might sit out there until government pay him."

All of this was news to Andrea. The government owing
him, why? She asked, and Sant told her.

"My God," said Andrea. "So why not stay on and help
him?"

"If I not go, like I say, he never go back Washington. But
he must. You see he think different . . . Maybe he make it
all work. But not alone."

Confusion riddled her senses. Whatever, thought Andrea, is really going on? Sinister.

"I've got to go back myself, Sant."

"Okay. But you stay until he ready."

"To go to Macao. I can't do tha—"

"No. I mean until he ready take care himself. Like
that."

"Yeah, fine. But since this affects me, don't you think
I'm entitled to know what's really up?"

Sant hadn't thought of it before in that way, yet he said,
"You must hear from him."

"That's a real laugher. Hear *what* from him? He thinks
he's a stand-in for God this year . . . It's been horrible, I
know, and we all feel sick and miserable about it. But, by
God, Sant, I've about had it with that man and—"

"What wrong between you and him?"

"Oh, nothing, Sant. Nothing that a kick at his rear
wouldn't help. Maybe not fix, but probably would help."

"Angry, eh?"

"You might say pissed, and in the spring-loaded position, too. I did something I probably shouldn't have, is all.
He wouldn't listen when I tried to talk it out."

"What is it you do?" asked Sant.

"I'd rather not go into it."

Sant had been walking up and down the library. Now he

stopped directly in front of where Andrea sat with her legs tucked under. With him standing, they were face to face.

"Don't run on him." Sant looked at her the way a marksman sights over a gun barrel.

"No, that's for you to do, I guess."

"Plenty important, what I try!"

"Oh, sure! And I'm just the house gadfly."

Slowly, Sant worked himself up to say it. "You be good to him. You never regret it. I not mean the man-woman thing. That always a battle. But not let him down, ever . . . I beg you once, Miss Andrea."

A nerve twitched in Andrea's knee. She straightened her leg. "But you shouldn't go like this. I can't do everything, you know."

"You take this." Sant unfastened a heavy gold-link bracelet from his wrist. "I not need it where I go." He handed it to Andrea. "Give to him and tell him for me, 'It all better than running guns.' He know what I mean."

"Oh, Sant." Andrea gave a little tremble.

"Good-bye, child." And with that, he was gone like a zephyr of black dust.

26

Bel Air

Andrea wasn't sure how long she sat there, her thoughts roller-coasting. Suddenly the power shut off. A stillness of the tomb. She pulled herself into a fetal ball on the chair until slowly her eyes came true and she could see vague shapes of furniture.

Hugging herself, she thought of Culhane. What was he up to, besides being insulting when she tried offering him the truth, showing him the realities of life—her life, anyway. The bastard. Where was he going? Up to what, exactly, and probably getting his directions from some wild calligraphy written in the stars. Should I go to him?

On my knees? The bloody hell with him, the lunk. Never! Love, ha! Cheap enough at the beginning, but the upkeep is the heaviest mortgage ever floated.

Andrea felt her way out of the room, down the hall, making a turn too soon and bumping blindly into a wall. She inched along, her hands guiding her, searching diligently, until minutes later one hand found a brass knob. She became petrified and wasn't sure why. The walls were like a Braille that spelled death and danger and everything evil that Andrea could imagine. Here, close to here, was where Karin was killed, wasn't it?

The terrace, she hoped, and turned the knob. The cool

feather of night touched her. She edged her way to the steps and, tentative as an infant, crawled down them with her knees bent in case of a fall.

Sideways, Andrea slid through the pool-house doors. She heard him, and jammed Sant's bracelet into her pocket.

"That you? I can smell you."

"Sorry," said Andrea. "Sorry, but I had to find someplace. The lights went out, along with God knows what else."

She heard something rustle, close by, but couldn't tell exactly where he was. His hand suddenly came from nowhere, brushing her thigh, making her start. Andrea squealed.

"Sorry, Andrea. I landed on you pretty hard the other day. Nerves shot . . . You caught me on the wrong wave, I guess." Culhane spoke in a very low, quiet voice.

"I only wanted you to know."

"What you said, well, it took bone. Not an easy thing to admit, and most people wouldn't, either."

"Most people aren't us, I like to think."

"Will you tell me what you gave out to Flickinger? I might have to know."

"And supposing he finds out that I did? That'd be really lovely for me."

Culhane thought of Metzilov and others he knew who traded on information for a living, or part of their living. Not quite the same thing, perhaps, but he wouldn't put too fine a point on it right now.

"I think I can understand how you got joined at the hip with Flickinger and his bunch," he said. "The only thing that matters now is what you're going to do about it . . . No, Andrea, I don't have to tell Flickinger what day it is. But then, I don't want you spinning more tales on me, either."

"That's a problem right there. He'll expect something, you know."

"Don't worry. I can cook pudding for him all day, stuff he'd *never* get his spoon into, either."

"Are we . . . Are you going back to Washington?" asked Andrea. Macao still tumbled about in her mind.

"A toss-up. I'm not sure yet."

And whatever Andrea could accurately remember, she told him, getting most of it straight. No more really than

sketches, she explained, and what journalists often do: a
personality piece made up partly of fact and larded with
plenty of impressions.

"And that's all?" asked Culhane when she was through.

"Basically, yes."

"Flickinger's got what passes for a mouth. Why doesn't
he ask me whatever he wants to know?"

"He only hinted at why."

"Make your best guess."

"Someone higher up told him to get a full brief on your
activities. Anything international that you're involved in.
Anything and everything."

"You mean the strategic stockpile trading?"

"That and anything else."

"What else?" asked Culhane, a lash in his tone.

"I really don't know, Rushton. They just don't like sur-
prises over there across the river."

Culhane was silent, busy estimating how much Halburton would know about the CIA's antics. Of how the wrong
thing, said in the wrong place, could leave his plans in rubble.

"Rush?"

"Yes."

"I'm beat, really tired." Andrea decided to say nothing
of her conversation with Sant. Enough was enough.

"I've made a bed on the flooor. It's not the Plaza, but it'll
do."

"Never mind. It's the Plaza."

A swishing noise of clothing sliding off in the dark, a
sound heard a billion times each night somewhere in the
world: in bordellos and bedrooms, on beaches and in palaces.

He wants me, thought Andrea, and this is one godawful
time for glandular fever—too much to resolve, nothing
really settled.

But he was hard against her. His mouth and beard going
everywhere, brushing and sucking her flesh. She feld cold,
none of the rubbery hotness of the other times in Washington, a distant century ago. No starbursts either, faking it
now, possessing while rejecting, with her body feeling
wooden like some windup and do-it toy.

Hardly their best night, and Andrea tried very hard to
forget the photos of Karin only a few feet away. By now she

knew this room abundantly well. Yet she imagined she lay on rocky soil of some forbidden grotto, committing a great sacrilege. Without novelty or even tender play, he was taking her like a rapist, with none of the lover's caresses of before. He hurt, and Andrea bit her curled lip to smother a whimper.

Nor would it be their best day when, late on the next afternoon, Andrea built up more courage and handed him Sant's bracelet while repeating, " 'It all better than running guns.' He said you'd know what he meant."

Culhane made her go through the conversation over and over again, with Andrea omitting only Sant's views of Karin.

Tracing the side of the pool in a fast walk, stopping, looking out against the firs, then resuming until rounding the pool twice, Culhane shook the bracelet in his hand like cold dice. It had been made in four colors of gold. Culhane had given it to Saxa years before as a Christmas present. A talisman. And Saxa, beaming at the time, had said he'd wear it always or until death asked for him. Culhane stopped in front of Andrea, loomed there, a flushed streak creeping up from the beard into his face.

"I've got to find him."

"He's doing what he thinks is right, Rushton."

"He ought to talk about it. That's the way we've always done it."

"Whatever is going on between you two? Are you running a darkroom or what?"

"Cave, they're going back to the cave, goddammit. They have to." Culhane was staring over the top of her head at nowhere.

"Who is? What is it, for goodness sake? Tell me."

"I can't. Not now and maybe not ever." Culhane caught Andrea's eye now, her distant and leery eye. "It's that way," he said.

Sant Saxa, that little bastard of a highwayman. Culhane was stunned, dismayed, yet mostly shamed. If the little one could risk that much, go that far, well . . .

Culhane's suspicions were confirmed at noon the next day. They sat somberly by the pool, with no music this time. Culhane was edgy, untalkative, buried in his privacy. Andrea couldn't break through to him, and stayed to herself, lazing in a chair, leafing through old magazines.

They both looked up as Captain Jack McTigue bounded down the steps.

"Hello, Jack." Culhane got up to shake hands, then said, "This is Andrea Warren from Washington. Andrea, meet Captain Jack McTigue of the Los Angeles Police."

"Rush, maybe we should step inside. Something's come up."

"Andrea's all right, Jack. Go ahead."

"You know a Gillis Prato of Gardena?"

"Sure. For a long time."

"You're aware then that Sant Saxa and she are friends?"

"Sure. Old friends."

"You think she's to be trusted?"

"What the hell's this all about?"

McTigue took one of the empty pool chairs, glanced again at Andrea, and started to pack a pipe, having switched today from his usual chain of cigarettes. "After the . . . The, ah, death of your family we began our investigation. We check on any possible suspect, no matter how remote. That includes Sant Saxa. You too, Rush, if you'd been in Los Angeles at the time. Anyone. That's standard police procedure." McTigue cracked a match with his thumbnail and drew on his pipe. "Seems like Saxa was visiting with Miss Prato on that particular weekend. So his story checks. Other people in Gardena confirm they were seen together on several occasions over the weekend. He stayed with her . . . But this morning she calls the homicide division and says she wants to change her story. We send down two detectives and they take a statement that puts a corkscrew into the whole case." McTigue paused, lighting his pipe again. "Prato says Saxa disappeared for five hours or so on that night. She stated that Saxa told her you owed him millions, had defrauded him, and that he'd asked for restitution or even a promissory note and you'd refused. So, he revenged . . ."

"That's nonsense, Jack. Absolute bull-crock."

"It's what she's sworn to."

"I don't give a damn what she's sworn to. He's been here ever since I got home. Hell, he was my partner. We were great, good friends."

"She's got two witnesses to confirm her side of it," said McTigue. "They were all having a little get-together and they all say Sant ducked out."

"Doesn't mean he did my family in. I can't buy that story, Jack."

"Try this, then. He came back to Gardena, according to what they're saying, just before daybreak. His clothes shredded, they say, and his eyeglasses busted and there was blood on his shirt. Mind you, people are swearing to this, Rush. Three of them."

Andrea gasped, and Culhane shot her a warning look. He knew how devilishly clever Sant could be. "I don't care if all Gardena swears to it. And why does Gillis step forward now?"

"She's mad out of her hat. Gave her the gate, she says, and stole her gold and what jewelry she had left."

Culhane reached into his shirt pocket, then showed McTigue Sant's gold bracelet. "He left this behind a day and a half ago. That sound like a thief to you?"

Inspecting the gold links, McTigue handed them back, saying, "Rush, no offense now, but I know a little about his background. It ain't exactly priestly."

"All a long time ago, Jack. Goddammit, you know him. There is no possible way he'd murder my family."

"An APB went out two hours ago."

Culhane whitened. Ice in his eyes. "Don't do it, pal, because he didn't."

"I've got no choice. In a homicide investigation there's damn little room for friendship. It's all gonna hit the papers, Rush, in a day or two."

"You'll have to stop it."

"I can handle things at the department, Rush, but not at the DA's office. They've a way of blabbing."

"I'll handle them," said Culhane. "You just cool your people down."

"And make it look like you're covering for a possible suspect in the killings of your own family? I wouldn't advise it," said McTigue. "The papers'll put a cinder up your tail for sure."

"The captain is right, Rush," broke in Andrea, fascinated now. No question, she thought, the little man is up to something odd, very odd, and salting his trail with chaos.

"There anything you can tell me that might spread some light?" asked McTigue.

Plenty I could tell you, thought Culhane—a ton, but I won't. I told Herbsant and now look. I don't double my mistakes on anything, unless this woman turns on me again.

McTigue blew out more smoke, waited for a minute, and got up, saying, "Okay, Rush. I'll let you know. We're on the hunt."

"Jack," said Culhane to the departing policeman, "you'll never find him."

Silent as a mummy, Andrea had lain back in the deck chair, keeping her own counsel. She was sniffing at the ripe spoor of a page-one story; several stories, connected. Incredible. She wanted a typewriter, a tape recorder, and the nearest rewrite man available.

"Andrea," said Culhane quite seriously, "I need some help."

"Certainly. What?"

"What time is it in Washington?"

She looked at her watch. "About six."

"In a minute I'll give you two numbers. One reaches the President's military aide, and the other will get an Air Force driver locally. Call them, upstairs there's a red phone in the library, and say we're coming back to Washington. They'll take care of the rest of it."

"Okay."

No Macao. Thank God for the first favor. And how do you rate a special phone here in California anyway, Andrea still wondered.

"In the top right-hand drawer of the desk up there you'll find a book of other numbers. Call Sarah Henry, that's Frank's wife. Tell her to come by tomorrow or whenever and select any one thing she'd like before the packers come to cart everything off. Do the same for Ellen McTigue . . . Take anything you want, if you care to."

"Isn't that expensive, the storage and all?"

"See if you can find out when the packers will come."

Culhane realized he would be clean out of Krugers now, when the movers demanded their payment. Flat broke.

"What about the house?"

"Over and done with."

"You can't just leave it . . ."

"I can't think of anyone who'd buy it, either."

229

Andrea let it go and asked, "Um, can I get on that plane, by chance?"

"As anything but pilot."

You'd be surprised, thought Andrea, who said, "When will we go back, do you think?"

"Soon as they come for us."

"Are we moving up to the house?"

"It's all over up there. I never want to go in there again."

He got up then, walked to her, tousled her hair, and said, "This won't fit me. Keep it if you like."

He handed her Sant's bracelet.

Culhane moved away toward the pool house.

Without really knowing, he could easily guess that Sant was somehow trying to help. Running loose, though, and playing with very live explosives ammunition that might detonate too soon. Forcing my hand, thought Culhane, who had decided yesterday that he must return to Washington or risk a blowup of everything: his courteous and quaint gambit for Russia, then Europe; the bargain with Halburton for returning three tons of gold; his chance, so highly prized, to rejoin the Shang-Magan.

Culhane worried. Half the time he was still under mud, with his head refusing to function, obey, do anything save torment him. He had to move now, fast, get out of here, or he would never shake it. The Mings—Richard and Jia—in China. He must see them, find Sant too!

PART III

27

Washington

"Are you with me?" asked Efram Halburton stiffly. "I keep thinking I'm facing a wall . . . I said that I have forwarded your trade proposals to China and Mexico under my signature."

"Oh, fine," said Culhane halfheartedly. "I want to send other copies to Richard Ming in Shanghai and Fausto Longorria in Mexico City."

"Who are they?"

"Friends of mine. And smart enough to figure out things that are usually beyond government people." Culhane didn't have to wait long to find out whether he'd scraped a nerve.

"Including me, I suppose."

"And me. And everyone else . . . Have you given more thought to putting Tim Rearden in as your Vice-President? This currency business has to get solved, you know." I'm going mad. I must be, thought Culhane.

"I'm not so sure that would solve it."

Culhane looked up, gazing directly at Halburton, thinking, He looks as bad as I must. "Is it possible all the gold we claim to have in Fort Knox and elsewhere isn't?"

Hesitantly, Halburton replied, "It isn't all there. It's a scandal that can't be explained, let alone defended."

"What happened to it?"

"I don't know, and if the Treasury does then it isn't saying."

"Well, send that idiot Squires packing and then demand an accounting."

"The accounting part is up to Congress, and they haven't authorized a gold audit in years. A few years ago, I'm told, some Congressmen asked for an inspection tour of Fort Knox and were refused outright."

"Sleight of hand?"

"Somewhere, I suppose. How far back is anyone's guess."

They searched each other with long looks, so silent, a mouse's squeak would have sounded like an explosion. Culhane buried his face in the palms of both hands, rubbed his forehead, and thought hard. Nothing came, except the notion that he was in a banana republic instead of the United States.

"We might have to reshuffle the cards," Culhane said.

"How?"

"I don't know."

Halburton adjusted the subject. "We're ready with the tankers and the grain freighters. The Navy says their special crews are trained up like monkeys."

"They'll need to be. They'll also have to slow down some until I can visit Amsterdam on my way back from Mexico and China."

"I don't understand Amsterdam. Why must you go there?"

"A little matter of getting some help. Schooling, you might call it."

Halburton didn't press it.

"Your funny money will be ready in a week or so. Soon enough?"

"Plenty. But somehow you'd better get a decent currency organized. Otherwise my exercise is pointless."

"You don't need to remind me every ten minutes," Halburton replied testily.

"Someone has to. You move like a snail."

"Pays to be cautious. We don't know how the Russians will react."

"Russia has a one-track plan—annex everything in

234

sight. They're damn good drinkers, but not so hot as planners . . . So don't get locker-room nerves now."

"How can you be so certain?"

"I've seen their stuff. Their so-called five-year plans.
Not one of them ever worked."

"You're asking me to risk plenty on you."

Culhane sensed the misty feeling coming on again before replying, "Halburton, there is a whole nation out
there putting their bets on you. Give me my gold and I'll
gladly go away."

"Very soon I should be able to do it."

"Spare me politicians' promises . . . You like Fats Wal-
ler?" An odd, vacant look came over Culhane's face.

"What?"

"The musician. Or Dizzy Gillespie?" Culhane reverted
again to another world.

"We were talking about Russia."

"They're no good at jazz, either. Jazz is original."

Halburton scowled, revealing how worried he was about
Culhane.

"When we've got them by the balls, their hearts and
minds will follow."

"Who? The musicians? What the hell ails you?"

"The Russians," said Culhane. "We're talking about
them, aren't we?"

"I'm not following you at all."

"Don't try. It's expensive sometimes."

"That's what I'm mortally afraid of."

"Stay afraid, stay safe, lose everything."

"I don't appreciate that kind of talk. I'm sorry about
your tragedy, but that gives you no right to—"

"You got appointed to act! So, goddammit, act!"

Both men were stunned: Halburton at the outburst and
Culhane at himself. Culhane shook his head, but it failed
to clear. A Salvador Dali painting up there, everything a
warped landscape.

"I'm sorry," said Culhane, standing. "If you'll excuse
me . . ."

"By all means."

Though when Culhane had departed the Oval Office, the
President's worries gushed. He mulled this new problem,
wondering whether the man was fit to carry out this make-

or-break assignment. Wearing a beard now, too. Did he think he was a monk in hiding?

Snow fluttered down in the dim of night as Culhane left the White House. Though not wearing an overcoat, he could feel none of it, neither the snow nor the bite of the air. He plowed his way toward the Hay-Adams, wondering if Andrea would be waiting there. Not if she was smart. Soon, Christmastime, and he didn't have one round Krugerrand to his name. Though never believing in money in any main way, he hated operating his life on the cuff. Stone-cold broke, the first time since he'd drawn his first pay at sea almost thirty years earlier.

Fear, yes, he had been raked by fear before. Most notably when losing the battle to keep the Chicago commodity markets open, losing a vast fortune of his own in that bloody skirmish. That was one kind of fear, the one of the tidal wave with its crushing power flattening everything in its path. But this fear of now was more subtle; he was naked, without capital and therefore without choices.

Hemmed in, Culhane found it impossible to sidestep the blade of desperation pointed his way. Or was it humilation? He wasn't certain.

Something was badly askew. Not just in my life, thought Culhane, but this whole rescue operation has a missing link, needs more leverage to force and control the reaction, a lot more.

What is it? And who cares anyway?

Early the following evening they walked along Pennsylvania Avenue in front of the Treasury, slogging through drifts of fresh snow. No other people were on the move, not even Army patrols, and all that Andrea and Culhane heard was the crunch of snow under their scuffling footsteps. Until bells rang out with a hymn from the National Cathedral; peerlessly clear, the notes carried with true pitch in the razored air. Andrea hummed along.

Everything was white: their vapory breath, the monuments, windows of buildings, streets, and the White House behind its black iron fence. Only the sky insisted upon a different color; it seemed in running argument with itself whether to dress in nun's blue or sinner's gray.

"I'm an outsider to Flickinger, an unknown, a man of no season." Kicking ahead through a drift of snow, Culhane turned back to her. "Flickinger is holding out on me, I think. I have a feeling he's short-circuiting me on some information I want."

"Like what?"

"Some records I think the CIA might possibly have on the New York Corporation. He dodges me whenever I ask about it."

Andrea's cheeks turned a deeper pink, her breathing going hollow. "Rearden country."

"You know them?"

"I know Tim Rearden, and wish I didn't."

"You know him?" asked Culhane, "or you *knew* him?"

Andrea understood the distinction immediately. "Both. And it's a sorry story I'd rather forget."

"Try me," insisted Culhane.

"Haven't we been through enough, you and I? You want to slice up my soul?"

Upset now, she knew she was going to tell him the truth up front this time. And she didn't think too highly of the truth just then.

"I had a very brief, uninspiring affair with Tim Rearden many years ago." Admitting it, Andrea wanted to die.

"Oh!" returned Culhane, disappointed. "It's none of my business, so let's forget it."

"Let's not. Tim Rearden is double-gaited and has good reason to be. Used to fag around with Brian Cowperthwaite of the British Embassy."

Culhane almost lost his footing on the ice-paved sidewalk. He asked, tentatively, "You sure of that?"

"Gospel truth. Ten years ago I made a bad mistake. I got taken in by the Borgia aura of the Reardens' political circle and made a damn fool of myself in the bargain. I lost out to Brian . . . I didn't really, but that's what happened."

"You're too classy to get tied in with the Rearden crowd." Culhane almost wished he hadn't asked her any of it.

"Not then I wasn't. The CIA was sweating for its life in Congress. It was just after Watergate, and the Agency's sins were coming up like porpoises. I was detailed to help enlist Tim Rearden's vote and power and his whatever else to derail the Senate investigations. I got suckered in good."

Stamping snow off their feet, they entered the hotel

lobby. Jenny Carruthers, perky and smiling, turned away as they walked in. It was common gossip among the staff now that Culhane was keeping the woman in his suite. Jenny disapproved of Andrea Warren. Shameless, so soon after the tragic incident, and who would ever believe it of Culhane. With a beard. Ugh!

Upstairs, Andrea sat rubbing her feet to restore the circulation. "What are you thinking about? You're off there dockwalloping somewhere," she asked.

"How well do you know Cowperthwaite?"

"He served with my father at SHAPE during the war. Sometimes he'd visit us in Long Island before my father died. Afterward, too." Sighing, Andrea went on, "Well, he's the most charming and dangerous fairy I've ever known. An Oxford don once and he's delightful, very delightful. Quite brilliant and nobody's fool."

"And he's also a set piece in British Intelligence dressed in diplomatic pants. Correct?"

"It isn't exactly talked about."

"Hear me . . . I'm going to set up a large trade for uranium ore with the British very soon. I'm also going to make it look like Rearden's New York Corporation is the supplier. Got that?"

"Yes."

"Then I'm going to make it look like old Joe Rearden reneged on the trade. Got that?"

"Not really."

"About four days from now, could you find a way to drop it to Cowperthwaite that the CIA has useful information on the New York Corporation?"

"Clumsy."

"But he'll want whatever he can get. That's the business he's in."

"And if he gets it, then what?"

"I'll know whether Flickinger has been holding out on me. If he has, I'll force him to hand the information over somehow."

"You're asking me to put a hustle on the Agency. They've been good to me. I'm sorry about what I did to you, but—"

"I'm asking you to huckster Cowperthwaite into asking the CIA for it. He'll have a legitimate interest, if I set Rearden up the right way."

"It's the same thing."

"Perhaps, Andrea, but I'm not asking you to get the information, only to help find out whether it exists. How painful is that?"

"Why do you want it? Is it a personal thing?"

"No."

"Why is it so important to you?"

"It may not be."

Andrea quivered a little. She looks disarming now, thought Culhane, a little fast maybe, and even dangerous, but she looks superb.

Andrea thought, I don't need to involve Cowperthwaite for this, yet making Flickinger cough it up could make rocks fall on me for years. And then what? Can I really afford that risk?

Survival instincts at guard, Andrea decided to pull off a little test. She needed, at that instant, some assurance of what she really meant to him. How deep did it go?

"Maybe I should go to my place for a few days. I need more clothes, anyway."

"You're leaving me?" Jolted, Culhane's face tightened up, as if it had just been slapped hard.

"It might be better."

"Don't go weak on me. I'm not the spy."

"You're getting to be more of one than you think, and I don't like that word."

"Just don't go, and I won't use it anymore."

"Promise."

"Andrea, don't go."

Standing there touching-close, they stared openly, trying to read each other. Dear God, she thought, is he trembling now? He's so afraid, yet he's all lava, smoldering power. And he's showing me, somehow, how this world tilts. Look at those eyes. They're sunset Rasputin. He can break you with those alone. They stood there, knowing full well that their next move was the end bet. Andrea knew that if she left now, he'd never come begging. Others had, but Culhane wouldn't. Yet how much do I answer for, apologize for, do for him now? she asked herself, gripped in the misery of choice.

Clay Flickinger's burred head faced the window in Andrea's apartment. Looking down upon the street below, through a filigree of icicled tree branches, he saw a guard dog urinating in the snow. It reminded him of the untidy contest he was having with her.

"You don't know what you're talking about," he said. Caution advised him not to look at her then. She might detect the guile in his face.

"I'm pretty close. I do know Ambros Piegar was approached and probably recruited by my father. At my suggestion, too," said Andrea, with a sudden urge to declare herself completely.

Flickinger's neck shortened imperceptibly, though not to him. A fraudulent laugh before he replied, "I couldn't imagine why your father would do that."

"Yes, you can. My father was trying to penetrate the Russian paymaster system that operated through the Swiss banks. Ambros was perfect. He distrusts the Russians as much as he hates his father."

Your father was one of *theirs,* Flickinger wanted to say, but instead he replied, "That proves nothing."

"Except that I happen to know the Reardens have some kind of an interest in Brunsweig und Sohn. So, there has to be a file somewhere in Langley on the New York Corporation."

Flickinger turned toward her. Everything in his face was hard, the mouth grim, the planes of his jaw thrusting out, the eyes unblinking.

"Leave it alone, Andrea. You're fooling with matters that don't concern you."

"Unless I want them to."

"What's that supposed to mean?"

"That I know you and my mother had a crummy little affair in Berlin. That the manner of my father's death was shushed up like it was dirty gossip . . . I can get that investigation opened up."

"Oh, interesting, how would you do that?" Flickinger bridled, completely ignoring Andrea's point about her mother.

"Have Rushton Culhane put a flea in Halburton's ear."

"Your father knew the risks. So don't think—"

"One call does it all, they say."

"Just who is it you're working for these days?"

"Not the Junior League, Clay. I can't continue my life on five-levels, bouncing my way through a maze all the

240

time. I can't take it." Andrea leaned back in the davenport, outwardly calm, melting inside, but glad she had finally said it.

"I'll do some thinking on it, Andrea. You should know
this may be the end of our business together."

"My position at the newspaper, I suppose, too."

"You're on your own there."

He looked at her very unevenly, as if Andrea were some
receding image about to disappear forever. Too much like
her father, he thought, walking deliberately to the front
door of the apartment. Flickinger didn't say good-bye, only
grabbed his coat and stalked off into the downy white day.

Andrea sat there blankly, asking herself what she had
done now. Loving a man she had once informed on was one
thing; turning against her benefactors was swift insanity
in these times. Was she mad? Mad enough, anyway, and
she was amazed at making a decision that could raise such
painful blisters. For love, doing this? A way of squaring
things with Rushton Culhane, who hides his own inten-
tions up blind alleys.

What about me?

As butterfly wings of steel flapped wildly in her stomach.

28

Washington

A car skidded to a curb near Kalorama Circle, a street once as moneyed as any in Washington. The lights dimmed but still caught the tendrils of snow blowing down like smoke on the city.

"I can get you closer than this," said the driver.

"No. Cruise around and meet me back here in twenty minutes or so."

"And if you're not here?"

"Then wait," came the curt answer.

A sound of the door handle as Flickinger got out, watching the car move off into the milky night. Snowflakes dropped against his neck, thawing into beads of water that drained down his shirt collar. He buttoned the top of his Burberry, looked around, then scuttled along the sidewalk.

It was the fourth house, a three-story brick affair, lavishly Georgian, off Massachusetts Avenue. A meager light shone from behind the heavily draped front windows. A tree branch creaked somewhere off to his right; then a dog growled from across a fence. A cold dog, perhaps. He rapped softly against the windowpane at the back door. A shuffle of feet, then a latch loosening, as the door opened. They stood there eyeing each other with the rapt attention of relatives who had owed each other money for too long.

243

The Frenchman's nose was as thin as the face that held it, and as arrogant. It was the face of every maître d' in Paris, thought Flickinger.

"A little coffee, with some Calvados?" Charm in his voice, almost warm.

"Be perfect," said Flickinger, pulling off his sodden coat.

"Come in, please. A beastly night, eh?" The diplomat led him to a pantry, where four chairs surrounded a small breakfast table.

Shortly the Frenchman returned, bearing a tray covered with a napkin, small cups of delicious-smelling mocha coffee, a half-filled bottle of Normandy Calvados, and glasses. He poured the apple brandy, and Flickinger swallowed his down in one take.

"So you have a problem, eh?"

"The Warren woman is threatening to open up the Berlin incident."

"A long time ago now. Hard to reconstruct, I'd say, wouldn't you?"

"The file is still open. They're never closed until resolved."

"Nothing points to you or you'd have been vetted by now. Not so?"

"I can't be sure what they have. I've never seen the investigative reports. I do know there were many of them."

The Frenchman sipped his coffee. He had yet to touch the Calvados. "You knew him well?"

"Very well, and enough to know he suspected my allegiances. Which is why he got kissed good-bye."

"Yes, I remember. And the wife, you were involved there, as I recall."

"We wanted to compromise her in case I was showcased," said Flickinger. "A small card to play, but one never knows."

The Frenchman pinched his great goshawk nose, then lifted the Calvados to dime-thin lips, too wide for the aquiline face. "So what does she want?"

"She wants a CIA file. An old and inactive one on the New York Corporation."

"Why, pray?"

"For Culhane. He wants it. She's guessed as to its existence. Culhane's wanted it for months. The woman thinks she's smart and is using the Berlin incident as leverage."

"And why do you suppose he wants it, and what's in it?"

"I'm not sure why he wants it. Private competitive reasons perhaps. As to what's in it"—and the Frenchman was given a brief reprise of its contents—"and it's also loaded with Piegar's involvement. Be the end of Rearden, depending on how it's used."

"Rearden and Piegar are of no particular interest to us anymore. It might even be useful to run Culhane against them without his being aware of it."

"Culhane is terribly tricky. I've warned you on that."

"An odd animal, isn't he?"

"He's in and out of five tunnels at once. I still can't track how he's securing these strategic items."

"A grave disappointment for a man with your record," chided the Frenchman.

"He works in a way that isn't possible to check or know about. He's used CIA fronts, but only as consignees on blanked documents. You can't—"

The Frenchman waved off more explanation. "I know. You've reported it before. Give Culhane the New York file. Scrub it a little, though not too much."

"It's all the way incriminating. Could bring a lot of trouble down."

"You must see the greater possibilities. Think more of how to get Culhane in your debt. Perhaps he will lead you closer to Halburton. Nothing is more important now. Nothing!"

"All right." But Flickinger wasn't convinced at all.

"If giving Culhane the documents doesn't quiet her, then she is a danger to us all. There's to be no investigation opened up under any circumstances."

The Frenchman nearly added that Flickinger was too important, too highly placed for the slightest chance to be run. It had taken years of stealth to place the right man in the higher precincts of CIA. But such compliments now could only end up costing more than the American was already getting paid.

"I don't think she'll be a problem."

"Advise yourself carefully on that point," warned the Frenchman.

"I'd better go now. I must get to Langley tonight." Flickinger shoved a hand into his breast pocket, pulling out an envelope. "Just in case my being here is ever questioned."

It was a receipt for two cases of French machine pistols

245

for the Cuban operation Flickinger was supervising in Florida. A good excuse, if necessary, to explain why he was visiting there. There was no reason to go over the Cuban matter, since, the Frenchman was fully aware of how Flickinger had cleverly undermined it twice now.

Snow flurried like a dervish as he made his way back. He was glad for the Calvados and the delicious coffee, yielding warmth now against the night. Yet Flickinger was not at all pleased with the idea of surrendering the files to Culhane.

Where would it lead?

And where would it lead if he disobeyed?

Easy enough to amend and copy the files; they contained nothing that would affect vital interests. Rearden's vital interests, yes, but no one else's, except possibly Culhane's.

Ah, Rearden, thought Flickinger, it comes to an end for us all. A given, on the day we are born it's a given. He hurried along as he saw the car up ahead. But he couldn't hurry fast enough to quiet the nerve pawing about under his scalp. At that moment he would have left the Warren women—unfaithful mother and unruly daughter—for dead behind the nearest hedge. Frozen dead, if he could, and frozen out of his life for good.

Predicting the outcome is impossible, decided Culhane, as he scratched rough notes on a pad. An old habit, it helped him jell his choices in the way others might attack a crossword puzzle. He drew a line under Hormuz, encircled China, transposing them both into a different order. Variables were everywhere.

As a rule, he was an early riser, finding morning the best time to work undisturbed. Dawn was a good time to think, as was the middle of the night, when the competition was usually asleep. Though, he admitted, it had taken some arguing with himself to slip out from beside the sweet warmth of Andrea an hour ago.

Swinging his chair around, he looked out the window into the wintry gray drabness. Too early to tell which way the weather would bend. Too early to tell a lot of things: how Mexico or China would decide, or why had Flickinger urgently called for a meeting at this hour.

The voice had sounded so urgent last night on the telephone. So did the footsteps Culhane heard echoing now in

246

the solitude of the outside hall; a clack-clacking of heel plates against the crushed-marble floor.

Where are you? Call me, damn you!

The door was open. Flickinger came through it at full stride, heaving his coat across the back of a stuffed chair.

"Tea, if you want any, down the hall," said Culhane. "And good morning." You fucking prick, he almost added.

"Not now, thanks." No "good morning" in reply.

Flickinger extended his lower lip, as if blowing steam out to kill the freeze in his weather-washed face. He saw Culhane's beard but made no comment.

"You have any luck with Maxaculi in Caracas?"

"Very helpful. Haven't had a chance to tell you."

Reluctantly, as if handing over his birthright, the intelligence officer passed a slim manila envelope to Culhane. "I've never seen this," said Flickinger. "It doesn't exist as far as we're concerned. References to certain operational matters have been deleted. Otherwise it's intact."

"I understand," said Culhane, reaching out, wondering what it was.

And he withdrew the envelope's contents. Noting that small deletions appeared at scattered intervals, he began skimming the unwieldly passages. He slowed to absorb a section that described Braunsweig und Sohn as one of twelve Swiss banks infiltrated to learn more about the KGB paymaster system in Western Europe. Another page stated that Braunsweig und Sohn was owned by the St. Gallen Trust, formed in 1948, with the "Trust" financed by monies believed to be cleverly diverted from the Marshall Plan—the aid program for Europe's recovery after the war. St. Gallen Trust assets, moreover, were administered by Braunsweig und Sohn, which was protected from normal scrutiny under strict Swiss laws of bank secrecy.

Culhane read and reread the part that fascinated him most. Here, at last, was the explanation of how Rearden's New York Corporation had managed to survive the Panic:

Joseph Aloysius Rearden, U.S. citizen, believed to be a resident of the State of New York, also Chairman of the Board of the New York Corporation, and members of his family appear as the sole beneficiaries of the St. Gallen Trust.

Failing abjectly to comply with provisions of the United States Tax Code, the above beneficiaries have never reported the "Trust's" assets and income with the appropriate U.S. authorities, see INT/AGY:

The "Trust's" assets currently consist of one billion of Swiss francs, depository receipts for four tons of gold bullion, deeds of numerous real-estate parcels within Western Europe, and various holdings of shares and bonds of several multinational corporations. The specific accounts used by the "Trust" at Braunsweig und Sohn are ten in number, (accounts 416-10 through 416-19). Persons authorized as signatories for these accounts are Joseph A. Rearden; his son, Timothy P. Rearden; and Hans-Otto Piegar, who was formerly the bank's managing director as well as the lawyer engaged in 1948 to draw up the terms of the St. Gallen Trust.

Boggled, Culhane was riveted by another key passage:

The St. Gallen Trust is, in part, a device for massive money-laundering activities. Over the years vast transfers of U.S. dollars and other hard currencies were funneled into the "Trust" from organized-crime sources, with the resultant monies temporarily invested and those investments later transferred at an agreed-upon discount to various offshore corporations known to be controlled by Mafia elements, see INT/AGY   . The "Trust," therefore, earned substantial commissions for its services and is thereby complicit in these illegal dealings.

Another audit trail points toward the St. Gallen Trust's financing of high-level distribution of narcotics, specifically the "White Dragon Pearl" heroin and No. 4 brown sugar heroin from the Golden Triangle area through Singapore. The "Trust" also receives kickbacks from various countries granted foreign aid from the U.S. Government, and which grants-in-aid are either approved or not, under various funding authorizations by Senator Timothy P. Rearden's Senate Appropriations Committee.

* * *

The last page was gobbledygook. Flipping it, he found a key taped to the cardboard backing of the file. He looked up at Flickinger.

"The key. What's if for?"

"Opens a safe-deposit box at the Crédit Lyonnais, Vendôme branch, in Paris. It's a bearer key. The box contains notarized copies of the St. Gallen ledgers, affidavits, and the like."

Culhane's thoughts tripped as if they were running over hot electric wires. Too good to be true, or was it? Now the final leverage fell into place.

"So now you've got Rearden where you want him," said Flickinger.

"How's that?" replied Culhane.

"Rearden. You've got him."

Piegar, thought Culhane, I've got you in the center of the reticule, the cross hairs right on your neck. You're the one I want.

"We always figured that you and Halburton, both having been involved with the Shang-Magan, were after Rearden," said Flickinger idly.

Only by the most sacred use of self-control could Culhane keep his wits now. Halburton? Shang-Magan? Had Halburton been their U.S. informant on trade matters? Surely not now that he was President. Before? Of course! When he was the U.S. representative in Geneva at the General Agreements on Tariffs and Trade. You slick bastard, Van Slyke. And Muldaur would have been in on it too.

"Oh, no," said Culhane blandly, "that's over and done with. It means nothing anymore."

"I see."

Hold yourself. Christ, don't give it away! "Why wasn't this material turned over to the Justice Department?"

"In my business you sometimes protect the barracudas so you can get at the sharks," offered Flickinger, quite ironically.

"You mean here's Joe Rearden financing all this heroin"—a flash of Karin—"then fronting for the Mafia and evading taxes. And you just let him gallop along . . . This listens pretty good. Keep going."

"The risk of revealing it is too high. That information concerns a very powerful political family. Americans. That

249

makes it domestic. CIA is expressly prohibited from engaging in domestic matters."

Interesting, that is. What am I then, a Mongolian? "There's always the FBI. Why not turn it over to them?" asked Culhane, guessing at the answer, but wanting it anyway.

"We'd be accused of running over their territory again. They'd likely complain, raise hell, and up we go again to Congress to get our ass belted around. We don't go looking for trouble over there, not with Tim Rearden chairing the Appropriations Committee."

And that must have been how Andrea got mixed up with Tim Rearden. A pawn. Some flesh for a vote. A trade, but a bad one.

"You people were on your knees begging for it, as I recall," said Culhane. "Chile, Iran, Guatemala, Uganda, Vietnam— you used them all to pick your teeth and won nothing."

"I resent that."

"And how do you think those countries felt?"

"Grateful, I hope. We went after the left-wingers, cleared the way—"

"For death. Spare me, Flickinger. You're all closet cowboys. You, the British, the Russians, the Germans, your whole mob. Enough of this, though . . ."

Flickinger was offended, off-balance. His heart pumped like a bellows. An expert at double-facing, though, he said, "I'll be on my way."

As in a market bluff of old, his most agile technique, Culhane said, "Here, you might need this someday."

He held out the St. Gallen file in his hand, praying that the other man wouldn't accept it. The key. Culhane had to have it, but wanted to appear disinterested, elegantly so.

"Never saw it before. Cinderella stuff."

"As you wish."

Seconds after the door closed, Culhane was in turmoil— Halburton, blast you, and Van Slyke, you conniving shithead. And Rearden, the crook! Can't make it on the straight, has to cheat, stealing the Jews' money, fronting the Mafia, funding drug operations out of Singapore too. Liu Wai's? And yes, Piegar, we're going to string you to the higher limbs.

29

Washington

By midafternoon Culhane finished up a lengthy meeting with the President. Mexico, apparently baffled, had signaled its agreement to mutual consultations. Culhane would go there, negotiate, attempt to move them toward a Memorandum of Accord, then return to Washington if nothing was heard from the Chinese by then.

They had discussed the world's grain reserves, especially those of the United States. Halburton, as usual, had disputed some matters; Culhane circled around any temptation to force Halburton's hand over his link with the Shang-Magan. That could wait, just as the Reardens could wait.

Going by the White House administrative office, picking up his air-priority document, tickets, and a packet of foreign currencies, he then met with his two-man staff for an hour. Culhane autographed forty different requisitions for various items from the strategic stockpile, while rejecting double the number. He'd be gone before the crowing and backbiting began.

No longer caring about the restrictions on the use of the red phone, he called Jack McTigue in Los Angeles, only to be told that there were no fresh leads in the homicide investigation, nor had they learned where Sant Saxa was nesting. Culhane advised that he'd be checking in from afar over the next weeks.

At 3:48, the wind tossing more wisps of snow, he lurched toward the hotel. Time to pack, arrange his luggage so as to smuggle one of the paintings abroad.

Spread across the bed, two suitcases lay opened; one for warm-weather clothing, the other for the colder climates of China and Europe, if he got that far. He blocked the clothing in one suitcase into a sort of square around its edges.

He heard the door open, and then Andrea's footfall outside in the sitting room. He hoped it would go well with her, but it gnawed at him just the same. Abrupt moves with no solid explanations never sat well with her.

"Hi," said Andrea, seeing him come through the door.

"Let me help you." Kissing Andrea, he took her coat, then told her, "There's warm water. If you want a bath, I'll bring a drink." She was wearing Sant's bracelet. He missed the brown one badly, but was glad to see the gold links on her wrist.

There was part of a bottle of Canadian whiskey left, more of Frédy's merchandise. Culhane poured it neat into two small glasses. Carrying them to the next room, thinking, he put the drinks down, sorted out some tapes, and played one of Hoagy Carmichael's medleys. A sharp wind pummeled the windows, rocking the frost-loaded panes until they groaned.

White mounds of bubble gel billowed around Andrea when he came in. Her hair was wrapped in a hand towel, turban style. The air cloyed and steam clouded the mirror over the wash basin.

"I traded a bread coupon to a girl in the office. Divine, isn't it?" She took a handful of the froth and blew it at him. "Want me to suds your beard?"

"Not now, thanks." Culhane smiled. "Want a taste?"

"Love it. Hold it for me, will you?"

He bent over, putting the glass to her lips, watching her mouth take the whiskey. Culhane sat on the edge of the tub.

"Flickinger came across this morning with the New York Corporation file. It's a beaut."

"Really," said Andrea.

"You pull a fast act. How'd you do it?"

"Could turn out to be the most expensive thing I've ever done in my life."

"Somehow, I'll make sure it isn't."

"Ummm. Another sip, please?" Something she wanted to mention then, had been holding in, wanting to spare him. She spoke slowly. "You know, Rushton, that you're . . . You've been into those nightmares again?"

"Bothers you, use the other bedroom."

"Baby, it's not me that's bothered, except about you."

"It's probably because we're not having enough sex."

"God, you're stubborn at times."

"It's the Aussie in me. They're pretty stubborn . . . I'll leave your drink here. Frédy is going to fix us dinner tonight."

"Gorgeous. What's the occasion?"

"There isn't one for us, I'm afraid. Soon, maybe." Culhane left her then.

He is a machine now. Even in bed, like a violent inmate too long in detention. Light up my life with another sand castle. Better yet, a bubble house, thought Andrea, as she blew a small tunnel through the foamy bubble gel. Anything, anything at all that doesn't exclude me from your world . . . Something interesting must be in that CIA file on the Reardens, she thought.

Frédy had outdone himself. Le Danielle was closed that night, but he'd opened it for them, and they dined at a small table with two candles teasing at the darkness. They ate illegally shot venison, pureed chestnuts, and roasted apple slices with raisin sauce.

". . . I don't know exactly, Andrea. It might take as much as a month."

"A month! Are you up to it?"

"Soon find out, won't I?"

"Will you be looking for Sant?"

"Sniffing for him, anyway. It takes time to make this sort of trip . . . You can stay here. I've arranged credit, and Frédy will look after you, and the suite is free, you know."

Andrea shook her head. The candlelight made her hair almost white; it shimmered like crystal.

"I'll call if and when I can," said Culhane. "It's easier to do if you're by the red phone . . . Up to you, of course."

"Then I'll stay here," said Andrea eagerly, reversing herself. "Just come back soon."

Her emotions must be running. He could detect a strong fragrance of the jasmine she wore.

"You'd better come back," insisted Andrea, thinking of Macao again. She gripped his hand, strongly, and he could feel pressure on his wrist.

"I may get as far as Europe," said Culhane. "If so, I'd like to meet your friend Ambros Piegar."

"You'll like him. I'm sure of it."

"In a few days use the red phone and tell him I'll call him when and if I near Europe. We can set a time to meet then. Only if he wants to, though."

"I think he'll *want*. Wish I were going with you," said Andrea wistfully.

"Next time. I've one more thing to ask."

"Fire away."

"At the National Security Agency," explained Culhane, "there's a Coast Guard commander by the name of Doug Brooks. He's a code specialist. Tomorrow evening, he'll be by here to pick up an envelope I'll give you later. It's the one Flickinger gave me this morning. Can you take care of that for me?"

"Certainly. May I . . . I read it?"

"I'll leave that up to you. After all, you sprang it loose."

"Just a girl's curiosity," replied Andrea, loosening her grip. Immediately he noticed the loss of warmth. "Look, isn't it fun? The walls are seeing the candlelight."

And it was true. The soft light brought out the polished knurled grain of the walnut. Quiet came between them as her eyes searched his face across the table.

"I owe you for a lot," said Culhane.

"You could try doing something for me."

"Name it."

"Well, you see, I levered Clay Flickinger by using your name in vain. I told him if he didn't come across then you'd ask the President to reopen the investigation about my father's death."

"You'd better draw me a picture."

"When my father was killed in East Berlin, Clay Flickinger was his regional control officer," said Andrea. "On the side, he and my dear wonderful mother were having a shabby little thing together. And I'd like to know what really happened."

"You've never been told? Hard to believe."

"Officialese blarney. And I'm reasonably certain Mother doesn't know that much either."

"Why have you never mentioned this, Andrea?"

"You weren't supposed to know that Clay Flickinger and I knew each other at all, remember?"

Looking fully at Andrea, he said, "If your threat produced the New York Corporation document, then he may be shielding something. Still, why wouldn't he just continue to stonewall me?"

"I wish I knew."

"Got to think on it, Andrea. Stay away from it until I get back."

"Him, yes, you, no. And I want to go upstairs."

Culhane was amused at her glib candor. She is a creature of the immediate, he thought, the angel of the instant moment.

Sleepy-eyed and loved out, on her way to the kitchen the next morning, she saw him sitting on the davenport. A screwdriver busy in one hand, he held the small Cézanne in the other, prying the canvas loose from its frame.

"What are you doing to *my* painting!"

"Got to get some money, Andrea. I'm all the way broke. So don't get sore."

"So what! You can't sell that, you said you'd *never* sell those paintings."

"I might not have to," replied Culhane, removing the last screw, springing the canvas free.

He looked up, feeling as if he'd just been accused of grand larceny. And the look he got in return was purely glacial.

Culhane told her, "The others are too big to pack."

She pivoted on one foot, angrily, and marched for the kitchen door.

Banging a kettle against the stove burner, she turned up the flame, and with it her own temper. Rarely given to outbursts, Andrea was fussed now and didn't care. The loss of the painting was bad enough. But that was not nearly so bad as Culhane's not having warned her. She'd put faith in

255

his word, the value of his promises. *"Those aren't for sale,"* he'd said many times. Men, the bastards!

An hour later, as she left for work, Andrea pressed a brief cool kiss to his cheek, stood back, regarded him as if he were diseased, then scurried out the door. Nothing else.

Later, having wrapped the Cézanne in several layers of tissue paper, one more of oilcloth, then a final binding of packing paper, Culhane shut the suitcases. He lugged them over to the door. Then he went to the desk and put some notes he'd been working on in the top drawer.

He thought of Andrea's huffy exit. Bad stuff. Yet why in hell did he have to account to anyone for his own belongings? The Cézanne was a treasure, but he needed hard funds now.

She was a full cut above most women he'd been close to: loyal despite her little Mata Hari games, very lovable, fun. A reverent and inventive lover. A damn good, capable woman, but still on the search to find the armlock she needed in this world.

The bell rang. Culhane knew the sound to well, the first round of thousands of air miles, ruses to come, agreeing on differences, using instinct, subtle bargaining, doing what he'd trained for, and doing it the best he knew how.

30

Shanghai

Slammed by clear-air turbulence, the aircraft's nose bucked upward and as quickly its port wing dipped. In a few frightening seconds the DC-9 plummeted two thousand feet.

A service cart banged its way down the passenger aisle. Glasses and bottles careened into seats as hats, coats, and packages tumbled from the overhead racks. A few passengers screamed. A young infant, held by his mother, sitting next to Culhane, spewed over the woman's navy blue silk dress. A warning buzzer sounded and a crew member spoke in nervous Cantonese to the passenger cabin as the aircraft was retrimmed and brought under control. Culhane woke up in the bedlam, thinking he was wallowing in another nightmare.

He looked out the window into a flamboyant sky. Clouds piled up like layered goose down, and greenish-orange shafts of light streaked down toward the somber earth below. China! He knew without being told, and his arteries seemed to fill with prickly heat.

He edged over in his seat, the smell of the infant's vomit souring the air even though the mortified mother was busy mopping up. His thoughts went back to Mexico and the past twelve days since leaving Washington. A procession of problems had arisen. Immigration questions came up, water claims, and other matters having nothing to do with the Trade Compact. Two days lost on those quarrels alone.

Had it not been for Fausto Longorria and a group of other top Mexican industrialists, the whole project might have failed. Probably would have, he thought. Immediately, they had seen the benefits for themselves, of course, and for their country and they'd gone into action.

A transfer through trade of 150 billion old-dollars' worth of American technology and expertise—in exchange for Mexican oil valued at 14 old-dollars per barrel. Natural gas at one fourth that price per thousand cubic feet. Mexico was loaded with it and needed the market. Not for dollars, but for advanced hardware and the knowledge of how to use it. Mexico was trading for a quantum jump of twenty years of progress.

Culhane recalled the last day of the meetings:

A great moment, Señor Culhane. *Yes. Muchas gracias.* De nada. Para todo! A drink to it, to everlasting friendship and pleasure, señor. *I've had all I can handle, thank you.* Perhaps it's the altitude? *You're right, I'm sailing very high right now.* And you will be our guest at Acapulco this weekend, the Minister had offered. *Terribly sorry but I must get to Australia.* Oh! Another negotiation with them perhaps? *No, just a small one this time with an old friend.* You are an excellent bargainer, Señor Culhane, muy fantastico. *I learned it by watching you gentlemen.* Oh, a diplomat too. Viva Mexico y Los Estados Unidos. *Yes, I'll have one more drink on that; it's only four in the morning, isn't it? (And please don't look now, Mr. Minister, but you gave away $2 a barrel you shouldn't have.)*

A bone-cruncher of a flight to Sydney, a pass by the barbershop to shave off the beard, then a long and pleasant dinner with Muir Tomlinson, the Shang-Magan's council member in Australia. Aging now, though the brain still as keen as a surgeon's blade, a man of magnificent manners. Tomlinson had been a great help in recent months. Culhane had wanted to thank him personally.

And one more thing: Could Tomlinson's House set up a barter trade of grain against Iranian sweet crude the Russians now controlled? The U.S. could release 400,000 metric tons of wheat or corn at very favorable rates. Would

Tomlinson deal for the oil on the best possible terms, though with the advantage purposely going to Russia?

Agreed. And also agreed that Culhane would call him in four days for the answer. Culhane was certain the shrewd old trader sensed a ploy, but was too much the gentleman to inquire about it. He was a trader, not a lawyer. And Culhane was only sorry that he couldn't reveal details of a gigantic grain trade yet to come.

Maybe. A maybe that was a hundred miles long. But that would have to await another day with Van Slyke in Amsterdam.

He thought of the big Dutchman now, and what it might take to arrange a blocking action in the world's wheat markets. In their private lingo, top-caliber world speculators used the term to mean seizing control of a market for any major commodity.

It all depended upon first-rate information, surprise, and the use of prime force at the exact right moment. When the real pros were at work, they always came hard and straight and didn't much care who was in the way. Culhane intended a full blocking action in wheat. He couldn't do it alone. No one could. For that play, so massive, you needed a melding of interests—a syndicated effort.

He thought of the two attempts while in Sydney to call Andrea, and the hell of a time patching them through the U.S. Naval Signal Detachment at Christchurch in New Zealand. No answer. He missed her.

And then it bubbled right up from nowhere. Something he promised himself he would never do: compare them as if they were racehorses, even paintings. Yet it couldn't be helped somehow, not when you had lived closely, passionately, with two women. Something magic, also killing, fiddled with your chemistry at two different times, and if that much craziness ever happened at once, it *would* kill you, absolutely.

Karin had been goodness itself: very good to him, to her children, often overly generous to others, and pretty good in front of a camera. And now Andrea, front row center, hello Andrea: beguiling, candid, a sense of humor, with more talent than she knew of and in the wrong line of work to prove she had it. Two lucky draws, and Culhane knew

259

he'd better let his thoughts drown or they might drown him.

Below, the sky was clearing. He could see a river meandering below a ravine cut out of the surrounding high country. Some carpeting of snow, too. The Fuchun River, he guessed, tumbling toward the Bay of Hangshou. China moved her whole country on rivers, not on wheels. These waterways stretched thousands of miles westward beyond the Gobi Desert into Tibet, even farther.

Water-beast trails and rice paddies next to more paddies as far as Culhane could see now. Green and yellow and then the sponge color of yellow umber. A billion people to feed down there. It was all so old, very much older than Rome and Carthage before it.

Ken-chou Ming. This was his land, the land of the Ming Dynasty.

He summoned the memory of Ken-chou again. The vibrant alive face, almost unlined, usually in peaceful repose when everyone else was agitated. A magnificent mind that ranged across engineering, philosophy, medicine, business, human nature. A marvel of a man with no discernible character defects, and the greatest trader Culhane had ever known. The writer of that Book, the man who taught Hong Kong how to become the greatest free-trading city of the world. Not the way Shanghai once was, but better than the city-state of Venice under the doges. All during the Second World War, when the Japanese had sent the British packing from their treaty colony, it was Ken-chou Ming who nursed the island people's spirits. He gathered their pride, lifted their hearts, and showed them what brute courage could deliver in foulest days.

A man in a century. And what he'd done after the war to revitalize Hong Kong's economy, give it fable, make it the trading haven it was, was a feat so extraordinary that even the British admitted it. He'd saved their colony, and for that they'd given him a pat on the back. And a silver medal.

A whirring of hydraulics as the wing flaps slowly extended, the engines singing lower now. A smocked stewardess walked the aisle to check seat belts. Shanghai, once the Paris of the East, a few miles ahead now as the aircraft swung its final approach to Honggiao Airport.

More than twenty years, counted Culhane, and once

again he would see Jia and Richard Ming. Do you start all over, everything new, kiss, shake hands, or what, after these many years? Almost half my life gone since living and working with them in Hong Kong. God almighty! Sant, you should be here, damn you. His throat went dry.

A rangy young man, broad-shouldered, tall for a Chinese, stepped forward just as Culhane entered the passenger terminal, carrying the smaller suitcase, the one with the Cézanne wrapped in bunting.

"Mis-ter Cul-sjane?" asked the young man, spacing the words cautiously.

"Yes." Culhane looked at the stranger carefully. High cheekbones, flowing black hair, brown eyes, and a complexion tinted white. A Eurasian.

A shy smile. "I Michael Ming—Ken-chou Ming, the less one—but some call me Michael." He shot a muscular arm forward to shake hands, Western style.

"Very glad to know you, Michael," said Culhane, amazed, returning the callused grip. "Are you . . . Whose son are you?"

"My father is Richard. My auntie is Jia."

"Well, I'm damned," said Culhane, shaking his head. "I didn't know. I'm sorry."

"Nothing to be sorry," said Michael, almost getting it right. "Please come. We get your cases and go home. My father badly sorry not to come. Apol . . . apologiza . . . much work. Auntie Jia at Fudan Uni . . . versity. Soon come home. We go, eh?"

"Whatever you say, Michael."

Surprisingly, they found his other suitcase as soon as they reached the claim area. Before he could put a hand on it, Michael Ming had easily hoisted it, sweeping the other one neatly out of Culhane's hand. He led the way through the milling crowd toward customs, where Culhane showed his diplomatic passport. The official studied it, observed Culhane acutely, and sputtered in rapid Shanghainese to Michael before waving them through.

"I'm not so familiar with your local dialect, Michael. What did he want?"

"He say you important to have paper you carry. No one tell him you are coming."

"Not so important after all, you see."

They walked toward the terminal doors, the boy handling the heavy suitcases as if they were balsa-wood bookends.

"My father say you very important."

"You must know by now how generous your father is."

"Auntie Jia say too. They very ex-cite see you."

"Me too."

"I have no money for taxi. We take bus."

"I think we can manage a taxi," suggested Culhane, who looked at the overflowing buses and decided he'd rather walk than grapple with that persecution.

When they'd turned into Honggiao Road, leading to the city, Michael asked, "You speak Chinese?"

"Cantonese and Mandarin. Not Shanghainese."

"I teach you, but now we speak Mandarin. I tell you what I do. Is easier to say than in English."

"Fine. I'd like to hear about your life."

"I've finished," began Michael in the Mandarin, "my fifth year of study at Fudan University. Soon I will receive a combined certificate in geology and engineering. Then, perhaps, I will be sent again to Western China, in the province of Xinjiang, to do more work there. I spend three or four months there each year."

"And what do you do there?" asked Culhane, his interest aroused.

"I have a small team and we search for certain rock formations, looking for mineral deposits. The work is difficult yet quite gratifying."

"I would imagine. You ever find anything worthwhile?" asked Culhane, staying as close to colloquial Mandarin as he could.

"Chrome deposits, coal, manganese, tungsten, and titanium. I think there are other traces too, but our exploration budget is very limited."

"Are these deposits large enough to develop?"

A brief silence. "I think so, but we must test and drill more," answered Michael Ming, who leaned over and gave some rapid-fire instructions to the taxi driver.

"How do you go about exploring that vast space with such a small team?"

A canny look brimmed over Michael's face, while the corners of his mouth curved into a sly smile. "I sometimes can secure permission to visit the region in the winter. Very cold then and snowy. I live with the Kazakhis, who

262

are Mongol nomads. They raise sheep. I hunt the wolves that kill their sheep. A wolf will kill ten, twenty sheep and sometimes a man even in broad daylight. Sometimes I even hunt on the Russian side of the mountains. There is a bounty on the wolves. The government pays in sheep. The bigger the wolf, the bigger the bounty sheep. I give the sheep to the Kazakhis and then some sample rocks and I ask them to please look for similar things as they traverse Xinjiang. They are very good at it."

Culhane was overwhelmed, proud too—an entrepreneur no less, the boy had founded his own intelligence system. "You are your grandfather." This is not a boy, he reminded himself, but a wolf hunter.

"No, not like what I've heard of him. But I try. You speak excellent Mandarin, Cul-sjane."

"I try," said Culhane through a smile. "Your Auntie Jia taught me, and the Cantonese dialect too."

The taxi approached the city's outskirts. People by the thousands teemed in the streets and on sidewalks. Bicycles everywhere or rickshaws made from them. Food vendors with carts and hawkers selling shoes and fountain pens. Street cleaners with straw brooms. Laundry hanging from window poles in the cool winter air. Culhane could see no beggars. Gay banners and posters were flapping in the breeze. Most of the roofs were tiled, and much of the architecture was in the European style, the buildings made of brick or stone or both. Culhane swept up every detail he could absorb.

The taxi moved along Fuxing Road, on past the Sun Yat-sen Museum, slowing as it reached the Yu Garden. In there, he knew, was classic Chinese landscaping, famous for its Halls of Mildness, for Watching Swimming Fish, of Serenity, and the Tower of Ten Thousand Flowers, the Treasury Tower, and the Emerald Pavilion. And here the Society of Little Swords, using the Hall of Heralding Spring as its headquarters, had once risen up against a corrupt emperor.

Culhane thought, This country wrote the bible of rebellion, as the taxi swung left into the old Bund.

"Michael, let's stop here for just a minute."

"Yes, of course," and Michael gave a clipped order to the driver, who pulled over.

Culhane got out. Now he could see what he'd been able

to get before only from pictures and books. The Bund. The best-known street in the East. Culhane saw the long line of buildings against the great avenue that curved along the Huangpu River.

He knew those buildings, even though he'd never set foot in one. The old Bank of Indo-China, the Glen Line, farther on Jardine Matheson (now of Hong Kong), then the Yokohama Specie Bank, the old office of Butterfield & Swire, the place where Sassoon of Baghdad made his fortune, and down near the end the old Palace Hotel and what had once been the offices of the *North-China Daily News*.

"You like it. I can see it in your face."

"I think I like it very much. Shall we go?"

In just minutes, the taxi cruised up to the old Broadway Mansions, once a very fashionable address for foreigners. "Auntie and Father live here. We go up."

"I can't wait." Culhane paid the driver as Michael beat him to the luggage again.

31

Shanghai

Stopping at the sixth floor, they walked down a wide hallway with silvery wallpaper of cormorants and lilies. Taking a key from his jacket, Michael opened the door, then ushered Culhane through a foyer that opened upon a sunken living room.

Culhane's heart soared when he saw her.

Jia arose, coming to him with that face that made his belly whirl. So serene, a face touching him with its invisible soft fingers, and eyes shaped like large marquis-cut brown stones.

Closer now, and he saw that she was still slender, the hair as black as ebony and swept back above the wide brow. Maturity had penciled a few shallow lines in her skin of smooth banana-ivory.

Old enchantment played new tricks as Jia said, "Twenty-two years, ten months, and eleven days. How we missed you."

"And how very beautiful you still are."

"Enough for an embrace?"

"A thousand of them."

He stepped the last few feet, threw his arms around her, and pressed so hard she gasped. Once again he smelled the jasmine fragrance. They held for a long time, dreaming old, saying nothing.

"I have the monkey tea for you after your long trip."

"I'd rather hug."

"You will kill me," she whispered, feeling Culhane's jarring strength, a strength she knew well from their Hong Kong youth. He loosened his arms.

"Is Richard here?"

"Soon," said Jia, inspecting Culhane's face minutely. "He is terribly busy and could not meet you."

"I was delighted to be met by your Michael. Quite a fellow." Culhane looked around, but the younger man had vanished.

"Our joy," said Jia fondly. "I will get the tea and we can have a twenty-year talk."

When she left, Culhane went to the window, passing by a few silkscreens on the wall and some intricately carved mahogany furniture. Two brass shelves held enameled cloisonné pieces and some red lacquered boxes. Hidden in one corner was a tired-looking television. A comfortable room, though with nothing of the grandeur of Ken-chou's villa high on the hills of Hong Kong. He looked down on the brownish river, then off to the harbor in the north. A dozen or more ships swung at anchor, and he thought of his early days at sea.

"Let's sit here," said Jia. He turned, seeing her pour the tea into yellow porcelain cups. "I cannot tell you how stricken we were to hear of this terrible thing happening to your family. I was blinded with tears."

"When I first mentioned it to Richard on the phone, he said you'd already heard about it. That surprised me."

"China has many ears, Rushton," said Jia, handing him a cup. "It must have devastated you."

"Every so often I can feel them with—with my hand." Culhane sat down next to her.

"When Father died, it was like that for me. Do you know, Richard told me of the park you bought on Repulse Bay and the statue dedicated to our father. Richard has seen it. What a wonderful thing for you to do. 'A perfect likeness,' he says, 'and twelve feet tall.' "

"I would have made it a hundred if they'd let me." Ten years ago he'd created that park, though it seemed only months.

"A grand thing to do. We are very honored."

"Not much, Jia, not for him . . . Tell me, did you ever marry? Do I know Michael's mother? Many times I wanted to contact you and Richard and I didn't for fear of getting you in trouble."

"For ten years, during the Cultural Revolution, it was a vulgar and dangerous time. You couldn't have found us," answered Jia, drawing a forefinger across her graceful throat. "And yes, I married soon after Father sent us here from Hong Kong. My husband was the commanding general of the Shanghai Military District. He died in North Vietnam."

"I'm sorry," said Culhane, noting her careful omission about Michael's mother.

"We hardly ever saw each other." Jia laughed sensitively.

"No children?"

"He was away a lot."

"A general, eh?" Culhane was pensive. "Was he good for you?"

"Sometimes."

"It's never meant to be all the time." Culhane let it go at that. He didn't want to know much more. "And what do you do now?" he asked.

"I'm teaching at Fudan University, where Michael goes."

"Teaching what things?"

"English, and translating English to Chinese for a local newspaper, the *Liberation Daily*."

Another newspaper bug, thought Culhane, a bit ruefully. "So many times I've thought about you and Richard. And when your father sent me to Africa and I came back to find you gone and him dead . . . It was a rough hour."

"It was time for us to come back here. Always that was his plan, and when the chance came he sent us."

"Why so important to come back?"

"At heart, you know, my father was a missionary. He abhorred the Maoists and always told us that we must come back, must be part of the force for change."

"And it helped."

"Things are changing," said Jia. "Though one week in China is a day anywhere else. Great resistance. You can't believe it sometimes."

A knocking sound from the hallway, like an object hitting the wall, and Jia tensed; her voice shook slightly with a barely audible "Oh."

Culhane followed her eyes as they went past him, coming to rest on Richard Ming. A wide familiar smile creased a face gone gray with exhaustion. Binocular-thick lenses rested on either side of the flaring nose, and his chest was sunken under a too loose suit of gray gabardine. A thin black tie skewed across his white shirt.

Richard Ming stumped forward awkwardly, holding a cane, unable to bend his knees. One arm was shorter than the other.

My old friend has sent his ghost, thought Culhane. God bedded in hell, what's happened! He shot up from the divan and moved swiftly to his almost-brother.

"Richard!"

The cane dropped. "My day and my year are both blessed. Ah, Rushton, so long for us." Richard Ming leaned his tormented body against Culhane.

"What's happened?" Utterly appalled, Culhane squinted now.

"Past troubles. All of them gone now. Let us sit and have some of Jia's tea. I have smelled it for an hour already. My nose is still perfect." Again the quaint grin as he looked at Culhane.

With laborious effort, which he insisted on making by himself, Richard sat on the floor to one side of the low tea table. His legs lay as inertly straight as two matchsticks. Culhane looked helplessly at Jia, who nodded very slightly.

"So," said Richard, raising his cup, "welcome at last to Shanghai. *Aii-oo,* we waited twenty cat's-years for you." Richard drank in the Chinese custom, slurping the monkey tea through his ever-present smile.

"A huge day for me too, Richard. And I'm impressed with your son, and I thank you for all the help over the past months. Made a great difference."

A fleeting look exchanged with Jia, and Richard said, "A good profit for our Shanghai Development Corporation, too."

"As it should be," said Culhane.

"You asked for some word on our old friend, Herbsant. It

cannot be true that he was involved in the despicable killing of your dear family?"

"It's a ruse of some kind, believe me. Has to be."

"A man of many ruses," said Richard. "Well, what I'm told is that he went to France. He made contact with a KGB resident agent in Paris. He disappeared somewhere and is believed to be out of that country."

Culhane jacknifed off the divan. He stood there, taut and nervous, then walked across to the window.

Sant knew the core of all the plans. Now the danger of discovery went off the scale. Culhane scowled into the dimming afternoon, watching a large junk tack its way across the river.

"Anything more?" Culhane asked, turning back to Richard, and barely noticing Jia now.

"No. Does it mean anything to you?"

"Yes and no. I could break his slippery head."

"Not a good place to be, with those Russians, unless, of course, he's seeking asylum . . . Interpol is alerted, you know."

"I do know. Tell me, Richard, what happened to you? I want to, hell, I just want to know."

But it was Jia who spoke up. "It was during the time of the Red Guards. For a while I was protected because of who my husband was. But Richard was imprisoned in a closet for a year, then beaten daily, and finally thrown into a bamboo cage for another year and forced to wear a . . . a big dunce's hat."

Culhane shook his head sadly. "Couldn't you have gotten word to me? I would have come for you. We could've helped . . ."

"Not a chance you'd set one foot in China. Not then," said Jia.

"Probably not," agreed Culhane. "But I could have sent men out of Macao. Or Shang-Magan would have ransomed you."

"We all learned something from it," said Ricahrd. "It was almost worth it."

"Learned what? What a broken head feels like?"

"That terrorizing is the whip of the truly weak. In the end they destroyed each other," replied Richard, adding, "and if you survive, as I did, you actually gain great face, and not a small amount of influence, too."

"A hell of a price to pay."

"Not as heavy as you think. Suffering is a good school for learning how to use one's remaining time on earth. And we've much to do here in China."

Compassion, like a cathartic, took hold of Culhane. Seeing this wreck of a fine man partly scrubbed him of his own sorrows.

"And where were you, Jia?"

"Michael and I hid on Shing-yun Dan Island. You can see it up the river, off to your left. The small one. We lived in a vault under one of the deserted homes for most of a year. Then we were found, and sent to work on a farm commune by Nanking."

"Mao set us back, but we became stronger," said Richard. "Everybody knew the Red Guards were out to ruin our civilization, our culture, everything we were trying to rebuild. In the end, as I say, they lost."

"But did you win?"

"I win," said Richard, "now that you are here."

"You're incurable." Culhane grinned at him.

"No, I'm a very sound businessman. And if I'm not, don't let anyone know it, or I'll be thrown out of my job," said Richard.

"Tell me about the Shanghai Development Corporation," he asked, as Jia slipped away for more tea.

Richard Ming ran him through the ropes of what this government corporation did: how it promoted trade for the Shanghai district, financed factories, and survived only by deceiving the central government in Beijing.

"And you are the managing director?"

"Yes, but my influence is really as a member of the Central Economic Planning Committee in Beijing. I was there all last week discussing your stupefying plan. And I spent an afternoon with President Deng, who is most, ah, interested, Rushton."

"Good."

"Many problems remain," cautioned Richard. "I must inform you the negotiators from Beijing will be delayed two days. They await final instructions."

"Because of the size of the undertaking?" A two-day delay, dammit!

"Beijing is one long train of suspicious bureaucrats.

270

Things are slow sometimes." Richard Ming tapped his head. "Up here."

Jia came back into the room. "We'll have *dim sum* soon," she said, "and then chicken in the Shanghai style. And no more business tonight." She spoke regally, very certain of herself.

Struggling to get up, Richard said, "Tonight and tomorrow you stay with us. When the others arrive from Beijing, it is better that you move to the hotel."

"Well, I don't want to inconvenience you."

Another toothy smile and Richard said, "I've talked already to the Jinjiang Hotel. They know you're not coming tonight. And we can see more of you this way."

"Where is Michael?" asked Culhane.

"At the student dormitory. You will use his room."

And they ate, talked, ate more, and drank rice wine until it was so late that Richard Ming was forced to excuse himself. An old circle of friendship was annealed again in those hours. A Ming trait. They were bred for loyalty, courtesy, and perpetuity.

Culhane awoke early the next morning under the fur of Michael Ming's wolf pelt. His mind turned to Sant, then to Muir Tomlinson. Three more days before he could call for the result, if any, on the grain-oil deal with Russia. Would they fall for it? And Andrea, what of her on this day, though it would be night for her now. The Blue Dollar! Van Slyke. So much to get done, all of it in different parts of the world, and time was his surest enemy now.

He kicked back the covers, strode across the cold wooden floor, and entered the surprisingly large bathroom. He wondered what English family lived here some fifty years earlier. Ten minutes later he was dressed in flannel trousers, a tan cashmere turtleneck, and a pair of bench-made Maxwell moccasins.

Leaving the bedroom, going down the hall, he heard stirrings in the kitchen. Entering, he saw Jia in a yellow woolen robe, puttering around an old wood-burning stove. Not one glossy black hair was out of place on her lowered head.

"So early," she said, looking up from the stove.

"A habit I can't shake."

"Some tea and pineapple? Or an egg?"

271

"Thanks, no. I'm going to take a walk, and you look lovely."

A demure look from Jia behind her smiling eyes. She was something, he thought, in a quick recollection of those days in Hong Kong, when they loved until limp as jellyfish.

"Richard would like to meet with you later at his office."

"Has he told you anything, Jia, of what I'm here to discuss?"

"We have no secrets from each other. A fantastic thing. Sometime I'd like to give you an idea or two. Is that presumptuous?"

"Not at all. I'll walk around and then we can visit. How about lunch at the Old Prosperity?"

"You know of that one, do you?"

"I've heard about it. A date?"

"Of course."

After he had gone, Jia sat on a stool by a small butcher's block. Picking up the *Liberation Daily,* she saw headlines blurting the news of an earthquake in western China, one thousand feared dead. China, she thought, the Heavenly Empire that was a constant maelstrom. And now Rushton Culhane.

Jia could feel the tiny flames licking away. To see him again was a breeze of sweetness; to feel him a typhoon of temptation. Absurd after all these years. Not the wild buccaneer he was two decades ago, but not far distant from it either. Yet misery tapped at the back of those dragon's eyes now.

He will have to *know* and *soon,* thought Jia, and she wondered how to broach this truth that he must know. How would he react? I must talk again with Richard, she decided.

Walking around for three hours, Culhane covered two of Shanghai's ten districts, crossing Suzhou Creek several times, then retracing his steps toward the harbor. Junks, drayage sampans, freighters flying enough colors to shame a rainbow; muddy waters, the aroma of refuse, the smell of sea life; memories, then, of a hundred ports he'd sailed into during his youth. But never this one—the Rotterdam of China.

Dragging himself away from a scene he loved, the living

portrait of trade, he walked onward to the Bund. He knew what went on behind the facades of those grand buildings some fifty years earlier. Drafts were exchanged, bills of lading drawn, ships chartered, compradors wheedled and fought for their hongs, alliances were begun and enemies earned. Glamorous women strolled under silk parasols on the wide walkways, while Daimlers and Rolls-Royces motored up the great boulevard and rickshaws were pulled everywhere by cone-headed coolies.

Drinks at the Shanghai Club, with the longest bar in the world, a hundred elbows leaning on it, where walrus-mustached Englishmen complained about business, the upstart Americans, and the deplorable French, who always had the most beautiful Eurasian mistresses.

To Culhane, it was a chapter he'd missed but had lived through somehow in other dreams. This is my city, he thought. And on he went, plugging his way along on the sidewalks clogged with people. The windows of the side streets were full of embroidered silks, watchbands, rock-and-roll tapes from Hong Kong, transistor radios. Small storefronts of dressmakers and palmreaders. Street cleaners sweeping the curbsides and painters up on scaffolding freshening the trim on brick buildings. Hawkers sold everything from fireworks to condoms.

Even more than yesterday, all of his senses were fitting into an alluring mosaic. Better and more fun than his first day in Hong Kong, half a life ago.

Now for Jia, and he quickened his step.

Two days later the negotiators arrived from Beijing, and Culhane had moved to the Jinjiang Hotel, in the center of what once was the old French settlement. Nixon and Chou En-lai in 1972 signed the Shanghai Communiqué there, though not much important had happened since between China and the U.S.

He'd met with them the morning after their arrival in a dingy government office building three blocks behind the Bund. Slow, deliberate talk, in the Mandarin tongue, and all of it in the classic Chinese style of bargaining: feint, outfox, close in on any slipup, however small.

You must appeal to their pride, their deep sense of nationalism. Right or wrong, they think of themselves as the eternal guardians, not as "Rice Christians." None of them

273

has forgotten the days of the unequal treaties when China had to give up her ports to foreigners. Remember, Shanghai itself was divided into four foreign concessions. Foreigners are still barbarians.

A size-up session. They were breaking for lunch and would meet again early the following morning. Tomorrow Richard would join them, a good signal, Culhane knew, as it meant they would finally get down to real business.

Culhane went back to the hotel, where he had arranged to meet Michael Ming. He climbed the winding steps toward the columned entrance. Michael stood at the top, his wavy dark hair blowing about in the slight wind, his face sturdy and resolute against the frosty air. He wore a dark blue anorak.

"Let's go up to Nanjing Road," called Culhane in the Mandarin high-song.

"It will be terribly crowded now," answered Michael.

"I know. That's why I want to go."

Michael bobbed his head dubiously and started down the stairs. "Aren't you cold?" he asked, seeing that Culhane wore only a blue pin-striped business suit.

"I have strange insulation. Usually I neither get cold nor too hot."

"Come to western China. You will change your mind perhaps."

"One day I'll go with you. You can bag me a wolf pelt."

"Auntie Jia said you walked through Africa once. Must have been interesting."

They dodged a truck loaded with live chickens and ducks in wooden cages as Culhane replied, "Quite interesting. I was doing some work for your grandfather. I doubt if I'd ever try that walk again, though.

"I see. What did you do last night?"

"I studied for a while and later on I ran through part of the city. Night is a good time to learn about a city. Long ago I learned about Beirut and Tangiers that way."

"What do you look for at night?"

"A hundred things, things like the rhythm of the city. But mostly to learn my way around. Last night, two policemen stopped me and asked if I was sick or lost or both."

Michael laughed discreetly. "What else?"

"I saw some of the night trade. Men were gathered around small fires on Dalian Road just above Lu Xun's

274

Tomb. They had their carts, full of what-all, and they traded. I watched. I couldn't understand everything they were saying, but I knew what they were up to."

"Way up there? A long way. It's illegal what they do."

"They trade to survive, Michael."

"I suppose," replied Michael, thinking of his own dealings in western China.

"One night we should get ourselves a cart and go up there. Watch out for that one!" shouted Culhane.

A small man was pushing a wooden cart pell-mell through the crowd. Stopping until it passed, they watched the pusher's powerful legs spinning around like a slot machine.

"We might not be welcomed up there. I'm only half Chinese, and you are none at all," Michael was saying amid the street noise.

They turned on to Nanjing Road, once the street of notorious nightclubs like Delmonte's and Farren's, opium dens, gambling casinos, and fastidious whorehouses. It was still the city's best shopping area, alive now, like a burning beehive.

Michael Ming was in awe. Beirut. Tangiers. Africa. He knew a good many things about Cul-sjane, hearing them often from his father and auntie. Especially from his auntie, who told him of how his grandfather had thought this American to be a natural talent. Here, now, was the man interested in so small a thing as Shanghai's night hawkers.

"Do you have a girlfriend?" asked Culhane.

"A good friend. Teng-li Fwen. She is a student in radio astronomy at Fudan University. Highest honors," added Michael, nobly, "and her father is a foreman at the Seagull Textile Factory."

They neared a restaurant, the Yangzhou, famous for its wild duck, which Culhane wanted to try.

"An astronomer, eh? C'mon, let's go in here and split a beer. I'd like to hear about your Teng-li. Bring her to dinner tonight."

They passed through the door into a din of frenetic talk and smells that were sweet, sour, fragrant, and acrid. A queer notion overtook Michael Ming. Some deep force drew him to this American.

32

Shanghai

The third and last round of the negotiations. Culhane had given the Beijing officials the floor on the day before, listening for what wasn't said, trying to find where the ballast of the deal could be shifted or couldn't. Their words were hobnails; a durable team of dealers, which told him they were interested ones.

It wasn't easy trying to paint new visions in the heads of men who'd spent their youth on long marches. Yet Culhane knew he must keep trying to persuade them. They were born doubters, the two of them from Beijing anyway. Meek and studious, Richard Ming sat at the head of the table, more or less silent, no smiles this time.

"No," Culhane was saying, "the minimum period is for ten years with a mutual option for another five. We both have something the other needs. That's where we begin. Look what you're getting: two hundred fifty billion old dollars' worth of all the technology and machinery you want. Handled right, you can enlarge your harbors, fix up your airports, your roads, your whole communications system. You'll have the best factories in Asia."

"And if we want other things?" said Xiang Xiao, the guant one, whose lopsided jaw must have been kicked too hard once.

"You can have milk cows if you want them," said Culhane. "There are sixteen hundred items we can supply you with. Take your choice up to two hundred fifty billion dollars. If we don't have it on hand, I'll get it for you."

"You are asking us to save your decrepit capitalist system with our oil," argued Xiao.

"Your oil but our know-how to get it out of Chinese waters and lands. You don't have the technology, and we both know it."

"Look at your country today. A shambles." More rhetoric from Xiao, the nut-cutter.

Stay on track, Culhane told himself. This bastard just wants his ass kissed.

"You've a billion people here. A billion brains with their two billion hands and legs. All of North America, Europe, and Russia taken together doesn't have as many. You have a resource in your countrymen that is immeasurable. You can lift them. You, you men, can do that. Look south to Hong Kong and Taiwan. See what your brother Chinese have done. You can do it better. You can be the greatest trading nation in the world."

"You do not understand China," said Zhang, the one with the moon face and lips that never seemed to close. "We progress a stage at a time. Firmly and without risk."

"I'll tell you what, Quo Zhang—ask the children of this country what they'd like. Ask of yourselves what sort of a country you will give your grandchildrn. China is indeed rich in tradition. Don't be blinded by it." A little warning hiss then from Richard Ming. "All your fears, your doubts and suspicions, are they to get in the way of your main chance?"

"And why would the United States do this for China?" asked Zhang.

Culhane went on unperturbed. "Simple. We want your surplus oil until we can develop long-term alternate energy sources. That's number one. Number two is we want to put our people back to work producing things you need."

"You talk here of a long-term alliance—ten years, you said."

"It'll take more than a year to get everything organized and flowing. It's different, yes. Large? Very. That means time. It's not a deal you'll get elsewhere. Certainly not in Moscow." Culhane dug that point in hard. "And if you think so, then you'd better go butter your rice with reality." A louder hiss from Richard Ming.

"What has Moscow to do with it?" complained Quo Zhang.

"You tell me. They've got over a hundred divisions massed on your northern borders. You'll never keep them at bay unless you strengthen your own defenses. To do that, you've got to improve your industrial base."

"Would the United States furnish us with weapons systems?" asked Xiao.

"Defensive ones, possibly. We're trying to get trade going, not another war."

"We must think and consult with others," said Zhang.

"Don't think too long. The fuse if burning."

"Where else would you go, Cul-sjane?"

"I've signed a Memorandum of Accord with Mexico—a hundred fifty billion dollars' worth. There are other places for us to trade."

"Such as?" asked Xiao.

"Such as that's my business," shot back Culhane, reaching for some fruit juice. His mouth felt as if it had spent half a day under a hair dryer.

Xiao stiffened. His low forehead seemed to drop another inch toward glowering eyes. "Your economy may not last ten or fifteen years."

"I agree," said Zhang. "That is a danger. Aren't you forgetting that, overlooking it?"

"Not at all, Xiang Xiao. We're in trouble, but we're going to work our way out of it. You—you've been in trouble for fifty years. More even."

Richard Ming closed his eyes.

"And now you are proposing a unity of opposites?" asked Zhang.

Culhane chuckled softly. "Yes. Yin and Yang. Very Chinese."

Now Quo Zhang blinked rapidly and observed, "I'm not so sure, Cul-sjane."

"As I say, ask your children. Ask them if they'd like to own a refrigerator, a four-room house of their own, or a fur coat. Go to Paris or London just once during their lifetime . . . If they say no, they wouldn't, then I agree we have nothing more to discuss."

Xiao and Zhang looked at each other, then at Richard

Ming. Finally, their collection of agate-brown eyes rested upon Culhane.

"We return tonight to Beijing. You'll have an answer within two days," said Zhang.

"Thirteen *old* dollars at the barrel." Culhane lifted his hands, opening them in a gesture of resignation, and smiled at Richard Ming, who just nodded gravely.

A short distance from the Jinjiang Hotel, the U.S. Consulate looked forlorn and lonely in its stone building. Late afternoon now, and Culhane bounded up the steps, unsure that he was ready for Muir Tomlinson's answer. Hormuz!

Showing his passport and a letter of accommodation signed by Halburton, he was immediately led into the counsul general's office. A fresh-faced man eager for something to do greeted Culhane like an undertipped doorman who had just found his mark.

A brief shake of hands, while Culhane asked, "I need a secure line to Sydney, Australia."

"You'll have to patch through our embassy in Beijing."

"Any way you can do it is fine," said Culhane anxiously.

The consular official picked up his phone, issuing orders to someone. Hanging up, he escorted Culhane to a soundproof room down the hall.

Eleven minutes later Culhane had his answer from the courtly Muir Tomlinson: the American grain was to be shipped to Murmansk; the crude oil would be loaded on U.S. tankers at Abadan, a port at the top of the Persian Gulf, north of the Straits of Hormuz. The Russians won the taller end of the trade, but they'd taken Culhane's poisoned bait to get it.

He spent the next call briefing a sleepy, apprehensive Halburton, then put in a third one to Andrea.

"Where are you?" she asked, gravel dust in her voice too.

"The Far East."

"I've been bounced at the paper."

A pause. *Flickinger, you son of a bitch.* "Just hang on. I'll be back in a week or two. Frédy will take care of you."

"The hell with Frédy. My career just got sewer-piped."

"I'm sorry, Andrea. I can't do much from here."

"Hurry home, Rushton, it's cold. Very boring, too, with nothing to do."

"Soon as I can. Bye. A kiss for love."

"What a mess!"

"We'll fix it somehow, don't worry. I'll call you soon."

He put the phone down. God, she must feel spiked all the way through. She needs a friendly rub. Bring her to Europe? Not enough time for it.

A southerly wind floated warmer air into Shanghai's fickle climate. An old woman poled a sampan through the choppy Huangpu River waters as night broke out with a rash of stars. The city's lights radiated even stronger beams, and from the harbor the running and mooring lights of ships and junks flickered like a computer display board. Red, green, a thousand twinkling whites, and the black waters reflected the lights as if they were shafts of burning fire.

Culhane crouched in the stern of the sampan. Next to him was Jia, and a few feet away and facing them sat Richard, with his legs extended. The old creased woman poling the boat stood on a stern platform, working her long oar in soft sucking sounds as water slurped against the sampan's low sides.

"Like Typhoon Shelter Bay in Hong King," said Culhane.

"Better food here," said Richard.

"Over there, that little islet, Rushton, is Shing-yun Dan, where Michael and I hid," said Jia.

He could barely see the island's rising outline. No light shone there. "I'd like to see it during the day sometime. Shing-yun means lucky, does it?"

"Tomorrow perhaps," answered Jia, her fingers tapping nervously on the seat. "Yes, it means lucky. Actually, it was called Shing-yun Dan—for Lucky Island—but the British shortened it to Shing-Dan, and the name stuck."

The sampan slipped smoothly into a cluster of others surrounding a kitchen boat. Pods and pods of the sampans, festooned with paper lanterns, extended for a mile or more. As the breeze changed direction, the smell of fish cooking was almost strong enough to land an airplane on.

"You like it?" asked Jia. "We thought it would be fun for you."

"It's enchanting. Perfect." Culhane smiled back at Jia:

281

she looked so China, a lotus flower with skin like the blush on yellow pear.

"I came here the first time with my father in 1947," said Richard Ming. "I can remember the year easily. Butter was seven hundred fifty thousand Chinese dollars a pound, and apples a million for the same weight. He owned six kitchen boats, which was the only reason we ate."

Culhane thought briefly of America, the inflation and hunger there. A lithe young waiter jumped from the next sampan to theirs. In Shanghainese, he recited a prodigious menu.

Jia ordered, and Culhane caught most of her words: stuffed sesame cakes, beef dumplings, clams in fermented black bean sauce, cockles in shrimp sauce, drunken sea bream, oysters, and eight-jeweled rice.

A raft bumped up against their sampan, and a bored lady offered drinks. They settled on liter bottles of Tsing Tao beer and tea.

A smaller boat sidled by with three musicians plinking notes on their two-string lyres. Shouts echoed from the next sampan, over the furious click of mah-jongg tiles. China, alive, older than Eden.

"Beer or tea?" asked Jia.

"Beer please," said Culhane. She poured for him and then tea for Richard, while the old woman put a board covered with oilcloth between them.

Taking Culhane's hand, Jia stared for a long moment at Richard, who nodded covertly.

"There is something important you must know, Rushton . . . It's about Michael."

"Go ahead."

"You are his natural father and I'm his mother," said Jia, directly and quickly, as if the words were too big to hold in her mouth.

Culhane's beer spilled. Seeing the truthful look in Richard's face, he was numb. Not so! Hammering in his head. An instant later—Oh, yes, yes, God, I hope so! Let this be! His shock was pinned with holy joy.

"I can guess at your surprise," said Jia calmly, watching him, "but there is more to it."

"I'd like to know it all." Giddy, a hundred sensations fought for supremacy inside him. A son, mine.

"When Father sent you to Africa," she began, "I learned

282

that a child was to come from us. Richard said I must tell Father. I did, and then he speeded the arrangements for our coming to Shanghai a month after the baby was born."

"Why . . . why didn't someone tell me, Jia?" asked Culhane, still weak.

"Father insisted on silence. But we tried anyway. No one knew exactly where you were. Even a call to Mr. Muldaur, and he said you were up in the Transvaal somewhere, headed for Rhodesia."

"I made the call," confirmed Richard.

"Why didn't you wait for me to return to Hong Kong?"

"Because Father said you would fight me there. And he wanted us back here to do the work he wanted done for China."

"God, he must have hated me," said Culhane, trying to regain himself, confused yet happy.

"No, he loved you, Rushton. You were his second son." Jia tightened her hand around his.

"Tell me, why does Michael think you're his aunt and that you, Richard, are his father?" Culhane could feel his breath shorten.

"An unmarried woman with a half-Chinese child would've had a hard time of it here. Michael might have been taken from me. So Richard agreed to claim Michael as his son by a white woman from Hong Kong. It was the only way."

"The sensible course," said Richard, "better for everyone. Besides, in those days you would not have been allowed into China, Rushton. That is why you weren't told."

Culhane could see the sense of it. But still, the revelation shocked him—a son he hadn't known about for over twenty years. Not the first time in history that had happened, he knew, yet it changed one's blood pressure all the same.

"Does Michael know, even gueas?"

"No, I think not," answered Richard, "and the three of us have an excellent relationship. He is my son in the way you were my father's son. But he believes I am his true father."

So Chinese, thought Culhane. Bred for loyalty, the family always coming first.

"And he should not know unless . . ." said Jia.

"Unless what?"

"Unless you decide to come live with us in China," said Richard.

"Here in Shanghai?"

"Yes, here," returned Jia innocently, her face empty of guile, and precariously angelic now.

"Technically speaking," said Culhane, "China belongs to Liu Wai's trading zone. So there's a Shang-Magan problem right off the top."

"Not at all," replied Richard. "China belongs only to China." And fervidly, Richard Ming imparted other information about Liu Wai's operations on the China-Burma border.

"That's actual fact?" asked Culhane.

"Liu Wai would never be welcomed in China. Not ever!" said Jia vehemently.

Culhane gazed at Richard, absorbing the implication, then said, "It would take a long-ton of thought."

"Even so, we must do nothing to upset Michael," insisted Jia. "I refuse to disillusion him. You can surely understand why."

"I respect that," replied Culhane, acutely aware of his own beginnings, the trauma of not knowing who he really was and where he belonged.

"We need you, Rushton," said Richard. "We may be the oldest nation, yet in some ways the youngest . . . An eternity of progress to catch up on."

"I tried to tell that to your pals from Beijing. They didn't seem convinced."

"You were more persuasive than you might think. A little tough, too, I might say."

"Stubborn boys."

"Believe you of me, though, it's not every day when a round-eye comes with two hundred fifty billion dollars of trade to discuss."

Culhane laughed. But it was of Michael Ming that he thought.

"What you are offering," said Richard, "could bring China a long way forward. President Deng knows it, I know it, so do others."

"You think Beijing will buy it?"

Richard Ming hung back for a moment, lifting his teacup, sipping. "It depends on whether they think the U.S. can finance its end. A proposition like that, well . . ." Richard shrugged. "Never before in history . . . China would lose great face if we signed and it all sank on us."

"Yes, and so would America."

"Can you?"

"We'll have to," replied Culhane. Blue Dollar! he thought. It all pivots on the bluff, the big gambit.

"We need help to develop our external trade. We don't have the experience, don't know the markets. We're essentially agrarian."

"You'll always do fine, Richard. On that score I have zero worries." Jia poured more beer, and Culhane casually saluted Richard Ming, who said:

"I am slowly going blind. Maybe a year from now, say the doctors."

Culhane had guessed as much, seeing the thick pink glasses Richard wore. "Have you seen . . ."

"From here to everywhere, including visiting specialists from Europe and Japan. It is a degenerative disease that can't be arrested. A nutrition problem."

"The Red Guard days?"

Richard nodded.

"The bastards."

"No, Rushton, I am happy. The work is very hard, but I truly feel I'm helping our people find their place." Richard Ming grinned, bone-white teeth showing. "A little mouth-to-mouth resuscitation, you see. And it is as my father would have wanted it . . . I hope you will come. We could wave a good baton together."

"Would your government really want me hanging around?"

"I have reason to believe so. You are better known in China than you think. They remember the archeological expedition you financed up on the Ancient Silk Road, and when you helped us with grain on credit . . . They don't forget."

Culhane guzzled more beer, thinking hard: Michael Ming and his pretty Teng-li, with whom he'd dined at the hotel two nights earlier. A future? China's future? Isn't that what I told the bargainers from Beijing today? Whatever in hell would Andrea say?

33

Shanghai

On the next afternoon Culhane and Jia strolled on the uninhabited islet of Shin-yun Dan, unaware that this would be his last full day in Shanghai. She'd taken him to the small island at his request, so that he could see where she and Michael had lived during China's lost decade. A sort of summer sanctuary for the wealthy French and British until 1939 or so; abandoned during the Japanese Occupation; for a while in the late forties used again by the Red Army.

"You say Red Army. Is that how you call it?"

"In front of you. Not the government, I wouldn't say it to them." Spiritedly, she went right on, "Those are some of the villas. The big one there was the residence of the Shan Chu of the British East India Company."

The porticos sagged, shutters had fallen to the ground, weeds grew waist high. But the masonry work, Culhane saw, appeared sound. They were ambling down a cracked walkway that bordered a long winding hedgerow. Below, the water rolled up against a wall of heavy rocks and cement slabs. A fine spray swiped off the rocks, some of it catching on Jia's coat until Culhane moved her away.

There she was, grandly, across the waters. Shanghai! Culhane thought of Marco Polo, yet this great city had been no more than a fishing hamlet during the Italian adventurer's time in China. Some little phantom, like a dream trying to break loose from a cocoon, knocked on the doors of his imagination.

"There's the old French Catholic church, what's left of it. Big arguments with the British over what kind of religion to have here." Jia looped an arm under his as they turned at the top of the islet. "That's where we hid, Michael and I." She pointed with her free hand toward a stone cottage with a big green door, set into a copse of tall poplars and barren cherry trees.

"In a vault, did you say?" he asked.

"A big wine vault—without any wine, of course. It was where the head of the commissary once lived. There's a sort of store there off to the side. See?"

"Yes." A low-slung building made of the same limestone, quarried in Nanking and sent hundreds of miles down the Yangtze to build the city of Shanghai. "Shall we sit for a minute?" suggested Culhane.

They found a weathered wooden bench, facing out to the much larger Chongming Island, and Culhane told Jia, "I'm honestly pleased you told me about Michael. It means everything to know I have a son left."

"Our son."

"And that you are his mother. You and Richard have done a wonderful job with him."

"He is our pleasure, always will be, and now yours perhaps."

Culhane changed the subject, asking, "How long has Richard got, Jia?"

"It's in God's hands. A few years with luck, if he doesn't kill himself with work first." Tears smeared her eyes. Culhane threw an arm across her shoulders. "It's why he needs you," snuffled Jia, "one reason, anyway."

"I need to really think about it."

"A woman?"

"Yes and no-yes. Other matters too."

"America, you wish to stay there of course?"

"I have nothing for or against America. It's a place. I was born in one of her territories, at least then it was, so that makes me her citizen . . . Not her puppet."

"Still, they must think much of you to send you on such immense mission."

288

Culhane smiled. "And they got me when I wasn't looking."

Jia made no answer. Culhane sat silently, scanning the distance. He watched as two gulls cavorted aimlessly over the sluggish brown waters. And he thought, That is how I want to be: free, unchained, able to do what I damn please. Yet always there seems some mystical tug of events that lassos my godforsaken life.

Jia nestled inside his arm, as she'd once nestled in his bed; the wonderful craving bed of youth.

"I'll think hard about coming here," said Culhane, breaking their quiet. "I can't make any promises yet. And much would depend upon your government . . . Can you do two things for me?"

"Yes, if I can. Of course."

And Culhane gave her the first of his requests.

Jia gasped, disbelieving her ears. "You mean that?" she asked.

"Just a preliminary inquiry. No more," cautioned Culhane. "You know how it's done."

A higher blush came at the compliment. Intrigued, Jia added, "It would take some finagling . . . My father was right about you."

"How so?"

"You somehow can see two worlds at the same time."

"You mean he could. Not me, I'm sorry to say."

"You're more alike than you might think . . . Now, what is the second thing?" asked Jia, still exuberant.

"Somewhere in Laos are forty-one missing American soldiers. Alive. They've been illegally held there since the finish of Vietnam. I don't care what it takes to do it, but I want them back home. That's a favor I need from your government, and it will never be forgotten by me."

He felt her move as she said, "That might be terribly hard. The Seventh Heaven would have to be moved."

"Then let's move it."

"Did you discuss this prisoner matter with the men from Beijing?"

"I wanted to, but there was no way I could make it a condition to the deal I proposed."

"I will try. But you mustn't raise your hopes. How do you know the prisoners are still there?"

289

"The Shang-Magan was told so by Liu Wai. His information is usually good."

"I must discuss it with Richard. You understand?"

"Yes, he would have to know," said Culhane.

Jia put a hand to his face. Both his arms encircled her slender body. This time it was no affectionate embrace of old friends. They went well into each other's mouths, deeply, and the flame of guilt seared at Culhane.

Dusk spread its gray guaze over the Bund's skyline as the sampan dropped them at a pier near the old Broadway Mansions. For those few secluded hours, he'd evicted Jia from the Chinese woman's traditional shell of reserve.

She had told him many things, interesting and subtle ones, and of her hopes, and of what dreams she spun. Paris, Hong Kong, London, none of those illusory places held the slightest charm for her anymore. She was Shanghai. China to the last stitch of the soles on her slippered feet, and with a native cunning, both Chinese and feminine.

Up the stairs they went into the Mansions, her hand in Culhane's and Jia not caring who saw it. Coming through the apartment door, they heard Richard groaning. And a few hurried strides later, saw him with his back against a wall, lifting weights. He was dressed in a crimson cotton sweat suit.

Slowly, evenly, he lowered the dumbbells to the floor, took a lungful of breath, and said, "A call for you, Jia, from the university." A ring of perspiration gathered around his mouth as he told Culhane, "Deng asks that you fly to Beijing tomorrow on the first plane. They will sign with one provision. They want proof America can finance her side of the trade."

Culhane knuckled his lower lip, calculating rapidly. "We'll do it in ninety, maybe sixty days."

"You are sure?" warned Richard.

"No, I can't be positive. But it's what I'd bet."

"There is another message for you, Rushton, over there. Michael has left on a field trip to Nanchang to observe shapes of something or other . . . I trust they aren't women," finished Richard Ming wryly.

Going to the table, Culhane picked up Michael's message. The thought of leaving gored at him. Not seeing Michael to say good-bye sank his heart too. Culhane gripped himself: no sooner had he found his other family again than he was forced to abandon it.

Alone again.

34

Amsterdam
London
Zurich
Oranienburg
Zanzibar

A third of the way around the world in little more than a day. Seeing the familiar landmarks of the city, Culhane knew he would arrive at Van Slyke's town house in a few minutes.

Strangely, he suffered no jet lag as yet, and supposed that adrenaline was still irrigating his system after Deng's ministers had conditionally signed the Memorandum of Accord. Of course, there still remained the question of a stable U.S. dollar. Yet he was reasonably certain an answer could be found, if only Van Slyke and the Shang-Magan could be enticed into a blocking action.

The inking of the Accord in Beijing had proceeded without fanfare. Afterward a small luncheon, a visit with President Deng, and Culhane left the country as quietly as he'd entered it. He had stopped briefly at the U.S. Embassy to dispatch the Accord to Washington under the seal of the diplomatic pouch.

Important, what he'd done? It could be. In a sense, a piece of new cloth was woven out of tattered threads. Though as he'd watched the receding skies over China, nothing churned his hopes more than discovering Michael Ming. A gift, pure of its kind and exhilarating in its promise.

Just three more blocks to go now. The green Mercedes 600 rounded Kalverstrat, a lovely and now winter-misted avenue ending at the Dam, where the royal palace kept stately watch over the city. The limousine sported unmannered luxury: buffed suede seats, a six-band shortwave radio, a television over the walnut bar, two phones. Outside, on the driver's door, was an intaglio of a solid gold cricket circled by a wreath.

The driver turned left and smoothly rode the Mercedes to a stop before the four-story, gabled, red-tiled town house. And there to greet them, his cave of a mouth making a smiling dark hole in the great wash of beard, was the gargantuan Piet Van Slyke. Wearing cavalier's black boots up to his knees, dove-gray pants, a green frock coat over a yellow ruffled shirt, he was operatic. A man for a past century, a man who defied convention.

Culhane got out, hearing the booming voice, "You dampt stranger, come here so Van Slyke can put you in his hand." Two steps at a time, the huge Dutchman bounded down to the cobbled street. A polar bear couldn't have seemed larger.

"Hello there, big boy," replied Culhane.

"Come, we go up. I'm glad you called when you did. We almost missed. I'm to meet in Zanzibar soon with the others and I was to depart today." Van Slyke threw an arm around Culhane and literally lifted him up the steps. Two housemen wearing black coats trimmed in orange piping made way for them.

"We could've met in Cairo. That's right on the way to Tanganyika."

"Bah! How can a man talk there in Egypt? It takes four hours to move two blocks, and twice as long to make a simple phone call."

They entered the front hallway, which looked up to a staircase sided with gleaming brass railings. Van Slyke

294

led him across a double-thick Tashkent rug of cerulean blue with silver and rose designs splashed on it. Then into a room Culhane had always liked, where the walls were planked and grooved with forty rare woods from as many different countries. Huge furniture of Javanese mahogany crowded the floor, and up above a skylight of stained glass depicted scenes of seven continents. The elegance, like its owner, was gigantic.

Van Slyke stood in front of a roaring fireplace, the flames casting an orange light against facing onyx lions supporting the mantelpiece. "So," he opened, "you've been busy, I hear." He talked in German, knowing that Culhane's Dutch was limited.

Culhane thought, Look at him, I'm damned if he doesn't look like a Viking against that fire. And he said, "You're going to need an extra ear for what I have to tell you."

"At the meal we talk business . . . Now, will you have some good Dutch Genever or that goat's piss from Scotland?"

"The goat sounds fine, Piet."

Stretching an arm the length of a short bullwhip, Van Slyke pulled on a wall cord. Seconds later a house servant arrived, took the drink order, bowed politely, and left.

"And how was China? A good trip?"

"You should visit Shanghai, Piet. It's ready for something to happen."

Van Slyke's eyebrows arched. "They've never wanted the Shang-Magan there. Odd as hell when you think that's where we began it all."

"Maybe that will change. Anyway, Piet, I need a personal favor."

"This house is yours. Ask."

"Herbsant Saxa, my comprador, is missing. He was last seen in Europe meddling around with the KGB in Paris. I need to find him, get him back."

Van Slyke ran his cucumber fingers into the drape of beard, then said, "A political matter if he's with them. We never involve ourselves, you know."

"I do know. I just want to find out where he is. I'll take care of the rest of it."

"Against Russia?"

"Against anyone."

An earthquake of laughter made the room shout back as

295

if it were only narrow canyon walls. Van Slyke's shoulders finally stilled. "Ach, I'm glad you are not my enemy. Sleep would come slowly."

The drinks came. Culhane's was Glenlivet, the first he'd had since the time at Andrea's house. He took a heavy pull, letting its burn run deep.

"Can you help me?"

"I can think about it, can't I?" answered Van Slyke, tauntingly.

"Just thought I'd ask."

"A tender business, these political dealings."

"And I'd say you and Halburton did a damn good job of admitting me to your classroom," returned Culhane, his eyes cold blue as he fished for truth across the room.

Van Slyke, if possible, grew another three inches. His head rose and the great wedge of nose widened as if offended by an odious smell.

"That's an odd theory."

"You and I don't bullshit each other, Piet. I'd hate for it to start now."

Still watching, Culhane drank, sensing that he'd cornered Van Slyke. Yet he wouldn't be rude about it. He wanted nothing more than the truth.

Van Slyke asked, "How did you learn this?"

"Is it true, Piet? First tell me that."

"It is true. How did you learn?" repeated Van Slyke.

"From an intelligence jockey with the CIA. Name of Flickinger. He forgot to check his premises one day and he made a mistake."

"Those ox-turded, fumbling Russians. Gott! What a nuisance."

"Russians?" asked Culhane, puzzled.

"Flickinger, we know all about him. He's been paid by the Russians and French for years now. He is no danger to us, but a fumbler just the same."

"You're sure it's the same man?"

"Unless there're two of them. He sounds like the same one who's on file at the Inspectorate. Muldaur reported on it once a few years ago when this Flickinger was doing stupid things with the French in Algiers."

Culhane thought hard. How much did Flickinger know, guess at? Especially now that the KGB had their thumb on Saxa, whom they could slice up like a ripe brown melon.

And a small starburst exploded in his whipping thoughts: Andrea! What did she really know? *Jesus!*

"Why that look on your face? asked Van Slyke.

"Just dismay, Piet. I honored every uncovered Shang-Magan trade on the Chicago Board of Trade before it closed up. You all got out sweet clean while I held the wall for you. Then you rig it with Halburton so I'm forced to go to Washington to pry loose what's already owed me."

"Ours is no gentlemen's club where polite rules are observed in times of trouble."

"Very friendly . . . All the shit missed you and hit me, Piet. When I really needed help, you all vanished and then set me up."

Van Slyke moved away from the hot fire. He threw a curious look at Culhane, whom he regarded as the coolest mind in the business. Only then did he say:

"My investiture as Shan Chu, which thank God comes to an end soon, compels me to do all in my power, call on every resource, to protect the various trading zones. North America could be lost as a market. And you, my friend, were the only solution at hand. No one believed, least of all me, that you'd go to Washington voluntarily. Not if your government had already settled a lake of gold on you. Would you have?"

"Someone could've tried asking me."

"And you'd have refused. Do you deny it?"

"How can I tell?"

"You wouldn't have gone willingly. So pressure was applied to force you out of your lair."

"And what of my family, Piet, did you arrange for their fate too?" asked Culhane, angered, his face hard and his eyes changing to blue hoarfrost.

"That is beneath you."

"Sorry. I didn't really mean that." Culhane told himself to get hold of his emotions.

"We've made efforts to find out who was behind the killing of your wife and children. Sooner or later we will know," promised Van Slyke.

"I can settle my own scores."

"Don't be too proud to accept help. You could not begin to mount the resources that Magan can."

"I wish they'd loaned me some when I needed it."

"Why would we do that? We needed you in Washington,

297

not in California trying to hold a trading operation to-gether in a country going to hell."

"I don't much like getting used in that way, Piet."

"Who does? But it's the zone that comes first."

". . . Last and always," rejoined Culhane, still upset, but knowing the rules as well as his host.

One of the housemen appeared at the door. Conversation stopped, while the man announced, "Dinner is served, Myjn heer."

A starved family couldn't have hoped to finish the amount of food served in Van Slyke's home. A sideboard, running the length of the dining room, was loaded with ham, a glazed duckling, a tureen of farmer's soup, wheels of cheese, four kinds of dark bread, three chafing dishes of vegetables, and an enormous baron of beef. All this for two people. A riot would have started in Washington just from the smell of it.

Van Slyke gnawed a mouthful of duck breast, washing it down with beer.

"Since we're trading bedtime stories, Piet, you ought to know, if you don't, that Liu Wai is probably getting his narcotics financing through Switzerland."

"That makes what difference?"

"I'm pretty sure the source of the funding is American Mafia money harbored in Zurich. Someday one or more governments are going to get wind of it and there'll be trouble. And there goes the reputation of the Shang-Ma-gan and everyone sitting on the council."

"You can document it?"

"In a day or so I believe I can.'"

"I'd like a copy of your proof and then I'll talk to him about it."

"Isolating him is better."

"How can you isolate a man who controls half the world's exportable rice crop?"

"Cut it out, Piet. The bastard is the Snow White of all time."

"Button up your hard-on. Lead goes into bullets, too. Are we supposed to shut down the lead mines?"

"I'm not saying that."

Van Slyke put his elbows on the table, his arms looking like bent hitching posts. "We're not the moralists of this world. We're traders. If there's a market, we supply it."

298

"Not, by God, in a death-peddler's trade. That crock of lard helps pay for a proxy army up on the Burmese border."

"Liu Wai says it hasn't anything to do with him. We've asked. Take his word, too, just as we do yours."

"Really? Well, I'm taking the word of a man whom I trust completely." Culhane thought of what Richard Ming had told him a few nights previously.

More duck breast disappeared into the middle of the red beard, preventing Van Slyke from answering. He munched away, and the beard bobbed up and down like the shuttle on a loom. A napkin the size of a flag got waved across the mouth, followed by more gulps of beer.

"I'd like to see what you've got," said Van Slyke.

"You can have the proof, Piet, just find Sant Saxa for me. And if you'd ask Monte Carlo to send me what they've got on Flickinger. Fair?"

"Sounds it."

"Now to real business, all right?"

"Yes, let's hear it."

"The United States has fifty to sixty percent of the world's grain reserves," began Culhane. "I want to tie up under option the surplus crops of Canada, the Argentine, and Australia. For two years. Will Shang-Magan make the trade and finance the options?"

"A monopoly position?" Van Slyke shook his mane of pioneer-style hair. "You want us to assist in a blocking action?"

"Yes."

"You realize the furor it would cause?"

"Only in Russia. We'd be willing to resell what is needed to other countries."

"Take billions of guilders. Besides, the Russians have sent out buying missions already."

"And you think they can outpace the Shang-Magan? I hadn't thought of that." Culhane needled as hard as he believed he safely could.

Van Slyke turned a full shade of carmine. The beard, the nose, the cheeks were all the color of bright rust now. "A rather tortured statement, isn't it?" he asked.

"I don't know. I only know that if Moscow isn't stopped, brought to its senses somehow, then Shang-Magan will no longer have zones to protect. There won't be any."

"We are not unaware of the problem. We are discussing an accommodation with Moscow."

"Here's to your requiem," said Culhane, raising his glass halfheartedly. "Metzilov will crack your *cojones*. He might be good here and there for information, but not for anything big. Nothing that will last." Culhane folded his napkin. Any more food and he was sure he'd have to be pumped out.

"If the United States wants to monopolize grain as a political tool, why does it need us?"

"No credit. And it would be politically impossible to use gold for that purpose. Besides, you can do it faster than I ever could."

"Who knows if it could be done at all?"

"I think I do, Piet. I've studied it for months now and—"

"I don't suppose the U.S. could approach those countries directly anyway."

"Not without showing its hand," agreed Culhane.

"Exactly what is it you propose?" Van Slyke took down at least a quarter-liter of beer. Culhane wondered that he didn't drown.

"The Shang-Magan options the grain for the account of the U.S. A two-year deal. Negotiate a fair premium for the extra year in exchange for a ten-percent reduction of the option price if the market falls."

"And how do we get repaid?"

"By buying up to two billion in Eurodollars. No more. You will clear the equivalent of six billion of old dollars within the year."

Another low rumbling roar spilled into the room. An inhuman noise, it sounded like a cataract emptying itself over Victoria Falls. "You're trifling with me," said Van Slyke between gasps.

Culhane stared rigidly at his host, a look that sobered the Dutchman. "I don't think you've ever known me to joke over a matter like this."

"Even if I believed you could restore the dollar that quickly, the others would never accept it. Explain the details to me."

Culhane shook his head. "I can't and I won't. But I think it's going to happen, Piet."

"That's extremely difficult to accept."

Culhane only shrugged, but his eyes lit up.

"You are quite serious, aren't you."

"I'm going to spike Russia, Piet."

"Who will believe you?"

"That won't stop me. But I need to control the grain."

"And that's not all, my friend."

"No, that's not all."

"Give me more to go on. Speak, and speak precisely, please."

"I'll give you the best thing I've got—my word."

Van Slyke got up abruptly and went to the sideboard. With a silver knife he cut a piece of cheese the size of a slice of bread. The cheese vanished while the giant paced up and down behind Culhane.

True enough, considered the Dutchman, Culhane made mistakes the way anyone could and did. But he was the best of the lot when it came to styling the big ones. Yet, in all his years in the business, Van Slyke had never come across anything so wildly ambitious. Tying up the world's grain supplies had never before been attempted. Nor was he sure it could be done. And there were bound to be political storms of which the Shang-Magan wanted no part whatsoever.

"Give me some sign," said Van Slyke, stopping next to Culhane.

"Of what. The Cross? My chop? The U.S. government owes me three tons of gold. I'll forfeit it to the Shang-Magan if I'm wrong."

"You'd do that, truly?"

Culhane nodded. "If it's ever paid over, of course. But that's the only condition I'd lay down."

Daring, unpredictable, often reckless. Against that motif, however, there is no textbook defense and Van Slyke knew it. What was the Californian really up to?

"I may give up my chair on the council permanently," said Culhane absently.

"You will be Shan Chu one day. Perhaps our next one. So don't be idiotic." Visibly perturbed, Van Slyke returned to the other side of the table. "So you're saying it's between you and Liu Wai. That's our choice, is it?" He leaned over the table, with only his hands supporting his massive bulk. Lucifer come up to earth, thought Culhane, who observed Van Slyke's shoulders rolling slightly as if the man were about to perform some incredible feat of

301

strength. Yet Van Slyke had spoken softly, exasperated but softly—the schoolmaster coaching his thick-headed pupil on the real alphabet again.

"Not at all, Piet. It's between me and me."

"You give up your chair and it might go to Joe Rearden."

"No, it won't." Culhane decided he'd said enough. He could feel his eyes going bleary, and his body was still several time zones to the east.

"Be careful of that decision," warned Van Slyke.

"I'll mull it over, as you probably will the blocking action for the grain."

"Camero might object to all that wheat under your hand. He's the biggest now, you know."

"And he'll be even richer if he'll come along with us. I know he's fond of money."

"How long will you be in Europe?"

"A few days. London, Paris, Zurich . . . Piet, I apologize, but I need sleep."

"Of course. There are two pretty Javanese girls staying on the fourth floor, if you're interested."

"Ah, Piet," said Culhane, getting up, "there'll never be another one like you. I'll see you in the morning, and thanks for the damndest dinner ever served in Europe."

Van Slyke looked at him speculatively, remembering the words of advice he'd spoken to Halburton months earlier:

First trust him. Tell him everything important. Drive him, push him . . .

Now the words showed their other edge. The loss of Culhane could bring about serious damage to the Shang-Magan's future, and Van Slyke was well aware of it. Youth! They needed it to survive the hard years to come.

A diaphanous dream of silken legs, strange flute music, and water splashing into a pool. A sky dark as a ripe olive and dropping lower by the moment, then the low wail of an Arabic song. Fragrance there too: the sweetness of pressed almonds, the waft of freshly picked citrus.

Culhane awoke, startled. He waited a moment before moving around in the large four-poster bed. The tangled dream cleared and he thought: Tangiers. I was just there. Was I? But London, today, if possible. He left the bed then and twenty minutes later was downstairs facing a houseman.

"We have ham, veal chops, herring, Irish bacon, eggs, wheat porridge, crêpes . . ."

"No, no," chuckled Culhane, speaking in halting Dutch. "Toast, juice, and coffee is fine."

"Very well. Myjn heer Van Slyke left this for you." A blue-vellum letter came forth from nowhere.

Culhane opened it, reading the flourishing Gothic script:

My friend,

A rude host, perhaps, but after our discussion yesterday I decided to leave early this morning. I am en route to Johannesburg and will visit there with our sensible friend, Muldaur. The others of the Council will meet with me in Zanzibar. In a week, possibly less, you'll have your answer.

You may have something. And you may not.

Think long and hard about your future with us. Think!

As to Saxa. Call Marit Toorenaar at my office in two days. Your answer will be ready by then. A small gift of my friendship and respect for you.

One of our smaller planes is at your disposal while you're in Europe. Use it.

> *Always a pleasure,*
> *—Van Slyke*

All joss to you, Piet. You've wined, fed, and slept me. In your inimitable style you've offered me the use of your women, and now you will fly me around Europe. Yet, if you knew what I think I know, you'd strangle me. I am going to make chaos of the world markets. Only for a while, but for that while it will make the most disastrous train wreck look like an altar boys' procession. Later, you'll forgive me. Remember, good friend, you were the one who gave me the dead hand. I've paid . . .

303

Before noon Culhane was walking along Bond Street, carrying the wrapped Cézanne under his arm. He went past Asprey's, where he'd shopped countless times; by Rose's, where he'd bought clothing for his children; on by Maxwell's, where he'd had his shoes made. On the street corners Christmas carolers serenaded the passersby with messages of hope and peace. People scurried everywhere in and out of stores, dragging children, clutching packages.

Culhane saw Lovet Meriman the moment he went through the door into the famed gallery. You couldn't mistake the art dealer. As nelly as they came, he wore a powder-blue coat and a creamy silk shirt topped with a lavender ascot. And a monocle.

Coming over on Van Slyke's Fokker aircraft, he'd tried to tell himself it wasn't so fatal, parting with the Cézanne this way. Now it seemed abhorrent, like shooting a favorite horse gone lame.

"A pleathure to see you again, Misther Culhane," said Meriman, lisping, talking as if his teeth were loose.

"And you, Meriman. Is that an early Dufy hanging there by the pillar?"

"Yes, 'tis. Care for a closther look?"

"Another time maybe."

"Shall we go to one of the rooms? Tea? Cuppa coffee?"

"No thanks," replied Culhane, following Meriman's birdlike walk across the marbled floor. They entered a private showing room where the walls were papered with seamless discretion.

"Yeth, now," spoke Meriman, taking a seat on one side of a square table, gesturing Culhane to the larger client's chair on the other side. "You wish to discuth the return of an old friend, is that it?"

"Approximately," answered Culhane, placing the package on a large cirle of dark felt. Overhead a cone of light stared down through a small glass eye in the ceiling.

"Shall I?"

"Please do."

Meriman opened the package quite carefully, sniffing at the amateurish way in which the Cézanne was wrapped.

"The affidavit of authenticity is in the oilskin there."

"Yes, I see it," muttered Meriman. Then he held the

304

Cézanne up with delicate, tea-party hands. "One of his best, I alwayth thaid. Still do." Meriman moved the canvas until it was centered exactly under the light, handling the painting as if it were the Eucharist.

Culhane remained silent. His thoughts were of Andrea's anger at his decision to let it go, and then of the ribbons of ruined paintings at the Bel Air home.

Meriman asked, "You recall your purchase price, Misther Culhane?"

"And I'll bet you looked it up within ten minutes of my call from Amsterdam."

"Quite. One point seven million in dollars on our records. You couldn't touch it today for eighty million."

"Like to make an offer for it?" asked Culhane, without warmth.

"In sterling?"

"No. In British gold sovereigns."

Meriman's eye blinked slowly behind his monocle before they narrowed shrewdly. "Three million would be our top limit, I should say."

Culhane slid his hands across the table, gathering in the painting and smoothing out the paper wrapping. Placing the Cézanne on the oilcloth, he began folding the edges over the canvas.

"Some dithcuthion certainly is in order," protested Meriman, his eyes quite circular now, alarmed that this treasure could be walked in and out the door so speedily. "Three point five million gold sovereigns. Sound more amusing?" A dainty cough punctuated this effort.

"And what would you offer in dollars?"

"Hong Kong or Canadian, you mean?"

"No. American."

Meriman wiggled in his chair. His mouth curled excitedly before the lips closed again, rubbing together, looking like two pink sea slugs in an act of wet love.

"Difficult to ethtimate under the circumstances . . . A figure perhaps of ninety million dollars."

"Here's what you can say yes or no to, Meriman. I'll take seventy-five million dollars and another million in sovereigns. Within six months, I have the right to buy the painting back for four million sterling and the return of your million sovereigns."

Meriman repeated the proposition, while fishing a rosy

silk square from his left sleeve and wiping his fingers with it. He was all of a rainbow today.

"Correct," agreed Culhane, "and I'll want the McKenna solicitors to draw up the contract under British law . . . I'll be in London until midmorning tomorrow."

Courtesies managed, an agreement reached, Culhane left the gallery and ambled up Bond Street once more, turning toward Berkeley Square and the Connaught. He was slicking Meriman, taking advantage of knowledge that the art dealer couldn't even guess at.

But Culhane was reminded of the time when Karin, as a surprise, gave him some Dürer etchings bought from Meriman. Forgeries. Meriman was left none the wiser that the clever counterfeits were discovered for what they were. Culhane had bided his time, letting the clock turn, before exacting his due. Much easier than mortifying his wife and creating a public ruckus. Now he had squared the books.

Later, in his room, he sat on the bed placing a call to the merchant banking house of Baring Brothers.

"Evelyn Ramsay please . . . Yes, I'll wait." A minute passed. "Rushton Culhane here . . . Fine, thanks, Evelyn . . . Overnight . . . Late today or at the opening tomorrow, Baring's will receive seventy-five million U.S. dollars and one more of gold sovereigns for my account . . . Yes, that's it . . . Please transfer half the dollars and four hundred thousand of the sovereigns to my account at Ferrier Lullin in Geneva with their advice of receipt to me at the Hay-Adams Hotel in Washington . . . Yes, Evelyn, it's a lunatic asylum there . . . Next, I'll need another hundred thousand sovereigns packed to leave London with me by noon tomorrow . . . Yes, here at the Connaught, and can you join me for dinner at White's tonight, say seven? . . . Wonderful . . . A favor now—find out all you can about the reputation of Ambros Piegar of Braunsweig und Sohn . . . Yes, the son of . . . I'll look forward to it too, Evelyn."

Culhane embalmed himself deeper in thought. How long would it take to clear Paris tomorrow, get to the Credit Lyonnais, and review the St. Gallen Trust documents? Zurich by nightfall tomorrow? Thank God for Piet's handy Fokker. And now what? A present for Andrea and some decent cigars.

No need to wait for a confirming call from Meriman, decided Culhane. He could spot the infant of greed a month before it was born.

And you, you son of a bitch, Kyril Nyurischev. Culhane smiled a little. I'm making a Christmas present for you, Comrade Nyurischev. A suppository that fits the strike zone of one Russian President's ass. Shredded glass in it, too. Cherish the feel of it forever. I'll have it done up of Baccarat crystal. My gift to you will do wonders for your posture, Comrade President. I guarantee it will add honesty to your soul . . . And where is Metzilov hiding?

An easy run of it through Paris. Van Slyke's pilot, a former mud wrestler from Hamburg's St. Pauli district, had him in and out of France within six hours. Motoring from Le Bourget airport to Place Vendôme, Culhane had presented the bearer key to the manager of the Credit Lyonnais and been shown to the CIA's safe-deposit box and offered a private room, and a Xerox machine to copy what he wanted.

Crucifying information, and enough of it to hang a whole list of high notables. He'd bought a small leather case at Hermes to hold two pounds of the incendiary papers. Along with the gold sovereigns, the papers were with him now at the Baur au Lac, where he'd checked in after arriving in Zurich.

An odd place to be on Christmas Eve, thought Culhane. What would the Mings be doing, and Andrea? She'd sounded like a lost lamb when he called her from London. And my gingerbread man, where in hell are you tonight? Tomorrow I'll know, and from now on you'd better quit plaguing my already overworried ass.

Night had fallen. He was waiting, looking out the windows and waiting, and seeing a filmy lace of stars flickering into life.

Which one are you on, Karin? Keep our little ones very close to you until I get there. I'm almost done now and I can feel it coming together. Shake some stardust down on me. I'm going in for the Nujitsu neckhold soon, and I'll need all that dust you can spare.

A knock then, twice, louder the second time. Culhane winked at the brightest star, then moved away toward the door.

"Ambros Piegar," said the man cheerfully.

307

"I'm Culhane. Thank you for coming, especially on this night." They shook hands as Ambros felt himself being eased through the door. "Can I fix you a drink of some kind? I'm having coffee."

"Mineral water, if you have it."

"Coming up." Culhane led Ambros to the small sitting room, then poured the drinks at a makeshift bar. Handing the glass to the young banker, he said, "Yesterday I talked to Andrea. She sends her love and holiday greetings and asks that you please send her a picture of your fiancée."

"Nice of her. She was my first puppy love . . . A long time ago, that was." Ambros blushed slightly, admitting it.

"She puts you up there in the rare air too. And so does the best banker I know of in Europe."

"Keep talking like that and I can fly to Davos tonight instead of driving . . . I can't stay long."

"Going skiing?"

"And getting married soon, and they're both a game of inches, I'm finding out," said Ambros pleasantly.

Culhane raised his drink and said, "Keep it a little dangerous. It's more fun and you'll live longer."

"And you, are you dangerous?"

"Have you any idea why I'm here?"

"I'd like not to guess over it, Herr Culhane."

"Let me lay it out flatly and quickly then. I plan to take over Braunsweig und Sohn. That means Rearden is out. I have reason to think you don't agree with the operating policies of your bank. Also, my friend Evelyn Ramsay of Baring's thinks you're a real comer. Since I don't intend managing the bank, I thought I'd talk to you about it, get to know you a little, get you to know me some. That's why I'm here."

Very American, thought Ambros, no subtleties, everything hitting at once. "I don't see how you can take over Braunsweig und Sohn."

"You will if you look in that leather case over there in the corner," said Culhane, pointing to it. "It's all the St. Gallen Trust stuff. Ledgers, the trust agreement, the deeds, the interlocks, the Mafiea deposit sequences, the hard evidence of how the Reardens conspired to beat their taxes, all of it."

Ambros's skin shrank a centimeter at a time. He tinkered with the ice cubes in his glass, and they were warm to his touch. "You could only have gotten those from one source," he said quietly.

"You're right. And I'm guessing that you were the man who originally provided them. Do anything else you want to but please don't lie to me."

"I've made a terrible blunder. I think." Ambros swore under his breath then, exhaling slowly.

"Not from where I sit you haven't. I'd like to ask you one question, Ambros. One of your clients is the Trading Company of Singapore. Do you know much about their business?

"Narcotics and rice and textiles and metals, I believe," replied Ambros evenly.

"I guess you know the trouble the narcotics part can cause. Your bank is an accomplice."

"I don't have the authority to dismiss them as a client, or some of the others, either."

"Supposing after *we* took over, you were put in charge of the bank. What then?"

Ambros took down an inch or so of mineral water. "I'd change many things. Those would be some of them."

"Would the financing of trade with China interest you?"

"If the terms were realistic. But I'm a trader in the currency markets. It's what I like best. Tell me, why are you going after Rearden or the fat man, Liu Wai? There must be a reason."

Culhane got up for more coffee, offering more mineral water to Ambros. "Like you, I'm a trader. I think it's the best fun in the world—a last hope, if you will. Anybody can cheat or play the rackets. When they do, they ruin it for the rest of us, because that's when governments move in and start telling you how to piss and in what color. They get in the way. That's why, Ambros. I want to be free and not doubted or be classed as a crook or told by anyone what to do. Getting rid of the Reardens and the Liu Wais is partial insurance."

"Under our banking laws you'd need a Swiss citizen who has fifty-one percent control of the ownership," said Ambros, worriedly eyeing the Hermes bag in the corner.

"That's why we're meeting."

Very seriously then, more doubt throwing its shadow,

Ambros asked, "Do you always approach people this quickly?"

"Faster sometimes."

"That may be too fast."

"You decide. Check up. Investigate. I'll be back in Europe before long, and you can decide then."

"You're in possession of information that could land me in jail. I suppose you've considered that."

"It won't. You can bet all you've got on it. And, meanwhile, stay well away from any fooling around in the dollar market. That's all I'll say."

"Why are you telling me this?"

"Because I hope we're going to be partners."

So something is happening after all, thought Ambros. Maybe there was time to make one more move. Maybe . . .

"I must leave soon. I'll think over your idea. I warn you, though, that some of these people who bank with us, some of them, are very unhealthy."

Culhane nodded his understanding. "One more thing before you go. When I come back to Europe, I'm going to have a rough session with your father. It has to be that way, because of who he is and what he's done. Up front, I want you to know it now. I'm sorry."

"Will there be legal trouble?" asked Ambros, panic toning his words, frightened for his mother.

"Not if your father sees daylight and does exactly what he's asked."

Ambros buttoned his suit coat, rose up from the chair and said, "You must be pretty rash if you're going after my father."

Ambros shook hands, looking at Culhane suspiciously. Nothing he'd heard about the American quite described the man's presence: like a wounded jaguar on the hunt, thought Ambros. A walk to the door, then, and the young banker was off for Davos, pondering and bothered.

Oranienburg. Gloomy, wet, the air was swollen with a marshy dampness just like Berlin's, a few kilometers directly south.

Wrapped also under gray, a blanket, Sant Saxa lay in a military hospital used by Russian and East German troops. Though chewing on genuine fear, his mouth didn't move at all. Surely age was withering him, but he was faking the severity of his illness. Whenever the going got too heavy, he'd do his eye tricks, rolling up the whites. He listened intently, eyes closed, his breathing shallow, as a doctor spoke to a man, who'd hovered about for days now.

"This patient lapses into occasional respiratory failures," said the doctor, tidying up a suction tube snaking from Sant's mouth. "So if you're going to beat on him, I won't be responsible for the consequences."

"Just get him so he can talk."

"I'm a doctor, not God."

"Can't you drug the little bastard with something? Why do his eyes go white?"

"We don't know. His blood pressure drops dangerously when it happens."

"Is that normal?"

"Hardly," replied the doctor.

"Has he said any more about Cuba or South Africa?"

The doctor stood up, wiping his hands on a towel soaked with mildly odorous disinfectant. "Why don't you try putting a microphone up his ass? You might be able to confer perfectly then."

Angered, the interrogator pounded a clipboard against the foot of the bed. Sound cracked out like a shot in the small room. Saxa started, the tube falling from his mouth, followed by a small roll of jellied cotton.

"Get the hell out of here. Now!" shouted the doctor.

White now with rage, his hairless head japanned with perspiration, the interrogator moved away toward the door. This was useless. Threatening, he turned, saying, "Get him talking by tomorrow or his balls come off just after we cut yours."

A deep groan issued from Saxa, and not because the tube was forced into his mouth again.

None of it made sense to the KGB agent as he shuffled down the hall. Culhane, Washington? Yes, the nigger's story had been thoroughly checked already. This black sewer rodent had been associated with the man, Culhane, who was somehow connected to the White House. How? That was an unknown. Doing what? Another unknown. The black one was just another defector, running and now wanted by the Los Angeles police for questioning. A murderer, was he? Couldn't squash a fly was what the KGB agent thought, but the basic facts of the story seemed to fit

311

so far. And facts so convincing made it doubly necessary to pry further, strip out the truth of every and any possibility.

But what of this other nonsense? An invasion of Cuba in the making? All right, an even chance of it perhaps. What Moscow demanded was the truth about the other dribbling: a joint assault by the Americans and South Africans, with the South Africans going into Zimbabwe, wheeling up to the Congo, and then a land-sea linkup with the Americans on Africa's west coast. Going for the unbelievably rich mineral lodes that Russia had struggled so hard for? The U.S. willing to sell its grain for Russian oil? A ridiculous story. Or was it?

But the KGB interrogator would keep on squeezing the black with the eyes of a live corpse. There was no room for the slightest mistake now. Moscow wasn't known for charity, never had been, couldn't even spell it.

Under a waning moon the big sailing junk, flying its long burgee of six dragons woven in six different colors, slanted on a port tack eighty miles off Zanzibar. Three times the signaler on the second watch had ripped up conflicting messages handed to him one after another. A hot-blooded wrangle was going on back there, and he thought: Geniuses unable to make up their minds; and he knew his own mind was still fogged over the tall Nubian woman he'd met a few days earlier in Zanzibar. A breathing black diamond! She'd turned his entire body inside out with all her sensual African wiles.

A door flew open, slamming hard against the bulkhead, and the Dutch giant strode in looking fearsome under the lime-green nightlight. Another message was handed over, a curt nod, then one more tremor as the door shut again.

One minute and thirty-two seconds later a signal burst went out to five different points on the globe. Lasting for only twelve seconds, it was the strangest message the signaler could ever remember sending. He tore the page from the encoding pad and burned it, dropping the dusty ashes into a chloride solution.

35

MOSCOW

Hans-Otto Piegar sensed he was about to gain the upper hand over Metzilov. "You must know," he was telling the crafty Russian, "their book losses alone would force Europe's banks to turn to BIS for temporary cover. We couldn't provide it in those amounts."

"You're not cooperating at all, Piegar."

"Much better to await the day when the Americans are forced to settle. Unless . . ."

"Yes?"

"Unless you agree to pledge your gold reserves."

"Don't be idiotic, Piegar. Remember, man, your position as president of BIS hangs in the balance."

"Perhaps, my dear Metzilov. But I wouldn't advise moving too hastily. Push things too hard and every shopkeeper in Europe will withdraw from his bank. There'll be nothing left to lend or borrow."

"We must finance the grain. And you'll have to come up with an answer!"

"I'll try, but more time may be your best answer."

"Our purchasing missions want clearance to commit. They want it now."

"Pledge your gold then. It's the only acceptable choice.

You've used all your unsecured credit by shorting the Eurodollar."

"You're not hearing one damn thing I've said!" stormed Metzilov. "We've got a minor problem that couldn't be foreseen. We expect help."

"It's not a *minor* problem. I can make inquiries of the other central banks, but—"

Metzilov interrupted, "Make the inquiries." He stood up, trying to figure out how to fudge his answers to Nyurischev. A war dance formed up in his neural centers. "Tomorrow then," he told Piegar.

"It'll take a few days. I'll start on it first thing tomorrow in Bern."

"I'm afraid your aircraft has been impounded for necessary repairs. So make your calls from here."

Metzilov smiled, almost sympathetically. Knowing his message was glycerin-clear, he wheeled about and left Piegar with the terrifying sensation that molten tin was pouring over his groin.

36

Straits of Hormuz

Six of the speedsters, only one with her motors idling, lay moored on station at the northern neck of the Straits. Very sleek, like whippets, the seventy-foot patrol craft were capable of maneuvering like armed sharks in all but heavy seas. But there was nothing swift about the duty pulled by the crews of these boats. Dull and listless, day running into day, as they watched and watched while a third of the world's oil moved through these waters in tankers as long as horizontal sky-scrapers.

An officer stood on the bridge of the flotilla's command boat, monotony picking at his empty face. Though he was dressed only in gray shorts and deck boots, a heartless sun rolled her scalding tongue over him, sending streams of sweat down his back.

He turned his sun-cracked face toward the shouts of an off-duty crew horsing around with a water-polo ball in the soupy water. A foot scraped on the bridge ladder, and the tanned face of a signalman appeared over the decking.

"The American tankers *Orion, Gideon,* and *Torrey* signal their approach to the southern channel buoy."

"Very well. Advise District Command and the port authorities at Abadan."

"Aye-aye, Comrade Senior Lieutenant," the signalman mumbled, disappearing down the ladder.

Grabbing a rail, the watch officer pulled himself up to a small platform with a canopy strung overhead to ward off the heat. Mounted on a brass tripod were powerful binoculars with coated lenses pointing directly across the Straits. He flipped up the lens shields, then pushed weary eyes against the cushioned eyepieces, sighting the binoculars on a red channel marker.

Ten minutes or so, he thought, and the *Orion* would come into view. A break in routine, at least; he'd never seen an American tanker in these waters during his two-year hitch. One small adjustment to the range now and soon he could count the rivets in the tankers.

The *Orion* poked her nose into the channel's final turn exactly nine minutes after the signalman's report. Leaning into the glasses again, the officer noted from the tanker's Plimsoll line that she was riding under two-thirds ballast. A flume of white wake, like a rooster tail, pitched up behind the *Orion*'s stern. An oceangoing tug was hawsered to the towering two-hundred-thousand tonner. The Russian's head snapped back. There'd been no mention of any tugs! Should he inquire? The hell with it, he decided, as he snugged into the binoculars once more. He saw the *Orion* slowing, losing way, then a hard turn to port as she broached the channel's northern opening.

Somewhere in the back of the Russian officer's head an alarm rang. Scaling ropes snaked over one rail of the *Orion,* as the tug moved up abeam now. Black figures in wet suits scampered like beetles down the lines onto the far side of the tug.

The officer slammed a fist against a large red button protected by a thin mesh of flexible wire. A klaxon horn bellowed its shrill scream, as he yelled orders into an intercom to the engine room, took one fast look around at the deck, then bolted for the bridge below. The patrol boat shuddered as the dual Smerilov diesels surged into life. Shouting at a gaping bosun to cut loose the mooring lines, the officer shoved his way onto the bridge, knocking over a helmsman on the way.

The tug was well away now, spewing frothy white wake, as the *Gideon* next slid into view. A wrenching tear of metal sounded as her bow smashed up against *Orion*'s stern.

The patrol boat's hull barely rubbed the water as it sprang like a crazed rabbit toward the channel, some two miles distant. So abruptly had the boat got underway that two sailors, sleeping below decks, were rolled from their bunks. One broke his ribs, the other suffered a concussion.

On the *Orion,* cleared now of its skeleton crew, the first explosive blasts pounded through six bulkheads. Semicircles of black smoke whoofed up through buckled deck plates as a tent of fire shot up her mainmast.

From the *Gideon* came an explosion of huge violence, a massive *karrooom-brom* ramming its shock waves across the narrow spread of water. A black funnel, like a huge cylindrical coffin, cartwheeled hundreds of feet up into the air. Another *whaaroom!* And the *Gideon*'s bottom imploded, caving in the hull, as a jagged cut ripped its length. Seawater by the acre forced itself into the *Gideon*'s bowels.

Coming up the line, the third tanker, her sparse crew already over the side, careened off the *Gideon.* Ash-colored smoke spiraled up into the sooty sky. Gray-fringed flame boiled underneath, seconds later going to orange, and finally to a brilliant reddish purple. Sea bubbled and hissed as if a volcano were erupting; and the chunky debris of railings, deck machinery, and plating flew up into the jet-black smoke like terrified albatrosses.

Gideon's hull buckled first in a mass of flame-licked carnage. With one last death rattle, she shuddered and sank. Two hundred thousand tons now littered the narrow channel, dredged to only a few fathoms deep.

Now *Orion,* followed shortly by *Torrey,* threw a combination punch of wicked force. Great hanging sheets of water flew up under the brutal sun until it all looked like a fire storm inside some enormous crystal geyser.

Hypnotized with rage, incredulous, the Russian officer slewed in too close. The rocking kicks produced by the joint explosions of *Orion* and *Torrey* snapped his boat as if it were no more than a toothpick. In his last moments, through blown ears, he heard, or thought he did, the chuff-chuff of helicopters. And in the space of a few minutes he'd made the long jump from boredom to death.

And an ending too, at least for a while, of the world's key oil lane. The most crucial stretch of water on earth, barely the size of San Francisco Bay, was now corked up by six hundred thousand tons of mountainous shrapnel—roughly the annual output of a fair-sized steel mill.

Western Europe would kneel first to inspect the damage, only to find her oilcan empty.

37

Washington

Flickinger was busily reading the Shang-Magan's file about himself. The KGB-CIA operator, or whatever he was, would be left in the dark as to the true source of this information. Now would he see the page Culhane had removed earlier: the one telling of Flickinger's ties to a French-Irish intelligence net used against the British.

Looking up blandly, Flickinger asked, "Where'd this trash come from?"

"The tooth fairy. Read it all."

Another few minutes and Flickinger thumbed the last flimsy, closing the file.

"You and I are going to do ourselves a small deal. Maybe a big one for you, though."

"Li-like what?"

"Anything you pass to Moscow in the future gets run by me first. You'll be a three-base man from now on, Flickinger, and if you pull one stunt on me you'll think you're burnt rubber on pavement. I'll run over you that hard. Understood?"

"Your screws are loose." Flickinger's lips hardly moved as he talked.

"Here's some more afternoon reading material," replied Culhane. From a drawer he took the two copies of the Na-

319

tional Security Agency's translation into Russian of the CIA's dossier on Joe Rearden, his New York Corporation, and St. Gallen Trust. "This is the verbatim Moscow chorus to the file you lost so conveniently for several months. You're to get one copy into Rearden's hands. Tell him you got it from Russian sources who picked it up from Piegar. The second copy goes to Piegar himself, with no explanation of where it came from. Got that?"

"And if I refuse? This crap you're passing me"—Flickinger pointed at the Shang-Magan's file—"is hogwash."

"Flickinger, I think you're one of the moles the CIA has fumbled after for years now. One look at that file and they'll use you to string a tennis racket. You know it, I know it."

Flickinger felt the sting of truth. He might figure a way to slip out of America, but he knew he'd never outrun the KGB; there weren't enough corners of the world. He pulled in his thin cheeks, and his mouth worked slowly as if chewing ice.

Culhane continued. "I'll want Joe Rearden in Washington before the end of next week. Before tonight you'll start taking pronto steps to get Herbsant Saxa moved to West Berlin. The KGB's got him closeted somewhere in Oranienburg. If he's in any way harmed, you're fish bait."

"I can't. I'd have to get leave from the Agency, and I haven't got the mon—"

"I'll underwrite the expense. You get what's left of your ass to Europe, and fast."

Flickinger's future, or whatever remained of his life, dangled on the fine thread of an easy decision, an easy one for Culhane to snip. Yet the turncoat still had his uses, valuable ones possibly.

"I've met with Cowperthwaite twice this week," said Culhane. "He's been very helpful in giving information on BIS's activities. The British are madder than hell at them."

"How does that fit in?" asked Flickinger crustily.

"I figure we owe Cowperthwaite a favor. For example, you're going to tell him how the French are penetrating Britain's MI-6 operations through the East Germans, who are in turn using the Irish." Culhane met the spy's widening face with a frigid glare, then told him, "And be sure to tell him his target is Liam Crossen. Don't miss that item."

A blinker lit up on the phone console, and Culhane picked up the receiver. He listened as one of Halburton's aides asked him to meet with the President in half an hour.

Flickinger's deepest instincts forced him to do the one thing he deplored—make a snap decision. Yet no real choice existed. Covetously, he looked at the incriminating file now lying so casually on the desk, the very desk on which he had laid the CIA's file on the New York Corporation a few weeks earlier.

"You don't owe Cowperthwaite."

"I decide who I owe."

"Dumb, very stupid, you'll get us all—"

"Here's some more dumb for you," said Culhane, in absolute bluff now. "I want to know, not *if*, but *why* you killed Andrea Warren's father. Getting on your case, was he?"

Turning white, Flickinger felt his throat constricting to the width of a straw. His mind, in shock, blotted out. Answers! he demanded of himself. But all that came up was: How much does he know? The French net! Metzilov! Warren! The KGB setup!

"Come across, Flickinger."

Long seconds ticked away. Flickinger averted his chalky face.

"Speak or I fish you, goddammit!"

"I-I was ordered to . . ."

"What?"

"Comprom . . . He was compromis . . ."

"So you put him away, is that it?"

Flickinger only looked away again.

"Stupid son of a bitch . . . You've got work on your plate. And you'd better call in every marker your holding."

The trap had worked. Feeding Flickinger enough he already knew about himself had left the spy uncertain as to what else might be known. But that wouldn't dig Frederic Warren out of the ground.

Getting up, Flickinger started for the door shakily, turned back, and said, "I don't understand why you're not shopping me."

Culhane replied. "Because I *know* who you are and I wouldn't know who they'd replace you with, would I?"

Outside, blending into the shadows of the barely lit hallway, Flickenger worked his head very hard. What did Culhane really know about the Hormuz affair? Unthinkable that his information could be so accurate. From where had it come? Jesus! The problems with the French ambassador, let alone the difficulties now faced with *serving* CIA and KGB. The wreckage of the net devised so exactingly to score on Britain's MI-6 would be a disaster the French would never forget. Now would Moscow.

Flickenger tried desperately to calculate the tasks ahead, and saw all of them through the veil of danger: Saxa, Rearden, Piegar, Cowperthwaite—a nightmare floating in a pisspot. The operation to recover Saxa alone would call for a high-wire walk over boiling water.

Despising Culhane, fearing him, Flickenger's thoughts played up against Andrea: How did that jet-setting cunt work into *this* picture?

Culhane entered the Situation Room in the White House basement. A projector, manned by a youngish naval commander, was set up in one corner; opposite, a screen was unfurled.

"All right, son," Halburton said to the naval officer. Light dimmed, and immediately the far corner of the room looked as if hell had instantly doubled itself, its lid bursting off; pyres of flame filled the screen, opening to a brief shot of the tankers piled up against one another. Frames later, black objects hurtled from nowhere into the smudge of pyrotechnic smoke. The aerial photography then caught the Russian patrol craft circling the wreckage. In less than two minutes, the film came to an end.

As the light was returned, the officer excused himself, quietly closing the gray door. Culhane stared at Halburton in wonderment, observing the President's ebullient mood.

"You couldn't get more destruction if you blew up an Aramco refinery."

"It's that Russian boat that saves the day," said Culhane. "You can claim anything, including a wanton torpedo attack."

Halburton rubbed his rheumy eyes, still smiling. "Nyurischev's been rattling the Teletype machine like a piano.

A threat a minute. I've promised a print copy to them, one day before it gets released to the media. It's damn certain going to make them look bad, if we keep hollering enough."

Culhane barely heard Halburton. "Damn near perfect. Did they ask how we got the pictures?"

"I told them our choppers just wanted to see our ships safely into the Straits. Then we got bushwhacked, or words to that effect anyway."

"Are they buying it?"

"I don't think they buy it, but they don't have any basis for a counterclaim." Halburton shifted gears, excited, and asked, "How are we coming on the grain business?"

"It's a tall order to execute, and it's never been done before."

"You think your friends would shy off if they knew the truth about Hormuz?"

"If you mean by *my* friends the Shang-Magans, the answer is yes. But then, I thought they were *your* friends too . . . especially Piet Van Slyke."

"So you—" began Halburton with an unsteady, though innocent, look.

"Yes, I know," said Culhane, "and also I know you manipulated me."

"Not many people liked the idea of me becoming President, and fewer yet offered to help. I turned to Van Slyke for advice . . ." The President's face spoke its own apology.

"I don't mind getting used. I like awful much being asked first," Culhane said.

"I couldn't be sure of you."

"We're even."

Halburton's eyes dropped to his hands. "I'll go along with taking on Tim Rearden, if it's mean ending the logjam on the Currency Reform Act."

"Don't do anything. Leave the Reardens up to me."

"Oh! And how do you intend—"

"Never mind for now. Just sit tight, please. You owe me that at least."

Halburton weighed his position. Culhane might very well be meddling in political matters. Hard to know. He was bold enough.

"You think you can make the Senator let go of that bill? I can't."

323

"Within two weeks, or at any rate before I go back to Europe," answered Culhane, trusting that Flickinger would set a furious pace for himself.

"What are we going to do about Secretary Squires? He's the logical person to conduct money discussions with the Europeans."

"You'll just have to keep him in the closet until the deal is set. Send him over later to do the John Hancock. That's not important."

"You ought to get credit if it works."

"You've specifically promised to shield me from publicity." And Culhane's expression made the point clear.

"Don't get riled now. Oh, here. I almost forgot," said Halburton, reaching inside his coat. A small packet wrapped in silver foil, bearing the seal of the Treasury, appeared in his hand. He handed it across the table. "Your comic paper."

"Is Squires the wiser?"

"I think not."

Culhane took the packet, saying, "I know you're not wild about this idea. I admit it's chancy, but there's no other way I can think of that's less chancy."

"And what if Europe refuses?"

"You've got to swing the tide somehow. Stun them. Band-Aids and crossed fingers aren't going to get it for you."

"Well, I'm worried," said Halburton. "I don't want to be laughed at either."

"No one's going to laugh, I can guarantee you. And remember, this is one thing you can do that doesn't require an okay from Congress."

"What I meant was—"

"I know. But we've been over it time and again, Halburton. If you've got a better way, now's the time to lay it down."

Halburton wiped his mouth. Once again he felt sidetracked, his power to shape events, let alone control them, endlessly diluted. "If only we could be more certain," he finally volunteered. "Your plan is . . . well, bizarre."

Culhane opened his hands, raising them, frustrated too. "But it isn't *my* plan. Only the wheat play with Shang-Magan is mine, if you want to put it that way. The Pentagon

324

dreamed up Hormuz. And the dollar rescue is only a swerve of the Treasury's old two-currency idea."

Halburton is weakening again, thought Culhane, and wants all the holes stoppered, every loose end nailed down. Can't be done, no conceivable way for it to be done.

"If it doesn't work, you don't know me anymore. Best I can do, I'm afraid . . . Tell you what, you sleep on it and I'll stay awake on it. Up to you, you're the President. But unless you can come up with a better light bulb, I'm leaving town."

"No, no, go ahead."

"Leave Washington?"

"Of course not!" Halburton protested. "I mean go ahead with your plan, and pray God it comes out all right."

"You'll have to get Piegar to meet me somewhere," said Culhane, who then suggested how to arange the matter.

Halburton pushed his chair back and got up, stooping, with all the cares of the planet lashed to his back. He opened the door, sauntering out to the noise of other chairs scraping, people standing up, Teletype machines chattering vigorously.

Light reflected against the shiny foil, and Culhane used it to make odd patterns against the tabletop. Along with all else he'd attempted to contrive, this was the paper key—the post-time bluff—that could change things for a long time to come.

His thoughts spliced with China. To Jia and Richard, of course, but mainly to Michael and the search his son was making for minerals on the western rim of that country. The deposits were there. Culhane knew it. He couldn't prove it, but his instict told him it was likely. He'd bet that way before. Thousands of times.

To run a decent survey, do tests and core drillings, would cost millions. Shortly, depending on how events swung, he could invest that amount. Would the Chinese give him a concession? Possibly. God himself wouldn't guess at the cost of excavation, if feasible deposits were found. Megafunding was a certainty.

Could history turn on its end again? Why not? he thought, listening to his imagination bubble.

His heart jumped as he broke the seal on the silvery packet. There they were, all nine of them. Each a ten-

325

thousand-dollar bill, a denomination no longer in circulation, and each bearing the grim likeness of Salmon P. Chase staring up at him.

But these were printed in blue ink.

38

Washington

No smell, sound, or feel of him. Nerves buried deep in her somehow crossed and Andrea awakened. Hearing the smooth chords of a Duke Ellington tune, she knew exactly where he was; contented, she breathed more easily.

Odd, she thought, how soon you get to know another's habits. Not the person, not the walls of their souls, a lifetime wouldn't do that for you. But a laugh, a look, a temperament, a mind was as exclusive as a fingerprint. Andrea rolled over, looked at the luminous dial on a cheap clock kept on the bedside table: 4:19, it reported. God! He's become a swooping owl of the night, my loner.

He's right square in the middle of it. I can tell. And he's trying so hard to pretend it's all as much of a surprise to him as anyone else. Hormuz: a tragic accident of unspecified cause, they say. Bullshitto!

That effing red phone! There it goes again. Shanghai Lil, or whatever her name is, grasping across six thousand miles for what, for whom?

In the sitting room four vigil lights burned. One of them threw its weak daub against Culhane's face as he hunched over a table, talking into the phone. Andrea moved quietly, trying not to disturb him, yet wanting to hear everything she could.

"Damn pity. Really," said Culhane.

"Well, at least he's out of intensive care."

"I just can't think of him being out of commission."

"Neither can he. But you can't carry on the way he does at his age and not expect the mule to kick."

"I suppose," said Culhane, truly sorry, asking himself if Hormuz was the cause of Van Slyke's heart attack.

"We're pretty shorthanded now. With Piet on his back and you on the sidelines, the beer is thin. This grain matter was put to the usual vote. It was very close run, Rushton."

"Yes?" Culhane's heart moved a mile.

"We're going to go it," said Baster Muldaur. "But the council wants a guarantee of ten tons of gold against the cost of securing the options on that much grain."

"I've already given you the way to profit tremendously by going into the dollar market."

"No one puts much store by that idea. Protection on the cost of the options is a *must* condition, Rushton. You're asking us to gather the oceans in a bottle, you know."

Culhane smacked the edge of his hand against his knee. He didn't have the authority to make good on a promise of that size. Halburton might not agree to it. Then what?

"You've got it, Baster."

"Your word still carries with us, but we'll need something in writing."

"I'll see to it. Should it be sent to you?"

"Please." Culhane heard a gruff sigh all the way from Johannesburg before Muldaur said, "Piet told me he advised you that the council posted a reward to get at the murderer of your family. Well, the reward was claimed recently."

"What do you have, Baster?"

"Interpol tells us, actually gave us a memorandum, that your Los Angeles police spread the word around with several threats. Somebody from one of those Chinese associations—the King Liet—has talked. The police seem to think the information tallies . . ."

"Go ahead," urged Culhane.

"It's all a bit thready. We were told that a Taiwanese, who worked for you and belonged to this Kung Liet, got mixed up with a blighter named Grasselli, who worked for—"

"Joe Rearden."

"Apparently. Both the Taiwanese and Rearden's man are believed dead, or in any event have disappeared. There may be some criminal people involved, too."

"Is that all of it?" asked Culhane, a throb beating unmercifully in the side of his head.

"It's all I have," Muldaur was saying. "There's an Inspector Matin with Interpol in Paris. You might care to check with him. All this information may be correct, though difficult to prove. But there it is."

"I owe you, Baster, for a number of things. Please thank the others for me."

"We'll be in touch then," said the Afrikaner.

"Baster, I appreciate everything . . ."

Lost completely in thought, he sat there trying to piece fragments together. Rearden, you son of all shitheads, I'll drag your guts through hell itself.

Only then did he hear Andrea's faint breathing from somewhere behind him. And heard her say: "I gather that wasn't Lotus-Flower this time."

"Lay off her, Andrea."

"Why isn't she laying off you? Or is that some other secret I'm not supposed to know?"

Now, thought Culhane, now is better than later. He got up, walked over to her, moved two of the vigil lights nearer, and sat down.

"Let's hear about these secrets," he said, bothered by her sarcasm.

"I don't think Hormuz was any accident. Nor your visits to Mexico and China, either."

"Of course they weren't. They were business."

"You're yanking big levers, though, aren't you?"

"Is that more CIA drivel?"

"No. No, it isn't. I stayed in this apartment for weeks, sort of made myself at home. And one cheery afternoon, after I'd been fired, I sat at that desk over there. I was going to write my mother a note. I found some scrap paper. Face up. All doodles and darts and arrows and little notes on Hormuz, China, Mexico, oil versus whatever. Grain. Then scribbles on the Eurodollar market. That was weeks ago. Am I aupposed to believe you're Nostradamus?"

Silence for what seemed like an hour. Culhane cursed

329

himself for carelessness. He wanted to trust her. But could she trust herself to stay absolutely tight-lipped?

"Some very, very large maneuvering is under way. That's all I can say for now," said Culhane.

"People have a right to know what's happening to them. Whether we're headed for war. Children becoming cinders. Little things like that." Acid in her voice now.

"Cut it out. There's a lot happening here and—"

Andrea pulled herself away. "I'd like the bullshit cut out. I'd like the story. I'd like to write it. And I'm going to."

"You'd create more problems than you can possibly imagine. You want that?"

"If there's a story in it, yes. Look what we've been through in this country—food riots, millions out of work. You can't even turn the damn lights on half the time. Army units in the streets . . . And I want my job back!"

"Forget that story. We'll find another one for you." Culhane smiled.

"How peachy. I nursemaid you at Bel Air and I force Flickinger to give you those damn Rearden papers. And what do I get? A kick right in the ass, that's what. My job and career kissed to nowhere. Thanks!" Her voice stung with cutting scorn.

His emotions reached out: to her nearness, to her problem, and to what she meant to him.

"I'll talk to someone about getting your desk back at the paper. All right?"

"No." Andrea shook her head until its golden feathers tumbled over her eyebrows. "I want it because I'm good enough to have it and keep it. I don't want the fix put in again."

"I'm going back to Europe," he told her. "Come with me. If things come together, I'll tell you the whole story as I know it. Meanwhile, you've got to forget it. Fair enough?"

"Europe again. I'm poor these days."

"We can manage."

"Thank you, Monsieur Cézanne."

"Quit goading me on that. It was necessary." He hadn't realized, not really, how obstinately attached to the painting she was.

"Can . . . Will I get an exclusive on the story?"

"If there is one, then yes, you can. As long as I'm completely left out of it."

330

"That might be hard to do."

"You'll have to agree. Understood?"

Raising her head, her green eyes shining even in that spare light, Andrea replied, "Yes, and yes, I'd adore going to Europe with you, and I'd like to hire a big red Ferrari and drive all over the Continent for a year."

Hating to disillusion her, hating not to, he said, "There's something else, Andrea, and I want you to brave it."

"Oh, yes, what?"

Hesitantly, bracing himself, Culhane said, "While in Europe, I learned that our gumshoe, Flickinger, is a double for the Russians and—"

"I don't believe you!" Andrea jerked away.

"It's hard fact."

"How do you know? My God, where did you find—"

"I can't say. You'll have to accept it on face."

"But that's incredible! I just don't believe it."

"I confronted him with the evidence. He all but signed it."

"And my father? Did you hear anything about him?"
Tell her, you must tell her Now . . .

Culhane inhaled. "Yes, and I'm very sorry. If Flickinger didn't actually do it, he probably set it up. I don't know the particu—"

Every plane of Andrea's face changed. Deep sobs, instantly, and then a dam of tears broke loose. Collapse, a whole beautiful body of collapse.

Culhane moved closer, swinging his arm around her shoulders. She shrugged it off as her head fell to her knees. He felt like a circus knife-thrower who'd missed.

Hiccups. Shaking. Keening wails. Andrea pulled her head back, clearing her eyes with a rub of knuckles. "I'll . . . I'll get him if it's my last breath."

"Sure. We both can."

"I'm going to kill the bastard!"

"There're better ways. Slower ways, too."

"I'm damned if I'll just ignore it." Andrea wiped her eyes again. "Even if it was years ago," she added.

"Among other things, he's one of the ringmasters for passing high technology to Moscow."

"I don't want to hear this!" cried Andrea.

She quieted again. She looked off somewhere in the hopeless dark as the flame of one vigil light expired. There was nothing to say. He could hold her in the way she had him in the gruesome days at Bel Air. Comfort her, try to make some ballad to her soul. They sat there, half embracing, until Culhane slid his other arm under her knees. He lifted her from the couch. An enormous strain on his legs and back, and he decided never to try it again.

Their favorite game. Culhane rubbed all of her with body cream; polishing Andrea's back and her long limbs, then exciting her sex to a pout. Hunger came up like steam heat inside her. Moist, trembling, impatient, she tried to straddle him. He rolled away. He would bend her, take her higher with mouth caresses, until Andrea knew a burn inside her womb that raged unbearably. Sometimes she'd go faint, whimper and groan, think she was on the verge of hysteria. She experienced hatred, told Culhane so, then panted heavily. Twice, she tried to manage orgasm without him. He stopped her, holding her hands over her head. Give and gave until pleasure became agony. At her first real scream, Culhane would know they reached the point of danger. Then, as now, he brought her strong legs over his shoulders, Andrea locking him inside herself, and their long delicious shudder began.

Afterward, as she slept, slivers of guilt festered in him. Too many times during their love frolic his thoughts had hunted elsewhere. The many elsewheres of Van Slyke, Rearden—mostly on Rearden—and then Halburton, who must be dealt with again.

Ten tons of gold.

39

Washington

"So it's creating a vacuum in the Council of Six. Muldaur is standing in for Van Slyke and he called to say they're optioning the grain for us."

Halburton beamed and said, "Now we're getting somewhere. I can't tell you how much—"

But Culhane stopped him with "They want ten tons of gold to cover their exposure on the options. And I agreed to it in your name."

"You'd no right! You're not running this country. I never agreed to anything like that." And for another half minute or so Halburton gave it his courtroom best, pouring it on pretty good.

"You're in all the way now, and you've got to see it through."

"You damn well know how sensitive this gold business is." Halburton was genuinely outraged.

"Why should the Magans trust us? You've reneged on me, and they're hardly what you'd call rookies. If you're worried, throw my three tons in with seven more. But for God's sake keep the deal straight!"

"You told me, you even assured me, you could finance those wheat options in other ways."

333

"I thought I could. But they didn't bite. So I had to go along with Baster the way he asked."

"Ten tons of gold! And while I've still got this whole Currency Reform Act with Congress hanging."

"I said I'd look after it and I will. But, dammit, you can't squirm out now. You must risk it."

Culhane pleaded, almost begged, but Halburton only replied with "Supposing I chose to go another way, and without you?"

He couldn't understand the man, this judge and lawyer; how do you work with a man who's got nothing really won yet and swings his decisions daily?

"All I'm saying is we should go slower, Culhane. It's my neck, not yours."

"Go *slower*, you say? You're buying the rights to the greatest insurance policy ever issued."

"I'm not so sure. And what's in it for them?"

"The Magans are covering for us. And they're only doing it because our interests and theirs are the same. They want Russia boxed."

"I can't give gold," said Halburton firmly.

"They're not asking you to transfer it tomorrow. They simply want a guarantee that, if called, it'll be paid."

"And if there's nothing to be had in writing?"

"Fool around with *my* word and they'll blot us out. You don't know what Muldaur is up against. Besides, they know too much now," said Culhane, arguing and forcing the issue.

Halburton shoved his hands into empty pockets, scuffed a foot against the carpet. A minute went by. Culhane unwrapped and lit one of the Montecruz cigars he'd brought back from London. Halburton lapsed into thought.

Culhane got up from the sofa. "Just stay very steady. And please write Muldaur. If it goes our way, you'll never have to deliver."

Leaving the White House, crossing the park to the Hay-Adams, he parried other dilemmas. Andrea? His life must change soon. He could sense it. How would she swim in those fickle currents? And one more item—the man Rearden, with whom he expected to play all-or-nothing ticktacktoe tomorrow, using Harlem knives to keep count.

So often he wished he could paint just one of these magnificent canvases. Standing before a Corot in the National Gallery, Culhane studied the intricate swirls left by the brushstrokes: the blue of twilight done so perfectly, and the other colors built so imaginatively of light and shade. Whatever had happened between the eye and the hand, no one knew, not even Corot himself. Marvelous.

He required peace—not absolution, just the simple peace painting offered him now. In Mexico and China he had used persuasion, played fair, gone for a balance. Now, though, and forever it seemed, he was doomed to pray up Halburton; Flickinger a strong candidate for more blackmail; gulling Van Slyke and afterward Meriman, but Meriman for a different sin altogether; now, in minutes, more of it, extortion this time.

Culhane looked up at the painting again, examining it carefully, afraid to examine himself anymore. Lies everywhere to be found, mocking him, the web drawing tighter, as it always must.

He heard her steps, intuitively guessing why.

"It's special, isn't it?"

"You wouldn't loan it to me, would you?" said Culhane, stepping back.

"I'm afraid that's beyond my province," said the pleasant-voiced young woman, a member of the curator's staff. "Your guests have arrived."

"Thank you."

He walked down the hallway. All of these many years and this would be the first time they had ever come face to face.

Culhane opened the door to a cheerful room used for committee meetings by the museum's trustees. Small, intimate, it was perfect. This wasn't the sort of rendezvous for government offices, or even the Hay-Adams apartment. Not for an affair this private.

He saw the back of Flickinger's head, then an incredulous popeyed expression on the face of Joe Rearden.

"Hello. I'm Culhane."

Immediately, Joe Rearden's gaze shifted to Flickinger, as he asked, "What's this all about?"

"I think you'd better listen to what Mr. Culhane has to say," answered Flickinger.

"My dealings are with you, I thought. And why in the devil are we here in a museum?"

Flickinger didn't anwer.

Rearden was across the table, sitting there like an abbot about to impose more rules on his minions. He was thin, noticed Culhane, thin-shouldered and thin-faced, his back straight as a pipe, the skin translucent, with imperious eyes as starched as a nun's underwear. He didn't appear criminal, decided Culhane, yet there are so few known prototypes to go by.

"It's better," said Culhane to Flickinger, "if you leave us alone."

"I'd planned to." Spinning his chair around, Flickinger exited in haste.

Culhane sat down, met Rearden's look, offering him a cigar. They talked for several minutes, generalities, trying to measure each other's inside weight. Having no facts, only suspicions, he wouldn't accuse Rearden of any conspiracy, along with his puppet Squires, to spur the government into withholding the gold it owed him. That was dusty history now, or soon would be.

"I keep wondering," Culhane was saying, "where you were hiding when the markets smashed up last year."

"Pulling in, the way any sensible man would."

"Pulling out is what you mean."

"Have it any way you wish. And frankly, I'm bored with this tête-à-tête."

"Your man Grasselli came down to see me. Never saw him again."

"Been busy traveling around."

You lie, I lie. Go at him now; you afraid?

"I was handed some interesting papers on you, Rearden. You could decorate palaces the way you've been handling it at Braunsweig und Sohn."

"My affairs are none of your business either."

"I suppose. But it's always *someone's* business, isn't it? I mean the St. Gallen ruse. Mafia and Liu Wai's connection. We don't even have to go into the billion or so in taxes you've evaded. Slick as a snake's ass, aren't you?"

"And I've been tricked into seeing you under false pretenses," fumed Rearden.

"What are those?"

336

"I was told the military wanted to discuss specialty metals. It's why I came to Washington."

"They usually do. But we're talking of something else, Rearden." Culhane was sure Rearden was under stress, the man's sneers were done so nervously. "Copies of all the documents can be put in the hands of the Attorney General within hours."

"I don't believe you. You've nothing at all."

"I'll lay any odds you'll believe *them* when they've got you balls in a bear trap."

"What is it you want, anyway?" Rearden glared, but the rest of his face soon went fish-belly soft.

"A turnover of Braunsweig und Sohn to Ambros Piegar and myself. Next, the government owes me about three tons of gold—about the same as what you've got on deposit in Zurich. That's mine now, free and clear."

"You're preposterous. The gold is a charitable-trust asset, anyway."

"Charitable, eh? Sell that notion to the tax people if you can. No, Rearden, you stole it from Uncle Sam, they stole it from me, so I'm going to take it back from you. Just moving the plate around, you see."

Rearden worried his chin with a finger, then said, "Where'd you get this larky infor—"

"Well, I won't say where I got it. But I think the Russians somehow rolled Piegar for it," lied Culhane. "It's all there. Even how Liu Wai gets moneyed for his dope trafficking and how you and the mob fit in."

Rearden knew panic. He had already read the Russian version on the St. Gallen Trust, having had hell's own time getting it translated back into English, only to find it was alarmingly factual.

"What are you driving at?" he asked.

"Not so fast. There's another couple of items on the list. You tell your son, today, to cut loose the Currency Reform Act in just the way the White House bill reads. Not one change to one clause."

Joe Rearden could feel the bones sliding out of his financial wings. Without gold guarantees, he could never swing control of Citicorp now.

"It's up to the Senate, not Tim, certainly not me," he countered.

"It's up to you both, or it's the rest of your life, and his, doing the laundry at San Quentin."

"You said there was a third matter." His mouth compressed into a penciled line.

"I want your man Grasselli. Very soon I want him."

"I . . . I don't think he's anywhere to be found right now."

"You don't think or you don't know?"

"I'm told he—"

"What you know is that he's dead. Isn't that right?"

Rearden bobbed his head, swaying in his chair: his son and himself threatened with prison, and now the cold enmity of a man he had reason to fear. Would Culhane ever believe the wiping out of his family was in insane mistake? *Squeezing your black fucking heart, Rearden aren't I.*

Rearden coughed, his speech jumbled. "A terrible mistake was made."

"What I'm offering you under the circumstances is a winner's hand or a sure loser's draw. Take your pick."

"Do I get the documents back?"

"You fill your side and I'll do mine."

"I need a guarantee I can depend upon."

"I'm of Shang-Magan," replied Culhane flatly, "and that's all the guarantee you need."

"When would I get th-the material?"

"When we get title to the bank, you can remove the originals and I'll give you what copies I have. You'll have to deal with Piegar senior any way you can."

"That bastard's gone over to the Russians."

"Don't worry, he'll be around for a while yet," said Culhane.

"What about those grain contracts I hold with your company's name on them?"

"The day the Chicago Board of Trade opens again is the day they get settled. Do we have a deal or not?"

"Jesus, Culhane, a man needs time to think. What the hell do you suppose—"

"You've all of a minute. Otherwise you get the losing draw, the laundry job."

"Can you quiet this Los Angeles police business?" asked Rearden.

"That was my family, Rearden!" Culhane's mouth

338

twisted into different shapes. "Were I able to prove, absolutely prove, then you'd be swinging—"

"I didn't do it. Believe . . . You've got to believe me."

Very clear images of Karin and his children coasted somewhere in Culhane's head. His muscles bunched, uncontrollably, all the way down. He wanted to reach across the table and tear out Rearden's throat now.

Instead, he said coldly, "Your minute is gone."

"You've overlooked one important thing about the bank." Rearden actually smirked now. "The bigger depositors are . . . well, different people. They won't want any changes they don't appr—"

"They go. Along with you, you fucking faker."

"I don't make myself clear? Culhane, those people can close up your life whenever they feel like."

"Worry about your problems, not mine." Culhane squeezed his knuckles so tightly one popped. "My family . . . Beautiful art that's . . . They're all lost forever . . . You're the goddamn bottom, Rearden. You're no trader, you're a grifter, a cheap flyweight."

"Culhane, I tell you it's dangerous. And besides, only something over two tons of gold is left in the Trust."

"Get out. Go see your Senator. Tell him it's all over. And start moving on the bank, and I'll take the two tons. Just move!"

Culhane's teeth clamped tight, his fury forcing him to his feet. Sickened, he almost bolted from the room while still able to fight his emotions.

Rearden tried to cry out after Culhane. But his voice deserted him. Betrayed, somehow he'd been betrayed by Grasselli and now the Piegars, for how else could Culhane have come by so many details of the St. Gallen Trust? Rearden smelled the bad breath of fear.

And what of the advice the turntail Piegar had given, and he had taken, to short the Eurodollar market with everything he could spare?

40

Washington

Even before the tragedy at Bel Air, he had spent long hours at the National Archives sifting out the facts. Culhane figured the amounts owed to the U.S., and years past due now, were enough to help set the trick. Although the same data was undoubtedly on file at Treasury, he chose to circle around Joshua Squires. The Secretary's link with Joe Rearden was too cozy to ignore. So why chance any possiblity of a fatal leak from that end?

Cowperthwaite had already handed over the other information: a rundown of those European banks actively shorting the dollar. Which was why he made sure the Britisher got advised of the French–East German–Irish activities against Her Majesty's intelligence services, whether Flickinger liked it or not. Debt incurred to Cowperthwaite; invoice, if any, zeroed out.

But his attention grappled with a much vaster debt: that trillion dollars floating loose in the financial markets of Europe. A deadly poison, one infecting the entire American money system, a system nearly dead and crying for swift remedies.

Sworn to secrecy, two lawyers from the White House general counsel's staff were going over the last pages of a document with Culhane. The lawyers insisted any further cutting would actually gut the agreement, making it useless. He was satisfied now. He only wanted the paper-work kept simple, absolutely clear, as easy to understand as the heading on the cover page, which merely read: LOAN AGREEMENT.

Reading the signature pages again, frowning, saying nothing to the lawyers, with a scratch of red ink Culhane crossed out the space for Finland. And then dismissed the legal talent as his thoughts hurried elsewhere.

What was Sant up to, for Christ-screaming-sakes? Was Hormuz really shocking Europe as much as the newscast-ers said? How was the Shang-Magan's blocking action on the wheat play coming along?

Culhane envisioned a trigger, one that was fingered with the shaky hand of Halburton. The next move was up to the President—the word to go ahead, get back to Europe, a meeting with Hans-Otto Piegar was finally arranged. A meeting that Halburton would suggest to the world's top central banker as one for informal consultations only.

41

Paris
Berlin
Geneva

Culhane took some Armagnac, easing it down slowly. He slid one hand far enough up Andrea's leg to get arrested in some countries.

"Feels better than anything they ever did at Lizzy Arden's," said Andrea, giggling.

"You're not wearing your racing silks tonight. How nice."

"You're crazy. Not here!"

Only a handful of people were gathered in the Rue Cambon bar at the Ritz Hotel. Mostly scattered, none of them close by, and Culhane was in the mood for impetuous fun.

"Lean back against the banquette," he persuaded her.

"They'll . . . They'll kick us . . ."

Andrea leaned back, though. Culhane kept moving his lips as if he were really talking to her. And he was, but only with the tips of his fingers. In delirium, she moaned with her eyes closed, not caring who heard it, as her thighs closed around his wrist.

"Stop, please," she said. When he did, Andrea covertly slipped the side of her dress down. "Did anyone see? God, you're awful!" Andrea pulled out her compact, studied her face, fluffed her hair.

"You're grooming the wrong end."

"Oh, hush! Really! You're bad."

"For the hell of it, would you like to snorkel around Montmartre tonight? See if we can scare up some music?" Culhane leaned over, touching her forehead with his.

"Like this?" she whispered.

"We'll throw on a sweater and dungarees and go play at the dance."

"Just us. Not the Mayor, or the Comte de Paris, or the keeper of the guillotine?"

"No way. This is a limited-membership outing."

"What are we waiting for?"

"Not the bill. Let's adios."

An upended night floated them across Paris. After an impromptu stop at Le'Creole, over a second bottle of champagne, he gave it to Andrea in easy stages. She had to know. So he told her about Michael Ming and of the mother, Jia, and the early years together in Hong Kong. Speechless for a time, Andrea was aghast when he mentioned his own tentative plans for China.

Yes, he assured her, he "loved her beyond all the known moons." She asked some hard questions, and he answered: "But, listen, in life anything can happen. Usually it does, the way you and I've lived it . . . Let's run with what we've got." Then he kissed her cold cheek once.

Andrea didn't drink another drop until just before dawn, when Culhane sat down at a good piano and played her favorite songs in a late-hour cabaret in Pigalle. Then she belted back the top of a Ramos fizz, and, letting go, plunked her Charles Jourdan shoes on the corner of a zinc bar. She cried a little inside, laughed to get rid of it, danced with the guitar player, whose flashy good looks reminded her of her father.

A friendly whore came in, wonderfully proud, and sidled over toward the piano. She had on more war paint than Geronimo in full battle dress: bright purple lipstick to match her dress and knee boots, deeply rouged cheeks, heavily mascaraed eyes, all under peroxided curls boiling all the way down to her slender waist. Culhane bought her rounds of champagne as he encouraged her to sing the salty dock songs of her native Marseilles to the smoke-screened dancers. People kept drifting in, more of them, like locusts, for no apparent reason other than to enjoy a little neighborhood party. A night feast, that was what he wanted, and some music and laughs with the whore, who sang badly but with heart.

Andrea danced by, stopped, backing away from her new-est partner, saying, "I'm still here you know." No smiles there, but a pretty sulk anyway.

"Up here," answered Culhane, "we'll play it together. C'mon up."

"Play it your way, you mean." Off she whirled again in smooth, heated rhythm.

And all the revelers drank until daybreak, when the pro-prietor threatened to call the police. But not before Andrea did a raucous shimmy on the bar, to shrieks of delight, as Culhane matched her tempo with the fastest keyboard he was capable of. When the police arrived, the cornet player was just finishing a crooning solo that brought on another stampede of applause.

Paris at dawn, flattering herself in pink.

And on that escapading night, *she* had sung out in fun too.

Mostly.

The quick and almost glamorous night, so gay after Washington, fled away too soon. Culhane spent his days memorizing and boxing up the St. Gallen Trust docu-ments. As he'd promised Rearden he would do, once a good-faith effort was made to transfer ownership of Braunswig und Sohn and the two tons of gold. Snags aplenty to over-come with the Swiss banking authorities; Culhane left it all up to Ambros Piegar with whom he talked daily.

Keyed up to a maddening state of excitement, Andrea kept Culhane at full trot. She lit up like a skyrocket, see-ing how her friends fell under his spell. She watched the women succumb to his dark masculinity. When their hints became too blatant, Andrea moved around to his rescue—and her own. A steady stream of visitors arrived at their hotel suite, so he engaged an extra room down the hall for privacy.

He lunched one day with the Chinese ambassador to France. Twice he called Shanghai to check on the progress of recovering the MIAs. Good movement reported in that quarter. They dined with the French defense minister and his wife, a chum of Andrea's, and Culhane listened to dourful omens brought on by the Hormuz incident. Andrea reacted skillfully, saying nothing either.

Still no call from Flickinger, and Culhane fell back to their agreed-upon alternative: if leaving Paris, he would check daily with the CIA's station chief at the U.S. Embassy on Place de le Concorde.

Monday came.

They checked out of the Ritz. Outside stood the red Ferrari Culhane had rented, its top down to show the interior of hand-rubbed black leather. Saying good-bye to some of the hotel staff, Andrea bolted to the car's side, supervised the luggage, and waited impatiently as Culhane settled their account.

"Can I?" she asked, when he appeared.

"I wouldn't dare drive that thing." Yielding to Paris's finer custom, he tipped seven hands lavishly.

"I'll do all of it."

"Keep it on the ground if you can."

"Baby, you're gonna see what snake hips are all about," said Andrea as she slid behind the wheel.

In Berlin, trudging his last block through a cold mist, changing taxis twice, Flickinger found what he was looking for. The safe house was set back in a dingy cul-de-sac, bordering a dirty canal.

Within three minutes, Flickinger was on to the station chief in Paris, saying, "When he next checks in, tell him his package has arrived at Klinik Augustiner, Khalenplatz Forty-one, West Berlin. Tell him I'm booked at the Kempinski."

"How do I log it?"

"You know who Culhane is?"

"Vaguely."

"He's Halburton's second asshole, that's who," said Flickinger sarcastically, then lying, "We're doing a courtesy job. So forget the logging part. Just get the message across."

Flickinger hung up, lighting the fourth cigarette he'd had in five years. Removing a small pad from his pocket,

346

he made a note of the time and date of the call, though not the number, then shrugged himself back into his raincoat.

All for a fucking little nigger, he thought bitterly. Back to the Kempinski, and he'd lie down for a time. Get up, then, and absorb a few drinks on Culhane's money and wait, but for what he didn't know.

Not far from Dijon they stopped at a small country inn for a late lunch. Before a roaring fire they tucked away chilled martinis followed by chicken roasted in apricots and mustard sauce. Coasting along in dizzying warmth, laughs, lots of them, and wanting it to go on that way forever.

He excused himself to call Paris, and a few minutes later came back with eyes and face telling her their intermission bell was ringing. She saw the change in him instantly.

"We can't stay here tonight. I've got to hightail it for Geneva and catch a flight for Berlin."

"Sant?"

"Flickinger got him out. He's in some hospital in the western sector. I'll be back after I call the Richemond and see if they can take us early."

Culhane turned away, leaving Andrea vexed with doubt. Their short honeymoon-without-strings was tripping over stones, and she could feel him pulling away again, off to his battles with no names.

And China. He wouldn't really, would he? she asked herself. She didn't care to think about that for long. Hope and then despair made her heart pound. Andrea motioned the waiter over.

Driving ferociously, whipping the Ferrari's engine into an angry whine, they streaked across the last length of France. Words, passing occasionally, mostly unheard, were buried under the louder sound of hurtling speed. Signposts blurred. Tunnels only howled their echoes. Once, the force of rushing air ripped a map from Culhane's hands. It didn't matter. Andrea knew the way like she knew her own birthday.

Reaching over, pulling up her collar, doing the same to his own, Culhane searched across the scree of the Juras. Everything moved at once: themselves, the willowy shad-

347

ows, and the changing angles of the upflung peaks in the distance.

Throat-squeezing speed as Andra caught Culhane up in the press of her excitement. He couldn't recall a more romantic night. Stopping once for gas, paying double the price of only one week earlier—Hormuz—they reached the Hotel Richemond before ten that night. Andrea arranged for their rooms, while Culhane saw to the Berlin flight with the concierge.

A bumpy two-hour ride, then ordered into a holding pattern before they were cleared to land at Tempelhof airport. Berlin, dreary and wet and cold. At the crossroads to nowhere, the limbo city, owned by no one and claimed by everyone, a Wailing Wall splitting its middle.

One flick of his official passport, and Culhane was quickly passed through customs. He waited in vain for a taxi, found one some ten minutes later, and gave the driver the Klinik Augustiner address.

North, through Kreuzberg, the diesel-powered Opel chugged along hitting almost every red light. Impatience mounting, Culhane thought about Sant for the fiftieth time. And finally arriving, he slapped D-marks into the driver's grasping hand, flung open the door, and raced up the wet pavement.

Astonishing, he thought, seeing Flickinger. The man blends into anything. There he was leaning against a pale green wall, looking like its natural extension.

"Where is he?"

"Follow me," said Flickinger.

"Is he all right?"

"Getting along, I guess. I'm no medic."

"How'd you get him out?"

"I discredited him, not easily either, and persuaded some very difficult people to offload him without a fuss. You want the script?"

"Later."

They reached a counter that ran around a small area filled with desks and cabinets. A crucifix stared down from one wall, one of its arms supporting a frond of dried palm. A ruddy-cheeked woman came over, matronly-looking in her floor-length blue habit. A veil covered her hair and a white crescent of linen bowed under her rounded though

348

firm chin. She spoke softly, in the Berliner patois, and Flickinger introduced her as Sister Marya Gertrud.

"May I see him?" asked Culhane.

"Yes, of course. But you must realize Herr Saxa needs rest."

"How about doctors, Sister? Do you have enough?"

"Quite adequate, we think."

"Can we go?"

"A moment please."

Sister Marya Gertrud returned to her desk, picked up a yellow folder, and said something to another woman there.

Culhane told Flickinger, "All right, good work and I appreciate it. Get on a plane for London and book a room at the Park Lane or the Berkeley. Sit tight until you hear from me, and remember the name Evelyn Ramsay of Baring Brothers. They're bankers. Got it?"

"How long will I be there?"

"When I know, you will."

Culhane entered the small room, seeing Sant lying as peaceably as you please, sipping juice through a bent glass straw. The eyes brightened, a grin came.

"What keep you?"

"What the hell have you been doing?"

"I resting. As you see."

"How are you feeling, Sant?"

"For while there I feel like pissed-on mosquito."

"Why the Russian zone, for chrissakes?"

"Throw some shit in air." Sant smiled weakly. His gold ear bead was gone. "I think I buy you little time. So I sell snake oil. They not buy, but have to listen anyway." Sant convulsed in a coughing fit.

"Did they pull anything from you? Any of what I told you in Bel Air?"

"Course not," replied Sant, insulted. "I phony it good, you know."

"You're positive?"

"Ask any woman who bed me."

"Too many of those to ever ask."

Culhane was greatly relived. He knelt down, bent over close, clasped Saxa's small dry hand, talked low into the shell of the brown one's ear. Covering the highlights of China and Mexico, then of Hormuz, he left out the Shang-Magan's bid for the grain options, also the part about the

349

Blue Dollar. But he did tell of Michael Ming and about Jia and Richard.

Finishing, Culhane took a chair again. Sant, looking as wan as a half-melted chocolate soldier, said, "The honey, she flow in rice bowl again."

"Maybe. We'll see."

Sant touched his nose. "This say different."

"Still a lot of rivers yet to cross."

A hard swallow as Sant said, "I lie on my ass and my ass give me time to think."

"And?"

Sant's face sagged away. He sucked more juice through the glass straw, belching lightly. Looking toward the open door, he said: "Remember we think how supply Communist factories so can make the black goods?"

"Yes," answered Culhane.

"I like try again."

"Pretty hard, Sant."

" 'Nother thing, Rush. Russia got thorium, silenium, other stuff you need one day."

"We'll figure out another way sometime," said Culhane.

"My way best, kid."

"How?"

"I not sure. If they not come across, we wreck caviar and vodka market." Sant peeled a weak grin.

"We haven't time to spare now."

"I start as gunrunner by myself and I like finish up myself."

"We're partners." Culhane's eyes darkened, searching Saxa's, questioning, checking.

"Wonderful thing about boy," said Sant.

"A gift really."

"I glad, Rush."

Culhane nodded, anxious to hear more of Sant's plans and the why of them. And why was Sant calling him *kid?* Not that it mattered, but he hadn't spoken that way since the Hong Kong days.

"When this thing all done, what then?" asked Sant.

"I think I'll go to China. And you'll love it, I hope."

"I got too much time on me. You see it, I feel it."

"China's just the place for you. I'll rustle you up a good herb doctor. A woman, of course."

They laughed. Sant coughed up some pink foam, shak-

350

ing his head slowly. "I deal with caviar and vodka people. That for me. I not going anywhere."

Culhane stood up, his throat tight, a thump under his heart. The spoor of the trail they'd traveled for so long sent up a different scent, gave off a stranger look.

Culhane heard steps, knowing they were Sister Marya Gertrud's and it was time to go. He squeezed Sant's skinny hand. "I'm at the Bristol Kempinski. I'll be back tomorrow."

"I be here . . . And, Rush?"

"Yes." Culhane looked down again.

"Teach boy in China good, eh?"

All through the night Culhane tossed about, dozing off at intervals. Twice he arose, sat at a table, and ran numeric series on a small pad. Morning came, almost unnoticed, and he checked his work in the early wash of light. All the estimates he could make were in loose register now; facts unknown he could do nothing about anyway. He was in play again. Where logic stumbled, imagination could take over. He needed to dare. The risks and challenges were the planks of his profession, and it was a source of deep pride that if he lost he was answerable to no man but himself. He loved speculating, the way some men must kill to prove themselves. Highest stakes, a sort of madness, so he controlled it the best he knew how.

And like any killer, any honest one, he was sometimes afraid he could miss, blow it. No second shot either. When it feels right you always go the whole bank and never hold back.

Waiting another hour, he started on the calls: Zurich first, telling Ambros Piegar to divide the two tons of gold now in his account, take half, and go long the dollar on margin; with the other half go short the major European currencies in various proportions, also on margin.

Next, calling Ferrier Lullin et Cie in Geneva, he instruced them to do almost the same thing with funds he'd transferred there from London when parting with the Cézanne.

And he'd do the same later with Baring Brothers in London, and tell Evelyn Ramsay what else to do when Flickinger checked in.

Afterward, Culhane ordered breakfast and rummaged in the hidden corners of his life. He'd become harder, more ruthless. He was lying and laying traps. Necessary, perhaps, but tawdry and unclean. A comprador, a real one, didn't lie; he fought his problems out with his brains, his courage, and his joss.

He'd need joss now, and plenty of it. By investing on margin, he was leveraging to the absolute fullest: the rough equivalent of four billion in Swiss francs—though in various currencies—putting himself at maximum risk. Betting hard the dollar would rise sharply in the weeks to come; and the European currencies would drop like a steel safe to the floor. One wrong-way bobble in the market and he'd be scrubbed dry again.

Over in the corner he saw the cowhide briefcase, a gift once from the King Ranch. The case held the document that would or would not cause the most massive shift of money in history. Bigger even than when OPEC drained the West of petrodollars. This one trade alone hinged on the biggest bluff ever run, was the key to the deals with China and Mexico.

Hailing a cab in the cool night air, Culhane was sped into Geneva. Greeted by the doorman at the Richemond, he was asked to see the concierge soonest. He went through the door, then across the lobby.

"Monsieur," said the concierge, "some messages for you," handing over an envelope and a folded slip of paper.

He read the slip first. A call from Muldaur marked urgent. From the envelope came a breezy love-dove note from Andrea, telling him, if he read this, to hurry on to Gstaad; and while Paris has no religious significance, the Ritz's beds were the world's best prayers. Culhane slipped both papers in his pocket.

"Can you arrange a car and driver to take me to Gstaad tomorrow?"

"I think so, monsieur. I'll try. What time?"

"Have him here at eight. Please ring the duty officer at the U.S. Consulate for me. Tell him I'm on my way there right now."

Only a dim light showed as he pushed the bell at the Consulate, announcing himself through an intercom to a surly security guard, who arrived at the gate carrying a cup of coffee. Culhane was ushered up more stairs, down a

352

hallway with its walls plastered with photo releases of the U.S. astronauts. Another fresh-faced, eager foreign service officer, dripping enthusiasm, catapulted out of his chair, saying, "Mr. Culhane?"

"Yes." A shake of hands, the man introducing himself, and Culhane showing his White House pass along with the note of accommodation from Halburton. He explained what he needed, and a few minutes later heard Muldaur's resonant voice.

"Sorry, Baster, if this is late. I've been on the move."

"Where are you?"

"Geneva. How's Piet?"

"Improving and agitated as hell. This Hormuz business . . . Are you on a safe line?"

"Yes."

"Created hellish pressures for Van Slyke in the European trading zone. It's got us all worried. Now comes word of the U.S. going back to the gold standard. Are you involved?"

"It's so, Baster."

"You'd better forget that one, Rushton."

"Why?"

"You already know why. It took years to get the U.S. off the gold standard . . ." Static. ". . . Would foul up trade all over . . ."

Now an echo on the line, then a longer buzz of static as Muldaur's voice faded once more.

". . . You there?" shouted Muldaur. "Goddamn telephones!"

"Right here, Baster."

"Somehow you'll have to derail whatever it is you're up to."

"I'm in deep now. Given my word, too."

"We can straighten that out somehow."

"It's bigger than that, much bigger. It may even mean a different future," said Culhane, hearing a heavy sigh from Muldaur.

"You'd better do as asked, Rushton." The tone became formal, threat hanging over each syllable.

"Baster, I'm sorry. I do it the Shang-Magan way. The word given is the word. I took the same oaths you did, remember."

"You'll be flirting with ruination."

353

A pause.

"Backing off on your grain commitment?"

"No. Unfortunately, those arrangements are mostly fixed now."

Superb, thought Culhane, replying, "I can't and won't back away from my deals either."

Another pause, longer.

"Then, by God, you're cancelled out with us."

"You're as good as they come, Baster. But I have to do it the way it's set up."

More heaving, then a final click. A life closed, too, and Culhane wanted to wail as he cradled the phone. A deep cry, inside, like the one he'd known when leaving Sant Saxa in Berlin only hours ago. Was there no end?

42

Gstaad

"Gstaad is one of the best. Agreed?" said the driver.

"I see it up ahead now."

"You've been here before?"

"Some years ago I skiied it with my wife."

"Beautiful, is it not?"

So was she, thought Culhane, answering, "I hope it can stay that way."

The driver made a horseshoe shape of his mouth. He looked in the rear-view mirror. But Culhane's attention was elsewhere, gazing out the window he was rolling down.

A triangular patch of sunlight shone high up on the rounded shoulders of the pearl-white mountains. Somehow, the light, under the canopy of bluish-white clouds, reflected against the powdery snow to make a great copper dome over the valley. A searing color, yet oddly soft. Of the thousands of paintings he had studied, none ever had captured light so perfectly.

Up ahead on a slope loomed the Palace, with its turrets on each corner. All of white, like marl, except for the gray stone roof, and the hotel surrounded by green firs draped in a hundred bridal veils of snow. It looked like what it was—an elegant playpen for the permanently amused.

As Culhane paid off the driver, an actress from Munich, who had appeared with Karin in two films, bounded down the steps. Garnished in furs and sunglasses, she grabbed his arms, exuberantly pasting both his cheeks with cousinly kisses. Haltingly, the actress talked of Karin, of how horrible the world was, of her newest movie release. They gabbed—promising to meet for drinks, knowing they wouldn't—until her yellow Daimler arrived to take her shopping in Col des Mosses.

He went in, escorted as if he were a maharajah, correctly guessing that Andrea had engaged one of the better suites. That was fine. He needed room, and privacy, for what he planned.

"Yes, Herr Culhane," said the receptionist, "your messages are upstairs."

"Miss Warren there too?"

"She's not been down this morning. I hope you'll have an excellent stay with us."

It hadn't changed much. The high-beamed ceilings, wood and brass attractively used to relieve the white stucco walls; even the red, green, and blue Persian carpet appeared the same, or was a good copy of the one he recalled.

Never surprise a lady in her boudoir, he reminded himself, walking over to the house phone. And then, a few minutes later, the sound of her purring voice still fresh in his ear, he walked into Andrea's arms.

"Baby, I thought you'd never get here."

"You've been skiing? You look all tanned up."

"Two days of it. We had Riviera sun, then it vamoosed somewhere."

"Catch up with your friends?" Culhane still held her closely.

"Some of them. Place is really popping . . . How is Sant, my little brown bunny?"

"He's getting over a respiratory problem. Sends kisses. And he also tells me he plans on staying in Europe."

"Why Europe?" asked Andrea, surprised.

"A long story. You'll have to wait, and so will I, I suppose."

Andrea said, "The von Thysseners are having a party tonight. I accepted for us. They usually put on real zingers, and I thought you'd want to go when Mitzi von Thyssener said the great and grand Herr Piegar is coming."

Culhane's attention rose. "Dandy. A day early, isn't he?"

"He's a *not*-so-dandy! I called my mother yesterday. She wants to come live in Washington with me."

"And you, have you thought about China?" he asked.

". . . Can you beat it?" Andrea went on, ducking his question.

"Wouldn't even try. Not today, anyway. I haven't eaten since Berlin. C'mon downstairs while I dig up a fish or something."

"You get ready and I'll phone down for a table . . . I mean, who the hell does she think she is anyway?" Andrea tossed her head, grimacing, in more moods now than a two-day rainstorm.

Dust of snow swirled, and the sound of steel runners crunching it. A tower bell pealed eight times as they arrived at the von Thyssener chalet by horse-drawn sleigh.

"You'll know everyone, so don't worry about me," said Culhane, helping Andrea down from the sleigh.

"I want to show you off." Andrea tugged her fur collar tighter.

"Why chance your ratings?"

"You're not in the mood for this, are you?"

"I'll watch you. I'm always in the mood for that."

A mild roar of party greeted them the moment they came through the door. People everywhere, prancing around like flamingos, or skating merrily along in the marijuana-sweetened air. There were Fleicks from Stuttgart, lesser Abruzzis from all over Italy, some minor French countesses with bought titles, a few Swiss textile barons, a Milanese silk manufacturer who Culhane knew to be an important diamond smuggler, a French armaments mogul he knew and didn't like, and a covey of Arabian princes. A melee, a cattle call for the glitterati.

A dozen fast handshakes and nods and smiles. A small breastwork of people, fussing around Andrea, lofted her away in a cage of chatter. She turned, made a funny face, beckoning at him to follow. Culhane blew her a kiss, admiringly; her moment now, and he wanted it for her.

357

Going down a flight of four steps, he went into a large room. Some fiddlers played gypsy music. Raftered ceilings, frescoes painted on them, a wide glass window at the end of the room, a long bar, and a longer row of faces aimed at it. Mostly strangers, though he saw three American industrialists he'd known casually, who had the money to leave the U.S. when the Panic came calling. A living blueprint manured with money idly glued to more big money. A long time since he had seen this garish a display, and for a moment it was amusing. Quickly, though, he found it somehow irritating, a gross insult even, as if you could be summoned, then bought. He heard snippets of hushed conversation about Hormuz.

Making his way to the bar through a strong waft of marijuana fog, Culhane asked for vodka. Down the bar, he could see faces weaving in and out, then three large swan-shaped ice molds filled with caviar. Chatter crisscrossed in four languages, three of which he could follow but tuned out anyway.

Off in one corner, on a small suspended stage, a male dancer gyrated sinuously. Painted head to foot in silver. Mardi Gras style, he wore only a leopard-skin jockstrap. Beside him, a very tall mulatto, with her head shaved and hips laced together in a red bikini bottom, nothing more, made suggestions with her sexy body to a fiddler trying to keep his bow against the instrument strings.

He was reminded of Andrea's antics several nights earlier in Paris. Yet this mulatto, lovely as she was, didn't have the same roll of timing to her moves. Very nice, though.

His drink came. He reached for it. Another hand, studded with pigeon-blood rubies, covered his free one. He turned to see a drape of matching stones around a slim neck; the sudden face was predatory, very aware with its midnight eyes and lips of flame.

"Andrea's friend, I gather?" she asked in an accent from anywhere in Europe.

"She's flown off on me."

"Ah, no." A deadly ravishing smile. "You don't enjoy yourself. I make you enjoy . . . You have lynx's eyes."

"You've got a few dozen of them," said Culhane, looking at her jewels again. "A local sale on?"

"You would enjoy me." She fingered her necklace.

358

"Even a blind man would."

"Order me Champagne."

Culhane flagged the bartender, asked for the wine, then said, "You're, let me guess, Hungarian?"

"Very good for an American. I'm Baroness Vilda-Marie Estinsy. Maja, my friends call me. And don't look around like you're going to leave me. S'not polite."

"Sorry, I get nervous around royalty. Always have."

"Are you here long?" asked the baroness. "A fortnight or so?"

"I'm afraid my visa is on a tight string."

"I'm sure I could straighten that out. Tell me, is your Andrea good to you, good enough to make you shiver?" A short chuckle, taunting, tumbled from her wide mouth.

Culhane fixed her eyes, carefully, saying, "Ever been to Longchamps to watch the races?"

"In Paris? *Naturellement.* Why do you ask?"

"Andrea. I'd bet her against the best fillies in Europe, if you get me." Culhane returned to his vodka.

"It's like that with you, is it? Charming." Her voice went inquisitive, half an octave higher now.

"Mostly that way and sometimes even better."

"If you're bored, I have one of the nicest chalets in Gstaad," coaxed the baroness. "We could always come back here later."

Culhane watched a man filter into a group at the end of the bar. He had seen photographs in Washington, so he placed the face easily. As he slid his hand out from under the baroness's, one of her blood-red fingernails gouged the top of his thumb. He didn't turn back to catch her scowl.

Culhane stood directly behind the banker, sipping his drink, waiting for Hans-Otto Piegar to turn. And then he did. "I'm Culhane." His voice was almost drowned by nearby laughter.

An aloof, antagonistic face, larded with good living, looked back at him. "An unexpected pleasure, I suppose," said Piegar, who failed to offer his hand.

"Can we talk, say at lunch tomorrow in my suite at the Palace?"

"No hurry, is there? Frankly, I'm exhausted, thought I'd ski tomorrow," said Pieger.

"Why not exhaust your way out of here? Get some sleep."

359

"I was advised by your President's office, which was odd, that you wanted some sort of interview. Is that it?"

"A little more than that, I'm glad to say."

"And I don't like what you're cooking up with my son, Ambros, either."

"Did you get the Russian work on all your thievery with Rearden?" asked Culhane quietly, referring to the translation of the CIA file.

In the opaque light Piegar's heavy face seemd to color, before closing up into a tight grimace. He made no reply.

"There's a lot to discuss, Herr Piegar. We're going to try one of those things that cannot be done but will be."

"I'll think about it."

"Come for lunch then. We'll order all your favorites."

Culhane walked away, moving into the crowd again. Tomorrow is soon yesterday and why am I here? Running his eyes over the raftered room, the quaint leaded-glass windows, the drinking glasses on their way up to burbling mouths, the glassy stares, he spotted Andrea. Surrounded by funsters, jubilant, her face so handsomely bright, she was obviously enjoying herself. No point in spoiling her night, and he began threading his way toward the door. He went by a clutch of people lounging on facing couches, who were passing around a gold snuffbox and a sniffing spoon.

Out in the night, he filled his lungs with clean, quiet air; cold, but clear as a raindrop. A low moon hung against the darker mountains, and he could easily see the Windhorn, the highest peak, towering ten thousand feet over the valley. Stars quivered around the moon. The higher-up trees, curtained in snow, looked like a million winter tepees.

He walked easily, thinking as he went along. Muldaur's rebuke continued to bore a hole, a deep one. Admittedly, he had told Van Slyke in Amsterdam that he might resign his seat on the council even if the suspension were lifted. But being run out, kicked out, was different. And he thought about the very rich, or nearly very rich. Culhane knew the wealth at the von Thysseners' to be largely inherited, or in some cases stole, even made in the bedroom like the baroness's. Some of them were in for a rude one. He felt neither good nor bad about it, just indifferent, the way Europeans had behaved over the plight of America. He drank more night air and wondered how high up on the

Windhorn the von Thyssener crown would bury him if they knew what was coming.

Up ahead he saw the Palace, stately, lit up like an opera house. By next year she wouldn't wear her evening dress quite so gaily. And that *would* be sad. A few minutes later, he brushed snow from his shoes and opted for a nightcap in the bar, small-talking with the bartender. Two drinks later Culhane went upstairs, and he slept until four in the morning. Awakening, he found no Andrea next to him and, though surprised, rolled over until dawn broke. Only later, dressed to go running, did he find a chair propped up against the other bedroom door. A note, written in loose scrawl, was pinned to the chair's cushion.

> *Didn't want to disturb the man voted most fascinating last night.*
> *In absentia, damn you anyway!*

43

Gstaad

Culhane was hanging up on a call to a staffer in Washington when he heard the subdued rapping at the door. Piegar. He checked to see if the door to Andrea's bedroom was shut.

The banker was dressed in town clothes and looked askance at Culhane, who wore dove-gray trousers, a beige turtleneck, and socks but no shoes.

"I've perhaps called at the wrong hour," said Piegar.

"Take off your coat if you like. This might be a long one."

He led Piegar across the room to a table, offering him a choice of chairs. On the tabletop were an envelope and a bound document with its legend reading: LOAN AGREEMENT.

"Coffee?"

"I've already had mine."

"I have a certain authority to speak for my government. Shall I get it authenticated for you?"

"Not necessary, I think I know who you are."

Do you now, thought Culhane, sitting down. "I'd like to go right to the heart of it all, Herr Piegar. No fuss, no frills. All right with you?"

"What is all this anyway? What are you up to, calling me here like this?"

"Off and on I've been doing some work in our National Archives. Various countries of Europe owe the United States about seventy billion dollars of past war debts that go back as far as 1917; at eight percent interest, compounded, that roughly comes to two hundred sixty billion dollars to date. We'll soon demand payment on all of it."

Piegar sighed. "Those debts are in moratorium. Have been for years now. And I'd like to know what this is all—"

"No longer. They're very much alive."

"Europe won't honor that sort of thing. Not without a plenary conference," promised Piegar. "Now, if you'll excuse me . . ."

"Only Finland paid what was owed us. She paid up. She's shiny clean."

"You'll never collect on the rest. If you've asked me here for this sort of nonsense—"

"Follow me carefully," said Culhane politely, "and you'll see how it works. Listen now."

The banker looked bored until Culhane reached for the envelope, opened it, and fanned out the blue ten-thousand-dollar bills on the table.

"These are blueboys. There's one here for every finance minister in Europe."

"Make yourself clear please." Yet Piegar leaned forward to inspect the bills.

"I plan to. We're ready to change the color of our currency. Everybody holding dollars, the green ones, in the United States will be exchanging them for the blues. The trillion dollars you hold in the Eurodollar pool won't buy anything in America, nor be gold-convertible. They'll just be green paper. Worthless souvenir money."

Piegar felt ice cracking underneath him. "This is absurd," he said. "An absolute breach!"

"Not when you figure what Europe's banks and the Russians played against us. And you too, Piegar."

"Herr Culhane, Europe is concerned with only one matter now—oil!"

"What oil?"

"When Hormuz opens again, of course."

"That might take years. And the Arab-Russian monopoly is over. Finito."

"Don't be ridiculous. Europe needs that oil."

"You'll be buying it exclusively through the United States. Whatever surplus we have to sell."

"You haven't enough, and Europe couldn't survive under that arrangement anyway."

"In a couple of years we'll have most of what we need, and probably what Europe needs to."

"I don't believe you. That's quite ridiculous on its face."

"Oh, you'll believe all right. By tomorrow you will, or maybe sooner."

"Even if it were so, which I doubt, Europe should buy its oil at the same price the U.S. does."

"Forget that one. No innocent passage for you. Great Britain, yes, and Finland, but not the others." And Culhane proceeded to tell just enough about the arrangements with Mexico and China to inflate Piegar's curiosity.

"Why the British and Finns?" asked Piegar, showing genuine concern.

"They speak our language, that's why."

"What price would Europe pay for oil?" More ice cracked under Piegar. His tongue washed his lips several times.

"Double whatever it costs the U.S."

"You can't expect—"

"You've nothing to negotiate with, nothing we want. You've all been Russian toys. Do you understand what's happening here, Piegar?"

A sullen morose look from the banker as he unbuttoned his suit jacket. He balled it up and threw it on an empty chair. His face hardened, turning aggressive.

"Culhane," he said, "we couldn't dry up the Eurodollar pool if we wanted to. The Russians alone are short the dollar by more than a hundred billion."

"Not *our* problem really, is it?"

"You'd ruin the European banking system," returned Piegar, galled, his voice rising again.

"You damn near ruined us, didn't you?"

"By God, I'd resign as president of the BIS before I'll be a party to anything like this." Piegar sat back, folding his arms.

"Oh, no, Piegar, you stay put where we can watch you every step of the way. Otherwise, I'll pass the word."

"What word?"

"All that stuff on how you conspired with Rearden so he could beat his taxes. How you both financed the distribu-

365

tion of illegal narcotics . . . It ought to sell a hell of a lot of papers."

Piegar flushed, recalling the furious whip of Joe Rearden's voice, days earlier, demanding explanations: How had all this damaging information leaked, and how had Moscow ever gotten it?

Piegar couldn't believe what he was hearing. It was more Metzilov coming at him again, but with a different harpoon this time. This casual, too-sure-of-himself, shoeless American was trussing him up. His throat went dry, and he asked for coffee.

"Want luncheon? A cigar?

"No." The cup rattled in its saucer. "I'd like . . . like to hear your whatever-it-is."

Culhane was standing up, leaning against the wall, lighting up a Montecruz. An urge to get it all done with visited, but there was a very long way yet to go. He pointed over to the table.

"What looks like a book there is a carefully drawn loan agreement. The U.S. will borrow back all the Eurodollars, being the difference between a trillion and the two hundred sixty billion already owed us. Europe gets repaid in the same currencies given us for future oil."

"Charge us double for the oil? You said that, didn't you? It means you'll be repaying us with our own sweat."

"Correct."

"There's Russia. They can't cover Eurodollars that no longer exist, and you'll ruin us. The banks. They'd be smashed."

"Russia is a different problem. You're going to tell Moscow that BIS will cover their short position . . . We'll reflow you enough dollars to do it. And the way *they* pay us back, through *you,* is in gold and platinum. We'll want ten years of their full production. By our count, not theirs."

"They'll refuse, naturally. So what good does it do?"

"No, they won't."

"They'll laugh you sill or worse. Probably worse."

"They can't. If they do, they don't eat."

Culhane explained, elaborately, how Russia would be starved, totally cut off from the world's grain supplies for the next two years. If she refused to pay up, the bellies of her two hundred fifty million people would shrivel.

"That's inhuman, monstrous even." Piegar paused. "You would do that?"

"No, I wouldn't. They'd do it themselves, the way they've done it to others. So in order to eat they'll have to pull out of Africa, out of the Middle East, Afghanistan, Poland, Hungary, and all the rest. You'll have to tell them, Piegar. We'll get to those details later."

"Me tell them!"

"Yes, you."

"I haven't the authority, never done anything like this before either. This is for diplomats."

"You're perfect, and there's no time left for a bunch of striped-ass diplomats to take the next three years screwing it up. You're the damage-control man here, the money man. Everybody understands a big money man, don't they? You're just to get the message on track, nothing more."

"How? I don't know how to—"

"We'll get to all that . . . But you don't do anything until Europe signs this loan agreement. There's a signature space in there for every country." Culhane came away from the wall in one swift motion, getting impatient. "You get Europe's various central banks to call in our dollars and remit them to the BIS. We'll tell you what to do from there."

"Dammit, we're not you chattels!" Piegar's jaw jutted out, as if he'd been hit on the back of the neck.

"You want oil, don't you? Without it there's no industry in Europe worth banking."

"Hormuz would have to be opened up, or we'd never have enough—"

"We'll open it when the Arabs agree to sell their output, all of it, to the United States."

"You're going to interfere with the normal operation of the Straits?"

"Not for me to say. But those Arabs got a little pricy with their merchandise. We need some big discounts, several years' worth, I'd say."

Piegar rose, sat down, got up again, awkwardly. His head spun dizzily and his nerves banged together like brass cymbals.

"You'll never get away with anything like this!" he shouted at Culhane.

367

"I already have." Culhane inserted his bluff, hoping it was sufficiently disguised. "Believe me, I'd rather persuade you than ruin you."

The loud voices awakened Andrea. She stirred in her bed, slowly putting a hand over her forehead, then felt around for her robe. Poking her sleepy head through the door, she startled Piegar. Already in mild shock, he knew her, but only when she closed the door, hurriedly, did his memory recover.

"Is that who I think it is?" he asked Culhane.

"I don't know who you think it is."

"The Warren girl."

"Better not call her a *girl* to her face. At least not that way."

"What's she doing here?" asked Piegar, looking again at the fan of ten-thousand-dollar bills.

"A little of everything."

"Isn't she a journalist?"

"Great chauffeur, too. Amazing woman really."

"I knew her parents years ago."

"She told me . . . But you and I, we've got work to do."

The small talk ended right there; now it became the language of the countinghouse. Far into the night they pickpocketed each other, with Culhane persuading Piegar that the blueboys were the real article. He had to watch it, and was under no illusion about who he was spiderwebbing here. Under all the bombast, Piegar was cagey and classed by some as one of the foremost money mechanics breathing, an artist even.

Occasionally, though, the precise dosage of lies and truth actually works.

America held, or soon would, the grain options and the purchasing rights those contracts conferred. Yet Culhane knew that the U.S. would hardly spend billions, even if it could, to covert options into hard cargoes for millions of tons it didn't need. Still, controlling the grain was the same thing as OPEC's grip on world oil—monopoly, pure and powerful, nothing less. And Culhane meant to run the power of that monopoly squarely at Russia, doing it through Europe's lower intestine. Nor could Culhane think of any sure way to convince Congress to change the color of the U.S. currency. Why do it? Yet, he gambled, Piegar wouldn't know that, not with certainty anyway. Piegar *would* know the U.S. Congress was already moving on the Currency Reform Act, had to; so it wasn't hard to convince him that the blueboys would have a part to play. A simple solution, therefore an almost perfect bluffing tool.

Piegar's power—or the BIS's—came from the Eurodollar pool itself. As long as the swamp existed, Europe could stop the U.S. from returning to a gold-backed currency, merely be cashing in Eurodollars for all of Fort Knox or more.

The loan agreement was real enough. Piegar could balk, hate it, but that carried no weight whatsoever; it was a perfectly legal government-to-government borrowing, an almost daily occurrence, only this time the amounts were colossal (getting back all those IOUs). If Europe failed to sign, she would end up with nothing.

And none of the blue-dollar bluff, that wicked and useful deceit, would have been possible without Andrea's having first yanked the St. Gallen tale out of Flickinger somehow; otherwise, there was no sure way of forcing Joe Rearden to make his son see the light (instead of a jail) and spring loose with the Currency Reform Act.

On the second day, chastened some by Culhane's charging style, Piegar offered fewer evasions. Yet, late in the afternoon over coffee, he said, "You're wrong on this grain business with Russia. You can't colonize them, you know. And how are you going to prove you have those grain commitments locked up?"

"Call Moscow and see how much they're able to buy over the next two years."

"The Russians won't take it!"

"Put it this way, Piegar. Nobody but a half-wit wants to colonize Russia. And nobody but a no-wit wants them colonizing the rest of us."

"They'll march, they will!"

"You know of armies that march for long on empty bellies?" Culhane made a sort of down payment on a smile, adding, "You think Russia's going to float armies across the oceans to take grains out of Canada, Argentina, Australia? Think harder." Culhane hunched his broad shoulders behind his next words. "So let me give you the most likely picture. When they're so hungry their guts sag, they'll come steal what food you've got in Europe. You'll see

369

tanks. And you'll see your churches and homes in rubble again."

"It's not in my scope. It's beyond anything I've ever done before," pleaded Piegar.

"Both of us, but so what."

"Where's the entry point? I don't know Nyurischev that well and—"

"Ever heard of Metzilov? Gregor Metzilov?"

"Yes, yes, I know that bastard, regrettably," said Piegar.

"Start with him. He's piped in, or was, and let him do the first rumba with Nyurischev."

"You're forcing us into their arms. You can see that surely. By God, we'd never have them out of our lives."

"Look at it their way. They'll be complaining before you know it that you're getting the best end of it."

"That's absurd!" said Piegar, and rubbed his eyes, before asking, "Supposing Moscow agrees, just suppose it, all right? How do you think they'll finance the grain they need? They can't do it. I know they can't."

"A one-hundred-percent sure way is for Europe's central banks to money it for them," said Culhane, wondering where Andrea was, dying to be with her.

"That would change everything. That means that we and the Russians would be in bed together for good."

"Fine, you're already next door. You're natural trading partners, too. I was told by a Britisher you were going to put your currencies together anyway. Might not be a bad idea."

"You can't mean this. You can't, Culhane." Piegar's face flashed up now, bright as a circus poster.

"Here's what I mean. The U.S. doesn't need Europe, or Russia either. And if Moscow wants a different kind of money, don't fight them on it. Give it to them, Piegar."

"We don't want them that close. Can't you understand it?"

"You didn't want us. Now you don't want them. What the hell kind of neighbor is Europe supposed to be?"

"Stop it, Culhane, you're not funny at all. You'd better lie down."

"What you'd better do is get it straight, Piegar, that they're your new lover. Kiss Russia up nicely."

"Dammit, don't you see, if you take all Russia's gold production they can't back a joint currency."

"Sure I see it. Your problem though, isn't it?"

"It is, is it?" asked Piegar. "Well, suppose we refuse to sign your loan agreement."

"You get no oil and Russia gets no grain. Where the hell's your head anyway?"

"Your government couldn't—"

"The hell with the govenment. Most Americans, I can assure you, don't care squab shit about Europe or Russia anymore. You're too much trouble."

"This, well, this will take months to work out."

"More like years, Piegar, before you'll see how it really works out. It'll be tough. But all you'll have to do is spoon the idea down their throats. And make no other side deals until you can bring Van Slyke into it."

"Van Slyke isn't, well, he isn't exactly a friend of—"

"That won't mean a damn thing," said Culhane. "He's the best mind in Europe for straightening out this kind of bugger's muddle."

They toiled away past the dinner hour. Culhane blocked every line of retreat Piegar tried; netting and returning all of the bankers' slippery eels.

Day three rolled in. Culhane, offering his last cup of courtesy, invited Piegar to lunch on the Palace's south terrace. A crystal afternoon with the sun burnishing the splendor of the mountains even as it reflected the chill in Culhane's eyes. But it was over, and Piegar knew it. Still, he tried to scrape up crumbs wherever he could find them, saying, "You know you'll be marked forever. Someone's probably going to kill you."

"Physically you mean? It already happened the other way," said Culhane, digging into his sausage, thinking of his children.

Baffled, Piegar dropped it, asking, "What plans have you with my son?"

"None at all," replied Culhane.

"Surely, you can tell me, I'm his fath—"

"Ask him. He'll soon be the boss of a bank." Culhane tried the beer, looking over it, very hard too, at Piegar.

Piegar wanted to curse, angry with himself, angered more at Culhane. He felt sick and pushed his plate away.

And Culhane said, "Remember, you've got a backdoor

371

job to do here. No ministers, no diplomats, none of that crap. This is a plain straight-out business deal where the rubber *has* to meet the road. And tomorrow is too late to begin."

"You're too hasty, Culhane. We should consult with other govern—"

"And don't slime it up with a lot of East-West politics. Don't make that mistake."

"But it is!"

"At your school maybe, but not mine."

With that Culhane got up, folded his napkin, and left, no more to say. Piegar remained seated, staring off across the valley, more sickened, wondering how he would broach it all to the governments of Europe. His dilemma was complete: financially, it was a choice between lobotomy and a heart transplant.

Piegar was cowed by the enormity of the task Culhane was cutting out for him. Cutting it from where? From sheep's wool perhaps, and certainly not from any tried and true compass bearing of the past. He felt violent and violently trapped. But he was a banker, a banker who knew enough to save whatever he could of the bad debt and run.

Run to where? Into the tentacles of Moscow? Mother, god, no! Yet, save for bombs and tanks, wasn't Europe the equal of Russia? In many ways superior?

And how was it that some men, *any men*, could maneuver the world's grain supplies, then use them as silent deadly cannons? Shoot, not lead, but the specter of hunger. Bloodless death, or the threat of it. Outrageous, yet Piegar couldn't bring himself to doubt Culhane, who was so outrageously sure of it all.

Culhane found Andrea upstairs, changing from her ski rig into a robe. He'd barely caught glimpses of her during the past few days. They shared the same bedroom again, but might as well have been staying in separate hotels. Other worlds for them, almost completely.

He went to their bar and poured himself a double Izarra. Her antennae seemed on full alert now, quite ready. Culhane dropped himself in one of the couches, propping his head against a pillow, tired, let-down, yawning. And he told her what he safely could about Hormuz, much more about Mexico and China, and what was likely to occur in

372

Europe, probably Russia as well. He went on for most of an hour, telling Andrea what only a few people in the world knew. He made himself another drink—this one for remembering, and for forgetting too. She asked questions, and he answered some of them. Wise to his evasions now, Andrea pressed for more, fascinated, all the way taken.

But he mentioned nothing about the St. Gallen documents, his future plans for Braunsweig und Sohn, or Rearden's implicit link to the murdering of his family. Nor anything at all about the two tons of gold he'd highjacked out of Rearden, the tons speculated fully now in favor of a rising dollar. Those were personal matters, private, the way a comprador might handle it, with discretion.

"So I was right after all, wasn't I?"

"About many things, Andrea, but what this time?"

"Those notes I found in your desk after you'd gone to Mexico and China."

"Yes. We're square too. You kept quiet and now you've got your story."

But her face wandered into a guarded pose as she said, "It's unreal, isn't it? I mean the whole thing when you think about it . . . So fast."

"In my life, for some funny damn reason, the big ones always happen quick. It's the little ones that take forever." Culhane raised his glass, saluting the oddity of it.

Andrea thought, thought more, and said, "I hate to leave here, Rushton. Really I do."

"Stay if you like, but I've got to head for Zurich and settle some things." Culhane meant to wash Braunsweig und Sohn of its underworld connections, and quickly.

"What about Nairobi? You said something or other, was it yesterday?"

"Right after Zurich. I'll fly down for a day to see Piet Van Slyke."

"Just a day?"

"That's all it'll take," answered Culhane, thinking he'd somehow have to clear the lanes with the Dutchman. He owed Van Slyke that much—not more, but that much.

"I should probably go to Capri and see what sort of shape Mother is in. She sounds dippy, sort of."

"Fine," said Culhane. "We can meet back in Washington."

"Sorry to ask like this, but can you loan me some money?"

"No loans, thank you, just take whatever you need."

And that reminded him to have Flickinger finish up the errand in London, then go home. He'd have to make arrangements through Baring Brothers for more gold sovereigns. Quite a few more.

Andrea got her wish. The heaviest snow in years fell, piling up at the rate of four inches every hour. Roads closed, and trains came to a standstill. Two more days went by before Culhane could hire a helicopter to fetch them from this fairy-tale valley, where he had pulled off what he considered a 24-karat confidence trick. Nothing less; nothing better, either.

44

MOSCOW

Days later other storms insulted Moscow: the lesser one of freezing sleet hurled down on the city like the Siberian Express; the second, by far the more important, dealt with alleged treason against the state.

On Saturday, Gregor Metzilov took lunch with his wife and daughter at their dacha, located on an ice-packed lakeside twenty miles or so from the city. A pleasant villa, mid-sized, made of good stone and wood, it was Metzilov's reward for past services to the party. Were he ever to obtain minister's rank, Gregor knew, an even larger villa awaited him. Along with the coveted prestige would come a problem, though—how to shift the cartons of rubles siphoned off from the underground market? The basement of this dacha was filled with them, carton on carton.

But his fears were elsewhere today. He brooded on Nyurischev's fitful rages over the failure to secure grain on the world markets. Then, of course, the Hormuz catastrophe. Nyurischev threatened his own war on every level of the bureaucracy and, demanding answers, had even sent an investigating team to the Straits.

Nyurischev's fury seemed to glue itself to Metzilov, the heat of it unrelenting.

Metzilov was only human. A brilliant and warped and

slick specimen, but still human. With each day's increasing pressure, he found his usually facile mind bumbling, and his temper going haywire at the slightest provocation.

Just as now when his daughter, Tamara, rounded the corner from the kitchen. She carried a tray laden with steaming beet soup, sliced hard-boiled eggs, and dabs of thick cream flecked with the best caviar floating on top.

Her breasts, large and unhaltered, shifted noticeably under the woolen jersey she wore. Placing a bowl of soup before her mother, an older Tamara, she heard a loud *crack!* Her father's fist whacking the table startled her; jerking, she spilled the hot liquid over her mother's lap.

"Uu-ooah," the young woman moaned, disgraced. Another *crack!* from the end of the table.

"You clumsy fool!" shouted Metzilov. "You can't even dress properly. Look at you! You walk around here looking like an Odessa field slut."

"Gregor, it was only an accident," said his wife soothingly, though plainly upset at the wet circle staining her dress.

"A slut, I say. And those damn, what are they, blue jeans! From the black market; you want jail, do you? Trouble for us all!"

Now another crack, more muted but still sharp, as a tree limb broke under the weight of the ice storm bruising the countryside. Tamara stood wide-eyed, trembling, shocked at the slur her father leveled against her. Her wide face began to burn before she dropped the tray, watching helplessly as the contents exploded across the floor as if they'd been shot from her hands. She tugged an apron to her eyes, burying her face.

The phone rang.

Disgusted, Metzilov ordered his daughter, "Stop your mewling. Answer the phone. God, there is never any peace!"

The daughter curtsied. Her mother got up to begin cleaning up the broken crockery, as young Tamara fled to answer the phone's insistent ring.

A moment later, returning, she told her father, "It is Pyotr Lanives. Very urgent, he says."

"What isn't!" said Metzilov, knocking over his chair as he went for the phone, cursing.

Tamara backed up, giving him a wide berth as he

charged out of the small dining room. She flattened against the wall, her big breasts heaving in fright.

Metzilov grabbed the phone, untwisting the cord, and again he swore. Outside, through the laced window, wet sheets of snow fell blindingly.

"Lanives!" he yelled at his assistant.

"Yes, Gregor. Have you heard?" asked a shallow, tight voice.

"Heard what!"

"Petchloff himself at the Finance Ministry was advised today by the Bank for Internal Settlements that all the U.S. dollars in Europe are to be redeemed by the United States. A special agreement of some kind."

"What's that! Say it again!"

Lanives repeated himself.

"When did this happen?"

"Several hours ago. It's already been reported on the BBC in London."

"It couldn't be! I would have been informed directly by Piegar." Metzilov's head shook.

"President Nyurischev has been with Petchloff all day. There is even a rumor there will be no rubles to buy grain. Very serious."

"It . . . can't . . . be," gasped Metzilov.

"We can't pay. There is no way to cover our dollar liability without the cooperation of the Americans. It's a crisis, Gregor. Worse than Poland ever was."

"I'll come to Moscow immediately." Metzilov threw the phone on the floor, breaking it in half.

He wept openly, shuddered and gasped more. The women lurked at the doorway, utterly confused, trying to comprehend Metzilov's shouting. One look at him, splayed there on his knees, and fear smacked them both with its invisible hand. Metzilov's wife scrambled to his side.

"Get away!"

"Gregor."

"Away, I say." An arm raised threateningly. And the daughter cried out again.

Slowly, with punishing effort, Metzilov raised himself as the daughter, scared, rushed to her mother's side. The women hugged each other.

Metzilov closed his eyes. All the grand strategies had backfired. Why? How? Who? he asked himself. Any thoughts of a ministry were now banished; the coveted Order of Lenin was gone too. No, just humiliation, a mock trial, years of desolation and digging tundra in some camp in the barren wastes of the Arctic. Torture; his health shot for certain. Death would be ecstasy.

Metzilov threw off an ugly look at his wife and daughter. They hugged tighter. He stumbled out of the room, hitting a wall as he went, knocking a picture off. Up the stairs he raced, the women hearing his pounding thud against the wooden steps. He ran, slipped, hitting his shoulder on a post, toward a storage room at the end of the hallway. Opening the door, he flung clothes aside, kicked a box out of the way, reached inside a boot, and gripped the heavy service revolver.

To the women, the noise sounded sharp, as sharp as two doors slamming shut, and as stupefying as the horn blasting outside in the wailing storm.

45

Washington

At 7:21 A.M., Culhane and Efram Halburton sat in the Lincoln Room, with only the trader knowing that it would be their last real business meeting. Sipping ersatz coffee, he watched the President fork down his favorite breakfast of buckwheat cakes. Culhane was tempted to light up a cigar.

"Rearden had some funny friends, you know."

"Shot down in cold blood! By gangsters, they say."

Culhane chose silence. Chasing the Mafia out of Braunsweig und Sohn had ended in someone going officially crazy, then swinging their barrel onto the New Yorker. Something must be done and soon to assure Ambros's safety.

"Madness," said Halburton.

"You ready to go into the rest of it?" asked Culhane.

"Yes, please go ahead." Halburton wiped his mouth.

Culhane told how the trillion Eurodollars could be funneled into the U.S. economy: so much for loans to fund the banks, as was once done in the thirties; so much loaned to industry to produce the wares exchanged for Chinese and Mexican oil; and so much to be taken out of circulation to satisfy the gold-to-currency ratios proposed under the Currency Reform Act.

"So long as politicians can't attach an engraver's plate

to a printing press anymore, then you can avoid a lot of problems," concluded Culhane.

Halburton grunted. His face looked as if it had just been introduced to horseradish, a lot of it, for the first time. Ignoring Culhane's bait, he thought it was perhaps time for compliments or cajolery.

"This currency-reform legislation is going to the floor of the Senate next week. Darned if they didn't push the bill like a bulldozer. How do you figure that?"

Culhane only smiled.

"I didn't hear what you said," said Halburton.

"There are some things you're better off not knowing."

"I'm President, in case you've forgotten."

"That's why," answered Culhane, thinking, God, I'm tired of this. Would Andrea never come home?

Halburton changed the subject. "I want you to go see this Yamani fellow in Saudi Arabia and discuss terms for reopening Hormuz."

But Culhane shook his head.

"Why not?"

"I've personal matters to attend to. Before long I'll be getting my mail in Shanghai anyway."

Halburton's hands fell from the table, while his mouth loosened. "China?" he asked in a whisper.

"That's where."

"With those Communists, you mean? What will you do there, if I may ask?"

"Tomorrow."

"What?"

"Work on tomorrow, next year, the next century."

"You can't run out on me now. We've got an understanding."

"I did my side. I'm paid up and then some," said Culhane.

"Certainly . . . Certainly you have, but we're just beginning."

Yet Culhane would have none of it. His books were balanced. He had one more dream to begin.

"You know something of the Shang-Magan. I want to talk to you about a different kind of an organization. Something we've touched on before."

"Go ahead," encouraged Halburton.

"We have a three-way trading link now with China,

Mexico, and ourselves. If we add Canada and Brazil and South Africa to the chain, you end up with an entirely self-sufficient community. All the strategics, all the oil, all the foodstuffs, everything you need you have. You need no one else. Even if you eliminate the United States from the group, it would be quite possible to get along just fine." Culhane allowed his words to sink in as an edgy look crossed Halburton's face. "If it's managed right, those six nations can dominate world trade for the next century and more. We can force countries to do away with their armies. If they don't cooperate, we can fix it so they get ticketed to the poorhouse. They'll listen, very closely, because they'll have to. Make Russia the first example, and while she'll bluster, she'll do it or starve herself out."

Lost in silence for a time, Halburton spoke up. "You really believe that can be done?"

"Worth a try. I like the percentages. You could help change everything in the world. What you've got now is a buy of some time. Two years, maybe. Make it a good buy."

"Getting into bed with the South Africans would raise the devil with our black people," observed Halburton.

"Not if it's explained right. Not if it means jobs and food." Culhane gave in and put a match to his Montecruz.

"What about the Arab-Israel thing?"

"On that score, I'd be willing to talk to Yamani and tell him the price for reopening Hormuz is final settlement of that question. And Israel, for its part, would have to give a fair shake to the Palestinians," said Culhane, instantly recalling how the Shang-Magans almost succeeded once in making the Middle East its own trading zone.

Halburton scoffed. "Four other Presidents tried it and failed."

Culhane moved from his chair to the window, his back facing Halburton now. "Nobody ever won a war anyway. We could have it in our power, soon, to make it stick . . . Think of it."

"And China? You think they'll agree?"

"The first in line. They can't afford a modern army. They've got a billion mouths to feed there."

"It's intriguing all right," said Halburton. "Needs thought, doesn't it?"

"Why don't you just once go for keeps, quit lawyering around and stick your neck out?"

"I tell you, I need to be elected President in my own right for anything like that," said Halburton defensively.

"You will be." And Culhane told Halburton, "The forty-two MIAs detained in Laos all these years are in Canton now. The Chinese got them out for you and have them hospitalized there. When you announce it, you'll have bought yourself at least ten million emotional votes."

"You can't mean it!" Halburton leaped up, starting over toward Culhane.

"Call Deng. He'll confirm it."

"How did you manage it?"

"I didn't. They did. And you can have the credit just for the asking."

Knuckles rapped on the door. A staffer, whom Culhane hadn't seen before, entered and handed the President a note. The young man exited as Halburton read the paper. He passed it to Culhane.

It showed neat rows of typed numbers, currency quotations on the London market. The dollar had risen to a three-year high against the pound, the D-mark, the Swiss and French francs. Culhane guessed that he'd profited in the scores of millions during the past two weeks alone. But he wasn't after money; he had made and lost hundreds of millions in his life. What really counted was being the best trader, and the money followed, plenty of it, more than he ever needed.

"I think you should rest this idea about China. I really do," said Halburton.

"I'll rest it in Shanghai."

"Who will negotiate the details of the trade agreements with China and Mexico?"

"I'll give you a list of qualified industrialists to represent the United States in the final bargaining with the Chinese and the Mexicans. And for Christ's-earnest-sakes keep the government people out of it, or you'll get soaked but good."

"Should Squires be involved?"

"What the hell's the matter with you, Halburton? Give the lunker his pink slip and be done with it."

"All right, all right," said Halburton, raising his hand placatingly.

A strained look bothered Halburton's face as he thought, I'd better take care of it. Be no budging him any-

382

way. Would there? Very doubtful. Pulling a paper from his pocket, he said, "Here, you'll want this."

Culhane took it and quickly read the Presidential Administrative Order instructing the Treasury to pay over three tons of gold to one Rushton Culhane.

"This was dated two months ago."

"I know," said Halburton, embarrassed. "I bring it along every time we meet, not knowing if it'll be our last one."

Culhane smiled, tempted now. But he reached for a pen and marked a notation—"Paid"—on the order, and scratched his signature and the date. Handing it back to a baffled Halburton, he said, "This washes us."

"I don't understand."

"Someone already paid it for you."

"Who?"

"Not important. It's settled, that's all."

"I don't understand you, Culhane."

"That's not so important either."

Unable to get a fix on what Culhane meant, Halburton offered, "There must be something I can do."

"Let me buy one third of the grain options from you."

"How do we arrange that?"

"Just another letter from you to Baster Muldaur. I'll take it from there," answered Culhane, wondering if the Magans would scream in blood.

Halburton grimaced. He'd already sent one letter to Muldaur guaranteeing the U.S.'s willingness to pay ten tons of gold to the Shang-Magan upon demand. Now this one. It ill befit the office of the Presidency to become involved in these transactions. It was disorderly, undignified, and circumvented the machinery of government.

"What would you do with all that grain?"

"Help feed China," said Culhane, seeing Halburton's eyebrows rise.

"Will I see you again?"

"I'll be around for a week or so. Think about the grain option, please."

"Oh, I will. I will."

Another arrow of thought hit Culhane. The White House press staff! One answer, wasn't it? He discussed it with Halburton, giving his reasons, asking for the favor.

"You might have a point," said the President.

383

"I don't think you'd regret it."

"Call me in a couple of days and I'll tell you what can be worked out."

Culhane left, and Halburton sat there, quietly, hearing only the tick of his mind. A new order, a fresh hope, with all the fears of the unknown to go with it. A different trade map. An outlawing of war or the fuse lighters would be shut out of trade. No more OPEC monopolies. Russia contained, on her knees, Europe and Japan brought into line again. Could it be?

Halburton wondered once more at the mystery of a Culhane, who his God was, if he had any, and what drove him. Like an oil wildcatter, the man was full of volcanic ideas, hunches, and bet-the-bank thinking. A doubly dangerous man, yet he had steered the U.S. by some of the most menacing shoals ever. And Halburton recalled again Van Slyke's words:

First, trust him. Tell him everything important . . .

Good Jesus! thought Halburton, what will it mean for the rest of us if Culhane sides with China?

Another walk, one of his last, back to the Hay-Adams. Damn lucky, thought Culhane, to have gotten away with even half of it; work yes, but Lady Luck's kiss too. Passing Jackson's statue, he felt earnest pleasure over one thing: the missing American prisoners now in China. Lost but not totally forgotten men, who would come home as complete strangers. But home at least.

The Chinese government, Jia Ming had told him, looked for no repayment against this gesture. A matter of goodwill, she had said, though the subtle hint that his presence in China would be appreciated was not lost on Culhane. They could have enlisted him a long time ago for the price of Michael Ming alone, for whom there was no price.

46

Washington

A key slid into the lock, making a slight scratching sound. The door swung open and Andrea walked into the apartment. She looks splendid, thought Culhane, like one of those enchanting faces on the old *Vanity Fair* fashion covers. A pink glow to her skin, a moist film lingering in her eyes, all the other lines in the right place, belonging there. Wanting to feel all of her, closely, hear of her trip to Capri, he hurried the call:

"I know it'll be difficult, Baster, but, Shang-Magan or not, we still have to be able to talk . . . I'm going to see Yamani next week . . . Yes, in Jiddah . . . Fine, I'll call you afterward."

Getting up from his chair, Culhane laughed exultantly. "Come here so I can kiss you in my three favorite places."

"You told me once there were at least a dozen," replied Andrea, almost flippantly.

"I'm only talking about the ones I see."

Laughing herself now, Andrea replied, "You need a keeper," as she stepped out of her slush-soaked shoes, slipped off her fur-lined raincoat, then a scarf. "You also sound like you've had a sun-kissed day."

"I do now. Almost two weeks. Seems forever," he whispered hoarsely.

Mouths met. A smoldering thirst, the deep kind that hangs there until the only answer for it is bed, more laughter, an argument, or all three.

"Your mother, she all right?" asked Culhane, when they broke apart. "I would've met you if you'd told me."

"I didn't know myself. Mother? She's fighting eternity with a vengeance, and headed back here next month. You should hear that soap opera."

"No, *gracias,* and you've never looked better."

A pert smile, not the usual wide one, as Andrea looked around the room. "What are all these suitcases doing?" Several of them lay opened, banked up against the davenports, telling their own story. She knew what they signified, hating it, but asking anyway.

"Time to go soon. How about a drink for new time's sake."

"Do me a double," said Andrea, behind a brave laugh. "A big double."

Andrea moved to a chair, slumped into it, and drew a sort of dust cover over her feelings. Turmoil tugged. A long hike of it from Rome yesterday, and she'd nearly had to sleep with the military reservations manager in New York to get a seat down to Washington today. Another struggle to find a taxi to drop the bags off at her own apartment. She felt emotionally cooked. *Walk or die.* Now she despised the words.

Culhane handed her the drink, then found a place for himself in the sea of luggage.

"You're going to do it, aren't you?"

"I've done everything here I can, Andrea. And California is, well, that's yesteryear."

"So very incredible, what you did, now that I've had time to think about it. Really." She took a hefty gulp of the drink to blindfold her nerves.

"You did a lot yourself, more than you think," and hearing it, Andrea thought he meant how she had kept his confidences before and during their trip abroad.

"I'll stick to my facts, thank you," she said.

"Started on your story yet?"

Culhane grinned, loving her, though knowing too she was going to refuse him, and feeling it very squarely.

"It's your story."

"Then I just handed it over. Write me out of it is all I ask."

"You boob, you're the second man in history to do the loaves-and-fishes trick. *You're* the story." Andrea was perspiring even in this cool room.

"One thing you've got to do is keep me out of print."

"Why? Really, why?"

"If I'm linked with too much of this thing, it could get very slippery."

"I figured that out in Capri. So I won't write it, and there goes my shot at the Pulitzer," said Andrea, sighing, yet showing no irritation.

"Come to China with me. You can write a thousand stories, and I'll get you wired up to all the right people."

"I've no doubt. But why China? Why not right here, Rushton?"

How to explain it? An encyclopedia couldn't cover it all.

"There's a lifetime of work to do there. They need railroads, harbors, airports, and tons of machinery to unlock China's resources and then trade them. It's all there, I think. I'm going to try reopening the Silk Road again, only in a different way. Don't you see?"

Andrea saw perfectly. She saw the rapturous look of the visionary at his pulpit, and the one of resolve as stubborn as a favorite sin. No pretense there at all. Her heart ached and ached more, and it hadn't stopped doing it for days on end.

"I could make you the happiest man who ever smiled. And I would too."

"You already have, many times. So come to China. They live longer there, you know."

"Are you never content, Rush? You have to become a wind-walker or something?"

"But I think I can help them," he answered very earnestly before his voice lowered. "At least I can dream there, and I must or I'll lose everything."

"You *have* to have it?"

"They say they want me."

"So do I."

"Let's try it together then."

Yet Andrea had come to understand the most important thing of all—a good bit of herself. China was Mars and

387

Pluto baked into one; mystery and strangeness and poverty stirred into unsavory soup.

"And me, Rushton, how do I fit in? A language I don't know, a completely different culture, no friends, not even an enemy yet. How does all that work?" She looked up, dearly wanting the enigma unlocked.

Culhane went over to her, sitting on an armrest beside Andrea. "Somehow, I'll take care of it for you." He took her hand, gently, then followed with "You can write a long, long story. A hundred newspapers would want it."

"You said it, friend!" Andrea looked away. "And you'd have to be five Pearl Bucks to try even a tenth of it." Her voice broke and its melody swam away somewhere.

Jokingly, sliding a hand behind her neck, pulling Andrea nearer, he said, "We'll find some Chinese ghosters for you."

The look in his eyes, burning like blue stars, pulled at her in the way she supposed China was calling to him. Andrea knew he was halfway across the Pacific already. Gone, like a fabulous dream flown by so fast you'd never get it back.

"You don't really care, do you?" A snuffle came.

"About you I do."

"I mean about your life and about the way you live it."

"I have a son there, Andrea. I owe him. Richard Ming, who Michael thinks is his father, has only a year or two to go. It's all the family I have."

"The boy, yes. It's the one really wonderful thing for you. And that woman, you loved her, didn't you?"

"Yes."

"And probably still do?"

"I'm quite certain I always will. I loved Karin, too, and I do you."

Shoulders limp now, a sob, sadness drowning her fine face, Andrea said, "I believe you. But you've a son there. And his mother was important in your life. How do you think I can stand up to all that?"

"Use me. What's the matter with that?"

"Nothing, sweetheart, nothing at all. It's just that I'd need all of you. And we can't lie to each other that it'll be that way."

Culhane gave her a deep look then, one Andrea could

388

feel almost stripping her bare, before he said, "There can't ever be another lie between us. It would ruin everything."

Her head moved and he could feel the swing of her hair give the answer before she said it. "No, my darling, I'm just not tough enough to go up against it all. You just told me you *loved* her."

"I'm not discussing bedroom arrangements."

A giggle then, a little float of honeyed laughter. "I could probably stand that part of it, I think. But I'd have to know it was me who owned you." She tilted her face upward, the moist streaks almost dry, then kissed his chin. "I really love who you are, and thank God you'll never be gentry. But I need someone who is mine alone. I'll never have children at my age. Mistake number one. Mistake number two would be going to a new country, where I won't be the one you need most. I'd make an awful bad mudder on the China track." Andrea clasped her hands together, looking down at her toes.

Culhane knew truth when he heard it. What was the point of sparring around? Aside from her harmless ploys under Flickinger's coaching, she'd been true blue the whole way. That was before. This was now.

"You're likely right," he told her.

"For me I am. I'm sorry, sorry-assed and sick about it."

But it sank in hard just the same. A healthy swipe at his drink didn't help any. A fluttering movement caught the corner of his eye, as a red bird alighted on the outside window ledge. Wanting to think for a moment, Culhane unwound himself from the chair and walked over to watch. The bird, scared, flew off, as the lovely one sitting behind him seemed ready to do.

Logic was on Andrea's side. He'd sensed her misgivings ever since Paris. Deep-freezing them, she had kept her own counsel. The long days and nights to come in China, that vast land, would be grueling. Nor would it be any simple matter for Andrea to finagle her way into Chinese society, such as it was. Change her from the silk-stockinged woman she is into a cotton-pantalooner?

And who am I, he thought in the silence, to ask her to come into a life so uncertain? I'm an orphan, turned bluewater sailor, then a bartender and nightstick for a Hong Kong club, a stockbroker in the same city, and a young trader for Ken-chou Ming. Money came, then admittance to Shang-Magan, the big time and the big bust. Now, perhaps, a chance to spin the wheel once more. So cut out the horsing around, take the heat off, and be good for her.

"Close your eyes." He turned, smiled, telling her, "And make a wish."

Culhane moved to a table and picked up a box made of heavy duck canvas trimmed with leather and brass buckles. Returning to Andrea, seeing her eyes still sealed, he placed the object on her lap.

"Okay. Open up."

"Me?" asked Andrea.

"Only for you."

One by one, she undid the leather straps, afterward tilting the box so the contents could slide out easily. Seeing it, pleasure welling up, Andrea burst out with "It's back! You got it back!"

"And it's yours now. Something we can have together, no matter where we are."

Andrea's head went faint; she touched the Cézanne gingerly, just like a first-time mother with a day-old infant.

"I can't. It's so beautiful. You're ma-mak-ing everything impos—" And the snuffles came again.

She was no crybaby. Yet when the strength of her face dissolved, the eyes swelling up, Andrea became even lovelier somehow. It made everything harder for him.

"Belongs with you, Andrea. Let's let it stand that way," said Culhane, without elaborating that he had brought the painting out of London with Flickinger acting as courier.

She cradled the painting. Excitement kept springing up, refusing to obey. "Take me, hold me again," she told him, afraid of crying again. The sobs came anyway, with more tears, until Andrea was wretched with embarrassment.

"We can't make this an unhappy time," said Culhane.

"So crazy, though, I feel crazy."

"I need some time with you. Our time."

"Oh yes, hours, days even . . . Oh, Rushton, what are we doing?"

"What's best, I guess. But it tastes terrible, doesn't it?"

"Godawful," replied Andrea, and reached up for him.

Afterward, the afternoon well gone by now, the musky smell of love clinging, they lay there and talked nothings to each other. Andrea avoided thinking of what it would be like without him. Better not, she thought, or I'll ruin it for sure. Yet it nagged like a nicotine fit. As they talked, she'd wanted to ask whether he had recovered the gold owed by the government. Never once in all these months had he mentioned it. Saxa had, that time in Bel Air, but never him. There must be reasons, and she dropped the notion, but not her curiosity. Flickinger's name came up once, very briefly, and he advised her what to do.

Thinking it the right moment, he suggested to Andrea, "I've an idea, if you'd consider larking around for the next year or so."

"That'd be easy enough. I don't even have a job."

"You do if you want to be assistant press secretary at the White House. Halburton's agreed to it, if you want it."

A quick flip of her long legs, a swirl, and Andrea lay across Culhane's chest, staring wildly at him.

"You've not serious. You can't be!"

"But I am."

"Halburton really agreed?"

"I'm not kidding."

"But he's doing it for you, isn't he?"

"Actually, I just fed him the idea. He went for it like a fly to honey."

"I'd love it!"

"You'd be perfect. You've got the whole kit."

"Oh, my God, I think I'm going to come again."

They laughed, very hard, roaring and rolling about, until the sheets, blankets, and pillows were in a tangled muddle. Convulsions, and more of them, until they could no longer stand it.

And recovering later, Andrea said, "Promise never to go a day without thinking of me."

"If I didn't, I couldn't make it."

"Promise."

"You don't even have to ask . . . Give a little thought to something."

"This is the right day for it," chided Andrea, though happily.

"It's a ways off yet, but let's meet next Christmas in Lamu."

"La who?"

"A lovely little Arabic island off the coast of Kenya. There's a fun hotel there called Peponi's on the beach. Gin slings and real good water and white sand so fine you can't

391

even hold it in your hand. Afterward, we can go to Venice for New Year's."

"Divine. Where do we stay there?"

"Suite 68–69 at the Danielli. Best one there."

"Very divine. And very interesting numbers, too."

"I knew you'd catch that. One New Year's I got snowed in in Venice. Had a hell of a good time."

"Wouldn't that be wonderful? But it can't snow there very often."

"We'll order it just for you. Those one-of-a-kind flakes and a gondola that's got a Saint Bernard just in case."

Sitting up now, Andrea was trying to straighten the bed-covers. Culhane admired her fluid movements, and her smooth and strong back, and the curve of her bathing-beauty breasts. They'd written their own waltz, he thought, and it was mostly good, about as good as it ever is. Proud, he was terrifically proud of her, and lonely about it too.

"I think I'll be seeing you in Lamu," said Andrea. "I like that idea."

"Wonderful. I'll take care of everything."

"You always do, Rushton."

Later, when Andrea heard him sleeping, her blond-lashed eyes went watery again. No Lamu or Venetian snow or anything else would happen. I know him. I've spent a good slice of my life profiling people, cataloging their pedigrees, occasionally the whole ticker tape of their lives. This one? Oh, damn you God, no! Not this one. He'll be off joining all the rivers of China or something. Me at the White House? How occult and perfectly smashing marvelous. I'll need a new wardrobe. Yet I'd rather be with my caliph, who sleeps soundly next to me. Damn him!

This whoever—Jia Ming—a million miles away. What good does it do to scheme and rage against that bitch? Who is she anyway? Some sorceress? I don't even know what she looks or walks like. Or how she—

Never a good way to die, decided Andrea, not even a merciful way to meet the living death of a love lost. And you should never start a man in your heart you couldn't finish up with, keep on a leash, or at least learn to follow no matter where. Sleep dared not approach her on that melancholy night.

47

Washington

"And you know him well, do you?" asked Halburton, enjoying the interview, a twenty-minute formality now ending.

"Mostly yes. Sometimes I'm not sure."

Halburton nodded. "A different stripe of man. Off the beaten track, you could say."

"Way off it."

"He certainly spoke highly of you."

"Well, he can be very considerate," said Andrea, holding it all in as best she could.

Halburton found himself absorbed by her womanly radiance; formidable, he thought, and quite sheer.

"Again I say I'm deeply honored," said Andrea sincerely. "I'll run all the fences to do a creditable job for you."

"You might find the going rugged for a while."

"I don't mind. I could sort of use it."

"That's what I like to hear, Miss Warren." Halburton beamed. Holding Andrea's elbow, he escorted her to the door.

"May I ask a favor?" Andrea gave him a smile that did everything except invent a new perfume.

"Most certainly."

"I've an acquaintance who works here. Could I see him in private for a few minutes?"

"Indeed. Do I know him?"

"Clay Flickinger. I think he's assigned to your National Security Council."

Halburton paused. "Isn't he the one who worked for our Culhane?"

"Yes, I believe so."

"See my secretary outside. Nothing to it, Miss Warren. And it'll be a pleasure having you on staff here."

Oh! But there is plenty to it, thought Andrea, as she shook Halburton's hand, again observing that avuncular face of cracked leather. So much of Halburton reminded her of an aging horse trainer in Ocala, who had once taught her how to sit a horse. The way the President gestured, the down-country accent, even the measured walk, added to the impression. Andrea could do nothing about the way her mind worked; it simply refused to ignore any front-pager ripe for a closer look, then a ranking.

She waited on a stuffed chair near a window. A month or so, Andrea thought, and the first buds of spring will come out. The cherry trees will flower, and perhaps so will a few other things, such as my life.

Andrea heard the footsteps. She never angered easily, but her temper was at blowtorch pitch now. She could even feel the fire in her blood blazing onto her cheeks.

"Well, well, who have we here?" said Flickinger buoyantly, sliding through the door.

Andrea stared at him disgustedly, then answered dryly, "Close the door, please."

Flickinger did, scouted out a chair for himself, then asked, "What brings you over here?"

"Never mind. And why did it take me so long to discover you're the uncrowned shitheel of all time."

Flickinger winced. "Pardon," he said.

"You killed or had someone kill my father! God damn your scummy treacherous hide," raged Andrea, half blinded. "You hang by a thread. Every day of your miserable life I want you to dangle on it, wondering who's going to cut it. You're venereal, you horrible bastard!"

Flickinger's chest sagged. One hand flew up to his mouth.

"And Rushton Culhane is going to have errands for you. You'll be hearing about those from me."

And now *her,* he thought, gagging on more sour bile rising in his throat.

48

Shanghai

Morning glory.

Legend told that all light touching earth from above falls first on China. A lilac blue of sky over Shanghai, streaked coppery red by rising sun, and the air pungently crisp like the smell of pepper trees after hard rain. A good day, a beauty really.

Everything around them was brilliantly vivid: fishermen unfurling the batwing sails of their junks, fleets of sampans chasing about, and the broken skyline of the great city itself. Shanghai came awake with a roar. A sharp blast split the air as a tug nursed a big Norwegian freighter up the taffy-stained waters of the Huangpu toward the harbor.

Culhane and Michael Ming looked across the riffling waters from the islet of Shing-yun Dan. The Bund, some tattered but all the way majestic, on the city's opposite shoreline stared right back at them.

"What is it like there in Arabia?" asked Michael, skipping a stone in the shallows with a powerful wrist throw.

"Rolls-Royces, a monopoly of sand, and dinosaurs of oil."

"Yamani, he is very powerful, I suppose?"

"Any man who uses his brains is powerful, Michael."

"I guess so . . . You know, Cul-sjane, I've not been back

397

to this little island since Auntie Jia and I hid from the Red Guards. Why are we here?"

Culhane motioned for Michael Ming to follow. They walked over mossy stones up among some trees, old ones, badly in need of trimming. Speaking in Mandarin, Culhane wanted to be very careful; there were a dozen meanings if you weren't, and he was still out of practice.

"Through your Auntie Jia and your father I've made arrangements to lease this islet from the City of Shanghai for fifty years."

Wide-eyed, perplexed, Michael said, "You have so much wealth you can use all this?"

"Enough anyway."

"Why will you do it?"

"I'm going to restore the houses and buildings here. This is where I'll live, where we'll do business."

Michael's look became intent, very serious, as he asked, "What business?"

"To build trade between China and the rest of the world. In several years, maybe less, this will be the largest trading city in the world."

"You will need people to help. Is that not so?" asked Michael slyly, his heart pounding.

"Soon we must scour China for its bests minds, young and old."

"Young? How young?"

"You can't operate anything without the young."

"You will need many permissions for all this to happen. Have you thought of that?"

"That's the least of our problems," said Culhane. Then he sprang the question. "Would you like to become a trader, a comprador like your grandfather?"

A Thousand Joys, thought Michael, answering, "I'm only a geologist," painfully subservient, his heart still beating wildly.

"Well, that's a damn sight more than Ken-chou Ming and I started with."

"You must be very careful, Cul-sjane, about using curse words when mentioning my ancestors," admonished Michael, liking this barbarian more every time he saw him.

"Accept my humblest apologies."

Dear Christ! thought Culhane, what an insane paradox. I never knew my father. This fine young man is my son. He

398

doesn't think he knows his real mother, and believes his father to be my great friend, Richard Ming. Fate throws the damndest dice. Loaded ones, too.

But he said, "What do you think?"

"I don't have to think. How long would it take me to learn? . . . Why are you laughing at me?"

Culhane wanted to hug his son.

"I'm actually laughing with you. And it will take your whole life, and even then you couldn't learn it all. That's not important, because no one else knows it all either. But you can become the best of your time, Michael."

"All my life," mused Michael aloud. "Like a soldier, you mean, or a monk?"

"More like a soldier, except you can pick your own uniform."

"You must be very good at this thing, Cul-sjane."

"Not like your grandfather, but I get by." Culhane smiled again, adding, "Something tells me you've got the right blood for it, anyway."

"A lifetime to learn. A long time. Where do I start?"

"Next week we go to Beijing to meet with Deng. We're going to get him to build a modern railroad across China . . . Soon you'll go to Switzerland for a year to learn about the commodity of money, then another year in South Africa for minerals, one more in South America, perhaps the one after in New York. We'll see."

"Deng! I'm too lowly for him to receive me. He is the Shan Chu of all China." Michael Ming was disturbed at the idea of any extended time away from Shanghai. Years!

Culhane stopped on the path. Resting a hand on Michael's shoulder, gazing right into the black centers of the younger man's eyes, he said, "Never hide from your own star. You are of Ming blood, and never forget that either. One day you will be a bigger boss than Deng ever was. Now's the time to learn how."

Michael didn't move, just stood there fencing with an idea beyond his grasp. What was the American trying to say? "This railroad to the west? As long as the Great Wall? Something like that?" asked Michael.

"Longer, and more useful, too. It'll run from Shanghai all the way out past the Gobi."

"So much money!" Michael's voice filled with doubt.

"Don't think too hard about money. Think about making your dreams work. They didn't build the Great Wall worrying about its cost, you know."

"Ah, yes, Cul-sjane, but you see the emperor had free labor then."

"We'll get Deng to loan us some of the Chinese army for a year. They can do something useful for a change."

Michael Ming let go with a low hiss, warning Culhane, "Be careful with your talk. You could get into trouble."

Pausing by the old wreck of the church, Culhane lit up his first cigar of the day, savoring its taste. He watched as the smoke tendrils floated away on the soft breeze, then saw big gray gulls teaching aerial ballet to their young over the water.

"Learn to speak your mind," he told Michael. "And always, always do it with me."

"Have you never lied?"

"More than I should admit to you. But I don't like doing it."

"You must tell me about those times," urged Michael. Culhane exhaled another pillow of smoke. It was very important that Michael understand one matter.

"Armies are hired to defend or seize economic advantage. So if the trader does what he's supposed to then we don't need armies. Try never to forget that, either."

Michael Ming, walking along, crammed that idea slowly into his head. A few steps later he said, "I will study those words more."

They ambled on, and Culhane said, "After Beijing let's go out to western China and meet with your friends."

"It's a very long trip."

"We'll rent a small jet out of Hong Kong and make it a shorter one."

It must be true, thought Michael, this Cul-sjane is touched by powerful and strange gods. Possibly dangerous ones. Who can think of it all? Switzerland, Africa, the Americas. A railroad. A visit with Deng! Jets to western China. Oh, oh, aiyee! A hundred mysteries to solve.

"We should take gifts to my friends in the west. Can you pay?"

"Never mention money again unless it's an emergency. It's a fatal flaw to think in those terms."

"I don't understand," said Michael.

"See if this helps. How much money to make another Auntie Jia or you?"

"No amount. That's ridiculous."

"Exactly. And that shows you the limits of money. Learn to make the other person think it's very important, his religion even. Try never to think small, as in money, or you'll end up doing small."

"I will try," said Michael dubiously, quickly adding, "But how can I leave China for all these years you speak of? No, I can't! What of my Teng-li? What of Auntie and Father?" A look like a dark cloud passed across his squinting face.

"Don't go cockeyed," cautioned Culhane. "That's always a mistake. Teng-li can join you when her studies are finished. And you'll come back to China three or four times a year so we can map our future."

"I'd need many permissions," protested Michael.

"Forget this damn permission stuff. You'll have a whole list of them." Culhane nearly became irritated, until realizing that this was indeed China. His son had never known true freedom.

"Auntie and Father trust you. So I will too. And what, Cul-sjane, will you call your business house?" A very direct look from Michael then, very Chinese, careful and sober and highly observant.

A big tug moved up the Huanpu pulling a dozen coal barges. Looking at it, Culhane made a mental note: I'm going to need a shipping line.

Then he answered, "We'll call it House of Ming. How does that sound to you?"

"No, honored friend. It must bear your name."

"If it has yours then it has mine," said Culhane to a bewildered Michael.

"House of Ming," repeated Michael in a low voice, his hair riding up with the breeze. "My grandfather would be immensely pleased. We honor him."

"He will bring us very good joss."

They moved off from a stone parapet where they had stopped briefly. Walking slowly, Culhane explained where he would live on Shing-yun Dan, and where Michael's house would be, where Richard would stay, and which buildings would be enlarged for offices and a very small museum.

And as Culhane exploded his plans, some hidden spirit, like the prayer of blood, stirred him. He was again in the crucible of family. So very much to do. He thought, Sant, I need your ass badly now.

He wanted to tell Michael his feelings. But of the five languages he could use, Culhane could not think of the exact right words in any of them. Looking above the straight line of the rising sun, he thought, *And You, I have never asked You for one thing, not once; now I ask You to give me some time, that's what I beg . . .*

There, right there, across the waters, on the Bund, one day those buildings would fill again with oil brokers, steel and coal agents, chemical and food people, textilers, mineral traders, chiefs and underlings. He could feel and see it. Shanghai, be with me, thought Culhane, and with my son, and we will wipe sleep from the eyes of this Kingdom.

Odd, thought Culhane, hundreds of years before it was the Emperor Ch'ung Ch'en who decreed that all Western barbarians be confined to the walled compound in Canton, go no farther. Yet here I am. Here *we* are, remembering that Michael was only half Chinese.

We will go up to Beijing and persuade Deng that China needs a first-class railroad, and that it will cost so many barrels of crude oil. He will argue. Let him. But we will offer to finance the hunt for minerals in the west, asking for a concession. He will ponder, delay. We will surrender vast tonnages of grains under the options secured by Shang-Magan and transferred to us by Halburton. Cheap grain that can be stored for years if necessary. Deng will ponder no more. He will dance. And that, decided Culhane, will be the House of Ming's first real trade inside the Kingdom.

"When will you start the work here?" asked Michael, breaking Culhane out of his reverie.

"It'll take a year or so. Jia will supervise it." He had dearly wanted to say *your mother*.

"You are fond of Auntie Jia?" probed Michael, again on the sly, yet too polite to go much further.

"Eighth Heaven, I'd say. Maybe the Ninth."

"There are only seven," said Michael, grinning.

"There may be a hundred for all we know. C'mon, let's go across. I want to meet this mayor of yours."

"Don't be foolish," said Michael. "We would need to apply for an appointment."

Now Culhane laughed.

"What the hell, Michael, we're his new tenants, aren't we? He'll want to discuss the rent."

Swelling with ideas, Michael's head was a birthday balloon filled with helium. Tonight, he would persuade Teng-li away from her astronomy studies, use his meager savings for a huge dinner at the Nine White Cats, her favorite. He would show her other stars, but ones of the earth and not the skies. House of Ming!

This intriguing barbarian, his life must have been so frivolous and easy. Why does he come to live in China? Cul-sjane comes with me to the west where I can see my friends again. I will test him to see if he's a wolf hunter. No! Impolite! He might be afraid of crossing into Russia and would lose face. I will ask Auntie Jia, whose face glows like incense when this American is near her. A score of gods are talking secrets to me.

Scrambling down a rock-strewn path, hand in hand, in the Chinese custom for men who are friends, they walked toward the sampan waiting at the quay.

Now the circle drew itself complete. Culhane, taught once by the very best, a Chinese, was here in this ancient Kingdom that first authored, centuries before, these tough compradors who breathed to risk, to trade, to put ribs and flesh on newer dreams.

Illegible dreams, except for the few.

NOVELS OF SUSPENSE AND INTRIGUE FROM AVON

THE TRADE by William H. Hallahan 57737-2/$3.50 Can./$3.95
An ex-CIA agent involved in the international arms trade is led from Cologne to Paris to London to Amsterdam in search of his partner's killer. Instead he falls into a neo-Nazi conspiracy leading to World War III—and into the arms of a seductive, lethal beauty.

Hallahan "graduates to the Ludlum-Follett class of writers with this crackling good thriller." *Publishers Weekly*

WAR TOYS by Hampton Howard 65557-8/$3.50
Set in Paris, WAR TOYS is the story of an ex-CIA agent who discovers that he has been set up as a disposable pawn by his own government—and decides to strike back with the very venom and calculated cunning that the CIA had taught him. This chillingly authentic espionage thriller takes the reader through a dazzling series of betrayals and counter betrayals, bitter vendettas and hairpin escapes.

"Gets off to a fast start...plenty of action."
The New York Times Book Review

KENSEI by Steven Schlossstein 69369-0/$3.95 Can./$4.95
At first, suspicion pointed to the Russians. Because whoever stole the top-secret 256K optical microchip—key component in the Pentagon's ultimate nuclear strike system—was risking all-out confrontation.

Art Garrett had staked his future and the success of his Silicon Valley firm to develop the 256K. Now he was gambling his very life, and the only woman he ever loved, for the survival of America...Against a fanatic Samurai military-industrial conspiracy prepared to conquer the world. Or die.

AV☮N Paperbacks